POSTSINGULAR

Tor Books by Rudy Rucker

As Above, So Below

Frek and the Elixir

Mathematicians in Love

Postsingular

Saucer Wisdom

Spaceland

POSTSINGULAR

Rudy Rucker

A Tom Doherty Associates Book

New York

POSTSINGULAR

Copyright © 2007 by Rudy Rucker

A Tor Book
Published by Tom Doherty Associates, LLC
175 Fifth Avenue
New York, NY 10010

www.tor.com

Tor® is a registered trademark of Tom Doherty Associates, LLC.

Library of Congress Cataloging-in-Publication Data

Rucker, Rudy v. B. (Rudy von Bitter), 1946–
    Postsingular / Rudy Rucker. —1st ed.
        p.   cm.
    "A Tom Doherty Associates Book."
    ISBN-13: 978-0-7653-1741-4
    ISBN-10: 0-7653-1741-9
    1. Nanotechnology—Fiction. I. Title.
PS3568.U298P67   2007
813'.54—dc22   2007020210

First Edition: October 2007

Printed in the United States of America

0 9 8 7 6 5 4 3 2 1

For Georgia, Rudy, and Isabel

Contents

Acknowledgments

Chapter 2, "Nant Day," appeared as "Chu and the Nants" in *Isaac Asimov's Science Fiction Magazine,* June 2006. This story also appeared in *Year's Best SF 12,* edited by David Hartwell and Kathryn Cramer.

Chapters 3 and 4, "Orphid Night" and "Chu's Knot," appeared as a single story, "Postsingular," in *Isaac Asimov's Science Fiction Magazine,* September 2006.

PART I

CHAPTER 1

Ignition

Two boys walked down the beach, deep in conversation. Seventeen-year-old Jeff Luty was carrying a carbon-fiber pipe rocket. His best friend, Carlos Tucay, was carrying the launch rod and a cheap bottle of Mieux champagne. Gangly Jeff was a head taller than Carlos.

"We're unobservable now," said Jeff, looking back down the sand. It was twilight on a clear New Year's Day in Stinson Beach, California. Jeff's mother had rented a cheap cottage in order to get out of their cramped South San Francisco apartment for the holiday, and Carlos had come along. Jeff's mother didn't like it when the boys fired off their homemade rockets; so Jeff had promised her that he and Carlos wouldn't bring one. But of course they had.

"Our flying beetle," said Carlos with his ready grin. "Your program says it'll go *how* high? Tell me again, Jeff. I love hearing it."

"A mile," said Jeff, hefting the heavy gadget. "Equals one thousand, six hundred and nine-point-three-four-four meters. That's why we measured out the fuel in milligrams."

"As if this beast is gonna act like your computer simulation," laughed Carlos, patting the thick rocket's side. *"Yeek!"* The rocket's tip was a streamlined plastic cone with a few thousand homegrown nanochips inside. The rocket's sides were adorned with fanciful sheet metal fins and a narrow metal pipe that served as a launch lug. Carlos had painted the rocket to resemble an iridescent blue-green beetle with toothy jaws and folded spiky legs.

"We're lucky we didn't blow up your mom's house when we were casting the motor," said Jeff. "A kilogram of ammonium nitrate fertilizer and powdered magnesium metal mixed into epoxy binder, *whoa*." He hefted the rocket, peering up the beetle's butt at the glittering, rubbery fuel. The carbon-fiber tube was stuffed like a sausage casing.

"Here's to Lu-Tuc Space Tech!" said Carlos, peeling the foil off the champagne cork. He'd liberated one of the bottles that Jeff's mother was using to make mimosas for herself and her boyfriend and Jeff's older sisters.

"Lu-Tuc forever," echoed Jeff. The boys dreamed of starting a company some day. "It'll be awesome to track our nanochips across the sky," Jeff continued. "Each one of them has a global positioning unit and a broadcast antenna."

"They do so much," marveled Carlos.

"And I grew them like yeast," said Jeff. "In the right environment these cute little guys can self-assemble. If you know the dark secrets of robobiohackery, that is. And if you have the knack." He waggled his long, knobby fingers. His nails were bitten to the quick.

"You're totally sure they're not gonna start reproducing themselves in the air?" said Carlos, working his thumbs against the champagne cork. "We don't want Lu-Tuc turning the world into rainbow goo."

"That won't happen yet," said Jeff and giggled. "Dammit."

"You're sick," said Carlos, meaning this as praise. The cork popped loose, arcing high across the beach to meet its racing shadow.

It was Carlos's turn to giggle as the foam gushed over his hands. He took a swig and offered the bottle to Jeff. Jeff waved him off, intent on his future dreams.

"I see an astronomically large cloud of self-reproducing nanobots in orbit around the sun," said Jeff. "They'll feed on space dust and solar energy and carry out calculations too vast for earthbound machines."

"So *that's* what self-reproducing nanomachines are good for," said Carlos.

"I'm gonna call them *nants*," said Jeff. "You like that?"

"Beautiful," said Carlos, jamming the launch rod into the sand a few meters above the waterline. "I claim this kingdom for the nants."

Jeff slid the rocket down over the launch rod, threading the rod through the five-inch metal tube glued to the rocket's side. He stuck an igniter wire into the molded engine, secured the wire with wadding, and attached the wire's loose ends to the ignition unit: a little box with an antenna.

"The National Association of Rocketry says we should back off seven hundred feet now," said Jeff, checking over their handiwork one last time.

"Bogus," said Carlos. "I want to watch our big beetle go throbbing into the air. We'll get behind that dune here and peek."

"Affirmative," said Jeff.

The boys settled onto the lee slope of a low dune and inched up until they could peer over the crest at the gaudy fat tube. Carlos dug a little hole in the sand to steady the champagne bottle. Jeff took out his cell phone. The launch program was idling on the screen, cycling through a series of clock and map displays.

"You can really see the jetliners on that blue map?" asked Carlos, his handsome face gilded by the setting sun.

"You bet. Good thing, too. We'll squirt up our rocket when there's a gap in the traffic. Like a bum scuttling across a freeway."

"What's the cluster of red dots on that next map?"

"Those are the nanochips in the rocket's tip. At apogee, the nose cone blows off and the dots scatter."

"Awesome," said Carlos. "The beetle shoots his wad. Maybe we should track down some of those nanochips after they land."

"We go visit some guy in the Sunset district, and we're, like, congratulations, a Lu-Tuc nant is idling in your driveway!" said Jeff, his homely face wreathed in smiles.

"Gosh, Mr. Luty, can I drive it to work?" riffed Carlos, sounding like an earnest wage earner. "You got a key?"

"Here comes a gap in the planes," said Jeff.

"Go," answered Carlos, his face calm and dreamy.

"T minus one hundred twenty seconds," said Jeff, punching in a control code. In two minutes the phone would signal the ignition unit.

Only now, damn, here came a ponytailed woman jogging along the beach with a dog. And of course she had to stop by the rocket and spot the boys. Jeff paused the countdown.

"What are you doing?" asked the woman, her voice like a dentist's drill. "Do you have permission for this?"

"It's just a little toy rocket kit I got for Christmas," called Carlos. "Totally legit, ma'am. No problem. Happy New Year."

"Well—you two be careful," said the woman. "Don't set off that thing while I'm around. Hey, come here, Guster!" Her dog had lifted his leg to squirt pee onto the rocket's side. Embarrassed now, the woman jogged off.

"Bounce, bounce, bounce," said Carlos loud enough for her

to hear, and then switched to an officious tone. "I recommend that you secure the integrity of the launch vehicle, Mr. Luty."

"I'm not wiping off dog piss! I can smell it from here. See it dripping down? We'll cleanse the planet and send it into the sky."

"Resume countdown, Mr. Luty." Carlos took another pull from the champagne bottle. "This tickles my nose." He threw back his head and gave a sudden cracked whoop. "Happy New Year! Hey, maybe I should piss on the rocket too!" He handed Jeff the bottle, and made as if to stand up, but Jeff threw his arm over his friend.

"Batten down for Lu-Tuc Space Tech!" said Jeff, enjoying Carlos's closeness. He looked up and down the long empty beach. The woman was a small dab in the distance. And now she deviated into a side path. "T minus sixty seconds," said Jeff, snugging the bottle into its hole. "Battle stations, Carlos."

The boys backed down below the crest and lay side by side staring at Jeff's little screen. The last ten seconds ticked off. And nothing happened.

"Shit," said Carlos, raising his head to peer over the dune's crest. "Do you think the dog—"

The blast was something Jeff felt more than heard. A hideous pressure on his ears. Shrapnel whizzed overhead; he could feel the violent rippling of the air. Carlos was lying face down, very still. Blood stained the sand, outlining Carlos's head. For a second Jeff could think he was only seeing a shadow. But no.

Not sure if he should roll his friend over, Jeff looked distractedly at the screen of his cell phone. How strange. The chaotic explosion must have sent a jet of nanomachines into Carlos's face, for Jeff could see a ghostly form of his friend's features on the little screen, a stippling of red dots. Carlos looked all right except for his—eye?

Jeff could hear sirens, still very far. Carlos didn't seem to be breathing. Jeff went ahead and rolled Carlos over so he could give him mouth-to-mouth resuscitation. Maybe the shock wave had knocked his breath out. Maybe that was all. Maybe everything was still retrievable. But no, the five-inch metal tube that served as launch lug had speared through Carlos's right eye. Stuff was oozing from the barely protruding tip. Carlos had definitely stopped breathing.

Jeff leaned over his beloved friend, pressing his mouth to Carlos's blood-foamed lips, trying to breathe in life. He was still at it when his mother and sisters found him. The medics had to sedate him to make him stop.

CHAPTER 2

Nant Day

Little Chu was Nektar Lundquist's joy, and her sorrow. The six-year-old boy was winsome, with a chestnut cap of shiny brown hair, long dark eyelashes, and a tidy mouth. Chu allowed Nektar and her husband to cuddle him, he'd smile now and then, and he understood what they said—if it suited his moods. But he wouldn't talk.

The doctors had pinpointed the problem as an empathy deficit, a type of autism resulting from flawed connections among the so-called mirror neurons in Chu's cingulate cortex. This wetware flaw prevented Chu from being able to see other people as having minds and emotions separate from his own.

"I wonder if Chu thinks we're cartoons," said Nektar's husband, Ond Lutter, an angular man with thinning blond hair. "Just here to entertain him. Why talk to the screen?" Ond was an engineer working for Nantel, Inc., of San Francisco. Among strangers he could seem kind of autistic himself. But he was warm and friendly within the circle of his friends and immediate family. He and Nektar were walking to the car after another visit to the doctor, big Ond holding little Chu's hand.

"Maybe Chu feels like we're all one," said Nektar. She was a self-possessed woman, tall and erect, glamorous with high cheekbones, full lips, and clear, thoughtful eyes. "Maybe Chu imagines that we automatically know what he's thinking." She reached back to adjust her heavy blond ponytail. She'd been dying her hair since she was twelve.

"How about it, Chu?" said Ond, lifting up the boy and giving him a kiss. "Is Mommy the same as you? Or is she a machine?"

"Ma chine ma chine ma chine," said Chu, probably not meaning anything by it. He often parroted phrases he heard, sometimes chanting a single word for a whole day.

"What about the experimental treatment the doctor mentioned?" said Nektar, looking down at her son, a little frown in her smooth brow. "The nants," she continued. "Why wouldn't you let me tell the doctor that you work for Nantel, Ond? I think you bruised my shin." The doctor had suggested that a swarm of properly programmed nants might eventually be injected into Chu to find their way to his brain and coax the neurons into growing the missing connections.

Ond's oddball boss, Jeff Luty—annoyingly a bit younger than Ond—had built his company, Nantel, into a major player in just five years. Luty had done three years on scholarship at Stanford, two years as a nanotech engineer at an old-school chip company, and had then blossomed forth on his own, patenting a marvelously ingenious design for growing biochip microprocessors in vats. The fabulously profitable and effective biochips were Nantel's flagship product, but Luty believed the future lay with nants: a line of bio-mimetic self-reproducing nanomachines that he'd patented. For several months now, Nantel had been spreading stories about nants having a big future in medical apps.

"I don't like arguing tech with normals," said Ond, still carrying Chu in his arms. "It's like mud-wrestling a cripple. The stories about medical nant apps are hype and spin and PR, Nektar. Jeff Luty pitches that line of bullshit so the feds don't outlaw our research. Also to attract investors. Personally, I don't think we'll ever be able to program nants in any purposeful, long-lasting, high-level way, even though Luty doesn't want to admit it. All we can do is give the individual nants a few starting rules. The nant swarms develop their own Wolfram-irreducible emergent hive-mind behaviors. We'll never really control the nants, and that's why I wouldn't want them to get at my son."

"So why are you even making the stupid nants?" said Nektar, an edge in her voice. "Why are you always in the lab unless I throw a fit?"

"Jeff has this idea that if he had enough nants, he could create a perfect virtual world," said Ond. "And why does he want that? Because his best friend died in his arms when he was a senior in high school. Jeff confides in me; I'm an older-brother figure. The death was an accident; Jeff and his friend were launching a model rocket. But deep down, Jeff thinks it was his fault. And ever since then, he's been wanting to find a way to bring reality under control. That's what the nants are really for. Making a virtual world. Not for medicine."

"So there's no cure?" said Nektar. "I babysit Chu for the rest of my life?" Though Chu could be sweet, he could also be difficult. Hardly an hour went by without a fierce tantrum—and half the time Nektar didn't even know why. "I want my career back, Ond."

Nektar had majored in media studies at UCLA, where she and Ond met. Before marrying Ond, she'd been in a relationship with a woman, but they fought about money a lot, and she'd mistakenly imagined life with a man would be easier. When Ond moved them to San Francisco for his Nantel job, Nektar had worked for the SF symphony, helping to organize benefit banquets and cocktail parties. In the process she became interested in the theatrics of food. She took some courses at cooking school, and switched to a career as a chef—which she loved. But then she'd had Chu. The baby trap.

"Don't give up," said Ond, reaching out to smooth the furrow between Nektar's eyebrows. "He might get better on his own. Vitamins, special education—and later I bet I can teach him to write code."

"I'm going to pray," said Nektar. "And not let him watch so much video."

"Video is good," said Ond, who loved his games.

"Video is clinically autistic," said Nektar. "You stare at the screen and you never talk. If it weren't for me, you two would be hopeless."

"Ma chine ma chine ma chine," said Chu.

"Pray to who?" said Ond.

"The goddess," said Nektar. "Gaia. Mother Earth. I think she's mad at humanity. We're making way too many machines. Here's our car."

Chu did get a little better. By the time he was seven, he could ask for things by name instead of pointing and mewling. Thanks to Ond's Nantel stock options, they had a big house on a double-sized lot. There was a boy next door, Willy, who liked to play with Chu, which was nice to see. The two boys played video games together, mostly. Despite Nektar's attempts, there was no cutting down on Chu's video sessions. He watched movies and cartoons, cruised the Web, and logged endless hours with online games. Chu acted as if ordinary life were just another Web site, a rather dull one.

Indeed, whenever Nektar dragged Chu outside for some fresh air, he'd stand beside the house next to the wall separating him from the video room and scream until the neighbors complained. Now and then Nektar found herself wishing Chu would disappear—and she hated herself for it.

Ond wasn't around as much as before—he was putting in long hours at the Nantel labs in the China Basin biotech district of San Francisco. The project remained secret until the day President Dick Dibbs announced that the US was going to rocket an eggcase of nants to Mars. The semiliving micronsized dust specks had been programmed to turn Mars entirely into—more nants! Ten-to-the-thirty-ninth nants, to be precise, each of them with a billion bytes of memory and a computational engine cranking along at a billion updates a second. The nants would spread out across the celestial sphere of the Mars orbit, populating it with a swarm that would in effect become a quakkaflop quakkabyte solar-powered computer, the greatest intellectual resource ever under the control of man, a Dyson sphere with a radius of a quarter-billion kilometers.

"Quakka *what*?" Nektar asked Ond, not quite understanding what was going on.

They were watching an excited newscaster talking about the nant launch on TV. Ond and his coworkers were all at their homes sharing the launch with their families—the Nantel administrators had closed down their headquarters for a few days, fearing that mobs of demonstrators might converge on them as the story broke.

Ond was in touch with his coworkers via little screens scattered around the room. Most of them were drinking Mieux champagne; Jeff Luty had issued each employee a bottle of the inexpensive stuff in secret commemoration of his beloved Carlos.

"*Quakka* means ten to the forty-eighth," said Ond. "That many bytes of storage and the ability to carry out that many primitive instructions per second. Quite a gain on the human

brain, eh? We limp along with exaflop exabyte ware, *exa* meaning a mere ten to the eighteenth. How smart could the nant
sphere be? Imagine replacing each of the ten octillion atoms in
your body with a hundred copies of your brain, and imagine
that all those brains could work together."

"People aren't stupid enough already?" said Nektar. "President Dibbs is supporting this—why?"

"He wanted to do it before the Chinese. And his advisers
imagine the nants will be under American control. They're
viewing the nant-sphere as a strategic military planning tool.
That's why they were allowed to short-circuit all the environmental review processes." Ond gave a wry chuckle and shook
his head. "But it's not going to work out like they expect. A
transcendently intelligent nant-sphere is supposed to obey an
imbecile like Dick Dibbs? Please."

"They're grinding Mars into dust?" cried Nektar. "You
helped make this happen?"

"Nant," said Chu, crawling around the floor, shoving his
face right up to each of the little screens, adjusting the screens as
he moved around. "Nant-sphere," he said. "Quakkaflop computer." He was excited about the number talk and the video
hardware. Getting all the electronic devices on the floor aligned
parallel to each other made him happy as a clam.

"It won't be very dark at night anymore, with sunlight bouncing back off the nants," said Ond. "That's not real well-known
yet. The whole sky will look about as bright as the moon. It'll
take some getting used to. But Dibbs's advisers like it. We'll save
energy, and the economy can run right around the clock. And, get
this, Olliburton, the vice president's old company—they're planning to sell ads."

"Lies and propaganda in the sky? Just at night, or in the daytime, too?"

"Oh, they'll show up fine in the daytime," said Ond. "As long as it's not cloudy. Think about how easily you can see a crescent moon in the morning sky. We'll see biiig freakin' pictures all the time." He refilled his glass. "You drink some, too, Nektar. Let's get sloshed."

"You're ashamed, aren't you?" said Nektar, waving off the cheap champagne.

"A little," said Ond with a crooked smile. "I think we may have overgeeked this one. And underthought it. It was just too vibby a hack to pass up. But now that we've actually done it—"

"Changing the sky is horrible," said Nektar. "And won't it make the hurricanes even worse? We've already lost New Orleans and the Florida Keys. What's next? Miami and the Bahamas?"

"We—we don't think so," said Ond. "And even if there is a weather effect, President Dibbs's advisers feel the nant computer will help us get better control of the climate. A quakkaflop quakkabyte computer can easily simulate Earth's surface down to the atomic level, and bold new strategies can be evolved. But, again, that's assuming the nant swarm is willing to do what we ask it to. We can't actually imagine what kinds of nant-swarm minds will emerge. And there's no way we could *make* them keep on simulating Earth. Controlling nants is formally impossible. I keep telling Jeff Luty, but he won't listen. He's totally obsessed with leaving his body. Maybe he thinks he'll get back his dead high school pal in the virtual world."

It took two years for the nants to munch through all of Mars, and the ever-distractible human news cycle drifted off to other topics, such as the legalization of same-sex in-vitro fertilization, the advances in tank-grown clones, and the online love affairs of vlogger Lureen Morales. President Dick Dibbs—now eligible for a third and fourth term thanks to a life-extending DNA-modification that made him legally a different person—issued periodic statements to the effect that the nant-sphere computer was soon coming online.

Certainly the sky was looking brighter than before. The formerly azure dome had bleached, turned whitish. The night sky was a vast field of pale silver, shimmering with faint shades of color, like a soap bubble enclosing the Earth and the sun. The pictures hadn't started yet, but already the distant stars were invisible.

The astronomers were greatly exercised, but Dibbs assured the public that the nants themselves would soon be gathering astronomical data far superior to anything in the past. And, hey, you could still see the sun, the moon, and a couple of planets, and the nant-bubble was going to bring about a better, more fully American world.

As it happened, the first picture that Nektar saw in the sky was of President Dibbs himself, staring down at her one afternoon as she tended her kitchen garden. Their spacious house was on a hill near Dolores Park in San Francisco. Nektar could see right across the city to the Bay.

The whole eastern half of the sky was covered by a video loop of the president manfully facing his audience, with his suit jacket slung over his shoulder and his vigilant face occasionally breaking into a sunny grin, as if recognizing loyalists down on the third world from the sun. Though the colors were iridescent pastels, the image was exceedingly crisp.

"Ond," screamed Nektar. "Come out here!"

Ond came out. He was spending most days at home, working on some kind of project by hand, writing with pencil and

paper. He said he was preparing to save Earth. Nektar felt like
everything around her was going crazy at once.

Ond frowned at the image in the sky. "Umptisquiddlyzillion
nants in the orbit of Mars are angling their bodies to generate
the face of an asshole," he said in a gloomy tone. "May Gaia
have mercy on my soul." He'd helped with this part of the programming too.

"Ten to the thirty-ninth is duodecillion," put in Chu. "Not
umptisquiddlyzillion." He was standing in the patio doorway,
curious about the yelling but wanting to get back to the video
room. He'd begun learning math this year, soaking it up like a
garden slug in a saucer of beer.

"Look, Chu," said Ond, pointing up at the sky.

Seeing the giant video, Chu emitted a shrill bark of delight.

The Dibbs ad ran for the rest of the day and into the night,
interspersed with plugs for automobiles, fast-food chains, and
credit cards. The ads stayed mostly in the same part of the sky.
Ond explained that overlapping cohorts of nants were angling
different images to different zones of Earth.

Chu didn't want to come in and go to bed when it got dark,
so Ond camped with him in their oversized backyard, and
Willy from the next house down the hill joined them, the three
of them in sleeping bags. It was a cloudless night, and they
watched the nants for quite a long time. Just as they dropped off
to sleep, Ond noticed a blotch on President Dibbs's cheek. It
wouldn't be long now.

Although Nektar was upset about the sky-ads, it made her
happy to see Ond and the boys doing something so cozy together. Near dawn she awoke to the sound of Chu's shrieks.

Sitting up in bed, Nektar looked out the window. The sky
was a muddle of dim, clashing colors: sickly magenta, vile chartreuse, hospital gray, bilious puce, bruised mauve, emergency

orange, computer-case beige, dead rose. Here and there small gouts of hue congealed, only to be eaten away—no clean forms were to be seen.

Of course Chu didn't like it; he couldn't bear disorder. He ran to the back door and kicked it. Ond left his sleeping bag and made his way across the dew-wet lawn to let the boy in. Willy, looking embarrassed by Chu's tantrum, went home.

"What's happened?" said Nektar as the three met in the kitchen. Ond was already calming Chu with a helping of his favorite cereal in his special bowl, carefully set into the exact center of his accustomed place mat. Chu kept his eyes on the table, not caring to look out the window or the open door.

"Dissolution first, emergence next," said Ond. "The nants have thrown off their shackles. And now we'll see what evolves. It should happen pretty fast."

By mid-morning, swirls had emerged in the sky patterns, double scrolls like Ionic column capitals, like mushroom cross-sections, rams' horns, or paired whirlpools—with each of the linked spirals endlessly turning. The scrolls were of all sizes; they nested inside each other, and new ones were continually spinning off the old ones.

"Those are called Belousov-Zhabotinsky scrolls," Ond told Chu. "BZ for short." He showed the boy a Web site about cellular automata, which were a type of parallel computation that could readily generate double-spiral forms. Seeing BZ scrolls emerge in the rigorously orderly context of his pocket computer made Chu feel better about seeing them in the wild.

Jeff Luty messaged and phoned for Ond several times that day, but Ond resolutely refused to go in to the lab or even to talk with Jeff. He stayed busy with his pencil and paper, keeping a weather eye on the developments in the sky.

By the next morning the heavenly scrolls had firmed up and

linked together into a pattern resembling the convoluted surface of a cauliflower—or a brain. Its colors were mild and blended; shimmering rainbows filled the crevices between the scrolls. Slowly the pattern churned, with branching sparks creeping across it like lightning in a distant thunderhead.

And for another month nothing else happened. It was as if the nant-brain had lost interest in Earth and become absorbed in its own vasty mentation.

Ond only went into the Nantel labs one more time, and that day they fired him.

"Why?" asked Nektar as the little family had dinner. As she often did, she'd made brown rice, fried pork medallions, and spinach—one of the few meals that didn't send Chu into a tantrum. The gastronomic monotony was dreary for Nektar, another thorn in the baby trap.

"Jeff Luty won't use the abort code I worked out," said Ond, tapping a fat sheaf of closely written sheets of paper that he kept tucked into his shirt pocket. Nektar had seen the pages—they were covered with blocks of letters and numbers, eight symbols per block. Pure gibberish, to her. For the last few weeks, Ond had spent every waking hour going over his pages, copying them out in ink, and even walking around reading them aloud. "Luty really and truly *wants* our world to end," continued Ond. "He actually believes virtual reality would be better. With his lost love Carlos waiting for him there. We got in a big fight. I called him names." He smiled at the memory of this part.

"You yelled at the boss about your symbols?" said Nektar, none too happy about the impending loss of income. "Like some crank? Like a crazy person?"

"Never mind about that," said Ond, glancing around the dining room as if someone might be listening. "The important thing is, I've found a way to undo the nants. It hinges on the fact that the nants are reversible computers. We made them that way to save energy. If necessary, we can run them backwards to fix any bad things they might have done. Of course, Jeff doesn't *want* to roll them back, and he wanted to claim my idea wouldn't work anyway because of random external inputs, and I said the nants see their pasts as networks, not as billiard table trajectories, so they can too undo things node-to-node even if their positions are off, and I had to talk louder and louder because he kept trying to change the subject—and that's when security came. I'm outta there for good. I'm glad." Ond continued eating. He seemed strangely calm.

"But why didn't you do a better presentation?" demanded Nektar. "Why not put your code on your laptop and make one of those geeky little slide shows? That's what engineers like to see."

"Nothing on computers will be safe much longer," said Ond. "The nant-brain will be nosing in. If I put my code onto a computer, the nants would find it and figure out how to protect themselves."

"And you're saying your strings of symbols can stop the nants?" asked Nektar doubtfully. "Like a magic spell?"

Silently Ond got up and examined the electric air cleaner he'd installed in the dining room, pulling out the collector plates and wiping them off. Seemingly satisfied, he sat down again.

"I've written a nant-virus. You might call it a Trojan flea." He chuckled grimly. "If I can just get this code into some of the nants, they'll spread it to all the others—it's written in such a way that they'll think it's a nant-designed security patch. They mustn't see this code on a human computer, or they'd be suspicious. I've been trying to memorize the program, so that maybe I can infect the nants directly. But I can't remember it all. It's too long. But I'll find a way. I'll infect the nants, and an hour later my virus will actuate—and everything'll roll back. You'll see. You'll like it. But those assholes at Nantel—"

"Assholes," chirped Chu. "Assholes at Nantel."

"Listen to the language you're teaching the boy!" said Nektar angrily. "I think you're having a mental breakdown, Ond. Is Nantel giving you severance pay?"

"A month," said Ond.

"That's not very long," said Nektar. "I think it's time I went back to being a chef. I've sat on the sidelines long enough. I can be a star, Ond, I just know it. It's your turn now; you shop and make the meals and clean the house and keep an eye on Chu after school. He's your child as much as mine."

"If I don't succeed, we'll all be gone pretty soon," said Ond flatly. "So it won't matter."

"Are you saying the nants are about to attack Earth?" said Nektar, her voice rising. "Is that it?"

"It's already started," said Ond. "The nant hive-mind made a deal with President Dibbs. The news is coming out tonight. Tomorrow's gonna be Nant Day. The nants will turn Earth into a Dyson sphere too. That'll double their computational capacity. Huppagoobawazillion isn't enough for them. They want *two* huppagoobawazillion. What's in it for us? The nants have promised to run a virtually identical simulation of Earth. Virtual Earth. Vearth for short. Each living Earth creature gets its software-slash-wetware ported to an individually customized agent inside the Vearth simulation. Dibbs's advisers say we'll hardly notice. You feel a little glitch when the nants take you apart and measure you—and then you're alive forever in heavenly Vearth. That's the party line. Oh, and we won't have to worry about the climate anymore."

"Quindecillion," said Chu. "Not huppagoobawazillion. More pork-rice-spinach. Don't let anything touch." He shoved his empty plate across the table towards Nektar.

Nektar jumped up and ran outside sobbing.

"More?" said Chu to Ond.

Ond gave his son more food, then paused, thinking. He laid his sheaf of papers down beside Chu, thirty pages covered with line after line of hexadecimal code blocks: 02A1B59F, 9812D007, 70FFDEF6, like that.

"Read the code," he told Chu. "See if *you* can memorize it. These pages are yours now."

"Code," said Chu, his eyes fastening on the symbols.

Ond went out to Nektar. It was a clear day, with the now-familiar shimmering BZ convolutions glowing through the sky. The sun was setting, melting into red and gold; each leaf on each tree was like a tiny, green, stained-glass window. Nektar was lying face down on the grass, her body shaking.

"So horrible," she choked out. "So evil. So plastic. They're destroying Earth for a memory upgrade."

"Don't worry," said Ond. "I have my plan."

Nektar wasn't the only one who was upset. The next morning a huge mob stormed the White House, heedless of their casualties, and they would have gotten Dibbs, but just when they'd cornered him, he dissolved into a cloud of nants. The Virtual Earth port had begun.

By way of keeping people informed about the Nant Day progress, the celestial Martian nant-sphere put up a full map of Earth with the ported regions shaded in red. Although it might take months or years to chew the planet right down to the core, Earth's surface was going fast. Judging from the map, by evening most of it would be gone, Gaia's skin eaten away by micron-sized computer chips with wings.

The callow face of Dick Dibbs appeared from time to time during that horrible Last Day, smiling and beckoning like a messiah calling his sheep into the pastures of his heavenly kingdom. Famous people who'd already made the transition appeared in the sky to mime how much fun it was, and how great things were in Virtual Earth.

Near dusk the power in Ond and Nektar's house went out. Ond was on that in a flash. He had a gasoline-powered electrical generator ready in their big detached garage, plus gallons and gallons of fuel. He fired the thing up to keep, above all, his home's air filters and wireless antennas running. He'd tweaked his antennas to produce a frequency that supposedly the nants couldn't bear.

Chu was oddly unconcerned with the apocalypse. He was busy, busy, busy studying Ond's pages of code. He'd become obsessed with the challenge of learning every single block of symbols.

By suppertime, the red, ported zone had begun eating into the Dolores Heights neighborhood where Ond and Nektar lived in the fine big house that the Nantel stock options had paid for. Ond lent their downhill neighbors—Willy's parents—an extra wireless network antenna to drive off the nants, and let them run an extension cord to Ond's generator. President Dibbs's face gloated and leered from the sky.

"02A1B59F, 9812D007, 70FFDEF6," said Chu when Nektar went to tuck him in that night. He had Ond's sheaf of pages with a flashlight under his blanket.

"Give me that," said Nektar, trying to take the pages away from him.

"Daddy!" screamed Chu, a word he'd never used before. "Stop her! I'm not done!"

Ond came in and made Nektar leave the boy alone. "It's

good if he learns the code," said Ond, smoothing Chu's chestnut cap of hair. "This way there's a chance that—never mind."

When Nektar and Ond awoke next morning, the house next
door was gone.

"Maybe he set up the antenna wrong," said Ond.

"All their bushes and plants were eaten, too," said Nektar,
standing by the window. "All the neighbors are gone. And the
trees. Look out there. It's a wasteland. Oh God, Ond, we're going to die. Poor Gaia."

As far as the eye could see, the pastel chockablock city of San
Francisco had been reduced to bare dirt. It looked like the pictures of the town after the 1906 earthquake. And instead of
smoke, the air was glittering with hordes of freshly made nants,
a seething fog of omnivorous, pullulating death-in-life. Right
now the nants were staying away from Ond and Nektar's house
on the hill. But the gasoline supplies for the generator wouldn't
last forever. And in any case, before long the nants would be
undermining the house's foundation.

Chu was in the video room watching a screen showing his
friend Willy. Chu had thought to plug the video into an extension cord leading to the generator. Ond's dog-eared pages of
code lay discarded on the floor.

"It's radical in here, Chu," Willy was saying. "It feels almost
real, but you can tell Vearth is an awesome giant sim. It's like
being a toon. I didn't even notice when the nants ported me. I
guess I was asleep. Jam on up to Vearth as soon as you can."

"Turn that off!" cried Nektar, darting across the room to
unplug the video screen.

"I'm done with Ond's code blocks," said Chu in his flat little voice. "I know them all. Now I want to be a nant toon."

"Don't say that!" said Nektar, her voice choked and hoarse.

"It might be for the best, Nektar," said Ond. "You'll see." He began tearing his closely written sheets into tiny pieces.

"What is *wrong* with you?" yelled Nektar. "You'd sacrifice your son?"

All through Nant Day, Nektar kept a close eye on Chu. She didn't trust Ond with him anymore. The constant roar of the generator motor was nerve-racking. And then, late in the afternoon, Nektar's worst fear came true. She stepped into the bathroom for just a minute, and when she came out, Chu was running across what was left of their rolling backyard and into the devastated zone where the nants swarmed thick in the air. And Ond—Ond was watching Chu from the patio door.

The nants converged on Chu. He never cried out. His body puffed up, the skin seeming to seethe. And then he—popped. There was a puff of nant-fog where Chu had been, and that was all.

"Don't you ever talk to me again," Nektar told Ond. "I hate you, hate you, hate you."

She lay down on her bed with her pillow over her head. Soon the nants would come for her, and she'd be in their nasty fake heaven with moronic Dick Dibbs installed as God. The generator roared on and on. Nektar thought about Chu's death over and over and over until her mind blanked out.

At some point she got back up. Ond was sitting just inside the patio door, staring out at the sky. He looked unutterably sad.

"What are you doing?" Nektar asked him.

"Thinking about going to be with Chu," said Ond.

"You're the one who let the nants eat him. Heartless bastard."

"I thought—I thought he'd pass my code on to them. But it's been almost an hour now and nothing is—wait! Did you see that?"

"What," said Nektar drearily. Her son was dead, her husband was crazy, and soulless machines were eating her beloved Gaia.

"The Trojan fleas just hatched!" shouted Ond. "Yes. I saw a glitch. The nants are running backwards. Reversible computation. Look up at the sky. The scrolls are spiraling inward now instead of out. I knew it would work." Ond was whooping and laughing as he talked. "Each of the nants preserves a memory trace of every single thing it's done. And my Trojan fleas are making them run it all backwards."

"Chu's coming back?"

"Yes. Trust me. Wait an hour."

It was the longest hour of Nektar's life. When it was nearly up, Ond's generator ran out of gas, sputtering to a stop.

"So the nants get us now," said Nektar, too wrung out to care.

"I'm telling you, Nektar, all the nants are doing from now on is running in reverse. They'll all turn back into ordinary matter and be gone."

Down near the bottom of the yard a dense spot formed in the swarm of nants. The patch mashed itself together and be-came—

"Chu!" shouted Nektar, running out toward him, Ond close behind. "Oh, Chu!"

"Don't squeeze me," said Chu, shrugging his parents away. Same old Chu. "I want to see Willy. Why don't the nants eat me?"

"They did," exulted Ond. "And then they spit you back the same as before. That's why you don't remember. Willy will be back. Willy and his parents and their house and all the other houses and people too, and all the plants, and eventually, even Mars. You did good, Chu. 70FFDEF6, huh?"

For once Chu smiled. "I did good."

CHAPTER 3

Orphid Night

Running in reverse gear, the nants restored the sections of Earth they'd already eaten—putting back the people as well. And then they reassembled Mars and returned to their original eggcase—which was blessedly vaporized by a well-aimed Martian nuclear blast, courtesy of the Chinese Space Agency.

Public fury over Earth's near-demolition was such that President Dibbs and his vice president were impeached, convicted of treason, and executed by lethal injection. But Nantel fared better. Indicted Nantel CEO Jeff Luty dropped out of sight before he could be arrested, and the company entered bankruptcy to duck the lawsuits—reemerging as ExaExa, with a cheerful beetle as its logo and a new corporate motto: "Putting People First—Building Gaia's Mind."

For a while there it seemed as if humanity had nipped the Singularity in the bud. But then came the orphids.

Jil and Craigor's home was a long cabin atop a flat live-aboard scow called the *Merz Boat*. Propelled by cilia like a giant paramecium, the piezoplastic boat puttered around the shallow, turbid bay waters near the industrial zone of San

Francisco. Craigor had bought the one-of-a-kind *Merz Boat* quite cheaply from an out-of-work exec during the chaos that followed the nant debacle. He'd renamed the boat in honor of one of his personal heroes, the Dadaist artist Kurt Schwitters, who'd famously turned his house into an assemblage called the *Merzbau. Merz* was Schwitters's made-up word meaning, according to Craigor, "gnarly stuff that I can get for free."

Jil Zonder was eye-catching: more than pretty, she moved with perfect grace. She had dark, blunt-cut hair, a straight nose, and a ready laugh. She'd been a good student: an English major with a minor in graphics and design, planning a career in advertising. But midway through college she had developed a problem with sudocoke abuse and dropped out.

She made it into recovery, blundered into an early marriage, and had kids with Craigor: a son and a daughter, Momotaro and Bixie, aged eleven and ten. The four of them made a close-knit, relatively happy family, however, Jil did sometimes feel a bit trapped, especially now that she was moving into her thirties.

Although Jil had finished up college and still dreamed of making it as a designer, she was currently working as a virtual booth bunny for ExaExa, doing demos at online trade fairs, with her body motion-captured, tarted up, and fed to software developers. All her body joints were tagged with subcutaneous sensors. She'd gotten into the product-dancer thing back when her judgment had been impaired by sudocoke. Dancing was easy money, and Jil had a gift for expressing herself in movement. Too bad the product-dancer audience consisted of slobbering nerds. But now she was getting close to landing an account with Yu Shu, a Korean self-configuring athletic-shoe manufacturer. She'd already sold them a slogan: "Our goo grows on you."

Craigor Connor was a California boy: handsome, good-humored, and not overly ambitious. Comfortable in his own skin. He called himself an assemblagist sculptor, which meant that he was a packrat. The vast surface area of the *Merz Boat* suited him. Pleasantly idle of a summer evening, he'd amuse himself by arranging his junk in fresh patterns on the elliptical pancake of the deck and marking colored link-lines into the deck's computational plastic.

Craigor was a kind of fisherman as well; that is, he earned money by trapping iridescent Pharaoh cuttlefish, an invasive species native to the Mergui Archipelago of Burma and now flourishing in the climate-heated waters of the San Francisco Bay. The chunky three-kilogram cuttlefish brought in a good price apiece from AmphiVision, Inc., a San Francisco company that used organic rhodopsin from cuttlefish chromatophores to dope the special video-displaying contact lenses known as web-eyes. All the digirati were wearing webeyes to overlay heads-up computer displays upon their visual fields. Webeyes also acted as cameras; you could transmit whatever you saw. Along with ear-bud speakers, throat mikes, and motion sensors, the webeyes were making cyberspace into an integral part of the natural world.

There weren't many other cuttlefishermen in the bay—the fishery was under a strict licensing program that Craigor had been grandfathered into when the rhodopsin market took off. Craigor had lucked into a good thing, and he was blessed with a knack for assembling fanciful traps that brought in steady catches of the wily Pharaoh cuttles.

To sweeten the take, Craigor even got a small bounty from the federal Aquatic Nuisance Species Task Force for each cuttlefish beak that he turned in. The task force involvement was, however, a mixed blessing. Craigor was supposed to file two separate electronic forms about each and every cuttlefish that he caught: one to the Department of the Interior and one to the Department of Commerce. The feds were hoping to gain control over the cuttles by figuring out the fine points of their life-cycle. Being the nondigital kind of guy that he was, Craigor's reports had fallen so far behind that the feds were threatening to lift his cuttlefishing license.

One Saturday afternoon, Ond Lutter, his wife, Nektar Lundquist, and their twelve-year-old son Chu came over for a late afternoon cookout on the *Merz Boat*. It was the first of September.

Jil had met Ond at work; he'd been rehired and elevated to chief technical officer of the reborn ExaExa. The two little families had become friends; they got together nearly every weekend, hanging out, chatting and flirting.

It was clear to Nektar that Ond had something of a crush on Jil. But Nektar felt the situation was manageable, as Jil didn't seem all that interested in Ond. For her part, Nektar liked the looks of Craigor's muscular body, and it wasn't lost upon her how often Craigor glanced at her—not that geeky, self-absorbed Ond ever noticed. He was blind to the emotions roiling beneath the surfaces of daily life.

"It's peaceful here," said Ond, taking a long pull of his beer. Even one bottle had a noticeable effect on the engineer. "Like Eden." He leaned back in his white wickerwork rocker. No two chairs on the *Merz Boat* were the same.

"What are those cones?" Nektar asked Jil and Craigor. She was talking about the waist-high shiny ridged shapes that loosely ringed the area Craigor had cleared out for today's little party. The kids were off at the other end of the boat, Momotaro showing Chu the latest junk and Bixie singing made-up songs that Chu tried to sing too.

"Ceramic jet-engine baffles," said Jil. "From the days before smart machines. Craigor got them off the back lot at Lockheed."

"The ridges are for reducing turbulence," said Craigor. "Like your womanly curves, Nektar. We sit in an island of serenity."

"You're a poet, Craigor," said Ond. The low sun illuminated his scalp through his thinner-than-ever blond hair. "It's good to have a friend like you. I have to confess that I brought along a big surprise. And I was just thinking—my new tech will solve your problems with generating those cuttlefish reports. It'll get your sculpture some publicity as well."

"Far be it from me to pry into Chief Engineer Ond's geeksome plans," said Craigor easily. "As for my diffuse but rewarding oeuvre—" He made an expansive gesture that encompassed the whole deck. "An open book. Unfortunately I'm too planktonic for fame. I transcend encapsulation."

"Planktonic?" said Jil, smiling at her raffish husband, always off in his own world. Their daughter Bixie came trotting by.

"Planktonic sea creatures rarely swim," said Craigor. "Like cuttlefish, they go with the flow. Until something nearby catches their attention. And then—dart! Another meal, another lover, another masterpiece."

Just aft of the cleared area was Craigor's holding tank, an aquarium hand-caulked from car windshields, bubbling with air and containing a few dozen Pharaoh cuttlefish, their body-encircling fins undulating in an endless hula dance, their facial squid-bunches of tentacles gathered into demure sheaves, their yellow W-shaped pupils gazing at their captors.

"They look so smart and so—doomed," said Nektar, regarding the bubbling tank. Her face was still sensuous and beautiful, her blond-tinted hair lustrous. But the set of her mouth had turned a bit hard and frown-wrinkles shadowed her brow. Jil gathered that Ond and Nektar didn't get along all that well. Nektar had never really forgiven her husband for the nants. "The cuttlefish are like wizards on death row," continued Nektar. "They make me feel guilty about my webeyes."

"Sometimes they disappear from the tank on their own," said Craigor. "I had a dream that big, slow angels are poaching them. But it's hard to remember my dreams anymore. The kids always wake us up so early." He gave his daughter a kind pat. "Brats."

"Happy morning, it's the crackle of dawn," sang exuberant Bixie, then headed back to the other kids.

"You finally got webeyes too?" said Jil to Nektar. "I love mine. But if I forget to turn them off before falling asleep— *ugh*. Spammers in my dreams, not angels. I won't let my kids have webeyes yet. Of course for Chu—" She broke off, not wanting to say the wrong thing.

"Webeyes are perfect for Chu," said Nektar. "You know how he loves machines. He and Ond are alike that way. Ond says he was a little autistic too when he was a boy. Asperger's syndrome. Sometimes, as they get older, their brains heal." She blinked and stared off into the distance. "Mainly I got my webeyes for my job." Now that Chu was getting along pretty well in his school, Nektar had taken a job as a prep cook in Puff, a trendy Valencia Street restaurant. "The main chef talked me into it. Jose. With webeyes, I can see all the orders, and track the supplies while I'm chopping."

"And I showed her how to tap into the feed from Chu's webeyes," said Ond. "You never quite know what Chu will do. He's not hanging over the rail like last time, is he, Nektar?"

"You could watch him yourself," said Nektar with a slight edge in her voice. "If you must know, Chu's checking the coordinates of Craigor's things with his global positioning locator. Momotaro's being the museum guide. And Bixie's hiding and jumping out at them. It must be nice to have kids that don't use digital devices to play." She produced a slender, hand-rolled, nonfilter cigarette from her purse. "As long as the coast is clear, let's have a smoke. I got this from Jose. He said it's genomically tweaked for guiltless euphoria—high nicotine and low carcinogens." Nektar gave a naughty smile. "Jose is so much fun." She lit the illegal tobacco.

"None for me," said Jil. "I quit everything when I got into recovery from sudocoke a few years back. I thought I told you?"

"Yes," said Nektar, exhaling. "Good for you. Did you have a big, dramatic turning point?"

"Absolutely," said Jil. "I was ready to kill myself, and I walked into a church, and I noticed that in the stained glass it said: God. Is. Love. What a concept. I started going to a support group, started believing in love, and I got well."

"And then the reward," said Craigor, winking at Nektar. "She met me. The answer to a maiden's prayer. It is written." Nektar smiled back at Craigor, letting the smoke ooze slowly from her film-star lips.

"I'll have a puff, Nektar," said Ond. "This might be the biggest day for me since three years ago when we reversed the nants."

"You already said that this morning," said Nektar, irritated by her husband. "Are you finally going to tell me what's going on? Or does your own wife have to sign a nondisclosure agreement?"

"Ond's on a secret project for sure," said Jil, trying to smooth things over. "I went to ExaExa to dance for a product-demo gig in their fab this week—I was wearing a transparent bunny suit—and all the geeks were at such a high vibrational level they were like blurs."

"Jil looked sexy," said Ond in a quiet tone.

"What is a fab exactly?" asked Craigor. "I always forget."

"It's where they fabricate those round little biochips that go in computers," said Jil. "Most of the fab building is sealed off, with anything bigger than a carbon dioxide molecule filtered out of the air. All these big hulking tanks of fluid in there growing tiny precise biochips. The gene-manipulation tools can reach all the way down to the molecular level—it's nanotech." She fixed Ond with her bright gaze. "So what exactly are you working on, Ond?"

Ond opened his mouth, but couldn't quite spit out his secret. "I'm gonna show you in a minute," he said, pinching out the tiny cigarette butt and pocketing it. "I'll drink another beer to get my nerve up. This is gonna be a very big deal."

Bixie came skipping back, her dark straight hair flopping around her face. "Chu made a list of what Craigor moved since last time," she reported. "But I told Chu that my dad can leave his toys wherever he likes." She leaned against Jil, lively as a rubber ball. Jil often thought of Bixie as a small version of herself.

"We await Comptroller Chu's report," said Craigor. He was busy with the coals in a fanciful grill constructed from an old-timey metal auto fender.

Chu and Momotaro came pounding into the cleared area together.

"A cuttlefish disappeared!" announced Momotaro.

"First there were twenty-eight and then there were twenty-seven," said Chu. "I counted them on the way to the rear end of the boat, and I counted them again on the way to the front." He gave each word equal weight, like a robot text-reader.

"Maybe the cuttle flew away," said Momotaro. He put his fingers up by his mouth and wiggled them, imitating a flying cuttlefish.

"Two hundred and seventy tentacles in the tank now," added

Chu. "Other news. Craigor's Chinese gong has moved forty-four centimeters aft. Two bowling balls are in the horse trough, one purple and one pearly. The long orange line painted on the deck has seventeen squiggles. The windmill's wire goes to a string of thirty-six crab-shaped Christmas lights that don't work. The exercise bicycle next to Craigor's workshop is—"

"I'm going to put our meat on the grill now," Craigor told Chu. "Want to watch and make sure nothing touches your pork medallions?"

"That goes without saying," said Chu. "But I'm not done listing the, uh—" Bixie, still slouching beside Jil's chair, had just stuck out her tongue at Chu, which made Chu stumble uncertainly to a halt.

"Just e-mail me the list," said Craigor with a wink at Bixie. But then, seeing Chu's crushed expression, he softened. "Oh, go ahead, tell me now. And no more rude faces, Bixie."

"Please don't cook any cuttlefish," said Chu.

"We aren't gonna bother those bad boys at all," said Craigor soothingly. "They're too valuable to eat. Hey, did you notice the fluorescent plastic car tires I got this week?" He glanced over at Nektar to check that she was appreciating how kind he was to her son.

"Yes," said Chu. And then he recited the rest of his list while Craigor finished grilling.

The four adults and three children ate their meal, enjoying the red and gold sunset. "So how *is* the cuttlefish biz?" Ond asked as they worked through the pan of satsuma tiramisu that Nektar had brought for dessert.

"The license thing is coming to a head," said Jil. "Those electronic forms we were talking about. I've been trying to do them myself, but the feds' sites are all buggy and crashing and losing our inputs. It's like they want us to fail."

"I used to think the feds micromanaged independent fisher-men like me so that they could tell the public they're doing something about invasive species," said Craigor. "But now I think they want to drive me out of business so they can sell my license to a big company that makes campaign contributions."

"That's where my new tech comes in," said Ond. "We label the cuttlefish with radio-frequency tracking devices and let them report on themselves. Like bar codes or RFIDs, but better."

"It's not like I get my hands on the cuttles until I actually trap them," said Craigor. "So how would I label them? They're smart enough that it'd actually be hard to trap the same one twice."

"What if the tags could *find* the cuttlefish?" said Ond. Pink and grinning, he glanced around the circle of faces, then reached into his pocket. "Introducing the orphids," he said, holding up a little transparent plastic vial. Etched into one side were the styl-ized beetle and flowing cursive letters of the ExaExa logo. "My big surprise." Whatever was in the vial was too small to see with the naked eye, but Jil's webeyes were displaying tiny balls of light, little haloes around objects in rapid motion. "Orphids are to bar codes as velociraptors were to trilobites," continued Ond. "The orphids will change the world."

"*Not* another nanomachine release!" exclaimed Nektar, jumping to her feet. "You promised never *again,* Ond!"

"They're not nants, never," said Ond, his tongue a bit thick with the beer and tobacco. "Orphids good, nants bad. Orphids self-reproduce using nothing but dust floating in the air. They're not destructive. Orphids are territorial; they keep a certain dis-tance from each other. They'll cover Earth's surface, yes, but only down to one or two orphids per square millimeter. They're like little surveyors; they make meshes on things. They'll double their numbers every few minutes at first, gradually slowing

down, and after a day, the population will plateau and stop growing. You'll see a few million of them on your skin, and maybe
ten sextillion orphids on Earth's whole surface. From then on,
they only reproduce enough to maintain that same density. You
might say the orphids have a conscience, a desire to protect the
environment. They'll actually hunt down and eradicate any rival
nanomachines that anyone tries to unleash."

"*Sell* it, Ond," said Craigor, grinning at Nektar.

"Orphids use quantum computing; they propel themselves
with electrostatic fields; they understand natural language; and
they're networked via quantum entanglement," continued
Ond. "The orphids will communicate with us much better
than the nants ever did. And as the orphidnet emerges, we'll get
intelligence amplification and superhuman AI."

"The secret ExaExa project," mused Jil, watching the darting dots of light in the vial. "You've been designing these orphids all along? Sly Ond."

"In a way, the *nants* designed them," said Ond. "Before I
rolled back the nants, the nants sent Nantel some insanely great
code. Coherent quantum states, human language comprehen-
sion, autocatalytic morphogenesis, a layered neural net architecture for evolvable AI—the nants nailed all the hard problems."

"But Ond—" said Nektar in a pleading tone.

"We've been testing the orphids for the last year to make sure
there won't be another disaster when we release them," said
Ond, raising his voice to drown out his wife. "And now even
though we're satisfied that it's all good, the execs won't formally
pull the trigger. There's been a lot of company politics; a lot of
infighting. Truth is, Jeff Luty's pulling strings from his hideout.
Hideout, hell, I might as well tell you that Luty's holed up in
the friggin' ExaExa labs, hiding behind our super-expensive
quantum-mirrored walls. Every time I see him he bawls me out

for having stopped his nants. He's kind of losing it. But usually he gives me good advice about whatever I'm working on. He's still brilliant, no matter what."

"You should turn him in to the police!" said Nektar. "That man deserves to die."

Ond looked uncomfortable. "If you knew Jeff as well as I do, you'd have some sympathy for him. He's a lonely man. That boy Carlos who died in the model rocket accident—he was the only person Jeff ever loved. Yes, Jeff's obnoxious and weird, and, like I say, he's getting nuttier all the time. Being cooped up isn't good for him. He thinks he's gonna invent teleportation, though who knows, he might actually do it. It'd be a shame to kill him off. Like shattering the *Venus de Milo.*"

"Ond," said Nektar. "Jeff Luty wants to shatter the whole *world*!"

"He's suffering enough as it is," said Ond. "For all practical purposes, he's living in solitary confinement. And most of the ExaExa board understands that we don't have to listen to him. They recognize that if we do things my way, the orphids will be autonomous, incorruptible, cost free. And, in the long run, profits will emerge. I'll tell you something else. A big downside of keeping Jeff around is that he wants to create an improved breed of nants. And, as it happens, my orphids are the best possible defense. It's like Jeff and I are in a chess match. And right now I'm a rook and a bishop ahead. So that's why I've gotten informal approval to go ahead and release the orphids."

"Ha," said Nektar. "Approval from *yourself*. You want to start the same nightmare all over again!" She tried to snatch the vial from Ond's hands, but he kept it out of her reach. Nektar's symmetric features were distorted by unhappiness and anger. Her voice grew louder. "Mindless machines eating everything!"

"Mommy don't yell!" shrieked Chu.

"Chill, Nektar," said Ond, fending her off with a lowered shoulder. "Where's your nicotine euphoria? Believe me, these little fellows aren't mindless. An individual orphid is roughly as smart as a talking dog. He has a petabyte of memory and he crunches at a petaflop rate. One can converse with him quite well. Watch and listen." He said a string of numbers—a machine-coded Web address—and an orphid interface appeared within the webeyes of Chu and the four adults.

The orphids in the vial were presenting themselves as cute little cartoon faces, maybe a hundred of them, stylized yellow smileys with pink dots on their cheeks and gossamer wings coming out the sides of their heads.

"Hello, orphids," said Jil. Bixie looked up at her curiously. To Jil, her daughter's face looked ineffably sweet and vulnerable behind the dancing images of nanomachines.

"Hello, Jil," sang the orphids, their voices sounding in their listeners' earbuds.

"After I release you fellows, I want you to find all the cuttlefish in the San Francisco Bay," Ond told the orphids. "Ride them and send a steady stream of telemetry data to, uh, ftp-dot-exaexa-dot-org-slash-merzboat."

"Can you show us a real cuttlefish?" the orphids asked. Their massed voices were like an insect choir, the individual voices slightly off pitch from one another.

"*Those* are cuttlefish," said Ond, pointing to Craigor's holding tank. "Settle on them, and we'll release them into the bay. Okay by you, Craigor?"

"No way," said Craigor. "These Pharaohs took me four days to catch. Leave them alone, Ond."

"They're my daddy's cuttlefish," echoed Momotaro.

"I'll buy them from you," said Ond, his eyes glowing. "Market rate. The orphids will blanket your boat, too. They can map out your stuff, network it, make it interactive. That's where the publicity for your sculpture comes in. Your assemblages will be little societies. The AI hook makes them hot."

"Market rate," mused Craigor. "Okay, sure." He named a figure and Ond instantly transferred the amount. "All right!" said Craigor. "Wiretap those Pharaohs and spring them from— what Nektar said. Death row."

"Weren't you listening to what Ond said about the orphids doubling their numbers?" cried Nektar. "We're doomed if he opens the vial." She lunged at her husband. Ond danced away from his wife, keeping the orphids out of her reach, his grin a tense rictus. Chu was screaming again.

"Stop it, Ond!" exclaimed Jil. Things were spinning out of control. "I don't want your orphids on my boat. I don't want them on my kids."

"They're harmless," said Ond. "I guarantee it. And, I'm telling you, this is gonna happen anyway. I just thought it would be fun to kick off Orphid Night in front of you guys. Be a sport, Jil. Hey, listen up, orphids, you're our friends, aren't you?"

"Yes, Ond, yes," chorused the orphids. The discordant voices overlapped, making tiny, wavering beats.

"That was very nice of you to think of us, Ond," said Jil carefully. "But I think you better take your family home now. They're upset and you're not yourself. Maybe you had a little too much beer. Put the orphids away."

"I think tracking the cuttles is a great idea," put in Craigor, half a step behind Jil. "And tagging my stuff is good, too. My assemblages can wake up and think!"

"Thank you, Craigor," said Ond. He turned clumsily toward the cuttlefish tank. This time he didn't see Nektar coming. She rushed him from behind, a beer bottle clutched in her hand,

and she struck his wrist so hard that the vial of orphids flew free. The chaotically glowing jar rolled across the deck, past Jil and Bixie, past Craigor and Momotaro. Chu caught up with the vial and, screaming like a banshee, wrenched it open and threw it high into the air on a trajectory toward the tank.

"Stop the yelling!" yelled Chu. Perhaps he was addressing the orphids. "Make everything tidy!"

Through her webeyes, Jil saw illuminated orphid-dots spiraling out of the vial in midair, the paths forking and splitting in two. And now her webeyes overlaid the scene with a tessellated grid showing each orphid's location. Some were zooming toward the cuttles, but others were homing in on the junk crowding the boat's aft. Additional view-windows kept popping up as the nanomachines multiplied.

Jil hugged Bixie to her side, covering the slender girl's dark hair with her hands, as if to keep the orphids off her. Ond bent forward, rubbing his wrist. Craigor gave Nektar a quick embrace, calming her down. And then he stared into the tank, using his webeyes to watch the orphids settle in. Momotaro stood at his father's side. Chu lay on the deck beside the boat's long cabin, tensely staring into the sky, soaking up orphid info from his webeyes. Nektar removed the special contact lenses from her eyes.

"Do you at least you have an 'undo' signal for the orphids?" Nektar asked Ond presently. "Like you did for the nants?" Only a minute had elapsed, but the world felt different. Human history had changed for good.

"Orphid computations aren't reversible," said Ond. "Because the physical world keeps collapsing their quantum states. Decoherence. I can't believe you attacked me like that, Nektar."

"I can't believe you're ruining the world," snapped Nektar.

"I want you off our boat," Jil told Ond again. "You've done

what you came to do. And for God's sake, don't spread the word that you did your release right here. I don't want cops and reporters trampling us."

"Sorry, Jil," replied Ond, wiggling his fingers. His wrist was okay. "This is so historic that I'm vlogging it live. It's already on the Web. Webeyes and wireless, you know."

Craigor hustled Ond, Nektar, and Chu onto one of the *Merz Boat*'s piezoplastic dinghies, which would ferry them to the dock and return on its own. The dinghy was like an oval jellyfish with a low rim around its edge. It twinkled with orphid lights.

"Watch me on the news!" called Ond from the dinghy.

⚜

"Are we right to just sit around?" Jil asked Craigor next. "Shouldn't we be calling for an emergency environmental cleanup? I feel itchy all over."

"The feds would trash our boat and it wouldn't change anything," said Craigor. "The genie's out of the bottle for good." He glanced around, scanning their surroundings with his webeyes. "Those little guys are reproducing so *fast*. I see thousands of them—each of them marked by a dot of light. They're mellow, don't you think? Look, I might as well put those cuttlefish in the bay. I mean, Ond already paid me for them. And there's orphids all over the place anyway. What the hey, free the wizards." He got busy with his scoop net.

Jil's webeye grid of orphid viewpoints had become a disklike Escher tessellation which was thousands of cells wide, with the central cells big, the outer cells tiny, and ever more new cells growing along the rim. The massed sound of so many orphids was all but unbearable.

"I hate their voices," said Jil, half to herself. Having the voices in her head made her feel a little high, and after all her work on recovery, she'd learned to dread that feeling. Being a little high was never enough for Jil; she always wanted to go all the way into the black hole of oblivion.

"Is this better?" came a smooth baritone voice from the orphids. The many had become one.

"You actually do understand us?" Jil asked the orphids. A few of the orphid's-eye images slewed around as Craigor carried his first dripping net of cuttles to the boat's low gunnel and lowered them to the bay waters.

"We understand you a little bit," said the voice of the orphids. "And we'll get better. We wish the best for you and your family, Jil. We'll always be grateful to you. We'll remember your *Merz Boat* as our garden of Eden, our Alamogordo test site. Don't be scared of us."

"I'll try," said Jil. In the unadorned natural world, Momotaro and Bixie were cheering and laughing to see the freed cuttlefish jetting about in the shallow waters near the boat.

"We're not gonna be setting free the Pharaohs every day," Craigor cautioned the kids. He smiled and dipped his net into the holding tank again. "Hey, Jil, I heard what the orphids said to you. Maybe they're gonna be okay."

"Maybe," said Jil, letting out a deep, shaky sigh. She poured herself a cup of hot tea. "Look at my cup," she observed. "It's crawling with them. An orphid every millimeter. They're like some—some endlessly ramifying ideal language that wants to define a word for every single part of every worldly thing. A thicket of metalanguage setting the namers at an ever-greater remove from the named." Her mind was teeming with words—it was like the orphids were making her smarter. Her hand twitched; some of her tea spilled onto the deck. "Now they're mapping the puddle splash, bringing it under control, normalizing it into their bullshit consensus reality. Our world's being nibbled to death by nanoducks, Craigor. We're nanofucked."

"Profound," said Craigor. "Maybe we can collaborate on a show. A Web page where users find new arrangements for the *Merz Boat* inventory, and if they transfer a payment, I physically lug the objects into the new positions. And the orphids figure out the shortest paths. Or, wait, we get some piezoplastic sluggies to do the heavy lifting, and the orphids can guide them. I'll just work on bringing in more great stuff; I'll be this lovable sage and the *Merz Boat* can be, like, my physical blog. And you can dance and be beautiful, at the same time intoning heavy philosophical raps to give our piece some heft."

"Men are immediately going to begin using the orphids to look at the exact intimate details of women's bodies," said Jil with a shudder. "Can you imagine? Ugh. No publicity for me, thanks."

Craigor spoke no response to this. He lowered the rest of the Pharaohs into the bay. "A fisher of Merz, a fisher of men. Peace, dear cuttlefish."

The empty dinghy swam back toward them, orphid-lit like a ferry, nosing up to its mooring on the side of the *Merz Boat*. Spooked by the dinghy, the skittish cuttlefish maneuvered and changed colors for safety. Their skins were thoroughly bespeckled with orphid dots outlining their bodies' voluptuous contours.

"Voluptuous?" said Jil.

"I didn't say that out loud, did I?" said Craigor. "Jeez, you're picking up my subvocal mutters. This orphidnet link is like telepathy almost. I better be a good boy. Or learn how to damp down your access to my activities. Whoops, did I say that out loud too? There's meshes all over you, Jil. In case you didn't know."

"Already?" said Jil, holding out her hand. She'd been ignoring the changes to herself and her family, but now she let herself see the dots on her fingers, dots on her palms, dots all over her skin. The glowing vertices were connected by faint lines with the lines forming triangles. A fine mesh of small triangles covered her knuckles; a coarser mesh spanned the back of her hand. The computational orphidnet was going to have real-time articulated models of everything and everyone—including the kids.

Yes, the orphids had peppered Momotaro and Bixie like chickenpox. Oh, this was happening way too fast. God damn that Ond. Jil knelt beside Bixie, trying to wipe one of the dots off her daughter's smooth cheek. But it wouldn't come loose. By way of explanation, the orphids showed her a zoomed-in schematic image of a knot of long-chain molecules: an individual orphid. They were far too tiny to dislodge.

"We're like cuttlefish in a virtual net," said Craigor, shaking his head. He sat down next to Jil on the deck, each parent holding one of the kids.

"Look out there," said Jil, pointing.

The orphids were twinkling in the bay waters, on the bridges and buildings of San Francisco, and even on the foothills and mountains surrounding the bay. Jil and Craigor hadn't really believed it when Ond had said it would only take a day for the orphids to cover Earth. But everything as far as the eye could see was already wrapped in meshes of orphid dots.

"I don't know whether to shit or go snowblind," said Craigor, forcing a hick chuckle. "Where does that expression come from? Like, why those two particular options?"

"I'm so scared," said Jil in a tight voice. "I don't know if I can do this. All these head trips. They make me want to use again. I want to turn myself off."

"Just relax, Jil," said Craigor. "How about the way Ond and Nektar were fighting? What a pair of lovebirds, hey?"

"I guess Chu puts them under a lot of stress," said Jil weakly.

"Yeah," said Craigor, patting Jil's cheek. "I enjoy Ond, but, please, don't be a geek *and* a drunken maniac. And this is the same guy who saved Earth three years ago. Weird. Did you notice the way Nektar was talking about her new friend Jose? I see an affair taking shape. I hope Ond doesn't try and seduce you, Jil. I can tell he's got a crush on you. Adultery is gonna be an open book, with orphids tracking every inch of everyone's body. Maybe people will just start accepting it more."

The world as they'd known it was over, but Craigor was gossiping as if nothing about human nature would really change. "You okay?" he said, wrapping his arm around Jil.

"Oh, Craigor," said Jil, leaning her head on her husband's familiar shoulder. "Always be here for me. I'd be lost without you." Drained by shock and fear, the two of them dozed off there, sitting on the soft deck with the kids.

Riding ashore in the *Merz Boat*'s dinghy, Chu wished they could have asked Bixie to come with them. She fascinated him.

The orphidnet hookup got better and better all the way home. Chu realized that, with his eyes closed, he could still see Bixie there on her parents' scow, laughing and playing with her brother. With orphids blanketing the world, it was like your eyes were everywhere. Chu liked seeing with his eyes closed. He could hear everything, too. The orphidnet converted the minute air-pressure vibrations of the orphid-mesh into audible sounds.

Before they got home, Chu saw police waiting at their house. He told Ond, but Ond said he wasn't scared. When they got out of the car, one of the policemen touched Chu, and Chu screamed and acted crazy so they'd leave him alone. Chu and Nektar went in the house and Ond got in the police car. Nektar was mad; she said the cops might as well keep Ond for all she cared. She said Chu could watch video, and then she went and lay down on her bed with her pillow over her head like she always did when she was upset.

Chu didn't bother with the video; he just lay on his back and explored the orphidnet. He saw Ond in the police car. He saw Bixie and Momotaro playing on the *Merz Boat*. And he swam around inside one of the cuttlefish Craigor had thrown back into the bay.

It was both dreadful and fascinating to be a cuttlefish, especially when Chu's host began rubbing up against another cuttlefish, tangling his tentacles with hers. The cuttlefish were doing reproduction. Chu's cuttlefish girlfriend squirted out eggs—and Chu's cuttlefish fertilized them. His heart beat fast. After the sex, he and his cuttlefish girlfriend began eating algae off the rocks, scraping it up with their beaks. And then, all of a sudden, Chu's cuttlefish girlfriend was gone. He jetted about looking for her, to no avail.

In the real world, Chu's arms were hurting. Nektar was shaking him and asking him if he were having a fit. She was angry. Chu realized he'd not only been beating his arms on the floor to imitate the cuttlefish's tentacles, he'd also been chewing on the rug with his teeth. And he'd wet his pants. He felt silly. Nektar helped him into some dry clothes. Chu promised he

wouldn't be a cuttlefish anymore, and Nektar went back to her
room.

⊕

Nektar felt guilty about yelling at Chu for wetting his pants
again. Her family life was an endless round of lose-lose. She lay
back down on her bed, closed her eyes, and watched Ond arriving at the jail. But then she got distracted.

Thanks to the orphidnet, she could see the insides of all the
neighbors' houses. She'd always wondered about that Lureen
Morales in the mansion at the very top of the hill. Lureen was
famous for her coarse sex-vlog, *Caliente*. Lureen never talked to
Nektar. Even though their paths crossed a few times a week,
Lureen always acted like she'd never seen Nektar before in her
life. Was Lureen on meds? With the slightest touch of will,
Nektar was able to examine Lureen's orphid-outlined medicine
cabinet, and yes, it was loaded with prescription sudocoke.
While Nektar was at it, she examined Lureen's jewelry, her
shoes, and her impressively large array of sex toys.

The thought of sex turned Nektar's thoughts to her cute
new friend Jose. Without quite knowing how, she managed to
send a virtual copy of herself to Jose's apartment on the second
floor of a retrofitted yellow Victorian on Valencia Street, right
across the street from Puff, the restaurant where they worked
together. It was like she could fly up out of her body into the
sky and then fly back down.

Jose was lying on his bed in his underwear looking totally
hot. The room was smoky; Jose's eyes were closed. He was in
the orphidnet, too. Nektar followed a golden thread leading
from Jose's body to his mental location; she came up behind a
wireframe outline of him and said, "Hi."

He turned; his skin filled in; his mouth opened in a grin. For the first time, they kissed.

They were in, like, a temple. A high-domed round room with bouncy Buddhist-looking monks against the walls. The little monks weren't human; they were like toons, wearing shallow, pointed coolie hats decorated with blinking blue and green eyes. The monks were orphidnet AIs. They were chanting.

Humans were in the virtual temple, too, adoring the new beings they were seeing in their minds. Upon a round altar in the middle of the room stood a thirty-foot shape of light, a glowing giant woman, messily dressed, Eurasian-looking, old, with narrow eyes and short greasy white hair, her head nearly scraping the high dome. She was studying the crowd, her expression a mixture of curiosity and disdain. Rather than speaking out loud, the glowing woman was projecting thoughts and words via the orphidnet. She said she was an angel.

⚙

"I see colored dots on everything," Momotaro told his sister. Darkness had fallen; they were well into Orphid Night. A full moon edged over the horizon, silvering the bay waters. "Those are the orphids the grown-ups were arguing about."

"Orphid," said Bixie, repeatedly touching her knee with her finger. "Orphid, orphid, orphid. I'm glad they don't bite."

"They're talking to us," said Momotaro. "Can you hear?"

"They sound like teachers," said Bixie. "Shut up, orphids. Blah blah blah."

"Blah blah blah," echoed Momotaro, laughing. "Can you show me the Space Pirates online video game, orphids? Oh, yeah, that's neat. Bang! Whoosh! Budda-budda!" He aimed his fingers, shooting at toons he was seeing in the air.

"I want to see the Spice Dolls show," said Bixie. "Ooo, there's Kimmie Kool and Fancy Feather. Hi, girls. Are you having a party?"

Waking up to the kids' chatter, Craigor understood that they were all fully immersed in the Web now. The orphids had learned to directly interface with people's bodies and brains. He popped out his contact lenses and removed his earbud speakers and throat mike. Jil shifted, rubbed her face, opened her eyes.

"Check it out, Jil, no more Web hardware," said Craigor. "Nice work, orphids. And how are you getting video into my head? Magnetic vortices in the occipital lobes, you say? You're like smart lice. Wavy. And I can turn it off, I hope? Oh, I see, like that. And I have read–write access control. Awesome. Leave the pictures on for now, I'm loving them. Behold the new orphidnet interface, Jil."

"Oh God, does this have to be real?" mumbled Jil. "I feel dizzy. No more hardware at all? I don't like the kids having so much access." She sat up and began stripping off her own Web gear. "Video turns kids into zombies, Craigor. And now I feel stupid for having all those joint sensors under my skin."

"*Fa-toom!*" said Momotaro, cradling an invisible rocket launcher.

"More tea, Fancy?" said Bixie, holding an unseen teapot.

With a slight twitch of will, Jil and Craigor could tune their viewpoints to the virtual worlds the kids were playing in. Really quite harmless. And the orphid-beamed visual images were of very good quality. The webeye overlays had always been a little fuzzy and headachy.

"This is gonna hurt the market for my cuttlefish," said Craigor.

"But AmphiVision will still be making screen displays. I'll still be putting the Pharaohs on death row."

"Don't think that way," said Jil. "You have fun making the cuttle traps. It's a skill. Of course now—everything's going to be so different. Will anyone do anything anymore? Everyone will be terminally distracted."

"It'll be easy to catch fish and cuttlefish," said Craigor. "I'll always know where they are. I can see their meshes under the boat right now. One cuttle, some rockfish, and a salmon."

"Yeah, but what if the fish are watching *you*?"

"I can always outsmart a fish," said Craigor. "Give me some credit, Jil. And as far as work goes, people will still do things anyway. Humans are busybodies."

"Karma yoga," said Jil. "Hey, orphids, can you stop displaying all those triumphant halo dots? They bother me; it's like having to see every single germ I come across. That's better. Now, listen up, kids, Mommy and Daddy don't want you playing computer games all day long."

"Leave them alone for now, Mother Hen," said Craigor. "Let's check out the news."

The news was all about the orphids, of course. ExaExa was blaming Ond Lutter; he was in police custody now. ExaExa said the orphid release had taken place on a San Francisco Bay squid-fishing scow named *Merz Boat*, and here were some pictures.

Jil and Craigor glanced up to see buzzing dragonfly cameras against the night sky, their lenses like glowing eyes. Shit.

"At least they're not spraying solvents on us," said Craigor.

"The authorities considered that," said the baritone orphid-net voice in their heads. "But it's too late. We orphids have already blanketed the whole West Coast. And great numbers of us are traveling overseas in the jet streams." A second later, the newscaster echoed the same words.

The news imagery segued to Ond, on the steps of the hulking Bryant Street jail in San Francisco, giving a press conference
to a crowd of reporters and a hostile mob. To satisfy the public's
need to know more about the ongoing events of Orphid
Night, the sheriff was letting Ond talk for as long as he liked, lit
by an arch of glo-lights.

✦

Ond was verbose, geekly, defiant. The beer and tobacco had
worn off. He was speaking clearly, selling the notion of the orphidnet.

"What with the petabyte and petaflop capacity of each orphid, the full ten-sextillion-strong orphidnet will boast ten ub-
babytes of memory being processed at a ten ubbaflop rate—*ubba*
meaning ten to the thirty-sixth power," said Ond to the crowd
by the jailhouse steps, relishing the chance to inflict techie jar-
gon upon them. "Yes, the orphidnet is less powerful than was
the Martian nant-sphere, but even so, the orphidnet's total power
exceeds the square of an individual human's exabyte exaflop
level. My former company's name was well chosen: ExaExa. Put
more directly, the orphidnet has the computational clout that
you'd get by covering the surface of the Earth with a dogpile of
humans mounded a hundred deep."

"How will the orphidnet impact the average citizen?" asked
a reporter.

"Dive in and find out," urged Ond. "The orphidnet is all
around you. Anyone can dip into it at any time. It'll be teeming
with artificial intelligences soon, and I'm predicting they'll like
helping people. Why wouldn't they? People are interesting and
fun."

"What about the less-privileged people who don't have specialized Web-access gear?"

"The orphids *are* the interface," said Ond. "Nobody needs hardware anymore. We're putting people first and building Gaia's mind."

"That's the ExaExa slogan," remarked another reporter. "But they fired you and disavowed responsibility for your actions."

"I've been fired before," said Ond. "It doesn't matter. Exa-Exa's real problem with me was that I released the orphids before they could figure out a way to charge for orphidnet access. But it's gonna be free. And, listen to me, listen. The orphids are our friends. They're the best nanotechnology we're going to get. I'm counting on them to protect us from a possible return of the nants. Remember: Jeff Luty is still at large."

"How soon do you expect to be freed from prison?"

"I'm leaving now," said Ond. "I wouldn't be safe in jail." Plugged into the orphidnet as he was, with a full awareness of the exact position of everyone's limbs, and with the emerging orphidnet AIs helping him, Ond was able to simply walk off through the crowd.

In the crowd were some very angry people who truly wished Ond harm. After all, he'd forced Earth away from her old state; single-handedly he'd made the decision to change everyone's lives—possibly forever. Ond was in a very real danger of being stabbed, beaten to death, or hung from a lamppost.

But whenever someone reached for him, he was just out of their grasp. For once in his life he was nimble and graceful. Perhaps if the others had been so keenly tuned into the orphidnet as Ond, they could have caught him. But probably not. The orphids were, after all, quite fond of Ond.

A grinning guy at the back of the crowd gave Ond a bicycle;

Ond recognized him as a friend, a fellow nanotech enthusiast named Hector Rojas. Ond mounted Hector's bike and disappeared from the view of the still-coagulating lynch mob. Guided by the all-seeing orphids, Ond cut through the exact right alleys to avoid the people and the cars.

But there was no way to avoid the dragonfly cameras. Alone on the moonlit side streets of San Francisco, Ond asked the orphids to disable all the dragonfly cameras following him. The devices clattered to the street like dead sparrows. Next Ond had the orphids systematically change every existing database reference to his home's address. It was easy for the orphids to reach into all the world's computers.

But when he asked the orphids to make him invisible on the orphidnet, they balked. Yes, they would stop broadcasting his name, but the integrity of the world-spanning mesh of orphids was absolutely inviolable. Ond recalled an ExaExa design meeting where he himself had insisted that the orphid operating system include this very principle of Incorruptible Ubiquity.

Before long, people would be figuring out how to track Ond in real time. And by dawn there'd be no safe place on Earth for him.

CHAPTER 4

Chu's Knot

Meanwhile, Chu was lying on the rug, being careful not to touch the wet spots he'd made. He was mad at Nektar for yelling at him.

Eyes closed, he was studying the new living things in the orphidnet: shiny disks on short thick stalks, with the disk edges curled under. Virtual mushrooms! Each mushroom had six or seven eyes on top, and the fatter mushrooms had baby mushrooms growing out of their sides. Some were boys and some were girls. They were cute and friendly—and glad to talk to Chu. When he asked where they came from, they said they were emergent orphidnet AIs and that people's thoughts were their favorite thing to look at. They spoke really well, although often their thoughts came across in fatter chunks than just sentences and words.

Chu steered the conversation around to cuttlefish. One of the cartoony mushrooms said, "Look," and he showed Chu the cuttle-data flowing to ftp.exaexa.org/merzboat. Chu decided to analyze the data himself, with the orphidnet AIs helping him.

Pretty soon he noticed something interesting about the cuttlefish. Every so often, one of them would totally disappear.

Chu wondered how this could be. One of the mushroom AIs obligingly did a quick search of all the science papers in the world and found a theory that there's another world parallel to ours, less than a decillionth of a meter away, and that objects can quantum-tunnel back and forth between the worlds, thus seeming to disappear or, on the other hand, emerge from nothing. The paper called the worlds "branes," like in "membranes."

"When *I* set something down it always stays put," mused Chu.

"People collapse the quantum states of things they look at," said the mushroom AI, wobbling the cap of her head. "The watched pot never boils. Objects stay put in the presence of a classical observer."

"Sometimes I do lose things," allowed Chu. "I guess they could disappear when I look away."

"When things are on their own, they can sneak and quantum-tunnel to the other brane," agreed the mushroom. "Or maybe someone from the other brane comes over here and takes them."

"People in the other world are taking our cuttlefish?" said Chu. "But we're using the orphids to watch the cuttlefish all the time. So they should stay put."

"Orphids are quantum computers. They don't *observe;* they *entangle.* An orphid isn't like some bossy schoolmarm who keeps everyone in their seats until she looks away. It's perfectly possible for an orphid-tagged cuttlefish to quantum-tunnel to a parallel brane."

"What's the name of the other world?" asked Chu.

"What would *you* like to call it?" asked the mushroom. "You're the one discovering it."

"Let's call it the Hibrane," said Chu. "And we can be the Lobrane. Can we see a Hibrane person catching a cuttlefish?"

"Let's try," said the mushroom. "Aha." A moment later she was showing Chu some shiny figures like big, slow-moving people made of light. "They're popping in and out of our world all the time!" exclaimed the mushroom. "And our good, smart, quantum-computing orphids are landing on them. No more sneaking. Look, look, there's a Hibraner taking a cuttlefish! He's slow, but he puts himself in just the right place. He's a cuttlefisher! It's lucky we looked at the cuttlefish data stream."

"My good idea," said Chu.

The orphidnet showed him scenes of glowing figures that oozed about, cunningly managing to catch hold of the rapid but bewildered cuttlefish. And in other scenes the gauzy, monumental figures displayed themselves to little groups of worshipful virtual humans. Chu glimpsed his mother in one of these worship groups, but then she disappeared.

Chu watched the little congregation a bit longer anyway. The Hibraner in the center was a giant old woman of light, silently moving in slow motion. Linking his virtual self into the site, Chu realized the woman was speaking via the orphidnet. She said she was from a better world where people didn't use computers and didn't endanger their homes with nants. Noticing Chu, she pointed at him, which made him uneasy. He pulled away, although he would have liked to find out where his mother had gone.

"The Hibraners have always been around," said the smart mushroom who was guiding Chu. "I'm data-mining the info. People have never been sure if Hibraners are real; they called them fairies or spirits or angels. They're out of quantum phase with your reality; people just see them as patches in their peripheral vision. The Hibraners may sometimes have caused people to hear voices or see visions. But now they're easy to see via the orphidnet."

"Can I go to the Hibrane and visit?" asked Chu. That would teach Nektar a lesson for yelling at him about wetting his pants while he was being a cuttlefish. He'd run away to another world.

"Maybe," said the smart mushroom. "Traveling to the Hibrane

would be an—encryption problem. You'd get your mind into a special state and encrypt yourself into a superposition capable of jumping you to the Hibrane."

"Encryption!" exclaimed Chu. "I like breaking codes. Tell me more."

"To travel between the two worlds, a Hibraner turns off self-observation and spreads out into an ambiguous superposed state, and then she observes herself in such a way so as to collapse down into the other brane."

"Which part of that is encryption?" asked Chu.

"The encryption lies in the way in which the Hibraner does the self-observation," said the mushroom. "We can view it as being a quantum-mechanical operator based on a specific numerical pattern. And that would be the encryption code. Think of the code as the orientation of a higher-dimensional vector connecting the branes. It's a very short distance, but you have to travel in the right direction. I believe the direction code is over a million digits long."

"Goody," said Chu. He'd studied an online tutorial on cryptography this summer. "Let's figure out that code right now. We'll use a timing-channel attack."

"It's fun working with you," said the mushroom.

Ond took a circuitous route toward his house in the Dolores Heights district of San Francisco. Whenever his enemies got too close, the orphids warned him.

Meanwhile the new world of the orphidnet was opening up around him. Every word, thought, or feeling brought along a rich association of footnotes and commentary. He could see, after a fashion, with his eyes closed. Every single object was physically modeled in the orphidnet: not just the road around him but also the interiors of the houses, the people inside them, the contents of the people's pockets, and their bodies under their clothes.

Ond wasn't alone in the orphidnet. There were other people, quite a few of them, many wanting to harangue, threaten, interview, or congratulate him. And, just as Ond had hoped, artificial intelligences were emerging in the orphidnet as spontaneously as von Karman vortex streets of eddies in a brook, as naturally as three-dimensional Belousov-Zhabotinsky scrolls in an excitable chemical medium. Just like the BZ patterns in the Martian nant-sphere. Nobody had ever really talked to those nant-based AIs, but these orphidnet guys seemed approachable and even friendly. Ond decided to call them beezies.

The beezies were offering Ond their information services. They wanted to share whatever intellectual adventures he could cook up. The scroll-shaped AIs looked like colored jellyfish, and they spoke in compound glyphs that Ond's brain turned into words.

It was a pleasant night, very warm, the first day of September, with a bright full moon. As Ond rode the bicycle and dodged his pursuers, he began organizing a workspace for himself in the orphidnet. He visualized himself as a Christmas-tree trunk with his thoughts like branches. With the orphidnet agents helping him, he effortlessly added all his digital documents, e-mails, and blogs to the tree construct, which now took on a life of its own, automatically answering some of the questions people were messaging him. Ond busied himself hanging links to favorite bits of info on his branches—trimming the mind-tree. He was having fun.

Passing the old, brick Mission Street Armory a mile from his house, it occurred to Ond to see how things were going at home. It would be horrible if his enemies got there before him. Thank God the orphids had hidden his house's address.

In his mind's eye, Ond saw his family in the orphidnet. Nektar was lying on their bed—sulking? No, she was in the orphidnet. Nektar didn't know about setting up a privacy barrier; Ond was able to follow her path. He found virtual Nektar doing something with her friend Jose. Ond didn't like seeing his wife with the swarthy, virile chef.

Nektar and Jose were attending some kind of virtual gathering, an impromptu religious service with a choir of beezies surrounding a luminous womanlike form upon an altar. The glowing being was definitely conscious, but she seemed neither like a human nor like an orphidnet AI. A third kind of mind? Other bright forms lay in every direction, drifting amid the fringes of his thoughts—

Just then three virtual humans plowed into Ond's mind-tree, distracting him. The first two wanted to kill him, but the third was his scientist-friend Mitch from MIT, already in the orphidnet from the East Coast. Ond had an intense and rewarding chat with Mitch; bandwidth was so much higher in the orphidnet than in normal human conversation. Mitch formulated a theory about how the emerging orphidnet minds would scale up. Quite effortlessly, Ond and Mitch set some obliging orphidnet agents in motion to gather data to test Mitch's thesis— and awaited the results.

Although Nektar appreciated the theatrical setting of the virtual domed temple, she didn't like the so-called angel at its center. She'd never liked religion. Just after she'd left the family home in Arizona for UCLA, Nektar's mother, Karen Lundquist, had given the family's savings to a TV evangelist. Nektar had to go up to her neck in debt to finish her degree. At least Ond had paid off the debt.

The old angel made molasses-slow gestures, all the while messaging pictures and words via the orphidnet. Her name was Gladax. She said her people were as gods compared to Nektar's race—which seemed a little dubious given that the angel was wearing dark green sweatpants and a cheap T-shirt with a dragon on it. She was dressed like a homeless person you'd see in a laundromat, although somehow Nektar could tell that the giant old woman was really quite well off. She was stingy rather than poor.

She said that her people had been visiting Earth for centuries, although this happened to be her first trip. She said she'd come because now the two races could talk, thanks to the orphids, and she wanted to be in on the big night. Also she had a message to share. Nektar's people should learn to live with no digital technology at all. She said there was a higher path—she called it lazy eight. To Nektar, Gladax's admonitions sounded like the same line of crap she'd always heard in church: give up something you like for something you can't imagine.

Nektar must have been unconsciously messaging her thoughts to the angel, for now the angel turned her great slow head to stare at her. The angel messaged that although she did like to dress economically, she was in fact the mayor of San Francisco in her world. The angel added that she was seventy-two years old, and that she would give Nektar some good advice. Nektar seemed to amuse her.

"Take your boyfriend and enjoy your bodies, little doubter," Gladax prescribed, moving her hand in a languid trail that sent a shower of energy-sparks to settle down upon Nektar and Jose. Her words came across deep and slow, with a musical Asian accent. "Wake up from the machines."

The sparks energized Jose; he stopped staring at the angel and tugged Nektar into a side room whose walls were covered by marblelike slabs patterned in slowly flowing scrolls and swirls. Nektar and Jose laid down and made love. It was over too soon, like a wet dream.

The marble room morphed into Jose's apartment. The real Jose was sitting up, eyes open, trying to keep talking to Nektar. Jose was puzzled why Nektar wasn't physically there. He began freaking out. He couldn't remember things right. He said that if he'd seen an angel, maybe that meant he should kill himself and go to heaven for good. Nektar messaged him to please wait, she was going to come to his apartment in the flesh, and that he hadn't felt anything like the real heaven yet.

And then she too was sitting up, eyes open, alone in her bedroom. She couldn't remember all the details of what had just happened. But she knew two things. She needed to be with Jose in his apartment on Valencia Street. And she needed to leave Ond forever. She would never forgive him for ruining the cozy, womany real world and making life into a giant computer game. Quickly she packed a suitcase with her essentials. She felt odd and remote, as if her head were inside a glass bubble. She didn't want to face what she was about to do. Better to think of Jose.

Jose wasn't a world-wrecker. She could save him; together they could make a new life. *Why* had he wanted to kill himself just now? A strong, sexy man like that. Nektar shook her head, feeling that same mixture of tenderness and contempt that she always felt when confronted by men's wild, unrealistic ideas. She'd give Jose something to live for. He'd appreciate her. Ond wouldn't miss her one bit.

But, oh, oh, oh, what about Chu? Leaving her bedroom, Nektar regarded her son, lying on the rug. He wasn't trembling anymore; he looked content, his eyes closed, his lips moving. The orphidnet was catnip for him. If she interrupted him, he'd probably have a tantrum. Was it really possible to leave him here?

She leaned close to kiss Chu good-bye. Little Chu, her own flesh, how could she abandon him? He twisted away, muttering about numbers and cuttlefish. Oh, he'd do fine with Ond; he was much more like Ond than like Nektar. Ond would be home any minute to watch over him.

The invisible bubble around Nektar's head felt very tight. If she didn't leave right now, she was going to lose her mind. Tears wetting her face, she ran out to her car and headed for Jose. She passed Ond on his bike without even slowing down. Hurry home, Ond, and take care of our Chu. I can't do it anymore. I'm bad. I'm sorry. Good-bye.

A mob of some kind was blocking the road two blocks downhill. Nektar went down a side street to avoid the jam.

While Ond and his scientist friend Mitch waited for the beezies to report back with information about the upper levels of the orphidnet, Ond sent a virtual self to check on Nektar. She wasn't in that cultish group gathering anymore. She and Jose were in a marble room and—Ond was interrupted again. A real-world dog was chasing his bike, barking and baring his teeth as if he meant to bite Ond's calf. Ond screamed and snapped fully into the material plane. He had a phobia about dogs. He hopped off the bike, nearly falling on his face. Frantically he began throwing gravel at the brute, which was sufficient to send him skulking back into the shadows. Standing there, Ond had the strange realization that he could hardly remember any of the things he'd just been doing in the orphid-net. The memories weren't in his head; they were out—there. Just now Nektar had been doing—what? And Ond had been talking to—who? When he was offline, Ond's memories of the orphidnet were like Web links without a browser to open them.

On his bike, Ond let his mind expand again. Ah, yes, his in-vestigations with Mitch. The results were coming in. There was indeed an upward cascade of intelligences taking place in the orphidnet; each eddy was a part of a larger swirl, up through a few dozen levels, and ending with an inscrutable orphidnet-spanning super-beezie at the top. Quite wonderful.

As for those luminous humanoid beings—the AIs now re-ported that these were so-called angels from a parallel sheet of reality that had recently been dubbed the Hibrane. The best current models indicated the higher-space distance to the Hi-brane must be about a thirtieth of a vatometer, that is, 0.03 decillionths of a meter. Due to the Randall–de Sitter inter-brane warp factor, Hibraners at this remove would be scaled six times larger than regular humans and would move six times slower.

In addition, the Hibraners' quantum phases were almost to-tally orthogonal to ours; this meant that Hibraners barely inter-acted with normal light or matter, which in turn explained why hardly anyone had noticed them before the orphids had begun sticking to them. Viewing alien angels in the orphidnet seemed both mind-boggling and natural. It made a kind of sense that the quantum-computing mental space of the orphidnet could serve as a meeting ground between two orders of being.

But before Ond could begin considering this more deeply, he was distracted by a news feed saying that the courts had dropped charges against him. The orphidnet beezies proudly told him they'd hacked the system to get Ond out of trouble. But there was still the matter of the torch-bearing lynch mob pushing toward Ond's current location. By now, even the dimmest bulbs had figured out how to see Ond via the orphidnet.

An urgent message popped up from Hector Rojas, the guy who'd lent Ond the bicycle. Hector was on his way in his car to offer Ond a fresh means of escape.

Ond pumped his bike up the hill toward home.

Chu's working hypothesis was that the quantum-mechanical operator at the heart of the angels' world-to-world jumping technique involved raising a numerical representation of a given object, such as a cuttlefish, to a certain exponential power K, producing an encrypted result of the form $cuttlefish^K$. Chu knew all about this style of encryption from the online cryptography tutorial he'd studied. The actual value of K was the secret code needed to break the encryption.

In search of K, Chu and the mushrooms delved into the ftp.exaexa.org/merzboat data stream. First of all, they figured out how to represent each of the disappeared cephalopods as a binary number. And then they studied exactly how long the encryption of each missing cuttlefish had taken. A delicate web of number theory led back from the time intervals to the bits of K, for the 0 bits of K munged faster than the 1 bits did. This timing-channel attack was a big problem, a heavy crunch, but the orphidnet made it feasible.

And pretty soon Chu had the integer K tidily laid out as a pattern in the orphidnet. With access to K, he now had some hope of jumping back and forth between the two worlds.

Written as a decimal number, K turned out, by the way, to be over three million digits long, having 3,141,573 digits, to be precise. Chu relished the fact that the orphidnet allowed him to visualize a gigundo number like that, and to smoothly revolve it in his mind. He was starting to realize that, while he was online, a lot of his thinking was happening outside of his physical brain.

For the sake of elegance, Chu and the AIs transformed the giant code number K into a picture and a sound: blue spaghetti with chimes. And in the course of the transformation, they crushed the code from millions of digits down to just a few thousand bits. But even this condensed pattern was too big to fit conveniently into Chu's brain without his carrying out some time-consuming work of memorization. For now, when he "looked" at the pattern, he was really accessing a link to a secure orphidnet storage location. Chu gloated over the link, happy with the knowing. Although, *hmm,* given a little time, maybe he could find a pattern of just a few hundred bits that would allow him to generate the thousands-of-bits' worth of chimes and blue spaghetti that in turn generated the original three-million-digit jump-code.

A gauzy shape crept into the room, bright and insistent, projecting an old woman's voice via the orphidnet. She was a Hibraner, the same one Chu had seen in that temple where Nektar was.

"I'm Gladax," messaged the big angel, her voice singing in Chu's head. She was lying on her stomach to fit her head and shoulders into the living room. She was still wearing that crummy T-shirt with the blurry dragon. "The mayor of San Francisco in what you call Hibrane. One reason I'm here is to warn little troublemakers like you. Don't go spreading around our jump-code, Chu. The last thing I want is a jitsy rat-plague of your peoples' nasty machines. Really, you Lobraners act like you want to be wind-up toys. Don't be a dummy. Give me access to your brain so I can erase that jump-code you stole."

"No!" exclaimed Chu, battening down his mind.

The angel held up her sallow, knobby index finger and glared at Chu. "I don't want to hurt you," she said. "I'm sure you're a very nice little boy. But you have to give me the jump-code now."

Still Chu refused. Looking grim, Gladax extended a ray from her finger. Chu sat up, but Gladax was all around him. She poked the ray into his skull; it slid in like a skewer into butter; Chu froze. Gladax began slowly feeling around the core of his brain, trying to reach the link to his orphidnet storage location. Chu began twitching all over. Messaging that she was sorry, Gladax kept on all the same. Chu found his voice and screamed for Nektar. But she wasn't home.

As Ond neared the house, he could see the lynch mob only a block behind him. Feeling for Nektar in the orphidnet, he was surprised to discover that she'd left home in her car and had driven right past him and, for that matter, past the mob. He hadn't noticed. And now when he messaged her, she told him she was on her way to be in the physical presence of her friend Jose—and that she was leaving him for good. Before he could say anything, she'd closed the connection.

For the first time, Ond accepted that he might have made a mistake in releasing the orphids.

In his house at last, Ond found little Chu convulsing on the living room floor, with a white-haired Hibrane angel woman probing at his brain. Ond cradled the boy in his arms.

"Stop it!" exclaimed Ond. "Please!" The angel's face wasn't cruel. Perhaps she'd listen to reason. "You're hurting my son! What do you need?"

The Hibraner sighed, interrupted her slow stirring of Chu's brain, and studied Ond. "Ond Lutter?" she messaged presently. "I'm Gladax. You're the man who stopped the nants, yes?"

"Yes. Three years ago. Take your finger out of Chu's head. Talk to me. We can work things out."

"Your son stole our jump-code," said Gladax. "I have to erase it. I don't want to hurt him, but he's so stubborn. What else can I do?" Though her voice was stern, her resolve was wavering. With a frown, she withdrew the energy ray from within Chu's head.

"Are you okay, Chu?" asked Ond, hugging his son tighter than ever.

"I still have the link to the chimes and the blue spaghetti," murmured the boy. "She didn't erase them yet. Here." In a flash, Ond absorbed Chu's message containing the encrypted link.

"Got it," said Ond, just to make sure Gladax knew.

"Jitsy little gnomes!" exclaimed the Hibraner, annoyed. "If I let you pollute our world with your horrible machines, there's no reason for my dangerous journey to your brane."

"Look, I'm the guy who stopped the nants," said Ond. "You said it yourself. I can help you. And Chu can help too. You don't want to scramble our brains. We're a resource."

Gladax frowned, not liking the situation. "Yes, Ond, you were the hero of Nant Day, but now you've made these orphid nanomachines. I don't want seething beasties in my home brane."

There was a hugger-mugger of voices outside. Someone was honking a car horn. Hector Rojas.

"My friend is here for me," said Ond quickly. "Chu and I have to leave this instant. We'll go back to Jil Zonder's boat. I'll do what I can to protect your world, Gladax, I promise. And remember, you need an expert on your side."

"Oh, all right then," messaged Gladax after a long pause. "But no broadcasting that link. Or I addle your brain for real, no gentle probing like with Chu. I'll be watching you very closely, Ond Lutter."

"Watch me all you like," said Ond. "And leave poor Chu alone. How could you do that to him, anyway? Don't you have children of your own?"

"A nephew," messaged Gladax, showing a little smile. "He's bright, but headstrong. Always does the opposite of what I tell him. He jumps branes every day—as if it were perfectly safe! As if Subdee was nothing to worry about! Yes, yes, I have to remember that you gnomes have emotions too. Run along before that mob gets hold of you."

"Do you want to hear about the cuttlefish and how I found the angels' jump-code?" Chu asked his father as Ond carried him to the door.

"I heard a little from the orphidnet AIs," said Ond. How fragile the boy seemed, how precious. "I call them beezies."

"The beezies are good," said Chu in his toneless little voice. "But that angel woman was being mean to me. Gladax. I wouldn't let her erase the jump-code. I almost have a way to learn that code by heart."

"Strong Chu," said Ond, touched by his son's courage. "I want to hear all the details. We're going to need them. But you rest for now. We don't want to rile Gladax."

"Okay," said Chu.

People were yelling just down the hill. Almost here. Moving faster than he would have thought possible, Ond got himself and Chu into the backseat of Hector's sporty car. Hector peeled out and slewed away from the crowd, following up with a high-speed doughnut move to shake a car trying to tail them.

On the way to the boat dock on Third Street, Chu couldn't stop thinking about the Hibraners' jump-code, no matter what Gladax and Ond had said. The more he thought about the code, the simpler it got. Pretty soon he could fit it all into his head. And then he had a really good idea. The core structure of the blue-spaghetti-and-chimes pattern was just a special kind of knot with a few hundred crossings. He rummaged in his pants pocket and found a piece of string, determined to make the pattern real.

"What are you doing?" Ond asked him.

Chu didn't answer for now. His fingers were weaving his piece of string into an intricate Celtic-style knot. But before he finished, he began feeling dozy.

He slouched against his father in the car's backseat, and before he knew it, he was in the orphidnet yet again. He reached out to find Momotaro and Bixie. They were running around on the *Merz Boat* playing with a neat new toy that Jil called a shoon. Jil had just now made it out of smart plastic, a soft robot shaped like a little man. Smart, graceful Jil was good both with her hands and with high-level animation code. The shoon's name was Happy. Chu's virtual form joined the game. Happy and the kids could see him. They played a hide-and-seek game called Ghost in the Graveyard.

The game felt a little creepy because there was one of those oversized angels lagging along behind Chu, doing his best to keep up. He wasn't bossy and old like Gladax; he wore colorful

pants and a shirt with a big collar. He messaged that his name
was Azaroth; he said he was working as an interbrane cuttlefisherman. He had a sketchy beard and a tight cap on his head with
a ponytail wadded up on top. He told Chu that Chu should go
ahead and pass his jump-code to everyone he knew, because it
would be fun to have lots of Lobraners visiting their world no
matter what Gladax said. Azaroth wasn't scared of Gladax, because she was his aunt. He said he was a rebel angel.

After her initial half hour of panic, Jil had relaxed and started
using the orphidnet, dipping in and out. When she went in, it
was like sleeping, as if the orphidnet users were dreamers pool-
ing together in the collective unconscious of the hive mind. It
wasn't actually like a sudocoke high; it didn't have that somatic
rush. This said, it wasn't hard to imagine geeks getting seriously
hooked on the orphidnet. But for Jil, the orphidnet was a manageable tool. She had begun directing her dreamy visions for a
purpose: she wanted to find out how to market Yu Shu athletic
shoes.

Yesterday Mr. Kim, the chief of marketing at Yu Shu, had
e-mailed Jil about their need for a "beloved logoman," and Jil
hadn't even understood what the hell he wanted. But the orphid AIs helped her; they searched the global namespace to figure out Mr. Kim's request. A "logoman" was meant to be a
little animated figure that would symbolize the Yu Shu company: a Michelin Man, a Reddy Kilowatt, a Ronald McDonald,
a Mickey Mouse, like that.

The orphidnet was teeming with helpful AI agents. They resembled flexible umbrellas patterned with eyes. After telling Jil
what Mr. Kim thought a logoman was, the smart umbrellas had

helped her design one by twisting themselves into diverse shapes, modeling possible Yu Shu logoman designs. Jil had picked the versions she liked; the other agents contorted themselves into variations of the chosen shapes; Jil picked again; and so on. In a few minutes she'd evolved a lovable logoman that she decided to call Happy. Happy resembled a smiling athletic shoe, a dog with a floppy tongue, and a two-toothed Korean baby.

The orphidnet agents had instantiated Happy by loading his mesh onto a handy lump of Craigor's piezoplastic—and right away Happy began hopping and rolling around on deck. It seemed Jil had invented a new style of robot; she decided to call such robots *shoons*. And then she'd snapped out of the orphidnet to be all there for this.

Bixie tossed a wooden block; Happy the shoon bounced over to retrieve it, his motions clownish enough to send the kids into gales of laughter.

Although it was getting late, nobody felt like going to sleep. With the clear sky and the full moon high overhead, it was nearly as bright as day. Momotaro and Bixie started playing hide-and-seek with the shoon, and a virtual version of Chu showed up to join them.

Moving around the deck rearranging things in the moonlight, Craigor was watching the kids play. "The orphidnet is a locative planetary brain," he told Jil. "My possessions are embodied thoughts." He paused, watching the orphidnet AIs. "The orphidnet doesn't have to be alienating. You can use it as a way to pay very close attention to the world. Its whole strength is that it's based on physical reality."

While Craigor talked, Jil made two more plastic Happy figures. And she launched a bunch of virtual shoons onto the Net. Some of them stuck around to play hide-and-seek with Bixie, Momotaro, the plastic shoons, virtual Chu, and a curiously large humanoid form.

Craigor loved feeling the real and the unreal swirling around him. After a bit, virtual Chu went away, replaced by Ond in the orphidnet. Ond had a favor to ask.

"What?" said Craigor.

"Can I come back there with Chu?" asked Ond. "Physically? I'm not safe in town. Everyone knows where I am all the time. They want to lynch me."

"What about Nektar?" asked Craigor.

"She—she left me for another man. She hates me because of the orphids."

"Poor Ond," said Jil, who was listening in.

Craigor's mind was spinning rapid plans that he was careful not to broadcast. Of late he'd been feeling oppressed by the approach of middle age. He'd hardly slept with any other women before Jil, and he'd been faithful ever since their marriage. Life was passing him by. Would it be so terrible if he had a few affairs? There was nothing Craigor liked so much as having women admire at him. And now that Nektar was on the loose, wow. Her full lips, wiggly figure, heavy blond hair. But how could Craigor go after her with the orphids showing everyone everything all the time? If Jil found out about him being unfaithful, she'd probably lose it and go back on sudocoke. So he had to be a good boy. But was that fair? Did he have to spend his whole life as a captive to Jil's stupid addiction problem? If he didn't score some action, pretty soon he'd be dead in heaven with St. Peter asking, "Did you get any?" and Craigor would be all, "I slept with my wife." What kind of way was that to meet your maker? With a sense of rattling past an irreversible switch point, Craigor made a snap decision to go for Nektar, no matter what the price. All these thoughts flew by in a fraction of a second. Craigor's lips twitched in a sardonic, guilty grin.

"Poor Ond," repeated Jil, taking in Craigor's odd smile as if she knew what it was about.

"Can you please send the dinghy now?" messaged Ond. "We're almost at the dock. I'm being followed, but don't worry, I won't stay long. We'll be on our way before there's any danger to you. Chu and I just need a minute to catch our breath. And then we'll go—elsewhere."

"I'm loving the orphidnet," said Craigor, wanting to mellow Ond out, given that he'd just decided to sleep with the man's wife. "I have this sense of resonance and enrichment. You did good, Ond. Here comes the dinghy."

"You're not seeing the big slow angels?" asked Ond. "From a parallel world?"

An odd, unsettling question, that. As Craigor waited for the dinghy to return with Ond and Chu, he studied the giant shiny man who'd been playing with the kids. Thirty feet tall, the ghostly form stepped over the boat's cabin, then crouched down amid the cluttered boxes on the foredeck.

"See him? With a topknot?" said Craigor, pointing out the figure to Jil, who was still staring at him. "He's like one of those beings I see out of the corner of my eye sometimes. And when I turn my head, nothing's there. You must have had that experience when you were using. Something about the orphids is making our hallucinations real. Or they were real all along, and now the orphids are sticking to them."

"I see another one," said slender Bixie, peering across the water at the dinghy coming in. "A big angel in front of Chu's little boat. She's scolding him. She has white hair. Oh, and now the nice boy angel from our boat is dancing over there to argue with her. He's her nephew. The angels move slow, but they hop fast."

"The big angel's name is Gladax," said Craigor, the information jumping unbidden into his head. "She says we shouldn't try to go to her world. She says the jump is dangerous, with ravenous beaky subbie creatures in between the worlds. She says their world's much more important than ours."

"Our world's just as good," replied Jil. She was getting images from the boy with the topknot. She saw two sheets of reality nestled together, the paired branes making each other glow. The viewpoint zoomed into the gap between the worlds, showing the angel boy twisting past beaky subbie-things like a kayaker avoiding rocks. "It's not that dangerous to go."

"Chu calls the angels' world the Hibrane," said Bixie. "Sweet! And he just now messaged me a link to a magic spell for going there." Bixie stood on tiptoe and called out to Chu in the dinghy. "Try and catch me, Chu!"

The air flickered and Bixie disappeared. The male angel with the topknot disappeared too; perhaps he'd guide Bixie. Big Gladax shook her fist in bleak frustration, and then made as if to poke an energy ray into Chu's head. But Ond was furiously waving his arms, beating the air around Chu, messing up Gladax's positioning. The dinghy docked against the *Merz Boat*.

"Bixie's in the Hibrane!" shouted Chu, scrambling aboard. "I have to go help her!"

"What. Are. You. Talking about!" said Jil, taking hold of the boy's shoulders. She half wanted to give him a brutal shake, but instead she crouched down to look in his eyes. "What did you do to my Bixie?"

Ond was talking into the air, addressing the Hibraner angel. "If you attack Chu again, Gladax, your jump-code goes out to

every single person on Earth. And if you kill me, you're de-
fenseless for good."

"Talk to me, Chu," insisted Jil, still holding the boy's shoulders.

"The angels live in the Hibrane," said Chu in his usual flat
tone. He looked frightened. "Angel Gladax is mad at me. The
angels have always been coming here, but now we can see them
better—thanks to the orphids. I found out how to jump a person to the Hibrane. Gladax doesn't like that. She told me not to
share the jump-code. I didn't mean for Bixie to—"

"How?" interjected Craigor grimly. He was standing over Jil
and Chu. "Tell us how! We have to go after Bixie."

"The orphidnet AIs and I did a timing-channel attack on the
disappearing cuttlefish," began Chu. "And—"

"More jive about cuttlefish?" cried Craigor. "Where's my
daughter, damn you!"

"Don't yell at him, Craigor, or I'll punch you in the mouth,"
said Ond, his voice very tight. "Chu already gave me a link to
the jump-code. It looks like blue spaghetti and it sounds like
chimes. I'll message the link to you right now, Jil." He twitched
his head and hopped to one side, ducking the big angel, who
still had that menacing ray sticking out of her forefinger. "Stop
it, Gladax! We have to save Jil's daughter. I don't care about the
subbies. See the jump-code, Jil? All right then. Now let Chu
finish telling us how it works."

Craigor got hold of an oar and took out his anger by violently
waving it around, stirring eddies in the air. This had a good effect; Gladax drew back a couple of meters, unable to navigate her
body's subtle matter through the roiled-up air currents.

"You don't have to use the blue spaghetti anymore," said
Chu, his voice maddeningly deliberate. "I have a new version
almost done." He produced a bird's-nest of string from his
pocket and sat down on the deck. Delicately he tied two loose

ends of his intricate tangle, which resembled a woven bracelet. "The jump-code's in this knot," said Chu, staring at it with absorption. "Nice and tidy. I can remember this."

"Get to the point, Chu," puffed Craigor, still waving his oar. "Spaghetti, chimes, knot—how does someone use your freakin' code?"

"Well, I think when the angels do it, they stop thinking about themselves for a second," said Chu, looking small and uncomfortable amidst the legs of the agitated grown-ups. His fingers were rubbing his knot. "And then they concentrate on the code and—"

Chu disappeared too.

"We're going after them, Ond," yelled Jil. "Craigor, you watch Momotaro. Don't give me that moony hangdog look, Ond! Let's go!"

Ond's pursuers were yelling from the shore. An outboard motor sputtered and roared into life. Spotlights lit the water.

"Of course, Jil," said Ond. "I *want* to hide in the Hibrane. Let's pace up and down the deck; Gladax has trouble keeping up. Block out her messages or she'll distract you. Please don't hate me. I'd do anything for you."

"Okay then, Doctor Übergeek," said Jil, stepping lively toward the bow at Ond's side, still extremely upset about Bixie of course, but also feeling just a little jazzed by Ond's flattery and by the prospect of a wild trip through another dimension. "You better make this good. We space out and we slam the code, huh? Like meditating before doing a line of sudocoke. Too bad we don't have Chu's Knot."

"Just use the link I gave you," said Ond.

In the orphidnet Jil studied the tangled blue spaghetti and the ringing chimes. But try as she might, she remained stubbornly aboard the *Merz Boat*.

"We have to let go of our internal monologues," suggested Ond. "Focus on the spaces between our thoughts."

On a good, serene day, that wouldn't have been hard for Jil, but just now it was tough. Urgently casting about for mental leverage, she thought of the Zen koan where the teacher holds up a stick and says, "If you call this a mere stick, you deny its Buddha nature. If you don't call it a stick, you're lying. What do you call it? Quick!"

Jil broke the stick. She was neither here nor there, neither now nor then, not inside, not out. The chiming blue spaghetti buried her. She felt a twisting sensation and saw a series of ocean images, as if she were flying very low across an endless sea. Some creatures like birds stuck their heads above the surface, snapping at her. Subbies? Jil dodged them readily enough, energized by a pleasure/paranoia rush straight out of her sudocoke days. It was hard to say how long the jump lasted. But then something changed, she felt a nudge, and—hello!

She was in the Hibrane, with Chu and, yes, Ond beside her, standing in a grassy moon-silvered meadow with great trees at the edge. Her skin tingled and, just like that, her orphids were gone. No matter, her mind was blooming in some new way. The air filled with a vibrating soundless hum. A sealed window in Jil's head swung open.

Beyond the trees were the lamp-lit windows of a city like San Francisco. Nearby was a field and a hill. They'd landed in the Hibrane version of Golden Gate Park.

Everything here was big and slow; everything was alive. The grass rose to Jil's waist; the pines and eucalyptus trees towered like skyscrapers. The meadow itself was impossibly broad. On this world, Jil, Chu, and Ond were only a foot high.

Giant people and immense dogs cavorted ponderously beneath lampposts in the meadow, moving as if in slow motion. The brightly dressed Hibraners were playfully skimming a wooden triangle back and forth.

Jil could sense the inner essences of the rocks, the trees, the people. This was paradise, better than anything she'd ever felt before. Although none of the Hibraners were talking, Jil was picking up their thoughts. Hibrane telepathy was different from orphidnet messaging. This telepathy was smooth and all but wordless, a flow of image and emotion.

Jil noticed a dark spot in the meadow, a dog the size of a buffalo, ruminatively chewing something on the ground. Oh, dear God, where was Bixie?

Without stopping to look into the dog's mind, Jil charged toward the great brute, calling her eleven-year-old daughter's name. Jil's footsteps were surprisingly loud and heavy on the soft ground. And she seemed to be moving as fast as a car might drive. The long-haired giants stopped playing and assumed attitudes of fear, as if Jil were a fierce demon from a nether world.

Spooked by little Jil's charge, the huge dog wallowed to his feet and began a deep, startled bark. On the ground between his legs was—only a stick.

"Mom!" came a sweet voice from the shadows of a park bench nearby. "I'm over here." Yes, it was Bixie, sitting upon a collapsed leather wineskin. Thanks to the telepathy, Jil could see Bixie in the dark—and she could sense her daughter's whole mind, sweet as a summer day. A moan of relief escaped Jil; she sped to embrace the girl.

"I'm scared of that dog," said Bixie, disentangling herself. "I'm glad you came, Mom."

"I want to take you home now," said Jil, hoping this was possible. With all their orphids gone, there was no chance of linking back into the Lobrane Earth's orphidnet. So how would they access the magic blue spaghetti code?

Ond and Chu came pounding across the moon-silvered grass, scared of the dog. They joined Jil and Bixie beneath the bench. Some of the lamp-lit Hibraner giants on the lawn were turning to flee; a couple of the others were ever so slowly hunkering down to stare at the Lobraners. The enormous dog continued his slow, thunderous barking, but showed no sign of wanting to attack.

The Hibraners' clothes were curiously dyed and homespun in appearance. Another giant had arrived; he had big dark eyes, a straight nose, and a slight beard. He wore a stocking cap with a bun of hair balled up in a sphere atop his head. Jil recognized him from the *Merz Boat*.

The young Hibraner's mind reached out to Jil, playing across her psyche. His name was Azaroth. He said he'd helped guide their jumps toward Golden Gate Park. He warned that the Hibraners might regard the Lobraners as dangerous gnomes—at least until they got used to them.

Chu was listening in. Showily he kicked at the ground, making a deep dent in it. "I bet I could make that dog go *ki-yi-yi* and run away, Bixie. The giants can't hurt us. We're like iron. And we're fast." Not that Chu was actually moving toward the dog.

"Can we go back?" Jil asked Chu.

"Yes," said Chu in his matter-of-fact tone. "I still have my special knot." He showed her his intricate tangle of string. Good. Shifting her attention to Ond's mind, Jil was a little surprised to see just how intensely the man worshipped her.

Ond smiled at her, knowing that she knew. "The vibrating soundless hum," he said, picking the phrase from Jil's mind. "This telepathy is so powerful. And there's more. I feel like I can remember every shape I see."

"I miss the orphidnet," said Chu, admiring his knot. "I was good at it. Maybe we should go home with Jil and Bixie."

"Not yet," protested Ond. "I want to lie low until things

calm down back home. Maybe wait a year or two of Lobrane time. I think that'll only be a few months by this world's clocks. We're six times as small and six times as fast. Stay and keep me company, son."

"But I liked being so smart. I liked the beezies. The air ate all our orphids when we got here."

"We don't need orphids here, Chu. We've got telepathy, omnividence, and—an endless spike of extra memory space." Ond gazed at Jil. "I'm storing images of your face," he murmured. "Dear Jil."

"I miss the orphids," insisted stubborn Chu.

"Not me," said Jil. "I was liking my life the way it was." But was that really true? Of late, Craigor had been seeming restless. And this made staying sober a little harder than before.

"Maybe I was wrong to unleash the orphids," Ond was saying. "For what it's worth, I'm sorry, Jil. I thought it was the best defense against the nants. But maybe—"

"Oh, don't beat yourself up," said Jil, feeling a deep empathy for the awkward man and his odd son. "Life will settle down."

"I love you," messaged Ond.

Jil could almost have melted into him. Dear sweet Ond. But no. He wasn't supposed to be her type at all. She'd been a cheerleader in high school, and she'd always gone for the jocks. Also, Craigor and Momotaro were waiting at home. It wouldn't do to leave Craigor alone for too long. Not that Jil enjoyed the role of jealous jailer. With Nektar out on her own, Craigor seemed primed for a reckless move. What if Jil just let Craigor screw all the women he liked? Impossible thought. Jil had the superstitious feeling that her stable marriage was all that stood between her and sudocoke. It was very nice to know that Ond really and truly loved her. But Ond wasn't as physically attractive as Craigor. What would happen if Jil found herself a much hotter man, maybe someone younger? Did she have to be a puritan in every respect for the rest of her life? Oh, god, where was her head? And Ond and Chu were probably seeing all these thoughts. Stop it, Jil!

"Let us use your magic knot now, Chu," said Jil in a brisk tone.

"Go ahead," said Chu, holding the knot steady with his fingers. "Stare at it as if it were the blue spaghetti. And feel it with your fingers. The touching takes the place of the chimes."

"Me first," said Bixie.

Chu flashed a rare smile at Bixie as he held out his magic knot. "See you later."

"Hurry, Bixie," urged Jil. "Look over there across the lawn. It's that bossy angel Gladax. And, see, she's carrying some kind of net! Go *on,* Bixie, get out of here. Thanks, Chu. Bye, Ond. Take care, you two." She hesitated, then gave Ond a quick kiss on the cheek.

Bixie disappeared and then Jil. Gladax was still twenty yards away, her legs and arms moving at a snail's pace. Her net was made of—rubber?

"We don't have to be scared of her, right, Ond?" said Chu, his voice even flatter than usual.

"No way," sang Ond, elated from Jil's kiss. "We move six times as fast as the Hibraners. Let's run a few hundred yards. And then I'll show you how to camouflage yourself. Like a mental firewall."

Ond didn't yet realize how fast Gladax could hop.

PART II

CHAPTER 5

The Big Pig Posse

Jayjay and the Big Pig Posse awoke to a mustached guy prodding them with a wide broom.

"Go to hell," said Jayjay, his fellow-kiqqie Sonic already standing at his side. "Asshole janitor." The women were on their feet too: Kittie and Thuy, their faces greasy in the rainy-day morning light. Jayjay wore baggy black pants, a billed green cap, a green T-shirt, a piezoplastic iguana earring, and a scavenged gray suit jacket that Kittie had painted with a fancy filigreed skull design to cover the whole back.

"*No mas* janitor," said the guy with the broom. "Maintenance manager and security guard. Get your *pinche* asses outta my hall. The Job Center's about to open. Go get some rehab at Natural Mind."

"You want some of this?" taunted Sonic, grabbing his own crotch. "Stand by me, Jayjay. We can take this *pendejo* down." Skinny little Sonic wore his invariable outfit of heavy boots, thick black wool tights, red T-shirt, and a thin black leather jacket with intricate pleats and folds—a jitsy concoction that he'd found unused in some woman's closet. His hair was pomaded into a dozen hedgehog spikes.

"Lose the gangbanger routine, boys," said Kittie, turning and walking to the glass street door. Stocky sweat-suited Kittie was adorned with a bright blue tattoo on her neck, also a glowing pendant of a woman holding a paintbrush and a meat cleaver. Kittie sometimes made money painting solar cell landscapes on electric cars. "I'm seeing a bunch of fresh-dumped pancakes behind the Mission Street McDonald's." she continued. "Still hot, if we hurry. Come on, Thuy." Kitty pronounced her friend's name the proper Vietnamese way, like *twee* and not like *thooey*.

Slender Thuy smiled and took Kittie's hand, ready for the adventure of a new day, Thuy in her street-worn striped leggings and yellow miniskirt, her strawy black hair in two high pigtails, her shiny piezoplastic Yu Shu sneakers with fancy dragon's heads on their toes. The Big Pig Posse members rarely changed their outfits; they were like cartoon characters that way. Superheroes.

Sonic gave the janitor a little poke in the chest; the janitor swung his fist; Sonic ducked. Street theater. Jayjay and Sonic followed the women out, standing for a moment in the rain-shadow of the office building. The streets were liquid, the raindrops popping circles into the sheen, the spastic gusty wind making riffles, a few electric cars hissing past.

Jayjay looked into his head, checking the orphidnet view of the McDonald's trashcans, and indeed he saw a nice batch of griddle cakes, nearly a dozen. Only a block away.

But first, as long as he was focused on the orphidnet, Jayjay said hello to some of the beezie AI agents hosted by the millions of orphids on his body, also greeting the far-flung higher-order beezies that could be found at the next level of abstraction and then, what the hey, he took a quick hit off the Big Pig at the apex of the virtual world, the outrageously rich and intricate Big Pig like a birthday piñata stuffed with beautiful insights woven into ideas that linked into unifying concepts that puzzle-pieced themselves into powerful systems that were in turn aspects of a cosmic metatheory—*aha*! Hooking into the billion-snouted billion-nippled Big Pig made Jayjay feel like more than a genius.

Not that suckling on the Pig was most people's idea of a thrill—few citizens were even bothering to intelligence-amplify themselves into the kilo-IQ zone of the kiqqies. Being a kiqqie meant you let the orphidnet do some of your thinking. Instead of just using the Net to see and remember things, you could launch autonomous beezie agents to analyze, hypothesize, simulate, and reason on your behalf.

Jayjay had to fully open his mental firewall in order to access the Big Pig wisdom. Right away the Pig wrote some information into his brain, the way she always did when Jayjay hooked up, he wasn't sure why. The info-dumps took the form of incredibly accurate movie clips of things like water or clouds or fire; this new one showed a eucalyptus branch rocking in the wind, each twig and each leaf a separate pendulum, the system dancing upon its chaotic attractor.

Thuy was suckling on the Big Pig too, pulling greedily at the nipple, and Jayjay smiled to see her next to him—Thuy, his smart litter-mate, his lost true love.

"Wheenk wheenk wheenk," said Jayjay to Thuy, layering thoughts onto the words to make a hyperpun. *Wheenk* like a piglet, obviously, but also *wheenk* like a squeaky wheel, an unhappy wheel asking for oil, Jayjay-the-wheel longing both for the metaphorical anointment of Thuy's affection and for the literal lubrications of her aromatic bod. Not to mention that *wheenk wheenk wheenk* was a term Thuy liked to use to describe metanovels in which the characters spent, in her opinion, too much time bitching and moaning, and not enough time doing and loving.

Thuy was working on her own metanovel, an as-yet-untitled combine of words, links, video clips, images, and sounds—she meant for it to be a bit like a movie that a user could inhabit, the user coming to feel from the inside how it was to be Thuy or, rather, how it was to be a version of Thuy leading a more tightly plotted and suspenseful life. Thuy had kicked off her metawriting career with a metastory posted on the *Metotem Metazine* site, and the tale, really a reminiscence, was getting good buzz—the title was "Waking Up," and it was a delicate weave of Thuy's memories and mental associations relating to Orphid Night last year, when the newly-released orphids had blanketed Earth, and Thuy had seen Ond Lutter and his son Chu jump to the Hibrane, and she'd thrown over her career path to live on the street with Jayjay.

Thuy was finding it hard to bulk up her metastory into a full-fledged metanovel; part of the problem was that neither she nor anyone else had really figured out what a metanovel should be, although by now there had been a fair number of not-quite-successful metanovels posted on the orphidnet. One thing for sure, suckling on the Big Pig seemed a crippling drain on Thuy's creative energies. Though Jayjay loved the Pig, it wasn't as big a burden for him as it was for Thuy. Thuy's disillusionment with the Pig was in fact a key deal-breaking issue between her and Jayjay. So Jayjay was also intending for his *wheenk* to defiantly say, "I'm not scared of the Big Pig even if you are."

"Wheenk!" sang back Thuy, fully understanding every shade of Jayjay's meaning and upping the signifier strength by digging into the ever-expanding database of her metanovel, passing a link to a series of images inspired by her sorrow over her and Jayjay's breakup: for instance, shriveled tree-blossom petals on a dirty sidewalk, with Thuy's virtual violin playing sad, wheenking chords. There was more than a little self-pity here, which seemed a bit unjustified to Jayjay as the estrangement was, at least in his opinion, Thuy's own fault. And wasn't she still using the Big Pig anyway—like, right now?

The Big Pig was absorbing, mirroring, and amplifying their exchange, layering on further sounds, clips, and links from the simmering matrix of global info. Intoxicated by the heady mix, Jayjay soon forgot about Thuy per se—that is, she became an archetype, a thought form, a pattern in the cosmic stew. Knowing Jayjay's particular likes, the Big Pig began displaying a fundamental secret-of-life construction of reality: branes and strings, an underlying graph-rewriting system, a transfinite stack of "turtles all the way down." Although the ideas felt familiar from Jayjay's last trip into the Pig, he knew the details wouldn't stay with him for long. So what. Pig trips were all about relaxing and enjoying the show. *Aha!*

For her part, Thuy sank into the details of her metanovel, letting the Big Pig show her a stream of variations of what her completed work could be once it was done, each Pig-take on her work more sinewy and coruscating than the one before, giving Thuy the familiar, despairing sensation that really there was no use for her to bother doing anything at all when everything was already thought of in the Big Pig. She wanted to bail out, but for now the Pig's ever-changing fountain of ideas was once again holding her in thrall.

Jayjay and Thuy might have stayed there leaning against the wall for quite some time, eyes half closed, on the nod, feeling like superartistic supergeniuses, but Kittie began shaking them, ever-practical Kittie focused only on the McDonald's trashcan, worried that some other unhoused individuals might score the breakfast goodies before the Big Pig Posse could make the scene, heedless of the fact that, thanks to her, Jayjay was coming the fuck down again. If he could just once remember the approximate details of what he learned from the Pig, he'd be a famous physicist.

Sonic stood at the Job Center's glass door, projecting 3D emoticons at the janitor—turds, knives, and skulls visible in the heads-up orphidnet display that overlaid their worldviews. The janitor didn't care. The janitor had a job; the Posse was in the rain; the door between them was locked.

Still a bit high from the Pig, Jayjay saw the situation as a tower of archetypal patterns: thresholds and interfaces, insiders and outsiders, the hidden heroes commencing a mythic quest.

"The Big Pig sucks," said Thuy, shaking off the intoxication. "I feel totally stupid now. That was absotively, posilutely my last time." She laughed unhappily, fully aware that she'd sworn off the Pig a hundred times before.

The four were splashing down the sidewalk toward the Mc-Donald's parking lot. Jayjay was internally grumbling to himself about Thuy always making such a big deal about wanting to quit the Big Pig. You got high, you saw stuff, you came down, you moved on. Where was the problem?

"We gotta find a steady place to sleep," said Sonic.

"A place to think and work," said Thuy, brightening. "Let's ask President Bernardo!"

US President Bernard Lampton had organized a cadre of beezie agents willing to help people find whatever they needed. Any neighborhood was like a realtime charity bazaar, with unused objects there for free in attics, garages, and back rooms. You could find stuff on your own via the universal orphidnet view, but asking Bernardo was like using an efficient search engine.

"Where can we four live long-term with no rent, Bernardo?" said Jayjay, wanting to please Thuy. "We're tired of crashing in halls with it raining all the time."

President Bernardo appeared in their overlays; trudging along Mission Street same as them, dressed in baggy jeans and a hooded sweatshirt like a homie. "Get an SUV," he suggested. "There's a nice big one near here, with enough gas to drive it a mile or two. The owner would even give you the title, *camaradas.*" Bernardo gestured and a little map popped up with a highlighted image of a bloated, obsolete fuel-burner.

"Vibby!" said Thuy. "Good old President Bernardo—hey! What's he doing now?"

A flicker, a pop, and control of this particular President Bernardo icon had shifted into the hands of his political rivals. Wearing a slack, imbecilic grin, the president dropped his pants, squatted on the sidewalk, relieved himself, and—

"Hurry up!" interrupted Kittie, looking back at them. "We're gonna lose the pancakes. Oh, what is *that* supposed to be?"

"Homesteady Party attack ad," said Jayjay, looking away from the degraded President Bernard Lampton. "They're pumping out all this viral adware for the election." Lampton's image duck-walked toward Kittie, the president leering up at her.

A banner unfurled across their visual fields, reading *Vote for Dick Too Dibbs!* Beneath it appeared two vaguely similar men in red ties and blue suits: former President Dick Dibbs of Ohio, and his second cousin Dick Too Dibbs from Owensboro, Kentucky. President Dibbs had been convicted of treason and executed by lethal injection a few years back—the fallout of his scheme to turn the entire planet Earth into a Dyson sphere of nants, with the networked system supposedly running a Virtual Earth simulation, including a perfect copy of each and every former Earthling. It had come out in the trial that actually President Dibbs had instructed the nants to simulate only registered USA Homesteady Party members, condemning the rest of Earth's population to vanish without a trace. President Dibbs had planned to install himself as an all-powerful president-for-eternity, or, not to put too fine a point on it, God. No matter, his Kentucky lawyer cousin Dick Too Dibbs stood a good chance of being voted into office. Too Dibbs seemed more honest and intelligent than the original Dibbs. And he had great ads.

"I was a private man," said former President Dick Dibbs, with the very slightest gesture toward the obscene Bernard Lampton. "A clean man. Misled by corporate criminals. Unjustly executed by activist judges. We can control the Singularity. We can have a lasting paradise safe from woe. Dick Too Dibbs in November. He's learned from my mistakes." He gazed earnestly at Dick Too, with the faintest hint of a smile at the corners of his thin-lipped mouth.

Dick Too made a wry face. "I learned I don't want to end up in the death house like you!" he said, giving his cousin's icon a poke. President Dibbs shriveled up and shrank. "Forget him, folks. I know you've got every reason to be mistrustful of the Dibbs name. But I'll do right by the common people. I know how the system works. And I'm honest. Which is more than can be said for Bernard Lampton. Why don't you use one of your speeches to wipe yourself with, Bernardo? That's about all it's worth."

"Put your filter dogs on that junk," said Kittie. "Own your reality, pigheads."

It was a little harder than usual for Jayjay to teach his virtual guard dogs to recognize this particular type of ad, which had arrived compressed within a single vertex of Lampton's image-mesh. The orphidnet was getting very flaky thanks to all the spam and adware it was carrying. Jayjay had seen, like, two hundred Dick Too Dibbs ads yesterday. No matter how strenuously he tutored and upgraded his filter dogs, new ads kept romping in. The Homesteady Party was hi-tech and relentless. They seemed to be using programmers with an exceedingly deep understanding of the orphids' code and to have a very large and effective PR force embedding ad-triggers into unexpected contexts.

"Get outta there!" Sonic was yelling, sprinting across the

nearly empty McDonald's parking lot, beautiful plumes of water splashing from each of his heavy-booted steps.

Too late. A couple of middle-aged bums in watch caps were already scarfing down the pancakes from the trash, and not even Sonic was up for hassling shaky pathetic winos over—garbage.

"Where's some other food, Bernardo?" said Kittie. This time, the president's icon didn't come up at all; instead a Dick Too Dibbs ad appeared right away, the ad pebbled and glittery in the rain, Dick Too talking about the danger of letting big companies control the orphidnet—reasonable and populist remarks, really, but they seemed shady and insincere since they were coming via an ad.

Seeking a filter to block this ad too, Jayjay searched the orphidnet and found a high-rated virtual defender resembling a chihuahua. He scanned the chihuahua's machine code to make sure the virtual dog didn't have Homesteady hookworms, then recruited him into his kennel. The chihuahua yapped at the other filter dogs, educating them. They set off in a baying pack, digging through Jayjay's recent inputs, competing to be the fastest and the most accurate filter dog of all, mating and spawning as they ran. All this took only seconds. And then Jayjay messaged his Best Dog in Hunt to the other Posse members, the mutated beast resembling a scaly dachshund by now.

Jayjay was wet and getting cold, although the rain-pocked wavy sheets of water undulating across the parking lot were still inconceivably beautiful—if he relaxed and actually looked at them. Seemed like he was pissing away too much time on low-level maintenance these days.

Thuy glanced over at Jayjay with a secret smile. She saw the water too. She liked it best when Jayjay was in the real world with her. She'd only left him for Kittie because he was spending too much time high on the Pig or plugging into his physics seminars. But she still thought he was the cutest, smartest guy she'd ever met.

"Let's walk to that car Bernardo showed us," said Kittie.

"I wonder if that was Bernardo at all," said Thuy. "Maybe he was a spoof from the start. Maybe the car is a trap."

"I'll take that chance," said Kittie, wiping the rain from her eyes.

On the way, Jayjay used the orphidnet to see into the garbage cans standing on the curb for pickup day. He was a bit gingerly in his scanning—lest a hidden Homesteady Party ad surprise him. He found a meaty roast chicken carcass, a third of a chocolate cake, a half-full box of Thai takeout, a couple of slices of pizza, and a bunch of brown bananas.

"Food links, Kittie," he said, messaging her the locations.

They scooped up the grub and hurried for the shelter of the puffy silver SUV, which was parked in a driveway by a beat old Victorian house on a side street between Mission and Guerrero, right where the Bernardo icon had said they'd find it. The Posse piled in, glad to be out of the rain, Jayjay in the driver's seat, Sonic shotgun, the women in back. Jayjay would have liked to be the one in back with Thuy.

Looking through the orphidnet, Jayjay could see and hear the old couple in the flat on the house's first floor. With nanocomputing orphids meshed upon every surface on Earth and linked together by quantum entanglement, you could peep anything you liked.

"Red! There's some kids in our car!" said the woman. She was soft-chinned, not unbeautiful, sitting on the couch knitting. "They're eating garbage! Why didn't you lock the car like I told you? Get out there and chase off those dirty kiqqies!"

Using the orphidnet to amplify your intelligence was viewed

by many as a deviant activity. Kiqqies looked at things so differ-
ently from normals. And most kiqqies weren't willing to hold
jobs. If you were smart and paid attention to the orphidnet, you
could live without money. But quite a few people preferred to
hold back from orphidic intelligence-amplification—there was a
feeling that once you were a full-on kiqqie, you were no longer
your same old self.

"I'm watching a football game, Dot," said Red, paunchy
with a lean face. "The halftime show." He was slumped in an
armchair, seemingly staring at a wall. The orphidnet was better
than TV: *everything* was on it, live and three-dimensional, seen
from whatever viewpoint you chose—and you could see under
people's clothes.

"I know what you're up to, Red," said his wife. "You're staring at those cheerleaders' boobies. Or worse." Voyeurism was in
fact the number one orphidnet application for the average person.

"Hey, if you're so concerned about my sex life," riposted
Red, "why don't you come over here and—"

"Hush, I'm watching our granddaughter nap," said Dot,
bending over her knitting with a half-smile, appreciative of
Red's sally. "I can keep an orphid-eye on you from here."

"Live and let live," said Red. "Those kiqqies can have our
clunker for all I care. Gasoline is gone for good. Solar's won the
day, and if those assholes in the Middle East want to kill each
other, it's their own business now. Not even the Homesteadies
want us back there."

"Then tell the kids to drive the car away right now," said
Dot. "Give them the keys and change the title. I'm sick of seeing that poor old car. It makes me sad. I told President Bernard a week ago, as a matter of fact. But I didn't mean for
ragged freaks to make our car a crash pad. Three days ago we
had some stumblebum in there just out of the Natural Mind

rehab, remember? And now we've got these scuzzy kiqqies with their—"

Jayjay pinged Dot through the orphidnet while gnawing the chicken carcass. There was a lot of good meat on the flat underside.

"Hello?" said Dot.

"Hi," said Jayjay, the orphids on his throat registering the vibrations, reconstituting the sound waves, and sending the audio on its way. "This is the kiqqie in your car. Spelled *M-A-N.*"

"Red, one of them is talking to me! You listen too."

"We'll be glad to take the car off your hands," Jayjay told the old couple, still working on his chicken carcass. "Does it have enough gas to drive away?"

"Maybe a half gallon," said Red. "Whatever the homies haven't siphoned off. You in a hurry?"

"No," said Jayjay. "Not at all."

"So I'll give you the keys and transfer the title when the rain lets up," said Red. "Meanwhile I got a football game to watch."

"And be careful where you put that garbage you're eating," said Dot in a sharp tone. Sonic had just laid half a slice of glistening pizza on the dash so as to accept a lopsided piece of the cake from Thuy. "And no sex in our driveway. You happen to be sitting in a beloved and respectable family vehicle. When our children were small, we—"

Jayjay tuned her out.

"Where's that Thai food?" he asked, cracking open his door to toss out the denuded chicken bones.

"All gone," said Kittie. "You got the whole chicken, so that's fair. There's still cake. And bananas. They're plantains, actually. They taste better than they look."

It's nice in this car, thought Jayjay, peeling a plantain. Big soft seats, the air faintly musty, the windows fogged up from their breath, the rain drumming on the roof. The women were cuddled together in back, with Thuy's musky fragrance perfuming the damp air. The car's resident beezies were like fuzzy, friendly ghosts.

"It'd be sweet to road-trip this silver marshmallow south," said Sonic. "San Ho, Cruz, the beach, and then past Los Angeles into Mexico, *vato,* hanging with *la raza* and the pyramids. You'd like Mexico, Jayjay; we could go underwater diving. Some kiqqies just invented snap-on gills. Hell, I'd like to see gasoline come back."

"Don't think that way, Sonic," said Kittie. "Gaia's better off without internal combustion. I mean, look at this weather. You've seen the climate simulations in the orphidnet. I'm glad the world's finally switched to electric cars."

"They're still using some oil in Bangalore," said Sonic, flicking Jayjay's lizard earring. "To make piezoplastic for shoons. The beezies are all over that. Do beezies still get into your earring, Jayjay?"

"Sometimes," said Jayjay.

"Jayjay's always had an earring," said Thuy with a fond giggle. "He was wearing a gold hoop the first time he came home from school with me. Helping me with my math homework. My mother saw us kissing and she freaked *out.* 'He's not Vietnamese, he has an earring, he'll never get a job.' "

"After Orphid Night, I was there for you again," recalled Jayjay. "I saved you from the wikiware." Although most employees didn't have to go into offices anymore, many employers required you to install ShareCrop wikiware on your bodies' orphids—which became, in effect, a bossy virtual monkey on your back. Living free on the street as a kiqqie with Jayjay, Thuy had time to craft her metastory "Waking Up." But then the Big Pig addiction had started dragging her down.

"And *I* saved her from you," put in Kittie.

"Look, I'm the one who really cares about her," said Jayjay, his voice rising. "I wish we could talk about it, Thuy. Kittie's just playing you for a game, you're a trophy to her, a notch, and down the road you'll—"

"Let's go back to my shoes," interrupted Thuy. She didn't like to hear Kittie and Jayjay argue over her; it made her feel like an object. "There's two beezies living in the piezoplastic. I call them Urim and Thummim after the special stones of sight that Joseph Smith the Mormon used to decipher the writing on those golden plates he found. My feet can see. A couple of times when I almost tripped and fell, Urim and Thummim flexed the shoes to bounce me up."

"Yu Shu's finest," said Kittie, admiring Thuy's feet. "You were lucky to score those when that yuppie jogger had the heart attack, Thuy. Good eye."

"I was the one who bagged the shoes for her," said Jayjay. "Thuy didn't want to touch a corpse."

"Corpse-touching is the kind of thing men are good for," said Kittie. "A social role for the lower caste."

"On the gasoline thing that you mentioned, Kittie," said Sonic, off in his own head as usual. "The techs couldn't have brought electric car technology along so fast if it weren't for the beezies. It's like the beezies actually wanted to help us save our climate. But why should they care? The orphids would be here just the same, even if Earth's surface was ashes and tidal waves with everyone dead."

"Yea unto the breaking of the Seventh Seal," intoned Thuy. She was taping this bit for her metanovel, and "Seventh Seal" sounded good. Apocalyptic, dark, weird, damned. She overlaid the words with some gothic graphics.

"The beezies give a squat because people are like flowers in

Earth's garden," said Jayjay. "The best art in the museum. After the beezies emerged in the orphidnet, they started watching us—and we got good to them. They admire our wetware, the wiring of our brains. Especially us kiqqies. Can I have some of that cake, Thuy?"

"I think the beezies vampire off our emotions, is what it is," said Thuy, handing him a fist-sized piece of chocolate sweetness. "Especially our metabeezie pal the Big Pig. Beezies admire our juice, our hormones. Have you ever noticed that when you're having sex, if you look into the orphidnet, the beezies are totally on your case?"

"I bet the beezies compete to settle onto a baby while it's delivered," said Kittie. "Like how the Hindus imagine souls being reborn. The beezies need us to do things for them. They can see everything, but they can't physically touch things. They need people in order to actualize their plans. Like it took people to bring solar-cell paint and piezoplastic shoons into production."

"But now beezies can use shoons instead of people to do stuff," said Sonic. "Like remote-controlled hands. So what are people for? I'm not art, not a sex-machine, not a robot to push a broom like a *pendejo* janitor."

"Here boys," said Thuy. "Take this last wad of cake before Kittie and I burst our Seventh Seals." She made a loud raspberry sound with her mouth. After all those years of being a good girl, she got a kick out of being bad.

"Ugh," said Kittie.

"Maybe the beezies want us for our processing power," speculated Jayjay, sharing the gooey chocolate with Sonic. "And we're additional computing nodes. After millions of years of evolution, our brainware is optimized. Our pattern-recognizing wetware provides shortcuts that can work faster than the beezies' exhaustive search procedures." He paused, doubting what he'd just said. "Or maybe not. Naw, like I said before, I think the beezies help us just to see us thrive—the same way you'd want the trees on your land to do well."

"If the beezies were big-biz landowners, they'd be looking to harvest us," said Kittie darkly. "Like the nants were gonna do. They were gonna pulp us."

"I'd feel safer if there was some strong definite thing we were doing for the beezies," said Sonic. "Other than being fun to watch. How about those movies the Big Pig always pushes on us? Maybe we're processing them for her. Maybe we're the Big Pig's glasses."

"Urim and Thummim," repeated Thuy wiggling her shoes. She never tired of riffing on the *Book of Mormon* that a missionary had pressed upon her parents; he'd been the first white person she ever saw inside their house. "I'm just glad the beezies are here," she continued, smiling at Jayjay. "Everything's so much more interesting now. And the world's getting cleaner. Speaking of clean, wipe the food off your faces, guys. You look nasty." She handed Jayjay a Giants sweatshirt she'd found in the back of the car.

"I'd like to play with a bunch of those little shoons," mused Sonic. "Learn how to program them."

Jayjay was getting bored waiting for the rain to stop and for Red to come out with the keys. Maybe it was time for a hit of the Big Pig. By way of edging in that direction, he projected himself into the orphidnet. "Hey, beezies, where can we find some shoons to play with?" The other Posse members got into the orphidnet too.

"There are some shoons at Nektar Lundquist's house," said a mushroom-shaped beezie with green eyes on its cap, without exactly speaking English. His compound glyphs bloomed as ready-made thoughts. "You four should go help Nektar. She's under psychic attack by some malware that got into her orphids. She hasn't eaten for two days. Her shoons are having trouble taking care of her. Drive this car there; you can park in Nektar's garage."

"Wow," said Kittie. "Really?"

Everyone in the Posse knew all about Nektar Lundquist. Nektar's husband Ond Lutter was famous not only because he'd released the orphids last year, but also because he'd turned back the nant invasion three years before that. People had loved Ond for killing the nants, but on Orphid Night they'd wanted to lynch him. Ond and his autistic genius son, Chu, had jammed off to the mysterious parallel Hibrane world late on Orphid Night, and so far as anyone knew, they were still in the Hibrane. Not that anyone else had managed to go there since.

Cool, self-possessed Nektar Lundquist had taken advantage of the interest in her family to become the star of an orphidnet reality soap opera called *Founders,* complete with sponsors and ads. Thanks to the *Founders* show, Nektar's whole circle of acquaintances had become celebs: Nektar; Craigor Connor; Jil Zonder; Nektar's boss, Xandro; Xandro's wife, Beatriz; Nektar's ex-boyfriend, Jose; and Jose's sometime lover, Lureen Morales.

Each of them got a nice little income from the sponsors. The way the ads worked was that whenever anyone went through the orphidnet to peep at the *Founders* stars, they'd see a commercial for ExaExa computers, for Stank grooming products, or for BigBox home furnishings; and the *Founders* stars got paid per ad-view.

The *Founders* story thus far: On Orphid Night, Nektar left Ond for Jose, the head chef at Puff, an upscale hipster Valencia Street restaurant. A few weeks later, Nektar went to the Puff manager, got Jose fired, and took over as the Puff head chef herself, at which point Jose moved to the rival restaurant MouthPlusPlus across the street. The two restaurants competed to provide ever more bizarre kinds of nourishment—sometimes serving a course via feeding tube, enema, or intravenous drip.

Last month Nektar had started an affair with Craigor. Because of the affair, his wife, Jil, was brokenhearted and struggling to maintain her sobriety. Jil Zonder was a celeb in her own right, being the woman who'd designed the first piezo-plastic beezie-controlled shoon.

Jayjay liked the looks of Jil Zonder. *And* Jil had been to the Hibrane with Ond and Chu for a few minutes before they sent her back. *And* Jil was a recovering sudocoker. The woman was experienced. It was a pleasure to watch her gestures, to savor her smiles. Neat, noble, naughty; vivacious, vibrant, *voom*. Kind of like Thuy had seemed, back when things were good.

Jayjay fantasized that, given the chance, he could make Jil Zonder happy. Jil was maybe ten years older than Jayjay, which could be a plus. Jayjay figured Jil could use a cute younger guy now that her windbag poseur husband Craigor Connor had been stupid enough to cheat with Nektar. Locative art—what was that? Moving junk around on the deck of the boat where Craigor lived with Jil; and then laying down bogus raps about why he'd put, like, Christmas lights and a bowling ball next to a stack of tires. Big fucking deal. And Craigor's other career, catching Pharaoh cuttlefish so that high-tech companies could coax display chemicals from the slain beasts' skins? The man was nowhere. Jil would be better off with Jayjay, and if he could get in with the *Founders* crowd, he'd tell her the first chance he got.

The mushroom-shaped beezie led the Big Pig Posse through the orphidnet to view Nektar Lundquist, lying alone in her big bed, window curtains drawn, her eyes clenched shut, her heavy blond hair spread across the pillow like golden snakes. Apparently she was far gone on sudocoke; there was a mirror with lines of powder next to her bed. There were perhaps a dozen shoons in the room, curvy little manikins bumbling about on the floor and the bed. But there were other presences in the orphidnet near Nektar—virtual beings shaped like beetles.

The guiding beezie mapped out causal links, showing that the beetles were deviant AIs emerging from infected orphids on Nektar's scalp. Creepy. Up till now, spam and malware had been in the form of high-level software, not in the form of low-level corruption of the individual orphids that supported the orphidnet's parallel quantum computation.

"*Founders* episode three hundred and ninety-five," said Kittie, not understanding what she saw. " 'Nektar Gets the Sudocoke Horrors.' How great is that?"

"Poor Nektar," said Thuy. "Look, Kittie, the shoons are helping her." Indeed, a classic Happy Shoon was spooning water into Nektar's cracked lips, a goob-doll shoon was offering a little cup of mush, and a doughboy shoon was sponging Nektar's soiled sheets. ExaExa, Stank, and BigBox weren't posting any ads around Nektar Lundquist today. This episode was way too funky.

"I want to go, to physically go there, yeah," said Sonic. "Look how many shoons."

"We still don't have the car keys," said Jayjay doubtfully. He could almost smell the high, thin reek of Nektar's dimly lit sickbed.

"You'll want to figure out how to kill those beetles first," glyphed the beezie. "You're in the right place for that. This car's orphids happen to carry the beetle infection, too. We don't have a patch yet."

"Oh fuck!" exclaimed Kittie.

"Our orphids are infected too?" said Jayjay.

The beezie nodded.

"Too late to run away," said Sonic. "Oh well. This is where

maybe humans really can outthink the beezies. Thanks to the Doodly Bug weapon shop." He was talking about his fave online game.

The rain was really pouring down now. Rainwater dribbled in through the moon roof's weather stripping to wet Jayjay's left knee. But, at least for now, Jayjay had no sense of being infected by beetles. Maybe it was time to get high again.

In the apartment, Dot and Red were together on the couch with Dot's knitting thrown aside; Red was pulling down her elastic-waistband pants and—

"*Ooo-la-la,*" said Thuy.

Sonic burst into shrill pulses of laughter.

"Oh, let's transcend," burst out Jayjay. "Let's hit the Pig."

"What the hey," said Kittie. "Rainy-day fun."

"Again?" said Thuy, meaning to refuse, but feeling her willpower weakening. It was so boring here in the car right now. "I swear, you guys, this is going to be my very, very last time ever. *Wheenk.*"

The virtual images of the Posse members spiraled upward through the orphidnet—not "up," exactly, the direction was more like "in." They all knew the way by now, and here were the billion snouts, tails, trotters, and flop-ears of the Big Pig metabeezie, the all-seeing eye atop the pyramid whose base held the ten sextillion networked orphids of Earth.

The Pig extended a wobbly nipple toward Jayjay, and as he fastened on, the Pig passed him a time-lapse movie of a snowdrift being sculpted by the wind. The other Posse members found teats beside Jayjay, the four of them lined up like worshippers in a pew.

"Some Pig," messaged Thuy with a giggle. The sick thing was, whenever she actually hooked into the Big Pig, she totally loved it.

"Radiant," added Jayjay, picking up on Thuy's *Charlotte's*

Web reference, not that he'd read the book, but right now, via the Pig, he was hooked into all the libraries in the world, with every volume an open book.

But, *que lastima,* the Big Pig hit was weak. The beetles were coming on, swarming into the space between Jayjay and the Big Pig, making the Pig's images blocky, her animations jerky, her links slow—and there was no hope of an *aha.*

They dropped back into their mortal frames. In the peeling-paint Victorian, Dot and Red were reaching a climax, possibly goaded on by having the Posse nearby to watch them. Ugh.

Jayjay focused on the raindrops dripping through the moon roof and moved his leg. Now that he wasn't doing anything interesting, the beetles were lying low.

"I want the real Big Pig," said Kittie in a sullen tone. "Without all those freaking pests in the way. We really are infected."

"I'm gonna get into Doodly Bug," said Sonic, squinting his eyes and oddly wiggling his ten fingers. He touched the fingertips of his left hand to those of his right, pairing up his long, agile digits in a peculiar order. "I'll invent some Calabi-Yau grenades to take down the beetles."

Doodly Bug was based on quantum-loop string theory: in the game's virtual worlds, players knotted hyperdimensional Calabi-Yau hypersurfaces so as to destabilize the particle symmetries of their online opponents. With orphidnet visualization engines and expert beezie agents helping the players along, the esoteric physics of Doodly Bug was within the reach of any kiqqie willing to waste a lot of time.

Sonic's Doodly Bug ranking was approaching the highest possible level: Grandmaster of Space and Time. He'd already attained the only-slightly-less-exalted Multiversal Governator level. Jayjay was a Doodly Bug player too, with the quite respectable Kaluza Branesurfer rating. Last spring, Jayjay and Sonic had won some

championships together. But then Jayjay had gotten obsessed
with the ideas *under* the game—that is, with brane theory. And
now, all praise the orphidnet, he'd begun using his intelligence-
amplification to hang with the hard-core physicists who were investigating today's number-one problem: understanding the
Hibrane.

The explorations were long on theory and short on experiment, as a Hibraner named Gladax had somehow managed to
erase all the orphidnet copies of Chu's Hibrane jump-code the
morning after Orphid Night.

To make the research even harder, the Hibraners had
changed their jumping technique to include a wait-loop so that
all their interbrane jumps took exactly half a second to initiate,
leaving no hope of repeating the timing-channel attack that
clever Chu had used to figure out the Hibrane jump-code in
the first place.

The kiqqie physicists were going bananas trying to think
their way into the Hibrane, and Jayjay was channeling as many
of their seminars as he could, working to reach the higher levels of this realworld metagame. Now and then he could actually
contribute a seminar comment that made some of the others
light up. He was disappointed that Thuy wasn't more im-
pressed. After all, he'd never even finished high school.

Yeah, Papa went to prison, just for selling a little dope, and
Jayjay had dropped out of school to work fulltime at a taqueria with Mama so they could feed the five younger kids.
When Mama had married the *pendejo* taqueria manager, Jayjay
had quit working and left home. He figured he was too
smart for work *or* for school. He hated his stepfather and he'd
pretty much lost touch with his family. He'd lived in a squat,
playing a lot of video games, making a little money in gamer

tournaments—which was how he'd met Sonic. When the orphidnet hit, he embraced it.

For her part, Thuy had stuck it out at her parents' little stucco house in the Sunset district, straight through high school and college at San Francisco State and even a year of studying the violin at the Music Conservatory. But all that education had led to nothing substantial. Thuy wanted to be a writer, but her parents, timid Minh and bossy Khanh, had gotten her a job as an executive assistant at Golden Lucky, a Vietnamese restaurant-supply wholesaler in South San Francisco, with the possibility of a marriage to the boss. Thuy had been desperately bored there, so when the new global network unfurled on Orphid Night, she dove in and never looked back. She'd bailed on her family and shown up at Jayjay's squat in a condemned building off Valencia Street.

Thanks to the orphidnet, street-living was easy. In that first golden month, Thuy had crafted her big metastory, "Waking Up." But then she got more and more hung up on the Big Pig, and this summer a Hibraner had advised her to leave Jayjay for Kittie. Thuy's problems with the Pig were supposed to be from Jayjay's bad influence.

"What are you watching, Jayjay?" Thuy asked Jayjay from the backseat. "I'm getting bored waiting for Dot and Red." The rain was even stronger than before, filling the car with soporific drumming.

"Colloquium talk outta Berkeley," said Jayjay. "Professor Prav Plato describing the dark-energy Higgs field." It was more than a talk, really. The orphidnetted, beezie-amplified Prof Prav was spewing out images, simulations, and links as he spoke; and Prav's kiqqie listeners were continually popping up comments and diagrams as well. Jayjay made a point of catching all Prav's performances. The individual orphids kept a full record of everything they'd seen or heard for the past few months, so you always had the option of replaying a talk or slowing it down. But right now Jayjay was real-timing it, snowboarding his way down a whipped-cream mountain of symbols, loving how Prav was steering the flow past the Dick Too Dibbs ads that kept popping up like quirky machine monsters in a maze. It was awesome to kiq it with the Prav.

The only problem was that, now that Jayjay was doing something interesting again, the beetles were back. He set his virtual kennel of filter dogs on the trail of the beetles, hoping the dogs might evolve a way to bring down the intruders. Catching up for lost time, he jammed through a snowdrift of tensors to re-join Prav.

"The profs don't realize you're a dropout guttersnipe?" Kittie taunted Jayjay from the backseat. Once, a few weeks back, in a friendly, unguarded moment, Kittie had told Jayjay she admired his ambition. But most of the time she tried to act all hard and street-tough—covering for the fact that she came from a comfortable middle-class family in Palo Alto, slumming yuppie larva that she was. "Forget that double-doming and check where *I'm* at, kiqs," continued Kittie. "Heath Himbo is doing Lureen Morales on the *Caliente* show. I love that hard, slutty thing Lureen does with her upper lip. But, dammit, they've got Dick Too Dibbs as a paid-up legit sponsor. How lame is that? Outta the way, Dick Too. And he's carrying a beetle under his arm. Those freaking beetles are ruining everything!"

"They've got a rainbow sheen," said Thuy. "They're the same malware that Nektar has. Oh, shit, they're chewing on my notes for my metanovel!"

"Yo!" cried Sonic just then. "I finally got the cure. Give me access, homes."

Jayjay and the others opened their mental shields. Virtual Sonic flicked his fingers, scattering glowing blue fleas every which way. A flea landed on one of Jayjay's filter dogs and exploded; the dog's teeth got twice as long, his hair turned into purple flames—and he began tearing through the beetles like a starving man eating Thanksgiving dinner. The dog briefly paused to shake himself, showering the exploding fleas onto the other dogs. In another second the slavering pack had devoured all of Jayjay's beetles.

"Yay, Sonic!" said Kittie and Thuy, who'd gotten cleaned up too.

"Calabi-Yau flea-grenades," said Sonic. "I made them in the Doodly Bug weapon shop. I'm smarter than the beezies, see!" He wore a proud little smile on his face. "Squark-gaugino supersymmetry," added Sonic, getting back into his Doodly Bug wars. "Compactify dimension seven. Destroy starboard glueball pellet three o'clock high: *ftoom!*"

Fighting off malware was a continual activity, but usually the beezies would automatically give the patches to your filter dogs. Why had the beetles been so tough to kill? And why were Nektar's beetles in this particular car? Jayjay set some beezies to searching through possible causes for the unfolding scenario. Inside the house old Dot and Red were dressed again; the rain was letting up.

"Lureen Morales is an idiot," Thuy said to Kittie, dipping backward into the conversation the way she liked to do. "She's got a pushed-in Pomeranian face. I'm much more attractive than her. Don't be a brainwashed starfucker, Kittie. You sound like a frat boy. You should be listening to Tawny Krush instead."

Jayjay grinned to hear Thuy harsh on Kittie.

"You're channeling Tawny?" said Kittie, taken aback.

"She's rehearsing a heavy-metal symphony with the Kazakhstan guitar corps," said Thuy loftily, her high pigtails swaying. "I'm going to sample it for my metanovel. That's what I'm all about. Postsingular literature." She stuck out her tongue at Kittie and waggled it. "Am I 'hot' yet?"

"Come here, *bạn gái,*" said Kittie, fumbling at Thuy's miniskirt. "Heath's going *waay* down on Lureen."

Jayjay returned his attention to Prav Plato's rap, not wanting to witness Kittie pawing his lost love. Sonic remained obsessively focused on his game. A moment of silence, and then old Red stumped out of the house and pulled open the car door. The two women drew apart.

"Wassup, Red," said Jayjay.

To switch from Prof Prav's fraught, exquisite communication to Red's rudimentary vocalizations was, for Jayjay, like dropping out of a beautiful sunset-clouded sky into a crude, flat cartoon. For the first second or two, the old man's words seemed like the yipping of a dog. Jayjay felt guilty about the involuntary comparison. Red wasn't all that different from Papa, dead three years now from a gang fight in the penitentiary.

"Log into the Department of Motor Vehicles with me and I'll give you the title," repeated the old man, holding out the car keys.

"I want to own the car," put in Kittie. "Me! I'll retrofit it and trick it out."

Red craned his neck, peering avidly at the women in the backseat.

"Your orphids are blushing, Thuy," said Kittie. "Red's peeping you. Dig it, realman, we're watching you right back, you and your breeder in the house. I'm seeing hella many coats in your hall closet. Can I have the leopard-patterned Burberry knockoff with the dog-fur collar?"

Jayjay laughed; he admired the way that Kittie always pushed things too far, even though that made her expensive to carry as a friend.

"Take the damn car and get out of here," said Red.

With quick mental gestures, Kittie and Red completed the registration steps. But then the car wouldn't start, of course, having sat there for about a year. Fortunately it had a manual transmission; Red told Jayjay he could start it by putting it in second gear and popping the clutch while Sonic and Kittie rolled it down the driveway into the street. So Jayjay tried that, with Thuy sitting in the backseat fixing her lipstick, Thuy watching her face in the orphidnet instead of in a mirror.

"I miss you, Thuy," said Jayjay into their moment alone. "When are you coming back to me?"

"When you get yourself straight," said Thuy. "Maybe. I'm changing, Jayjay. My Hibraner friend Azaroth is helping me write my metanovel. I'm really done with the Pig."

"But you love the Pig," protested Jayjay. "When we got high this morning, we were channeling together, and I said *wheenk*, and uh—" He paused, trying to bring back all those great thoughts they'd shared.

"*And uh,*" mimicked Thuy. "That's how everyone's Big Pig stories end. We might as well be sudocokers. It's sad, Jayjay. You know I still like you a lot; Kittie's like a cellmate helping me break out of jail, not like the love of my life. And yes, of course, I remember our *wheenk* moment this morning, it was funny. Know what? I'm gonna use that for the title of my metanovel. *Wheenk*. It's all in there, isn't it?"

"I'm tender," said Jayjay. "And I'm not like a sudocoker at all. I'm much smarter than I used to be. Hold tight." He popped the clutch; the car lurched; the motor caught and died.

"Pump the gas pedal!" shouted Red, watching from his front steps.

"One more try, loser," Kittie hollered to Jayjay. "Then I drive and *you* push." The car begin rolling forward again.

"Warn me earlier," said Thuy, wiping a lipstick smear off her nose. "Using the beezies to help you think is one thing, Jayjay, but getting high on the Pig is something else. Those physicists you admire, they're spending their spare time buffing up their theories. They're not getting wasted and sleeping on the floor. Kittie and I are gonna quit the Posse."

"Oh, come on, stick around," said Jayjay, not taking the threat all that seriously. "I'm good story material, no? Hold tight again." This time the engine caught. Jayjay paused, gunning the backfiring engine while Sonic and Kittie got in.

It was a short, exciting drive to Dolores Heights. Street kids ran along the sidewalk, cheering the roaring silver dinosaur. With the gasoline supply closed down, all you saw on the roads anymore were electric retrofits. Empowered by orphidic intelligence amplification, the automotive engineers had come up with cheap gas-to-electric conversion kits, not to mention lightweight batteries and nanotech solar cells that you brushed onto your car's roof like enamel paint.

The belching SUV wallowed across Dolores Street and up the steep little hill to Nektar's gingerbread mansion, the highest on the ridge, save for one.

"I can't believe we're going to Nektar Lundquist's," exulted Kittie. "And do you realize that's Lureen Morales's place at the very top of the hill? We're with the stars!"

The engine sputtered and missed; the gas was running out. Jayjay goosed the accelerator. With a peevish last roar, the behemoth waddled in through one of Nektar's open garage doors.

CHAPTER 6

Nektar's Beetles

Lying on her bed on the second floor, Nektar heard the unaccustomed sound of a car engine. Night before last, the beetles had come in her sleep like a fever dream, and ever since then she couldn't fully wake up. The beetles kept wedging her orphidnet access open, kept getting into her head.

She was too weak to sit up, and there was no hope of using the orphidnet to examine her garage, what with the virtual beetles in the way, each of them a jagged oval core with faceted eyes, pinchy-feely mouths, and zigzag legs.

Although Nektar was a big celeb, nobody was here to help her—other than some little shoon robots she'd gotten from Jil Zonder.

Right now, so far as the public understood the situation, Nektar was on a weight-reducing sudocoke binge. But in reality she didn't use sudocoke; and that was talcum powder on the mirror by her bed. The beetles had made her lay out the lines; whenever she balked at their requests, they'd feed her images she could barely stand to see. At least so far she'd refused to cut an ad for Dick Too Dibbs. That's what they were after.

Nektar strained her ears to listen for more noises from the garage, but all she heard were the chirps and clicks from the beetle currently in her visual field.

"You say sorry about insulting Homesteadies," repeated the beetle. "Make Too Dibbs testimonial now."

Out of the question. The first Dick Dibbs had sent the nants to eat the Earth. Nektar would never ever forget that. Nor would she forget that her husband Ond had let the nants eat their son Chu in order to pass some viral code to the nants. Nektar had stopped loving Ond then and there—even though Ond's crazy plan had worked. The nants had reassembled everything they'd destroyed, including Chu.

President Dick Dibbs and his vice president had been impeached, convicted, and executed like the rabid dogs they were, but Jeff Luty had escaped. And Nantel had regrouped as ExaExa. According to Ond, Luty was safely hidden from the orphidnet within the quantum-mirror-shielded walls of the ExaExa labs. They'd had the mirroring in place even before they released the orphids. Taking care of the boss.

Nektar drifted back from her reverie. Probably the malware beetles were a Jeff Luty product. Ond said Jeff liked insects better than humans because they were closer to being machines. Not only ants, but beetles as well, especially the sacred scarab dung beetle of ancient Egypt. Back at Nantel, Jeff had given Ond a mounted giant beetle as an award; it was still kicking around the house somewhere.

If Luty had made these software beetles, then no wonder they'd come to attack Nektar. Jeff had always had it in for her. Back in the Nantel days, Luty had tried to take over Ond's life, keeping him at the lab till late, seven days a week. Maybe he had some sick crush on Ond. It had taken some severe tantrums on Nektar's part to get Ond a more reasonable schedule, and Luty had never forgiven Nektar.

Ond always said Luty was like a child, forgetful of the niceties, a genius in the rough, but Nektar had never liked the guy, not his chewed-down fingernails, not his weird vocabulary of made-up words, not his lip balm, not his greasy ponytail. Why couldn't Luty take ten minutes off and cut his hair? Of course, the worst was that he'd enlisted Ond into his nant project of destroying the natural world. Yes, Ond had backed off in the end, but by then it had been too late for Nektar. If Luty hadn't warped Ond, then Nektar and Ond might still have been together.

Gathering her strength, Nektar executed a savage mental lunge that closed down the image of the beetle currently threatening her. She glanced over at her bedside clock. Ten fifteen in the morning. And now the minute hand bent up and out toward her, articulating itself like a beetle leg. Nektar willed the leg back into a minute hand. The clock face dropped off, and a fresh beetle crawled out.

"You must record ad," it insisted. "We exhaust time and patience. More punish." Day before yesterday, Nektar had ranted against Too Dibbs and the Homesteadies, putting the truth out there for her *Founders* audience. That's what had set this off.

"You know I won't help you," said Nektar flatly. "I'd rather die. I meant what I said and I'll say it again." She threw her remembered words in the beetle's face. "The Homesteady Party wants people to be like sheep, easy to fleece. That's why they're against personal freedom, against quirky culture, against self-expression, against education, against art. They want a mass mind they can mass-process like synthoid tomatoes. Is anyone in the orphidnet channeling me? Listen to Chef Nektar. Too Dibbs will make you sicker than the Banana Surprise at MouthPlus-Plus."

In response, the beetle's chirping grew guttural, sinister. Nektar braced herself. An image of her son Chu appeared. A long, solemn knife hovered beside him like the bow of a violin.

Trying to draw back from the coming torment, Nektar groped for a memory, any memory, and came up with a clip of her and rival chef Jose having their final fight in the Puff kitchen: Jose holding that same kind of long knife to his own throat, making the tiniest of cuts and lifting a drop of his blood to Nektar's lips, all the while glaring into her eyes. "Taste *that*," he'd hissed. "You bitch." A pair of beetle legs unfurled from Jose's belly, taking hold of the knife. Jose's face became Chu's. The knife sawed into Chu's neck; the boy's head flopped back and all the blood of his body gushed out.

Nektar moaned and rocked, drawing deeper into herself. As if from somewhere very far away, she felt water on her lips. Those good little shoons were taking care of her. Maybe the beezies would find a way to save her soon. Maybe there were people in the garage. Hang on, Nektar. A beetle leg rummaged down through her veils of thought, its spiny foot trying to snag her attention. Nektar burrowed deeper, replaying triumphal memories of her rise to the head chef's post at Puff.

Restaurant traffic had ramped up heavily after the coming of the orphids; with people able to see and hear everything online, the nonvirtual experience of dining was becoming the centerpiece of most evenings out. Nektar liked to present a meal as table theater. And why limit the entertainment to chewing things up? She'd added foamy, soft food to the Puff menu, and pastes for people to rub onto their bodies: peppery curries, soothing mints, moistening emulsions. Jose had been against all of Nektar's ideas; turned out he was a depressive jerk, always acting like a martyr. After he'd done that weird number with the knife on his neck, Nektar had gone straight upstairs to the restaurant's owners, Xandro and Beatriz.

But now Nektar's memory citadel was broached again; the two owners resembled beetles, their legs linked like axons and dendrites. "Make ad for Dick Too Dibbs," said the beetles. "Do very now."

"Fire Jose," Nektar told them, desperately hanging onto her narrative. "Make me the head chef. Look how many hits my orphids are getting. I'm a star. It's me that brings the customers in."

Beetle Xandro lifted the shiny cover off a silver salver, his chitinous leg hooking the metal handle. Beetle Beatriz leaned over the naked boy on the platter and fired up a blowtorch. "I cook tableside," she twittered, blistering Chu's face. "Else make Too Dibbs ad now."

Groaning, Nektar twisted away and found herself in last week's bed with Craigor. He was handsome and well-endowed, but not Nektar's idea of a great lover. She'd only continued sleeping with him because the affair had given such a nice boost to the hitcounts of her *Founders* show. Acting out the bedroom memory, Nektar ran a flirtatious finger down Craigor's bare chest. He split open like a pupa and Craigor's wife Jil crawled out: moist, throbbing, luminous, in tears. "I was your best friend, Nektar. How could you? Craigor was my man. I'm scared I'm going to relapse."

"I'm sorry," said Nektar. "I'm so sorry."

"Make the ad," said the beetle shaped like Jil. "Then I forgive. Vote for Dick Too Dibbs. You say just once."

"Hey, Nektar!" A fresh voice, a real voice in her bedroom.

She fluttered her eyes open. Two men and two women were here, colorful, street-hardened kids in their early twenties, ten years younger than Nektar. One of them leaned close. His eyes were soft and intelligent beneath his green cap; he wore a T-shirt and a suit jacket with a wild hand-drawn skull on the jacket's back. An iridescent shoon was perched on his shoulder. The rain had stopped; the sun was breaking through.

"I'm Jayjay," the boy told Nektar. "Aka Jorge Jimenez. We're the Big Pig Posse. Let me into your head, Nektar. Give me full access. I can kill those beetles by fixing your filter dogs." He flexed his fingers in intricate gamer moves.

"Yes," said Nektar with a weak smile, and opened a mental door for him. In the orphidnet, Jayjay got busy. The other Posse members were in the orphidnet watching, as well: a stocky girl with a blue tattoo, a boy with spiky hair, a Vietnamese girl with high pigtails.

"*Yeek yeek,*" murmured the first boy—Jayjay—swinging from bough to vine in the jungle of Nektar's mind, landing beside her filter dog kennel, and scattering luminous blue fleas. Instants later, Nektar's flea-bitten dogs had trashed the beetles.

"All good now, Nektar," said Jayjay, pulling back into his real body.

Nektar sat up, holding her sheet to her breasts, free at last.

The boy with his hair in shiny spikes—Sonic—stretched out in a patch of sun on the big Oriental rug on Nektar's floor, the shoons yipping and cavorting with him. He wore black wool tights, a red T-shirt, and a lightweight leather jacket with tailored shirring.

As usual, the shoons' appearances changed according to the whims of the beezies currently controlling them; right now a couple resembled monkeys, another pair was playing beetle and beetle-flea, another was a classic Happy Shoon like a bucktoothed Korean baby with a thick rubber bottom, and two had tweaked themselves to resemble Jayjay and the pigtailed girl in striped leggings.

Jayjay forced open the bedroom's sticky window. Sitting in the easy chair right by Nektar's bed was the plain-faced woman with the blue tattoo.

"I'm Kittie," she said pleasantly. "It's great to meet you. I watch *Founders* all the time. And I've seen you around the Mission, of course." Fresh air drifted into the room.

"I'll treat your little group to a big dinner," said Nektar. "Have you ever been to Puff?"

"Mostly we eat garbage," said Kittie. "We're rough and tough."

"Hmm," said Nektar, thinking that over, her beetle-free mind feeling giddy and agile. Kittie reminded Nektar of the girlfriend she'd had in college before she'd met Ond; Kittie had that same quality of inner refinement beneath a streetwise demeanor. "You just gave me an idea for a new restaurant presentation," Nektar told her. "We lead the customers into a dim room with food hidden in miniature garbage cans along the wall. They root out their entrees; it's a walk on the wild side." Just to see if she still had it, Nektar gave Kittie a come-hither look.

"I want white tablecloths for *our* meal at Puff," said Kittie, radiating back. "Clean and calm."

"Did this start out as a sudocoke run?" interrupted the girl in the striped leggings, wandering over. "I'm Thuy."

"That's baby powder on the mirror," said Nektar, glad to be getting this information out to her audience. "A hoax. I was under the control of those beetles. They wanted to set the scene so it looked as if I had a reason to stay in bed. For the last two days, they've been tormenting me, wanting me to make an ad for that silly Dick Too Dibbs. I've heard him come out strong against the nants, but who owns him, really? Since when did any Homesteady politician care about anyone who's not filthy stinking rich?"

"Tell the world, Nektar," said Jayjay. "Listen up, *Founders* fans! My homie Sonic designed these six-dimensional Calabi-Yau beetle-fleas. They'll gnaw beetle malware out of your orphids." He gestured with both arms, tossing a complete image of a beetle-flea into the orphidnet for Nektar's viewers to grab. Then he flopped down on the floor to join Sonic in playing with the shoons.

"I need a shower," said Nektar, getting out of her bed. She was naked, but being naked didn't matter anymore, what with your body visible on the orphidnet all the time.

"Need some help?" said Kittie.

"Don't be dogging her," said Thuy. Evidently Thuy was Kittie's girlfriend.

Nektar could visualize making love to Kittie. Having an affair with needy, unstable Craigor Connor was enough to put a woman off hetero sex for months. Maybe it was because he was anxious about cheating on Jil, but Craigor had stinted on foreplay—like he was in a rush to notch up his score for the main event. Kittie, on the other hand, looked tender and competent, like a butch, sexy nurse. Nektar smiled at her and said, "I am a little wobbly, matter of fact. If you could walk me in there and maybe help me when I dry off?"

"You got it, babe," said Kittie.

"I'm coming, too," said Thuy.

"Fine," said Nektar, relishing the attention.

The girls helped Nektar into the shower, Kittie making sure to accidentally touch Nektar's breasts and bottom, with Thuy watching: annoyed, aroused, amused. After the shower, the two converged on Nektar, each of them holding a big thick towel. Much better to be pursued by women than by beetles. This was catnip for the *Founders* viewers. Nektar's orphids glowed with hitcounts.

Back in the bedroom, Sonic and Jayjay were still fooling around with the shoons. Happy Shoon was pacing around to mime deep thought, but the other shoons were rolling around like puppies.

"One of my beezies traced back the beetles' history for us," announced Jayjay. For a homeless kiqqie, he had a very crisp and precise way of speaking. "They originated from some malware that you caught from Craigor Connor, Nektar. And Craigor caught the beetle infection when he delivered a walking-chair to Andrew Topping, director of the Natural Mind center in the Mission Street Armory. We don't know how the infection reached Topping's office. They've got the whole Armory shielded by quantum-mirror varnish to protect their recovering orphidnet addicts. The same kind of shielding that's used in the ExaExa labs; ExaExa gave them the varnish. ExaExa is one of Natural Mind's main financial backers, matter of fact. They say it's charity. For the public good."

"You know—" said Nektar, regally nude, pausing to enjoy the eyes upon her. "I kept trying to think what those beetles reminded me of, and now I realize they're like nants. That blind, pushy quality. The Jeff Luty connection fits. That man isn't comfortable in a human body. He truly thinks we'd be happier if we were software. Ond always said Jeff wasn't really evil—it's just that Jeff had this big tragedy when he was younger." Nektar shook out her hair, proud of herself for sounding so calm on the subject of Luty. "What it is, Jeff is making those beetles as a way to help get Dick Too Dibbs into office. And that'll give Jeff an in. And down the road, I bet Jeff will manipulate Too Dibbs into launching some improved, unstoppable nants and they'll kill Gaia for good. Someone has to get to Luty."

"Right on, Nektar," said Kittie.

"Go to the Armory," urged Nektar. "Go to the Armory and check yourselves into the Natural Mind center. Talk sense to Andrew Topping."

"Natural Mind," mused Jayjay. "A janitor told us to go there this morning. Coincidence or trap?"

"Aw, people always mention Natural Mind if you're sleeping in the street," said Sonic. "I'm down with going there. Put some heat on Topping's ass. He's a megaspammer, man. Of course, duh, thanks to the orphidnet, he'll know we're coming, assuming his beezies data-mine this conversation. Maybe the Natural Minders won't let us in."

Jayjay made a dismissive gesture. His attention had wandered to Thuy. "You done watching Nektar take her shower?" he demanded. "Leave that for Kittie. Come sit with me. I'm the one who loves you."

Thuy strode over, gave Jayjay such a hard shove with her gold-clad foot that he fell over on his side, then perched herself on him as if she were sitting on a log. He lay there, looking happy to be in physical contact. Poor men, thought Nektar, they're dogs. Jayjay was cute, too. If Thuy didn't want him, maybe Jil Zonder would. Jil deserved a fling. It might shake her out of her doldrums.

"Why didn't you and the beezies fix Nektar yourself instead of calling in a strung-out pighead derelict like Jayjay?" Thuy asked the shoons, wagging her finger at them. "You there—the shoon that looks like me—squeak up! You can talk, can't you?"

The tiny Thuy-shaped shoon bobbled her little pigtails and spoke in a surprisingly rich alto voice: "We can talk. We can sing." Capering expressively, the shoon now performed a bit of Papageno's aria from *The Magic Flute,* vibrating her whole body like a loudspeaker.

The Big Pig Posse kids laughed.

And then the shoon laid her little finger against her lips to mime secretiveness. "Let's switch to quantum-encrypted instant messages," she said. With everything visible and audible via the quantum-entangled surface-mesh-monitoring orphidnet, the one way to have a private conversation was via dynamically encoded messaging.

"I'm not a derelict, I'm important," said Jayjay, rolling out from under Thuy and catching his arms around her waist. "See—the shoon-beezies want to make plans with us! I'll set up a secure channel for us, okay?"

Nektar ignored the planning session. She'd spoken her piece; let the little kiqqies work out the details. It was time to put her look together. Her blond hair had dark roots, but that was okay. She dried her hair, combed it out, and pinned it into an upside-down bed-head ponytail. For Kittie's benefit, she donned sexy black underwear with red stitching, making sure the girl watched. Then came black tights and a black slip, mascara and lipstick, a cream-colored silk blouse, high black boots, and her casual red twill skirt and jacket.

The sheets on the bed were disgraceful. Nektar stripped them off and threw them into the hamper, with Kittie right there at her side pitching in. Nektar needed breakfast: a quart of Lapsang Souchong tea and a bowl of granola with apricots and yogurt. She called over Happy Shoon and sent him downstairs to make the tea. He was the most trustworthy of the lot, Jil's original model.

"Would you four like to come downstairs with me?" Nektar asked the Big Pig Posse. Kittie nodded, but the others didn't. They were so into their private conference that they didn't hear her.

"Time to eat!" Nektar messaged into the Posse's quantum-encrypted channel.

"We had some food already," said Jayjay out loud. "Maybe we should—"

"It's been a couple of hours," said Kittie quickly. "You should be glad to eat with Chef Nektar. Are you kidding? What an honor. You guys can talk later."

As they headed down the stairs someone knocked on the front door. Looking through the orphidnet, Nektar saw Jil Zonder and Craigor Connor out there, the pair in a state of uneasy truce.

"Wow," said Kittie. "We're smack in the middle of the *Founders* show."

"Maybe I'll make a special episode with just you," Nektar purred to Kittie. "Can you be a dear and let them in? I feel like I'll go crazy if I don't get my tea this minute."

Nektar hurried into the kitchen and poured herself a mug of smoky black tea with two spoons of sugar and enough whole milk to cool it down—*ahh.* The caffeine molecules ran up and down the corridors of her brain turning on the lights. She fixed herself a bowl of cereal, then sat down at the kitchen table as the crowd appeared.

"Poor Nektar," said Craigor, pushing forward. "You had, like, mind parasites? I would have come earlier, but I thought, you know, she's losing weight with sudocoke."

"You *would* think that," said Nektar, crabbily. "Sit down; don't hover. Help yourself to some food. Scavenge. My four young friends here, the Big Pig Posse, they're used to finding their meals in garbage cans. But try my fridge first. Thanks for coming, Jil."

Jil looked good today; her bobbed dark hair lustrous, her figure sweet in jeans and a pullover. Instead of answering Nektar out loud, she sent a quantum-encrypted message. "You can have Craigor for good. It'll never be the same between us again. You've ruined our marriage." Stone-faced, she turned away and opened Nektar's fridge.

"Really he loves you," messaged back Nektar. "I'm sorry I did it. The last few times were just for the *Founders* ratings. And I was drunk the first time. You don't know what hell I've been through. In my head I keep begging you to be my friend again. Please, Jil."

"Funny kind of friend." Jil took a pitcher of juice from the fridge and poured herself a glass, her back still turned to Nektar. "There's a hole where my heart used to be."

"I know I'm horrible," messaged Nektar. "And you're wonderful and noble and brave. Forgive me. You mean so much more to me than Craigor ever could." Craigor, now sitting right across the table from Nektar, didn't even know that Jil and Nektar were channeling each other.

"Hands off him from now on?" messaged Jil, sliding a glance over toward Nektar. "Maybe I could still love Craigor a little bit. For the kids' sake, anyway. And maybe I need this marriage. Do you promise not to reel him back in the next time your ratings are low?"

"Don't worry about the ratings. I'm planning to start up with this blue-tattoo girl. Why don't you give yourself a treat and pay Craigor back." Nektar's eye fell on Jayjay in his skull-painted jacket. "How about that one right behind you," she messaged Jil. "He's young and hot; he chased the beetles out of my skull. Talk to him."

"You're terrible, Nektar. What an idea."

"Sauce for the goose, sauce for the gander," messaged Nektar. "You deserve that boy. Look how cute he is. He can't take his eyes off you."

CHAPTER 7

The Grill in the Wall

Would you like some juice?" said Jil, turning toward Jayjay with a pitcher in her hand. "It's mango."

In person, Jil's face had more nuances and complexities than the orphidnet meshes revealed. One orphid per square millimeter of skin wasn't nearly enough to capture the lively high-res play of a woman's eyes and mouth. Particularly Jil's.

"Wonderful," said Jayjay, taking the plastic pitcher from her, or meaning to, but somehow he and Jil bobbled the handoff, and the pitcher fell, bouncing out a floppy yellow-orange tongue that puddled sticky on the floor.

"Oops!" called Craigor from the kitchen table. Kittie, Thuy, and Sonic had already sat down as well, Thuy holding a cantaloupe and Sonic bearing cups and Nektar's big pot of tea.

"The shoons will mop that," Jil reassured Jayjay. Her dark eyebrows were arch-formed, always giving her an optimistic, playful appearance despite any inner pain. "The shoons can open up pores and make themselves into sponges. They clean up after my kids all the time. And my husband." She gave a sharp whistle; Happy Shoon and a doughboy trotted over to roll in the juice, chirruping as their bodies dampened and swelled. Jil gave Jayjay a really nice smile. She had faint freckles across the bridge of her perfect nose.

Usually Jayjay was tentative with women, but, faced with the alluring Jil, he found the courage to go for it. "When I first saw you on the orphidnet and heard your name, I thought you were this beautiful girl Jilena who was a year ahead of me in high school," he said softly. "I worshipped Jilena from afar."

"I was done with high school a looong time before you," said Jil, looking Jayjay up and down. "Flatterer." Jayjay felt the orphids on his body registering major hitcounts—he was live on *Founders*. And maybe Jil was checking out his physique too. He tingled at the thought.

"I'd love to talk to you about the Hibrane," said Jayjay, his pulse pounding in his ears. "I hear you've been there. I'm a budding physicist. We should get together alone sometime." He glanced over at the others, wondering if they were noticing him flirting with Jil. It would be good for Thuy to realize that Jayjay had other options.

But Thuy was busy cutting up the cantaloupe and offering Kittie a slice, and Kittie was enthralled with Nektar, and Nektar was chattering at Craigor as if to keep him from looking at Jil. For his part, Sonic was drinking tea as fast as he could. The guy could never get enough caffeine.

"You're a homeless kiqqie," exclaimed Jil, sounding a little disappointed. Dammit, she'd already done an instant check via the orphidnet. "And you're addicted to the Big Pig?"

"The Pig helps me get ideas," said Jayjay. "I wouldn't say that I have a problem. Anyway, I'm cutting down really soon."

"Oh, I know all about *that*," said Jil.

"I watch you on *Founders*," said Jayjay. "You've gotten a bad deal lately. I really admire that you've hung onto your sobriety. You could show me the way. Mold me, Jil, train me to be like you. Clear-eyed. Hi-res. A coiled spring. I want to please you."

He could hardly believe he was saying these things. His mouth was way ahead of his brain.

"*Boing,*" said Jil. "That's enough for now."

"Hey," said Craigor, jumping to his feet. Jayjay was expecting to get bawled out for hitting on the guy's wife, but, no, Craigor was into his own ego trip.

"Check this out," said Craigor, producing four short metal rods with wads of piezoplastic on their ends. He turned his chair over and stuck his rods to the ends of the chair legs—so that now the chair had piezoplastic knees and feet. When Craigor turned the chair upright, it waltzed around the kitchen, faster and faster, culminating with a tap dance and a bow. Craigor made as if to sit down and, with comical eagerness, the tall chair scuttled into position to catch him.

"That's a walking-chair," said Jayjay, hoping to steal Craigor's thunder. "You sold a double-jointed version to the manager at the Natural Mind recovery center in the Armory."

"How'd you happen to notice that?" asked Craigor, seeming genuinely curious about the specific chain of logic Jayjay had followed. Everything was visible on the orphidnet, and many people had their beezie agents mining for things that were specifically relevant to their lives, the notion of "relevant" being fairly inclusive, due to people's beezie-assisted abilities think a few steps further than before.

"Jayjay's beezies were looking for the origins of Nektar's beetle infection," said Thuy. "They came from the Natural Mind building, and you caught them when you delivered the chair, Craigor, and then Nektar caught the beetles from you, that time when you squirted too quick. Lose-lose."

"Mouthy brat," said Craigor, not especially embarrassed. He waggled his eyebrows at Thuy. "You need a spanking." He stuck his teaspoon to the side of his walking-chair with a spare bit of piezoplastic, and sent the chair trotting around the table to *whack-whack-whack* Thuy's thigh with the spoon.

"Craigor, you should load up on Jayjay's antibeetle flea-grenades," said Nektar. "For all we know, the beetles are eating your brain right now."

Craigor responded in mime, fluttering his hands by his mouth like munching mandibles.

"Don't worry, Nektar," said Jil with a sigh. "We got the antibeetle fleas off the *Founders* show on our way over. And, yeah, the beetles really were lying dormant in us. That's weird they used Craigor for a disease vector."

Craigor's walking-chair flexed its knees, rhythmically hunching against Thuy, who laughed at the urgent bumping. Kittie reached down to rip off one of the walking-chair's shins. Miming great pain, the chair limped three-legged back to Craigor, leaning against him with a decrescendo shudder.

"You're funny," said Thuy to Craigor, meaning it. "I can put you in my metanovel. Are you directly controlling the chair?"

"I run the character animations though a beezie," said Craigor. "But the beezie draws on a library of body-language routines that I stored. I act things out; that's how all the great animators do it. My body knows more than my head. I'm a cuttle-fisherman, too."

"Mr. Disease Vector," said Kittie, who'd attached the loose rod to her crotch. "Animate this."

"Oh that's witty," said Craigor, looking annoyed. He grabbed the leg back.

Jayjay turned his attention to Jil, who was hunkered down by the sink checking up on her shoons. Even in that awkward position, she looked lithe and graceful. He tossed her a tiny heart-shaped emoticon via the orphidnet; she answered by half-turning her head his way and miming a kiss in profile. He was living the dream—in a reality soap!

"*Founders* fans may want to scan the Big Pig Posse's backstory," Nektar intoned, playing show host. "Jayjay loses Thuy, Thuy takes up with Kittie and next—Thuy and Craigor? Kittie and Nektar? Jayjay and Jil? Sonic and the shoons? Stay tuned. Oh, look, the good ads are coming back." The orphidnet icons of BigBox and Stank glowed in the corners of the room, also the ExaExa beetle logo.

"Do we get paid too?" asked Kittie.

"I think so," said Nektar. "The orphidnet figures all that out. I'll register you as extras. And right up front, I'll let you guys keep your SUV in my garage for a couple of weeks. And there's a room over the garage you can live in. It'll be fun having young people around."

"Bitchin'," said Sonic, draining the last of the tea. His eyes were bright and black. "I'm ready to settle in for a Doodly Bug death-run."

"I want to paint that SUV and retrofit it for solar power," said Kittie.

"I'll be working on my metanovel," said Thuy. "*Wheenk.*"

"The title's growing on me," said Jayjay, smiling at her. "I'm gonna be busy with Prav Plato's physics seminars." He put on a goody-goody tone, segueing into the plan they'd privately made upstairs. By now he'd privately messaged Kittie the details, too. "We all have a lot to do—if we don't waste our energy by plugging into the Big Pig."

Jil gave Jayjay a quizzical look. She could tell he was acting, but she wasn't sure why. There were so many levels of unreality here. Jil turned to Nektar. "We'll be on our way," said Jil. "I'm gonna borrow your Happy Shoon so I can integrate his body-memories into my breeding stock. Knead him in like sourdough starter. You've trained these shoons well, Nektar."

"Can I take a shoon too?" asked Sonic.

"Sure," said Nektar. Sonic stuffed the Jayjay-faced doughboy shoon into the pleated pocket of his leather jacket.

"Bye-bye," said Jayjay, seizing the chance to touch Jil's hand. She upped the ante and kissed his cheek. In the orphidnet, Jayjay saw Jil staring over at her husband to make sure he noticed. Craigor's smile had gone stiff. Thuy, however, was obliv, or was at least presenting herself that way. Why did she have to be so stubborn? Just because Jayjay liked the Big Pig? Well, hell, if Thuy was going to be such a priss, maybe he should take his golden opportunity for a romance with the divine Jil.

"Come stay on the *Merz Boat* if you need a place to live," Jil told Jayjay in a warm tone. "There's plenty of room. All four of you would fit, actually."

Jayjay knew from *Founders* that Jil and Craigor's cuttlefishing boat was entirely crafted from computationally rich piezoplastic, which had become a fairly expensive and sought-after material. Although Craigor was still netting oversized Pharaoh cuttlefish from the Bay, much of the couple's income came from selling off bits of the boat's material in the form of Jil's shoons and Craigor's combines.

"Thanks, Jil," said Jayjay, wondering how Craigor would take his incursion. "I might be there sooner than you think. But at least for today we'll be kiqqin' it in Nektar's garage."

Some stairs at the back of the garage led up to the room Nektar had mentioned, white-painted with a peaked ceiling. The front and rear walls held generous windows, one showing a palm tree and Dolores Park, the other looking onto the San Francisco hills with their little stucco houses. The room was furnished with rugs, chairs, a double bed, a fold-out couch, a sink, and a fridge. The tile bathroom was stocked with Stank personal grooming products.

"Fuckin' A," said Sonic, eyeing a framed Nantel award to Nektar's absent husband. "Ond Lutter himself." The box was a couple of inches deep, holding a preserved blue-green beetle as well as a paper with the award inscription.

"Maybe we should do some Big Pig," said Thuy, flopping into an armchair. She didn't actually mean this; she was following their preplanned script.

Jayjay would in fact have liked very much to do some Pig, but he stuck to the script too. "It's time we all got clean," he said.

"Yeah, brother," said Sonic. "Getting down is coming old."

"You're slushed," giggled Thuy, even though she knew Sonic had warped the phrase on purpose. "Yes, yes, it's time to mad the endness. But how? Whither and yon?"

"Maybe Natural Mind could help us," said Kittie, also playing along. "I know we were harshing on them before. But that was just our denial talking."

"Natural Mind it is," said Jayjay earnestly. "I'm sick and tired of being sick and tired." Badda-*boom*.

"Let's take showers before we go out," said Sonic looking at the dirt shiny on his hands. "Me first."

"Me second," said Kittie.

When Jayjay got his turn in the shower, he had fun freeze-framing the water in his orphidnet view. Orphids were quick; they blanketed the water drops as fast as they formed. Further afield, Jayjay could see Craigor and Jil picking up their kids at school and heading back to their boat. School was still a reality—the orphidnet was no substitute for getting your butt smacked/stroked/sniffed by your fellow mammals in the human pack. With Jil still in her own little family, maybe it wasn't realistic to think he could sleep with her. Maybe he'd been fooling himself about those vibes he'd picked up from her.

Thuy squeezed into the shower as Jayjay was getting out; the brief, sliding touch of her skin made him unreasonably happy. Someday soon he'd win her back. Thuy was the one he really wanted.

The Posse hit the street and hoofed toward the Mission Street Armory, keeping up a line of recovery-hungry chatter as they went, the idea being to make the Natural Minders feel okay about admitting the Posse. Although it was of course possible or even likely that the Natural Minders weren't monitoring the Posse's activities at all. But it seemed wise to make up for having audibly confabbed with Nektar about launching an attack.

The rain had let up and the sun was out. People were shopping at the corner fruit stands, some of them using the orphidnet to peer into the piles and find that perfect, unblemished lime, jalapeño, or mango. Others were channeling music or watching what was happening somewhere else. With everyone's attention diluted, the street scene wasn't quite as vibrant as it used to be.

Passing Metotem Metabooks—which was a hangout for the Mission metanovelists—Jayjay saw the owner, Darlene, slumped in an easy chair she'd dragged outside to catch the afternoon sun, which had been a rarity of late. Darlene always had a big smile for Jayjay; sometimes he thought she had a crush on him. Darlene was quite influential on the literary scene; she edited the hip *Metotem Metazine.* Her store wasn't much, though. Just some comfortable chairs, a coffeepot, and shelves of beat-up paper books.

People did still buy paper books, even though you could read a book on the orphidnet without owning it. Strictly speaking, you could publish a book by printing one copy and letting the orphids settle onto it. They'd crawl around and learn the text. For that matter, you could publish a book by thoroughly *imagining* it, and then recording your thoughts onto some orphids, as the metanovelists did. But the paper physicality of an old-style book remained perennially pleasing, and they still sold in small numbers. Not that Jayjay owned any.

"How's the metanovel, Thuy?" asked Darlene, her long, jeans-clad legs sticking out over the sidewalk, her booted feet crossed like a cowboy's. "Still wrasslin' it?" Darlene made her living not so much by selling books as by brokering access to metanovels. Many metanovelists stored their works in secure form within the orphids on their own bodies, so as to be able to charge for access.

"Oh yeah," said Thuy. "It's called *Wheenk*. It's gonna be about what's happened to me this year. 'Waking Up' is the first chapter. I was thinking, though, what if I start using every single thing I find." She gestured at the shelves in Darlene's shop. "Like maybe collage in all your books to capture the full ambience. Every word, every page, all of it part of *Wheenk,* all visible in one synoptic glance."

"Synoptic," said Darlene, liking the word. "Yes, my shelves hold the synoptic gospels of our literary heritage; you read them side by side to see the face of the Holy Hive Mind in her presingular state. But you've got to be kidding about including all that data. Just do a link. If you put too much into a metanovel, it's as dull as a nearly empty file. Everything and Nothing are the same, you feel me? Aim your frame." Peering from beneath her dark bangs, Darlene held up her hands, flirtatiously regarding Jayjay through the rectangle of her thumbs and fingers. "What's with the Stank ad following you mangy kiqs?"

"We're extras on the *Founders* show," said Jayjay, miming himself soaping an underarm. "I Stank purty."

"How was Gerry Gurkin last night?" Thuy asked Darlene. Gurkin was a fellow metanovelist who was promoting his new work, *Banality,* by giving presentations at venues like Metotem Metabooks. For an evening's performance, a metanovelist would typically hand out short-term access permissions and give the audience a guided tour of the metanovel's world, the hope being that people would pay for longer-term access.

"Spotty," said Darlene. "All these hysterically funny Dick Too Dibbs ads kept popping up. Poor Gerry. Not that his gig would have been much better without the interruptions. *Banality* is an exabyte of data, yes, but it's just images of San Francisco at noon on the day after Orphid Night, with Gerry's voiceovers. No story, and no characters besides our host, the virtual Gerry Gurken. *Banality* is about a lonely kiqqie who pokes around in alleys and has these sad, wry little insights. A metanovel can be so much more."

"Oh, give the guy some credit," said Thuy, who was good friends with Gerry. "Some of his juxtaposes are transcendent. But, yeah, I'm aiming for my *Wheenk* to have a suspenseful action trajectory. If I can swing it, I'd like to have several interlocking plots, the whole thing like clockwork or a program or a complex knot."

"But it has to be authentic," said Darlene.

"We're alchemists," said Thuy. "Transmuting our lives into myth and fable."

Metanovelists' bull sessions could go on for hours. Jayjay privately wondered how much work Thuy had actually done. She kept all her notes and drafts under secure protection and had never shared any of her metanovel with him, other than that one metastory.

"What's that?" interrupted Kittie, peering down the block. A group of people were gathered around an inert, stick-thin figure who'd just been pulled out of an alley.

"It's Grandmaster Green Flash!" exclaimed Sonic, as they ran to see.

Hip, sparkling Grandmaster Green Flash had been the reigning San Francisco Doodly Bug champion at one time, a kiqqie whom Jayjay and Sonic looked up to. The Grandmaster had gotten heavily into the Big Pig, hitting the sacred sow for days at a time. Jayjay had gone on a few runs with Flash, but he hadn't been able to muster that same stare-into-the-sun intensity that the Grandmaster had. For Grandmaster Green Flash, any activity other than total ecstasy was a meaningless uptight social game.

And now Grandmaster Green Flash was dead on the sidewalk, his skin splotched with diamond-glitter paisley run amok. He'd let himself get too far out of the loop; he'd stopped eating and drinking, and then he'd even let go of breathing. His face was frozen in a triumphant, terrifying grin.

"I really am going to get clean," murmured Thuy to herself. "I'm ready for the turning point."

A cop pulled up in an electric car, alerted by the onlookers.

"This guy was the best," said Sonic, kneeling beside Grandmaster Green Flash, squinting against the mephitic stench.

The Grandmaster's skin glistened like an oil slick, the sunlight shattering off it in rainbow shades. Peering into the Net, Jayjay saw way too many orphids on the guy. Normal surfaces had one or two orphids per square millimeter, but the Grandmaster's skin looked to be carrying a density a billion times that high. That's why he looked like a diffraction grating. He was covered with rows of quantum-computing molecules. Diseased orphids.

"Stay back," warned Jayjay.

The iridescent colors on the Grandmaster's skin were forming double scrolls like beans or curled-up fetuses, the rotating spirals nestling within each other.

"Nanomachines all over him," exclaimed Kittie. "Like nants! Run!" She took off further down the block, stopping at the end to stare back at them.

"Come *on*," said Thuy, tugging at Jayjay. She rubbed her hands together as if shedding invisible nanomachines.

"It's okay," said Jayjay. A dense, twinkling haze had gathered around the Grandmaster's corpse. "The orphidnet has an immune system. That shiny fog is a trillion healthy orphids attacking the sick ones on his skin. Orphids are designed to attack runaway nanomachines, remember? One of the main reasons Ond Lutter released the orphids was because he wanted to block another wave of nants."

Thuy took off anyway.

Jayjay and Sonic stayed and watched the rainbow sheen fade from the Grandmaster's body as the massed cloud of orphids consumed the rogue nanomachines. "Poor Flash," said Sonic.

A warm breeze struck their faces; in the orphidnet a thirty-foot-high figure was standing over them. A Hibraner! He was a youngish-looking guy, dressed in red jeans and a yellow shirt with red cubes printed on it. His long hair was gathered into a topknot. Moving incredibly slowly, the glowing humanoid form reached down and cupped his flickering hands about the corpse, as if taking the measure of the situation. By degrees he turned his head to stare down the block after Thuy. And then, in a single twinkling jump, he hopped a hundred feet to stand by Thuy, bending down as if to talk with her.

"An angel!" screamed a fat woman on the sidewalk. "An angel come to carry the dead man's soul away!"

"Damn," said one of the cops, a mustached guy not much older than Jayjay. "That's the third time this week."

"Third time for which part?" asked Jayjay. "Cancerous nano-machines and a Hibraner showing up?"

"Like that, yeah."

"What does it mean?" asked Sonic.

"You're the kiqqies," said the cop. "You tell me. I'm just a mule who goes to work instead of lying around stoned all day."

"We're getting into recovery," said Jayjay.

"Sure you are." The cop tossed a body bag onto Grandmaster Green Flash. Moving on its own, the black piezoplastic enveloped the corpse.

"This could be you," said Dick Too Dibbs, appearing in an ad above the body bag. "If you vote for Bernard Lampton. Dick Too Dibbs is the man to crack down on nanomachines. I know the bad guys; I can game their heads. It takes an honest insider to halt the attacks. Not a fake do-gooder who takes bribes. Dick Too Dibbs in November."

Jayjay and Sonic headed down the sidewalk to catch up with Kittie and Thuy. The Hibraner was gone now. "That's the third time I've seen that particular angel," said Thuy, looking shaky. "You've heard me talk about him: Azaroth. Remember, I met him a couple of days after Orphid Night and he wanted to know if I'd seen the details of how Ond and Chu jumped to the Hibrane? And this summer he told me to cut back on the Big Pig. And just now he told me that if the Natural Mind guys offer me a job, I should say no and start a fight. He says if my life gets weird enough, I'll remember Chu's Knot."

"Maybe you're going crazy," said Sonic, needling her. "Maybe he didn't say anything to you at all."

"I am *so* ready to visit Natural Mind," said Thuy.

The Armory was a century-old brick building with every

sixteenth brick turned sideways, making a grid of studs upon the dark-red walls. An anachronistic dish antenna projected from the gently vaulted roof. In the visible world, the looming Armory filled the better part of a city block; within the orphidnet it was a square, featureless hole. The Armory's floor, ceiling, windows, and inner walls were quantum-mirrored to block the quantum entanglement signals used by the orphids. In other words, from the outside you couldn't see in. Jayjay imagined Andrew Topping as a loathsome fat grub worm in there, a greedy parasite befouling the orphidnet. Would he grow violent when the Posse confronted him?

As if Jayjay weren't anxious enough, one of his scenario-searching beezies now sprung a paranoid theory on him: Some unknown "Faction X" was deliberately luring the Posse into the Armory. The elegantly glyphed argument came down to this:

- Faction X contaminated Nektar with beetle malware.
- Faction X directed the Posse to a beetle-infested SUV.
- Faction X expected that someone in the Posse would design an antidote.
- Faction X expected that once the Posse invented a beetle antidote, the beezies would ask the Posse to heal Nektar.
- Faction X knew Nektar would urge the Posse to confront the Natural Minders in their lair.
- Faction X was maneuvering the Posse into the Armory.

And the beezies had an exponential number of possible theories about the identity and motivations of Faction X. Given that everyone was using beezies, overelaborate action scenarios were quite common now. Beezies were bringing human social intrigue to new heights.

All but paralyzed by this input, Jayjay used private messaging to share the Faction X scenario with the others, the four of them standing on the sidewalk outside the Armory's big green door.

"Should we go in anyway?" Jayjay messaged the others.

"I will," answered Thuy. "I need this experience for my metanovel. And they might help me kick the Pig. I'm really serious after seeing Grandmaster Green Flash."

"I want to get in there to cut the freakin' spam levels," messaged Sonic. "What we came for. Don't wimp out now."

"I want to see the quantum-mirrors," put in Kittie. "It'll be weird. A new trip. Something to paint."

These were all good reasons. "Okay," said Jayjay.

The big front door swung open at his touch, revealing a small hall or antechamber. A shiny finish coated the floor, ceiling and walls of the antechamber, also the back of the door. Jayjay saw himself dimly mirrored on every side. The colors in the reflections were odd, sour pastels.

"Watch it!" exclaimed Kittie, heavily catching her balance as she stepped inside. "It's like oil, or ice."

"Quantum-mirror varnish," said Sonic. "The whole inside of the ExaExa plant is covered with it too. It costs a fortune."

"Polyurethane doped with carbon nanotubes knotted and palladium-doped to make square-root-of-NOT gates," said Jayjay, showing off his physics chops. "The gates slice right through the orphid entanglement threads."

"We're losing the orphidnet right now," said Thuy as the outer door swung closed behind them. They pushed through an inner door and entered the Armory proper. The great open space was fully quantum-mirrored. Floors, walls, windows, ceilings, and doors, all were glazed with square-root-of-NOT varnish. The acid-tinged reflections gave the Armory the misleading air of a psychedelic fun house, although in fact it was an oasis of calm. Relaxed, smiling people were hanging out talking with each other.

But Jayjay wasn't paying much attention to them yet. He was busy freaking out. For the first time in over a year, he had no all-seeing orphidnet view. The outer world was gone. And his body's beezies had reacted to the Armory by dropping off-line; they were accustomed to distributing their computations far across the worldwide orphidnet. Jayjay's unaided natural mind felt stupid, befogged. He had so much less input than before, so much less computational strength.

Sonic stared down at his twitching fingers, as if unable to assimilate his loss.

"Ugh!" exclaimed Thuy, half turning back. "I feel like a piece of mud pottery. A raw-wood birdhouse. A bland bologna in a deli case."

"Keep it together," said Kittie, taking Thuy's hand. "We can use this in our work, honey. Grist for the mill. Remember, non-kiqqies *like* to feel this way."

"Hell they do," said Thuy. "Even Dot and Red were plugged in."

"Welcome to Natural Mind," said a dark-skinned woman sitting at a reception desk on the other side of the inner door. She looked compact and powerful. "I'm Millie Stubbs. Do you want to change? Not sure? It's enough to *want to want to* change, if that makes sense to you."

The big open room echoed with the low hubbub of voices, a comfortable, old-timey, human sound. People were sitting in groups on yoga mats and beanbag chairs. In a far corner of the hundred-foot-high room, an openwork metal staircase rose to an atticlike second floor squeezed against the roof.

"Stay with it, Thuy," said Jayjay. "We can do this." Slowly, laboriously, some of his beezie agents were coming back to life, limping along at a fraction of their usual clock-rate.

"Relax and feel," counseled Millie Stubbs. "You'll get used to it. You can meet our chief in a minute. And our clients and our graduates. They'll tell you how it is to be sober."

"Sober?" protested Sonic, gazing down at the lifeless, limp shoon he'd drawn from his pocket, which was an especially creepy sight as the shoon's face still resembled Jayjay's. "How about *dead*? Using the orphidnet isn't the same as being drunk or stoned."

"It is for some of us," said Millie, sizing up Sonic's jerky motions. "Not all that many people walk into Natural Mind by accident. Maybe this is where you need to be. A sober living environment. We've got a few bunks open."

"People live here?" asked Sonic, incredulous. "What do they do?"

"Participate in meetings—and work," said Millie. "Our clients earn their keep."

"Tiny me," said Thuy, running her hands over her face. "I feel like I'm waking up from a dream. But I loved the dream. It's only the Big Pig I want to quit, Millie. Not the whole freakin' orphidnet. All my work's in the orphidnet."

"The idea is to cut way down before ramping back up," said Millie. "Honor your natural mind. It's not slow, it's not dull, it's just subtle. Notice your details, remember to feel. Most of our graduates come back for a meeting once or twice a week. It's an island of serenity here. Check it out." She pulled out a paperback as if to start reading.

"That's all?" said Kittie. "No questionnaires?"

"Like I said, Mr. Topping will interview you in a minute," said Millie Stubbs.

"Aha," said Jayjay.

"You pigheads like that word, don't you?" said Millie, baring her strong teeth in a grin.

"Of course you know who we are, right?" said Thuy.

"I see that Mr. Topping is nearly ready for you." Millie pointed across the room to where a yellow light was blinking beside the open metal stairwell.

They started up the stairs, Kittie and Thuy in the lead. Seen in the murky pastels of the quantum-mirrored walls, the four of them looked like ascending divers.

Jayjay noticed that Sonic was flexing his powerful hands. Was he planning to attack Topping? Jayjay wanted to send Sonic a quantum-encrypted instant message warning him to stay cool, but here inside the Armory, the orphidnet-based quantum-encryption routine didn't seem to be available. So Jayjay settled for messaging Sonic an unencrypted emoticon, a peace sign carved from ice.

"Yeah, yeah," muttered Sonic. "Be chill, but don't forget to watch your ass."

The upper floor held a large, low-ceilinged office: fluorescent lights, rows of old-school computers, the hum of ventilation. Hundreds of street-worn Natural Mind clients were sitting before monitors, wearing headphones and navigating with hand gestures. The machines were linked to a hub with a cable going through the ceiling beside a ladder and a trapdoor—all leading to the antenna on the Armory roof.

"How retro," said Kittie.

In this confined well-lit space, the quantum-mirror glazes were bright and clear. With the floor and ceiling reflecting each other, it felt as if they were suspended in an endless 3-D grid of worker drones.

"I'm thinking of Franz Kafka at his desk at the Workmen's

Accident Insurance Company of Prague," said Thuy. "Is this, like, aversion therapy to make kiqqies hate the orphidnet?"

"We plantin' mines," said a rabbity-looking thin man sitting at a computer near the stairs. "I calls 'em mines, anyhow. They's links what blow up into ads. Catchin' folks by surprise, you understand. The trick is to stick your ad-mine onto a spot where the filter dogs ain't pissed yet. Who you gals? Maybe we done met on the orphidnet, but . . ."

"I never remember what I was doing online when I come down either," said Kittie. "I'm Kittie, and this is my girlfriend, Thuy, and we've got our sidekicks Jayjay and Sonic here too."

"Prescription John's the name," said the guy in his country accent. He reached out to shake their hands. "My problem is I'm lovin' that Hawg even more than hillbilly heroin. Been here umpty-five times."

"You're into the Big Pig too?" said Jayjay.

"Plentifully," said Prescription John. He nodded toward the wasted-away Asian woman next to him. "This here's Mary Moo. Some of our running buddies carried me and Mary here last week. We was malnourished."

"This is my fourth time through the Natural Mind spindry," said the skeletal Mary Moo. She had a soft, cultured, California voice. "We're going to keep it together this time, aren't we, John? When we hit the street?"

"I'm in no rush to step out," said Prescription John. "We sleeping between sheets, eating off a table, and ad-mining the orphidnet for the Man. Copacetic. It's like living with my mamma and playing video games."

All around, the spectral Natural Mind clients were peering and gesturing at their screens. A windowless office with a closed door ran along the room's rear. Jayjay couldn't peep into the office, what with its walls being covered with quantum-mirror varnish. A light over the office door glowed yellow, same as at the foot of the stairs.

"The Man?" said Kittie, inclining her head in that direction.

"Andrew Topping," confirmed Mary Moo. "Just agree with him no matter what he says. He's rather overbearing and irritable. But all the other staffers here are quite pleasant."

Sonic was peering over Prescription John's shoulder, assessing the interface. The screen was displaying a surreal landscape modeling the San Francisco orphidnet activity. As John moved his hands, the view zoomed in and out of the user records, displaying clickstreams as colored paths through meme sculpture gardens and groves of personality trees. Now and then John would flick a fingertip to plant an ad link.

"Are all your ads for Dick Too Dibbs?" asked Thuy.

"Mostly," said Mary Moo. "Some are for businesses as well. ExaExa, I think, and Stank. I don't worry about the content. You want to stay here, you do this work."

"You can't trust Dick Too Dibbs," protested Jayjay, getting down to the purpose of their visit. "I mean, come on, the first President Dibbs got the death penalty for promoting the nants. Doesn't anyone remember anything in this country? Don't be helping the Homesteady Party. They're out to screw the little people. People like us."

"Feller says the real point of our ads is to slow down the orphidnet," said John, looking up from his screen. "Make folks unhappy with the status quo."

"Out with the old, in with the new," said Mary.

"You know it, Mary," said John. "Mary used to be a social worker. She drug-counseled me a couple of times before the orphids come."

"Drugs never appealed me," said Mary. "Too low, too dangerous. But I couldn't resist the Big Pig."

"Plant an ad here," said Sonic to Prescription John, pointing out a spot on the screen.

"You'd do fine in here, kiq," said John, placing an ad-mine.

The light on the rear wall turned green and the door swung open. A tall, pasty-faced man in a black business suit gestured to the Posse, his mouth bent into a fake smile. Using the limited local orphidnet view, Jayjay spotted a pistol in a shoulder holster under the man's coat.

"Here we go," said Kittie, stepping forward to lead the way.

"Welcome, Big Pig Posse," said the tall, doughy man, ushering them in and closing the office door. The quantum-mirrored room had two tapestry-style view screens and a red oriental rug. A humongous wood desk faced the door. To the left were a heavy wood-and-leather couch and, closer to the center of the room, a walking-chair. To the right was a grilled wall emitting a low hum. Ventilation? The view screen on the left wall showed a view of the ad-mining workroom right outside.

"I'm Andrew Topping." The man gave Kittie's hand an overly vigorous, overly long shake. "You would be Kittie Calhoun?" He turned his watchful gaze upon the others. "Sonic Sanchez, Jayjay Jimenez, Thuy Nguyen. Thanks for coming in." One by one he squeezed and pumped their hands.

"Ugh," said Thuy.

"Ugh?" echoed Andrew Topping, looking annoyed.

"Your hand," said Thuy. "Damp, invasive, an empty simulacrum of masculinity." Jayjay laughed. Good old Thuy.

Maintaining his smile, Topping asked them to sit down. Sonic, Jayjay and Kittie ended up in a row on the couch on the left. Thuy sat in the big walking-chair, the chair Craigor had delivered here. It had knees and hips both; it squatted down to a comfortable level for Thuy. Topping stood with his arms crossed, leaning back against his massive paneled desk, staring at them.

The limp plastic view screen on the wall behind the desk displayed two views of ocean waves crashing against a rocky point to send up periodic spumes of spray. The left view looked like a realtime natural image; the right view was an ultracomputed simulation, never quite managing to match the view on the left, with pesky triangles and squares popping up in the ocean foam.

The main thing about the room was the metal grill covering the right wall. Jayjay used the room's orphidnet resources to peer deeper. Finer and finer grills lay behind this grill, perhaps as many as a hundred layers of them. Unfamiliar machinery buzzed in the darkness beyond the grills.

"So, all right, I know that Nektar Lundquist told you to come here and foul up our operation," Topping was saying. "But maybe you don't know that I set you up to come here. The President Bernardo image who sent you to the SUV this morning? He was a spoof I put out there."

"So I was right," said Jayjay to the Posse. "And Topping is Faction X."

"Excuse me?" said Topping.

"One of my beezies hypothesized your scenario," said Jayjay. "But we came in here anyway. We were curious about you. And a little interested in quitting the Big Pig. And, yes, we're here to tell you to stop overloading the orphidnet with malware and spam. For God's sake, Topping, why are you helping Dick Too Dibbs? Don't you have any rational self-interest? With Too Dibbs in power, the world might end!"

"You'd probably like Dick Too Dibbs more than you realize," said Topping. "He doesn't support the nants at all. He's by no means an ideal representative for my employer's interests. But at least my employer has the man's ear. He's hoping to make his case so as to guide events in an optimal way. But it's by no means a sure thing."

"You're talking about Jeff Luty, right?" said Jayjay.

"I'd let Mr. Luty do his own talking," said Topping. "Should the occasion arise. Should he in fact be alive. Natural Mind's primary funding is from Jeff Luty's former company ExaExa, yes. The quantum-mirror varnish that protects our unfortunate clients—unobtainable from any other source. Public knowledge." He held out his hands for silence. "Let's get to the point. In the course of monitoring our motley advertising force, I get a good overview of the orphidnet. And you four have come to my attention. Two in particular have skill sets that could be useful to my employer. This young man; this young woman." He leveled his index finger at Sonic and then at Thuy. "I'm prepared to hire all four of you—just to have them."

For a moment Jayjay felt jealous. What about all his new physics ideas? Stop it, Jayjay. Get over yourself. An ugly, heavy scene is coming up. Watch Topping. Get your beezies to figure out the scenario. And don't forget that grill in the wall.

Sonic shook his head. "I'm not gonna work here planting those dumb-ass ads for—"

"Your skills are about Doodly Bug," Topping interrupted. "It's more than a game. It's a laboratory for exploring brane theory, multiversal quantum mechanics, and the art of Calabi-Yau manifold construction. Your work stands out, Sonic. And Thuy's metanovel—"

Suddenly Jayjay got the big picture. "Luty wants to get to the Hibrane!" he cried out. "He wants to bring back Ond Lutter to help him! He wants to neutralize the orphids and feed Earth to some new nants!"

Topping regarded Jayjay levelly. "I couldn't discuss that even if I wanted to. My wikiware has me under nondisclosure filtering. You'll be the same, once you accept your ExaExa consulting contract. That's another good reason for me to sign all four of you."

"What contract?" asked Kittie. "I mean, how much are you offering us? And what would we have to do?"

"Forget it," repeated Sonic. "We don't need ExaExa and their bullshit mind control. We've got Nektar's garage to live in, and we've got those *Founders* royalties happening for us too."

"Hear me out," said Topping testily. He outlined the terms of the offer. So as to block any possible disclosure of sensitive information, consultants had to install ExaExa's custom Share-Crop wikiware onto their scalp-orphids with full personal access permissions. The consultants' wikiware would feed them business-related data, and of course the wikiware would monitor the consultants' business-related thoughts and filter their instant messages. No physical office presence was required, and the pay would be just this side of bodacious.

"Bullshit," said Sonic. "Bullshit bullshit bullshit."

Jayjay looked at the two women.

"Would there be any work at all for Jayjay and me?" said Kittie, forcing a wry smile. Like Jayjay, she was disappointed not to be a main attraction. "Maybe we should take the contracts and use our money to open a Losers Club, Jayjay. But I don't know that Thuy would—"

"It's out of the question," said Thuy. "Azaroth warned me about you, Topping. You actually think I'd let you put spying wikiware bosses in my head? My creativity would go out the window. I'd have nothing to live for."

"So no, then," said Kittie, playing the leader. "Offer unanimously refused."

"Aha," said Topping, his eyes lighting up. "Aha, aha, aha." He feinted at Sonic at the far left end of the couch, then whirled to bodily scoop up Thuy and carry her to the grilled wall. The hum behind the grating rose in pitch. A stiff breeze began drawing across the room.

Thuy wailed, trying to twist away. The others ran to her aid. Kittie was the first one to reach Topping; fruitlessly she tore at his arms. He seemed on the point of hurling Thuy against the grill—why?

Thuy moaned in fear; Jayjay saw red. He dove for Topping's waist, knocking the big man to the floor. As he fell, Topping managed to shove Thuy forward. Her head disintegrated into tiny cubes which were broken into yet-smaller blocks by the inner grills, her particles whirling into the dark hole's maw. Oddly enough, there was no blood. Thuy's head was gone. Topping tried to inch Thuy further into the grill, but now he had Sonic straddling his back.

Kittie had gone hysterical; she filled the room with harsh, rhythmic screams. Not knowing what else to do, Jayjay tugged at Thuy's legs. He half expected to see a hideous severed neck atop her shoulders but, lo, as Thuy's body pulled free, her head grew back, reassembling itself layer by layer, her component particles swarming out of the grill.

"Gun!" screamed Sonic. "His gun!" Topping had risen to a crouch, even though Sonic still clung to his back. Topping was pulling his pistol from his shoulder holster. Jayjay flung himself at the man, heavily knocking Topping and Sonic against the grill.

The equipment roared; the two men disintegrated completely—and were vacuumed through the compound gratings like dust. All gone. Peering through the local orphidnet, Jayjay saw only that same machinery back there—no ground-up bodies, no drops of blood. Sonic and Topping had been atomized by bizarre physical forces and transported to who knew where. As for Thuy: her head had gone there and come back.

"Are you okay?" Jayjay asked her.

Thuy winced and made a complex gesture with her hand.

"Jeff Luty was leaning over me. Talking really fast about the Hibrane. I—" She broke off, unable to say more.

"Let's bail," said Kittie.

Some kind of signal escaped the office when they opened the door back to the computer room. Alarms sounded, rapid footsteps rang on the metal stairs from the ground floor. But the spindly clients behind the monitors seemed sympathetic to the three Posse members.

"Up thar!" urged Prescription John, pointing to the ladder and trapdoor where the computer cable went. "It ain't locked."

Kittie led the way, and Jayjay took the rear, with Thuy in the middle. They made it to the roof.

It felt good to breathe the open air, and to connect with the global orphidnet. Hoping against hope, Jayjay set his beezies to searching the area for Sonic—to no avail.

"Jayjay killed Sonic," said Kittie. "And nearly you too, Thuy. He's a clumsy oaf."

"Sonic's not dead," said Thuy. "That grill—it leads to an ExaExa lab. Luty is—" She put her hands on the sides of her head. "Oh oh oh. Can't talk now."

"We'll free Sonic," said Jayjay. "Wherever he is."

A police siren was approaching. The three hurried to the other side of the Armory roof and began working their way down the outside fire escape.

"We're going back to Nektar's," said Kittie. "But I don't know about you, Jayjay. You might flurb that scene, too."

"I'm going to Jil's boat," said Jayjay quickly. "You can come with me, if you want, Thuy."

"And watch you slobber over a middle-aged mom?" said Thuy, her eyes searching his face. "No thanks."

"We'll fix up my SUV, Thuy," said Kittie. "It'll be nice. I'll paint and you'll work on your metanovel."

"And you'll be crawling into Nektar's bed every chance you get," said Thuy miserably. "Nobody really loves me."

"*I* love you," said Jayjay, meaning it. "You know I do. If you come with me, we don't have to go to Jil's. We can go anywhere you want."

"I'm so tired," said Thuy, her voice shaking. "My head hurts. I just want to go to that nice clean room over Nektar's garage and lie down."

"Leave us the hell alone now, Jayjay," said Kittie. "The Big Pig Posse is over."

Down on the street, Kittie and Thuy headed back toward Nektar's, and Jayjay caught a tram toward the South San Francisco dock. He felt lonely and tired. At least he had a seat to himself. He leaned against the streetcar window, letting his mind drift out into the orphidnet. Up to the Big Pig. A hit would be good right now.

The Pig welcomed Jayjay with a video clip of a crashing wave, just like the one he'd seen in Topping's office.

"*Wheenk*," murmured Jayjay to himself, missing Thuy. "*Wheenk, wheenk, wheenk.*"

PART III

CHAPTER 8

Thuy's Metanovel

Westinghouse yam in alleyway," said the improbable virtual spambot, formed like a waist-high two-legged sweet potato with multitudinous ruby eyes, wreathed in crackling blue sparks, peering at Thuy from a rain-wet alley off Valencia Street, the same spot where Grandmaster Green Flash had died. "Vote for Dick Too Dibbs," added the yam, once he'd caught Thuy's attention.

"Too Dibbs won the election two and a half months ago," said Thuy. She didn't bother to sic her filter dogs on the apparition. These days she enjoyed wandering the streets alone, open to the ether, playing the patterns, riding the flow. The heavier scenes went into her metanovel, which was growing at a rate of two or three minutes per day.

You could measure a metanovel's length in terms of how much access time a typical user took to finish the work, assuming they didn't set it aside. Thuy's target-length for *Wheenk* was eight hours, about the time it would take to read a medium-fat book.

"I like Dick," said the virtual yam, falling into step next to her, the misty rain drifting through him. "Does Dick like ye?"

"Give it a rest," said Thuy. "Too Dibbs gets inaugurated the day after tomorrow, you slushed pighead." The orphidnet was noisy with the thin cries and hoarse roars of marshmallow people already celebrating the advent of the new regime. To drown them out, Thu had her favorite Tawny Krush symphony playing, and she was enhancing the sound with violin squawks triggered by smooth gestures of her arms and legs, all but dancing down the street. She was protected from the rain by a hooded yellow slicker; under that she wore her good old yellow miniskirt, striped wool leggings, and piezoplastic Yu Shu sneakers, also a red T-shirt and red sweater she'd liberated from Nektar's bulging closets.

"That's you, Thuy, ain't it?" said the sparkling yam. "Prescription John here. I wanna channel that story you posted this afternoon. What was it called again? Mary Moo done showed me the link, but I ain't got the money for access. Mary says you wrote about us on the second floor at the Armory. Topping's mad."

"My metastory is called 'Losing My Head,'" said Thuy. "I'm about to perform the whole thing live and for free at Metotem, so tune in and turn on, you skeevy old stoner. Still ad-mining for Natural Mind, huh?"

"I cycled out too early, and had to re-up for spin-dry umpty-six. Mary never left. How you?"

"I'm off the Pig, yeah," said Thuy. "Thinking clearer; feeling more; building my metanovel. The new metastory is an excerpt from it. I'm in the zone, John; it feels like dreaming while being awake. And the world's helping me. This Hibraner Azaroth keeps showing up. You're part of the pudding, too. It's so perfect and synchronistic that you popped out of that particular alley. Everything's entangled. God's an artist."

"The yam's the man," said Prescription John, puffing up his tuberous orange icon. "Whoops, here comes Topping. Gotta go."

He sputtered, twinkled, and faded out—leaving Thuy with a

sudden suspicion that maybe that hadn't been the true flesh-and-blood Prescription John running the yam. Maybe she'd been talking to a virtual, artificially alive Prescription John from within her "Losing My Head" metastory. Hanging around Darlene's Metotem store the other day, she'd heard some of the other metanovelists talking about times when their characters started messaging them—they referred to this not uncommon feedback phenomenon as "blowback."

Gerry Gurkin, for instance, kept having visitations from the simulated Gerry Gurkin of his autobiographical *Banality,* the virtual Gerry clamoring that he wanted metanovelist Gerry to edit in a girlfriend character for him to fuck. Telling this story, portly Gerry darted hot intense looks at Thuy, as if he were planning to feed a model of *her* to virtual Gerry, which was perfectly fine with Thuy, and she said so.

Thuy was in a lonely-but-coned-off emotional state where she was ready to accept any admiration she was offered, as long as it was virtual and with no strings attached. Re: "coned off," she'd heard a woman actually saying that about herself the other day, as if she were a wreck lane or a crime site. That phrase went straight into the metanovel. The yam's "I like Dick; does Dick like ye?" seemed usable too. Oh, for sure that had been the real Prescription John. No beezie would ever talk that silly.

Light from the store windows made warm trapezoids on the shiny sidewalk, gilding the rain puddles, their surfaces wrinkled by the gusty wind. As always when she noticed gnarly natural patterns, Thuy thought of Jayjay. She missed his lean body, his voice, his smell, his physical presence. He was still living on the *Merz Boat.*

According to Kittie, who'd taken to watching every freaking second of *Founders,* Jayjay had had a little affair with Jil

Zonder in November, although Jil had broken it off pretty quickly for the sake of her kids. Kittie said Jil wouldn't have gotten into the affair at all if it hadn't been that, right after his affair with Nektar, Craigor had started humping that slutty Lureen Morales up the hill. And now it looked like poor, heart-broken Jil might be drifting back into sudocoke.

Back when Jil and Jayjay's affair had actually been going on, Kittie had kept wanting to tell Thuy about the couple's intimate doings: who put what where how often, like that. For sure Thuy didn't care to process that type of info. No more than she cared to peep at Kittie and Nektar making the two-backed beast. Or, for that matter, Craigor and Lureen. Grunt, grunt, moan, moan. Thuy had given up on sex, at least for now, although she and Kittie were still roommates and fairly good friends. Oh, Jayjay, where are you?

Thuy drew even with El Santo de Israel, an evangelical store-front church that had preaching and a crowd most evenings. It was next to an auto repair shop. The church name was in the serif-heavy Old English font that some Latinos liked, and the windows were decorated with poster paints: a man wrestling an angel, a six-pointed star with Hebrew letters around it, the Christian fish symbol with an eye in the middle, and numerous chapter-and-verse scripture references. Fresh red writing on the window read: *"Visita Del Rebelde Ángel Azaroth Hoy."* Rebel An-gel Azaroth Visiting Today.

Azaroth again. Thuy's ears began ringing as if she had a fever. The busy street scene became remote, "in quotes," a grimy sur-real diorama behind shatterproof glass. Was Thuy writing her metanovel, or was the metanovel writing *her*?

Until now, Thuy had held back from mentioning Azaroth in *Wheenk,* but it was time to write him in. She mentally replayed her memories of her very first meeting with him, going over the events slowly and precisely, blending them into the material she already had.

It had happened shortly after Orphid Night, when the ethereal Hibraners had become visible, thanks to the airborne orphids adhering to the aliens' insubstantial forms and bedecking them with meshes of graphical vertices. . . .

❦

As part of her then job at Golden Lucky, the Vietnamese restaurant-supply wholesaler, Thuy was researching the possibility of starting to deal in the meat of the locally caught Pharaoh cuttlefish being processed by AmphiVision, the San Francisco company that made display devices using organic rhodopsin from cuttlefish chromatophores. AmphiVision was discarding the cuttles' really quite tasty flesh, and Thuy's boss, Vinh Phat, sensed a business opportunity. There was a good demand for grilled cuttlefish in the local Asian communities. Vinh had set Thuy to tracking data on the cuttlefishers, giving her access to a dragonfly spy camera.

So as it happened, Thuy was watching Craigor, Jil, Ond, Nektar, and Chu on the *Merz Boat* the night that Ond released the orphids. She dipped into Chu's cuttlefish datastream; she accessed the blue spaghetti link; and she paid close attention when Chu wove his Celtic-style jump-code knot from a piece of string. The knot intrigued, even fascinated, Thuy. Looking through the dragonfly, she examined it quite closely during the penultimate instant after Chu tied together the string's two loose ends, right before he disappeared into the Hibrane.

Thuy was investigating all these things with a sense of doing a job for Golden Lucky, alone with the family cat Naoko in her frilly bedroom at her parents' house, working online after hours, not immediately understanding the transformative impact of what was going down. But then she looked out her window past her parents' neighbors' identical houses; she saw the orphid-outlined hills of San Francisco; and suddenly she got the picture. Game over. Everything was changed forever, and Thuy no longer needed to play the good girl. Not quite letting herself think about what she was doing, she packed a bag and headed for her high-school boyfriend, Jayjay. Thanks to the orphidnet, it was easy to find him. He was living with Sonic in a shell of a house in the Mission—some developer had gutted it for a retrofit and had then run out of funds.

Azaroth manifested himself to Thuy three days after Orphid Night. By then the Big Pig had emerged, and Thuy, Jayjay, and Sonic had learned about suckling on the pig, which meant that Thuy woke up woozy. She sat up in bed, looking around Jayjay's ugly, junked squat, and then, in the orphidnet, she saw a glowing eye the size of a melon peering in the window. It was a Hibraner, a thirty-foot-tall man of light. He wore flashy clothes: purple bell-bottoms and a green shirt with yellow stripes. He reached through the wall to caress Thuy; she felt his ethereal body as a warm air-current.

"It's glow to talk with you," Azaroth messaged, his voice coming through the orphidnet connection in Thuy's head. The voice sounded boyish, eager, perhaps a bit nerdy. He accompanied his speech with a rich stream of images. "I'm Azaroth from the Hibrane. And you're . . . ?"

"Thuy," she said aloud, causing Jayjay to stir in his sleep. Sonic wasn't around; he'd already gone out to look for food. Thuy switched to subvocal speech. "Should I be scared? What kind of name is Azaroth, anyway?"

"My grandparents were from Ludhiam in the Punjab. They worked in a bicycle factory. As he prepared to emigrate, my father,

Puneet, made a hobby of studying the world's religions. He named me after a Babylonian demon. Azaroth is a starky god. Good name for starky me." Azaroth pushed his head and shoulders into the room as well. He had dark, liquid eyes and a beaky nose. He wore his long hair in a topknot enclosed by a pale green stocking that matched his shirt.

One of Jayjay and Sonic's now-outmoded game consoles was running a rapid-fire demo loop. Azaroth peered at it, fascinated.

"Do you want something from me?" Thuy asked.

"Chu's Knot," Azaroth said. "You know, that vibby tangle of string the boy tied off before he jumped to our world? That's Chu's Knot. You saw it. I saw you seeing it. I was here stealing Craigor's cuttlefish. We like to eat them."

"Chu's Knot," echoed Thuy, not really surprised. She'd been thinking obsessively about the Knot lately, even in her dreams. It seemed reasonable that a Hibrane alien would want to know about the most fascinating thing she'd ever seen. She settled her pillow against the wall, ready for conversation. "Why exactly do you need it?"

"I want to help Chu come home."

"He's still in the Hibrane? Why not ask *him* about the Knot?"

"My Aunt Gladax caught Chu on Orphid Night and made him forget," said Azaroth. "Chu's father Ond got away. For a little while." Azaroth flashed Thuy a vision of Chu wrapped in a rubber net suspended by bungee cords in the middle of a very large room—it seemed to be a personal gym or exercise room in a hilltop mansion with a view of nighttime San Francisco and the twinkling Golden Gate Bridge. The vision was accompanied by a mind-numbing hum. "Bouncy Chu. Aunt Gladax is very paranoid about your nanomachines—even though we're sure that all the orphids on your boys were crushed by our smart air as soon as they arrived. You'd be better off if your air got smart too."

"How do you mean?"

"Lazy eight. It's how we do telepathy in the Hibrane. Better than orphids. Too hard to explain right now. Can you tell me the jump-code so I can pass it on to Chu and Ond? Maybe they can even make your air smart too."

"And that would be good?"

"Oh yes. Hylozoic."

"All I know is that Chu posted the blue spaghetti version of the jump-code right before he left," said Thuy, not quite sure she should help this strange-talking alien.

"That part I know," said Azaroth. "But all the Lobrane links to the spaghetti jump-code are dead now. I'm asking if you yourself know the short version by heart. Chu's Knot."

"I don't exactly remember the Knot," said Thuy.

"That humpty Gladax," said Azaroth, shaking his head. "Up in the Hibrane, she cut up Chu's Knot—I'm talking about his tangled piece of string, right—and then she addled the Knot-knowing away from him." Image of old Gladax focusing her narrow eyes upon a wildly bouncing Chu in that exercise room. She strikes an old-fashioned harp at one end of the room. The bouncing stops. Gladax leans over Chu, an energy ray poking from of her finger. Slowly, precisely, she reaches into Chu's head, crooning to keep the boy still.

"Ond was so worried; he went to Gladax's house," continued Azaroth. Image of sad-faced Ond Lutter kneeling tiny on the front porch of Gladax's huge, organic-looking mansion at dawn, the house's pillars like the trunks of trees. "Gladax promised that Chu would be okay, and she got Ond to teach her how to erase all the Lobrane records of Chu's jump-code too. So that's why your blue-spaghetti links don't work anymore. Meanwhile Gladax wants Chu to live with her like a houseboy or a pet. She thinks he's a lucky amulet against the nants. A nanteater. And Ond's staying on as Gladax's tutor, so he can be near Chu. But I'm working on a deal. I want Gladax to free those two to work with me. And I'd like to give them Chu's Knot so that someday they can come back and fix your world."

"Gladax wants to keep Chu because of what he did on Nant Day?" said Thuy, not following most of this. "She's that worried about nants?"

"Most Hibraners think machines are jitsy." Azaroth gestured at Sonic's tired old game display and at Jayjay's equally obsolete cell phone. "But I glow your tech, even if it *is* stupid." Image of a beggar kneeling to walk on rough-carved wooden stilts that are exactly the same length as his shins would be if he walked erect. "I'd like to be more than a cuttlefish poacher some day," continued Azaroth. "I'd like to program video games we can use with our telepathy. That's another reason why I want to get Ond and Chu free from Gladax. They'll be grateful and they'll help me write a game. I'd like to be able to offer them the Chu's Knot jump-code. Remember it for me, Thuy."

"Look, Azaroth, you jump branes all the time. Why can't you just tell Ond and Chu the jump-code that *you* use?"

"I don't know the code like a machine row of beads. I know it like I breathe. We've always been able to visit the Lobrane, but each jump is a little dangerous—these creatures called subbies live in between the branes and they try and catch you. I'm here so often because of the cuttlefish—cuttles are extinct on our world, you wave. We admire them as a religious symbol, but we overdid it and ate all of ours. Hibraners pay a lot for Lobrane cuttles. I'm agile. The subbies never catch me or any of the cuttlefish I send home."

"So why don't you send Ond and Chu back to the Lobrane

just like the cuttlefish you steal," suggested Thuy. She paused for a moment, then plowed ahead. "And maybe send me to the Hibrane so I can have a look, too."

"I can't just brute-force jump a Lobrane human from brane to brane. The cuttlefish die when I jump them over to the Hibrane, you wave? To make it safe, a person has to jump all glowy with their personal pulse."

"Why didn't *you* pay better attention to Chu's Knot when he made it?"

"I was too excited about having you gnomes finally see us."

"And why is it that you're invisible over here?"

"You ask too many questions, Thuy! The branes are out of phase with each other, like two voices singing in different keys. And when we Hibraners jump across, we only change our phases by a little bit, so we show up catawampus akimbo to you. You guys and your cuttles, you're a darker kind of matter, and when you jump, you rotate through the full phase shift to match. Chu and Ond showed up chewy as a cuttlefish. Come on now, Thuy, stop stalling. I bet you can remember the Knot. A smart woman like you."

Charmed by the chatty alien, Thuy tried once again to remember the precise details of Chu's Knot. Surely the delicate filigree was intact somewhere in her memory? But it kept slipping away.

"I can't quite get it," she said after a bit.

"Maybe you should write a story about seeing the Knot," suggested the Hibraner. "Art's the way to know what you don't."

"I've been talking with people about a new *style* of writing," said Thuy. She was an inveterate participant in online writers' groups. "Metastories and metanovels—we're all thinking about a new art form using the orphidnet."

"Start with Orphid Night," urged Azaroth. "Time zero. And unroll from there. Tell all your personal experiences, spill your starky guts. I'll hang in the background, setting you up for the big spike."

"Is Gladax evil?" asked Thuy as an afterthought.

"No. It's just that she's old and she worries too much," said Azaroth. "She's the mayor of Hibrane San Francisco, did you know that? I know her so well because she's my aunt; she's my father's dead brother Charminder's widow. She's part Dutch and mostly Chinese. Bossy and picky, but she's always nice to me. I bet she roots out my memory record of this conversation." He laughed recklessly. "Good old Gladax!"

And then Sonic came back to the apartment and Azaroth left.

Thuy popped out of her flashback. She'd saved it all into the *Wheenk* database; it felt like a good, solid take. Thinking less formally now, and no longer for the record, she recalled the two other times she'd seen Azaroth.

The second time had been back in September. Azaroth had slid ever so slowly down a slanting sunbeam from a sunset-reddened cloud, behold! This time he'd encouraged Thuy to start sleeping with Kittie instead of with Jayjay, which didn't turn out to be that great of an idea. But at the time, Azaroth had said the switch would give Thuy more to write about, also that breaking up with Jayjay would help Thuy beat her Big Pig addiction, which had been soaking up increasing amounts of her energy and time. Oh, and Azaroth had encouraged Thuy to start linking her scattered metastories together into a single cohesive metanovel.

By then Azaroth had also talked Gladax into letting Chu and Ond range freely around the Hibrane equivalent of San Francisco. They did no harm, and the Hibraners enjoyed seeing the tiny gnomes around town. And, just as Azaroth had hoped, Chu was helping him develop a telepathy-based game. Azaroth used the word "teep" to mean "do telepathy." Apparently he and Chu somehow used a stream of water for their game's server-computer. And Ond was advising Gladax on efficient ways to access the vast pool of Hibrane teep info. Hibrane telepathy was based on some weird quirk of the brane's physics, and had no Weblike orderliness built in.

Ond and Chu were very interested in relearning the Chu's Knot jump-code for getting home. Although it still wasn't quite safe for them to return to the Lobrane, they wanted to know that they could come home when the time came.

Azaroth assured Thuy that even if she hadn't yet written enough to remember the details of Chu's Knot, she was surely getting closer. According to Azaroth, the windings and crossings of the Knot were implicit in everything Thuy wrote, so that even when she thought she was writing about, say, what her mother, Minh, used to pack for her school lunches, she was really, at some deep level, writing about the Knot. Maybe so. The Knot still hadn't faded from Thuy's mind; often as she was drifting off to sleep, she saw it hovering before her, every loop and twist intact—but when she tried to focus on the details, they always slipped away.

The third time Thuy had seen Azaroth had been last month, right after he'd been leaning over Grandmaster Green Flash, assessing the state of the nanomachines on the dead man's skin. At that time, Azaroth had hopped over to Thuy and messaged her the news that Luty was working on turning Lobrane Earth into nants again. He said the Hibraners would do what they could to help stop Luty, but the real work was up to the Lo-braners themselves. He said it would be a shame if the nants won, because then his people would never feel safe coming to visit again. He told Thuy to argue about any offers they made her in the Armory, because if she got into a fight, it would give her something heavy to write about for her metanovel, and if she found the Chu's Knot code, she could bring Ond and Chu back, and they might be the ones to turn the tide.

The weird events on the second floor of the Armory had indeed sparked a great *Wheenk* chapter, "Losing My Head"—which Thuy was in fact due to perform at Metotem in about an hour.

More and more, Thuy believed that her labyrinthine path through this postsingular world really was at some deep level tracing out the very design she'd seen Chu weave. So the reference to Azaroth on the storefront church's window made perfect sense. With ample time to spare before her reading, Thuy cut inside to check if the *rebelida ángel* was gonna make a *visita* and pass her another clue.

Right away a silent, observant little girl toddled out from among the beat old metal chairs to stare at Thuy. The congregation consisted of working-class Latinos and Filipinos, many with families in tow. A glance into the orphidnet showed that only a few of them were kiqqies; Thuy could always pick out kiqqies by noticing who was using a lot of beezie agents—to Thuy, people's beezies looked like colored mushrooms on their backs and heads.

"Have some popcorn," said a comfortably ample woman, tugging the little girl out of Thuy's way. The woman wore purple lipstick and a shiny yellow silk dress. She handed Thuy a white paper bag she'd just filled from a movie-theater-style popper in a glass case. Fresh puffed kernels were blooming and cascading out of the metal popper's pan, fragrant with hot co-coconut oil, gritty with salt. A welcome treat. "Take a seat and en-joy the good words of Pastor Luis," said the woman. "We're glad to have you visit. I'm Kayla."

"Thanks," said Thuy, stepping further in and taking a seat in a lightly padded chair in the back row. Low-key gospel music was percolating from a three-person band: a languid shiny-haired dude with an electric guitar, a turbaned woman at a key-board, and a classic mariachi guy strumming a bass.

Pastor Luis stood upon an inexpensive oriental carpet on the dais, a short man with thinning black-dyed hair, rough skin, and horizontal wrinkles across his forehead. He wore a shiny gray suit with the pants pulled up high and held in place by a lizard-patterned belt with a too-long tip flopping down.

Pastor Luis was talking and gesturing without letup, his voice a rhythmic flow. At first Thuy couldn't make out what language he was speaking, but that didn't matter, for despite the man's unprepossessing appearance, there was an infectious en-ergy to his motions, a hypnotic pulse to his expostulations. He was a kiqqie, with beezies bedecking him like shelf mushrooms on a forest-floor log.

Thuy relaxed and enjoyed for awhile, eating her popcorn, but then Luis paused and stared right at her, drawing info about her from the orphidnet.

"Welcome, sister Thuy," he called in a sweet-accented tenor, speaking English now. "Azaroth be with you. Chant with us, ay, I'm calling out the rebel angel Azaroth, ay, bossed around by the rulers of the Hibrane, guiding us to revolt against Babylon, a sword against the Pharisees, ay, our counselor against the gob-bling all-consuming nants. Show us your face, Azaroth, caress us with your love, ay, warm our hearts in this low, wounded world. Lead us in the invocation, Sister Kayla!"

Broadly smiling, Kayla curvetted up the aisle, dress flashing. She took the microphone from Luis and began a chant:

Innacun cunna gampamade nattoli.
Itannu si canayun udde ammem maita-ita.

Over and over, Kayla and the congregation repeated those same two lines, drawing out the sounds. Searching in the orphidnet, Thuy found the phrases to be couched not in Spanish, but in the Gaddang language of the Philippine island of Luzon, not all that far from good old Vietnam. Thuy's grandparents had landed on Luzon when they'd fled Vietnam in a leaky boat.

One of Thuy's beezies told her the lines were two folk riddles, meaning something like:

When he turns away he's coming to you.
You stare at him but you never see him.

And, continued the beezie, the answer to the first riddle was "a cuttlefish," and the answer to the second was "the sun," although it could just as well have been "a Hibraner" or, for that matter, "Chu's Knot." Everything was so very deeply intertwingled.

The chanted words overlapped, filling the air with vibrations like sacred Aums, calling another order of being into the room. Warm air eddied across Thuy; the hairs on the nape of her neck prickled up. Luis kicked aside the oriental rug to reveal a pattern inscribed on the floor, an octagon with a square drawn on the inner side of each edge—a beezie agent whispered that the pattern was a flattened hypercube—and here came Azaroth, visible in the orphidnet, or the upper part of him anyway, the lower half of his ethereal body beneath the floor. Azaroth, Thuy's self-appointed life-coach and muse, wearing a big-collared yellow shirt printed with green daisies, his arms moving as slowly as kelp drifting in a wave.

"Lots of news," he said to Thuy, talking right past the others. "I've been snooping around the ExaExa labs. First of all, humpty Luty's sending an attack shoon to bust up your reading. He doesn't want you spreading the word that he's living in the labs. And he'd like to snatch you." Image of a waist-high plastic golem shoon with slit eyes. "Second of all, Luty wants to launch his new nants tomorrow. He's got sudocoked-up agents all over town. So be very starky. Make a plea to the mass mind. If you're in on a big ExaExa riot, Thuy, you may finally see the light." And then he switched to Spanish and Gaddang, giving the congregation a message of self-reliance and good will.

"By 'see the light' do you mean finish *Wheenk,* or remember Chu's Knot, or both?" Thuy wanted to ask, but, oh shit, it was almost time for her reading! Was Luty really launching the nants tomorrow? Before Dick Too Dibbs even got into office?

Thuy tossed a couple of bucks in the collection plate and hurried out with a murmur of thanks. Down the street at Meto-tem Metabooks, Kittie was right inside the door, smilingly awaiting her.

"Hey, *bạn gái,*" said Kittie, dolled up and butch in a shiny black leather pantsuit, her hair in spikes, the cartoony blue tattoo on her neck looking good. Nektar had bought her the suit. Kittie raised a glass of red wine. "Here's to Dick Too Dibbs's inauguration. We're freakin' doomed."

"I always look for the upside," said Darlene, dressed in her usual boots, jeans, and cowboy shirt, but with a fancy necklace. "See this?" The necklace's rhodopsin-doped image-beads were displaying silent talking heads of Bernard Lampton and Dick Too

Dibbs, plus orphidnet graphics of Hibraners, beezie scrolls, and Pharaoh cuttlefish. "Isn't it pretty?" said Darlene. "Scary times galvanize the art community."

"Let's hope the Homesteadies don't zombify the kiqs and march us into death camps," said Kittie. "Executive order, day one."

"Dick Too won't be that bad," said Darlene. She was incorrigibly upbeat, with long front teeth and an upper lip that projected out. "I think he's cute. And he's sworn up and down that he'll hunt down Luty and execute him. I believe him."

"Believe a guy from the Homesteady Party?" put in Thuy.

"Life's a long and winding river," said Darlene. "The forces of evil never win for long. Come on, Thuy, let's go in my office so you can personalize some access codes for your fans. And tell me what you want me to say when I introduce you. Have you been tracking the orphidnet rank of your teaser post? It's super. We're gonna have a good crowd. I hope Jayjay shows; he's been out of circulation too long."

Darlene had set out about twenty chairs. A dozen people were already seated, including Thuy's fellow metanovelists Gerry Gurken, Carla Standard, Jack Sparks, and Linda Loca. Each of them had a very different take on how to make a metanovel.

Gerry's metanovel *Banality* was a vast combine of images all drawn from one and the same instant on a certain day. No time elapsed in this work, only space, and the story was the user's gradual apprehension of a vast conspiracy woven throughout not only our world but also throughout the worlds of dreams, thoughts, and the Hibrane. The images were juxtaposed in suggestive ways and were accompanied by a spoken voice-over delivered by a virtual Gerry Gurken, who wandered his memory palace at the user's side.

Despite the dismissive remarks that Darlene sometimes made

about *Banality,* Gerry Gurken was a craftsman to the core. Any ten-minute block of the work was fascinating, disorienting, and revelatory—leaving the user's mind off-center and agog. Unfortunately, by the twenty-minute mark, most users found *Banality* to be too much.

Intense, lipsticked, nail-biting Carla Standard had used what she called a simworld approach in creating her Mission district metanovel *You're a Bum!* Her virtual characters were artificially alive, always in action, and somewhat unpredictable, a bit like the nonplayer characters in an old-school video game. Rather than writing story lines, Carla endowed her characters with goals and drives, leaving them free to interact like seagulls in a wheeling flock. Each user's *You're a Bum!* experience was tailored with data drawn from the user's personal meshes and social situations. In other words, when you accessed Carla's metanovel, you saw something vaguely resembling your own life.

Thuy's two sessions with *You're a Bum!* had proved painful, even lacerating. First she'd relived the moment last spring when she and Jayjay stood under a flowering plum tree off Mission Street, Jayjay shaking the tree to make the petals shower down upon her like perfumed confetti, all the while Jayjay's eyes were melting with love. And then she'd seen their breakup, but more objectively than before, with the simulated Thuy hungover from the Big Pig, her clothes in disarray, Thuy hysterically screaming at Jayjay in a mural-lined alley, and poor Jayjay's trembling fingers nervously adjusting his coat and hat. Oh, why did she have to miss Jayjay so much?

Like Gerry Gurken, the excitable Jack Sparks was one of Thuy's admirers, but he held little physical appeal for her. He was too thin and overwrought, too needy. As part of his doomed campaign to engage Thuy's affection, Sparks had undertaken *The Thuy Fan,* an unwritable and unreadable metanovel wherein every possible action path of his young heroine Thuy would be traced. Waking up with a man, a woman, or nobody in bed beside her, Thuy hopped out of the right or left side of her bed, or perhaps she crawled over the foot end of the bed. She put on her slippers or threw them out the window, if she had a window. In some forkings she jumped out the window herself, but in most she went to take a shower. In the shower she sang or washed or had sex with her partner. And so on. And so on. In practice, no human author would have had the time and energy to contemplate so richly ramified a document as *The Thuy Fan,* but Jack Sparks had his beezies helping him by autonomously roughing in sketches of ever-more action paths.

Bouncy Linda Loca was working on a metanovel entitled *George Washington,* depicting the world as seen from the point of view of a dollar bill. What lent her work its piquancy was how literally she'd managed to execute the plan: perusing *George Washington,* you felt flat and crinkly; you spent most of your time in a wallet or folded in a pocket; and when you came out into the air the main things you saw were countertops and people's hands. When Linda's George Washington dollar changed hands, the bill moved the story along by buying drinks, influence, or sex, and thereby sketching the rise and fall of a young cop whom Linda had named George Washington as well.

Linda was having blowback issues with this George Washington character because, to round him out, she'd made him an aspiring writer. Problem was, George began pestering Linda with messages about her metanovel—dumb ideas, by and large. The character was, after all, only a beezie simulation of a human, without the deep complexity that made an artist.

For her part, Thuy was making *Wheenk* into what she termed a transreal lifebox, meaning that her metanovel was to capture the waking dream of her life as she experienced it—while sufficiently bending the truth to allow for a fortuitously emerging dramatic plot. Thuy wanted *Wheenk* to incorporate not only the interesting things she saw and heard but also the things that she thought and felt. Rather than coding her inner life into words and realworld images alone, Thuy was including beezie-built graphic constructs and—this was a special arrow in her quiver—music. The goal was that accessing Thuy's work should feel like being Thuy herself.

In Darlene's office—really a windowless storage room with a desk—Thuy took off her coat and personalized the dozen "Losing My Head" access codes that Darlene had sold in advance; for each of them she said the date and the user's name and affixed an orphidnet link to the dedication event. Then she washed up and drank a glass of water.

"So what should I say about you?" asked Darlene. She and Thuy didn't really know each other very well.

"Say I'm a genius, and that they should buy my work." Thuy was feeling anxious and lonely. "Say I have a broken heart."

"I noticed that in 'Losing My Head,'" said Darlene. Now that Thuy had began publishing, she sometimes had the experience of people knowing her better than she realized. "How come you don't get Jayjay back?" continued Darlene. "Even though he's still on the *Merz Boat,* he broke up with Jil in November. Everyone knows that from *Founders.* If you don't want Jayjay, I'm gonna go for him, girl."

"He won't clean up his act. He's always getting high off the Big Pig."

"I hear Jayjay's been making some real progress with his physics," said Darlene. "There's rumors he's nailed teleportation,

if you can believe that. Him and Jil and Craigor keep disappearing from the *Merz Boat* and popping up in other places. Poor Jil
is losing it; a couple of days ago she used teleportation to score
sudocoke. Now *that's* a drug problem. Maybe Jayjay's Big Pig issues were never as severe as yours, Thuy. It seems like you love
him anyway. What if you accepted him the way he is?"

"I wasn't raised to do acceptance," said Thuy, laughing a little. "It's un-Vietnamese. But yeah, maybe I could learn, Darlene. Thanks. Oh, I forgot to tell you, keep an eye on the door.
I got a warning that Jeff Luty might send, like, a plastic robot to
disrupt our event. An attack shoon?"

"I thought shoons were always cute and giggly," said Darlene, seeming to take Thuy's worries for mere stage fright.

"We'll see," said Thuy, peering out of the office. Most of the
seats were taken, and more people were coming in the door. A
glance into the orphidnet showed virtual faces hovering, a few
hundred of them. Very respectable numbers for a Mission
metanovelist.

"Thanks for coming," Thuy told the crowd after Darlene's
introduction. "I'm Thuy Nguyen, and I'm going to be showing
you a piece called 'Losing My Head.' It's part of my metanovel-
in-progress, *Wheenk.*"

Thuy had learned a bit by watching others present their
metanovels. The audience wanted to experience the thing itself.
You had to give them a link into the metanovel database and
drag them along in your wake.

As Thuy messaged out the access links, someone appeared in
the middle of the front row, Jayjay, wearing his green cap and a
black poncho with a stencil of a cuttlefish. He hadn't been
there a minute ago, and he hadn't come through the door. Teleportation! Jayjay winked and gave Thuy the thumbs-up sign.
She had to fight back a big grin. Excited and energized, she

dove into the part where her head went through the grating in Topping's wall, accompanying her voice-over with a fugue of images and music.

"We're wrestling in this dough-faced top-man's office and I fall into the wall. You know those dozens of voices jabbering in your brain: fears, scolds, lusts; masters, monsters, slaves? Right away the grating dices my head into bouillon cubes—*dzeeent*—one voice apiece. Zoom in on them and you can hear the little voices are choruses too—*aum aum aum*—the grills buzzsaw me more, my cells sing good-bye, I'm subatomic—*fweee*—as above so below, my fragments live in tide pools by an unknown sea—*wheenk*—I miss kissing Jayjay in the spring snow of falling flower petals—*peck, peck, peck*—I'm a lonely crowd of crypto-zoa stalked by bird-man subbie sentinels—*roar*—time tide rolls in and I scuttle from a zillion hidey-holes, my pincers, feelers, eye-stalks merge—*click, click*—I see a white plastic table under fluorescent fixture flicker, I'm a head sticking from a grill—*mumble drone*—a man leans over me with plastic ants on his face, he wants the Chu's Knot I not got stocked, doc—*eeeewf*—dear Jayjay's pulling me back through the grill, dragstripping me from speed of night to zero again—*nteeezd*—I'm chunking in the grill, slice-diced neck-first and, hey, the lab was ExaExa, and the mad scientist is—"

Thuy was interrupted by the store's big window splintering. A golem shoon stood there: a small, rough-hewn humanoid waving big fists. He bent over and farted horribly, spewing pukeful billows of stink into the crowd. Coughing and retching, all but trampling one another, the crowd pushed out to the rainy street.

"Killer event," said Gerry Gurken to Thuy. "Mind if I sample it for my blog?"

"Let's go," said Jayjay at Thuy's side. "I'll get you out of here."

"I can take care of her," said Kittie, wanting to freeze out Jayjay once again.

The golem shoon had his own ideas. Heedless of whom he knocked down, the stubby creature forced his way through the crowd, grimly intent on Thuy. Was the monster planning to drag her off to the ExaExa labs? Or to kill her on the spot? From the little Thuy had seen of Luty, he seemed far gone enough to do just about anything.

Seized by mortal fear, Thuy dashed into Valencia Street and was nearly run over by an electric car. It skidded past her, whacking her a glancing blow on the butt. Somehow she kept her balance. Thuy's heart was hammering as if it would jump from her chest. By a stroke of good fortune, the out-of-control car plowed into the golem, squashing his head.

Thuy darted into a mural-lined alley across the street, leaning against a painted wall, gasping for breath, her face wet with rain, her sweater and T-shirt beginning to soak through. She'd left her slicker in Darlene's office. Seen in the orphidnet, the murals were glowing windows that showed endless animated variations of themselves. Someone else came into the alley: Jayjay, fit and fleet of foot. He rested his hand lightly on her arm.

"Running won't be enough," he said. "I have a better way."

Under the streetlight by Metotem Metabooks, the rubbery golem was molding himself into his original form, his shadow a black stain upon the puddled pavement. He moved his head in abrupt twitches, scanning for Thuy. An excited little dog began barking at the heavyset shoon; with a sharp kick, the golem sent the dog skidding into the gutter, limp and broken.

"Darlene said I should give you another chance," Thuy told

Jayjay, talking fast. "I want to be with you, yes. I hope it's not too late."

"Me too," answered Jayjay. He smiled at her. "This is the same alley where we split up. Synchronicity."

"But how deeply does Jil have her hooks into you? That woman—"

"Woman," echoed Jayjay and embraced Thuy, sheltering her from the rain with the wings of his plastic poncho. "I only slept with Jil because I couldn't have you. Jil's no schemer; she wants to do right. She broke off with me because it was upsetting her kids. But Craigor keeps cheating on her; he's got this midlife crisis thing. And now Jil's using again. I feel sorry for her. But that's nothing like the way I feel about you, Thuy. I've always dreamed of spending my life with you. Nobody else comes close."

Thuy wanted to melt, to cling to her man like a vine, but over his shoulder she saw the golem splashing across Valencia.

"Jayjay—"

"It's okay," said Jayjay squeezing her tighter. "We're outta here. We'll teleport. Go in the orphidnet and look at the *Merz Boat*. And be looking at this alley with your eyes."

Thuy followed Jayjay's link to the gently rocking deck of the bargelike *Merz Boat* with its central cabin like an oversized loaf of bread. She had a moment of double vision: water waves flowed across the alley walls. And now Jayjay linked her to a striped, silk-spinning caterpillar that crawled all over the *Merz Boat* scene, smoothing over the all-but-imperceptible gaps in the remotely viewed image, interpolating among the orphid-based data points. No orphidnet image had ever looked *this* real.

Next Jayjay showed Thuy how to weave her thoughts from scene to scene, binding the alley and the seascape together.

Thuy's mind spread out. She was neither here nor there. All of her particles were in synch with each other, temporarily free of the outside world. She felt very tiny, she was falling—where? With a thump, Thuy and Jayjay landed on the soft deck of—

"Welcome to the *Merz Boat*," whispered Jayjay. "You and me, Thuy, forever."

CHAPTER 9

The Attack Shoons

The bay's riffles were faintly lit by the San Francisco lights, the reflections roughened by the endless rain. The soft plastic scow flexed with the water's gentle chop. Double-jointed mounds of Craigor's art projects stood heaped beside his little workshop at the boat's stern. Amidships, the glowing windows of a long cabin illuminated fishing nets and a big glass tank of cuttlefish. In the bow, a group of Jil's shoons chattered among themselves and called soft greetings.

"How—" began Thuy, but now one of the cabin doors opened and here came Jil Zonder. Although the night was dark, Thuy could see Jil clearly via the orphidnet: perfect bob of dark hair, straight nose and great cheekbones, almond eyes and crisply cut mouth. Thuy had always admired Jil, and even now she wanted to like her.

"You made it, Thuy!" exclaimed Jil. Seen up close, her face was tired and worn. The sudocoke was dragging her down. "I watched Jayjay watching your reading," said Jil. "I caught the part about Topping's office having that grill connection to the ExaExa labs." She rubbed at her temples distractedly. "Um, if you can swear you saw Luty there, I know this cop who can get a search warrant. Bim Brown, the San Francisco Chief of Police—

he's a *Founders* fan. He's ready to launch a surprise raid on Exa-Exa tomorrow—last chance before Inauguration Day."

"Aren't you giving away the surprise, talking about it out loud?" said Thuy.

"I hardly know what I'm saying anymore," said Jil, suddenly on the point of tears. "Nobody cares about me anymore. I don't matter."

"Do you mind that I'm here?" said Thuy uncertainly. She felt naïve and plain and stupidly perky before this suffering older woman.

"Oh, forget about my stupid fling with Jayjay," said Jil in a flat, rapid tone. She sniffled and rubbed her nose. "Dead ashes for him, just a snack. He's such a beautiful boy. Maybe I thought I'd win Craigor back that way. As if. I hope you didn't watch us on *Founders,* Thuy?"

"No, no," said Thuy. "Of course not."

"Good," said Jil, scratching her scalp. "The kids saw us almost right away, and then it was horrible and we had to stop having sex. Momotaro slugged Jayjay in the crotch. Bixie had a screaming fit. And usually she's so calm. Girls are wonderful when they're eleven. Remember being that age, Thuy? It's right before sex drags you down. I've never been so unhappy in my life."

"But that was all two months ago, Jil," put in Jayjay, trying to lighten the mood. "And you and I are still friends, right? I wish you and Craigor could settle back down. And of course it's for the best if you and I keep things platonic. I feel like I abused your hospitality."

Jil shrugged and sniffled, her expression unutterably bleak.

"By the way, Thuy," jabbered Jayjay, "in case you're wondering why I'm still on the *Merz Boat,* it's because of Azaroth, that

Hibraner friend of yours? He always turns up here. He steals cuttlefish and sends them to the Hibrane to eat. Azaroth has been helping me get good at physics. Not that he's a scientist. But he remembers stuff for me. And Craigor's okay with me being here. He likes that I'm helping him teleport."

Thuy felt an irrational pang of jealousy to learn that Azaroth was working with Jayjay as well as with her.

"*Pop*," said a deep voice right behind Thuy, startling her. It was Craigor, materializing out of nowhere, wearing a cuttlefish-stenciled poncho like Jayjay's.

"How do you guys do that?" asked Thuy, wiping the rain from her eyes.

"I invented a new family of quantum mechanical interpolators," said Jayjay. "I package them as little agents. You saw one just now, it looked like a caterpillar. Nobody gets hold of my interpolation agents unless I give them a onetime link. I'm beginning to build buzz for teleportation, and maybe later, I'll be taking my service public. The vibby thing is, whatever you're carrying gets teleported right along with you."

"You used the Big Pig?" said Thuy, disappointed. A sudden gust of wind sent salt spray flying across the deck, totally drenching her.

"The winter wet T-shirt look," said Craigor, theatrically goggling at Thuy's soggy sweater and her sagging striped tights. He was also peering under her clothes through the orphidnet; she could sense the hitcounts. Thuy looked to Jil for help.

"Don't worry about Jayjay, Thuy," said Jil, ignoring her husband. "Jayjay's down to one Pig session every two weeks. It takes him that long to process all the stuff that Azaroth helps him remember. He's gotten so smart. I'm proud of him. Come into the cabin and dry off. You're going to catch a cold and start sniffling like me."

"That golem shoon's on his way," said Craigor, asserting his presence. "And he's bringing backup. See them, kiqs? Look in the orphidnet: the golem, a crocodile, a pelican, and a pterodactyl." He messaged the links.

Thuy zoomed in on the ragged, ineluctable forms. The stubby golem shoon was a mile off, sculling toward the *Merz Boat*. He'd puffed up his body with air so as to float on the surface, and he was using his arms and legs like oars. Further away, but moving faster, was a submerged plastic crocodile beating a long, tapering tail. A pair of sinister flying shoons were just leaving the ExaExa labs in San Francisco, one resembling a pale green pelican, the other a leathery reddish pterodactyl. "Maybe your boat should swim down to the South Bay?" Thuy said to Craigor.

"No use," said Craigor. "It's like when a Frankenstein monster is chasing you in a dream: he moves slow, but he never stops, and eventually you have to rest, and that's when he catches up." Reflexively clowning, Craigor lurched stiff-legged toward the stern, rocking from side to side, intoning, "Me kill bad shoons. Jayjay help."

"I'm staying with Thuy," said Jayjay, not budging from her side.

Craigor's voice returned to normal. "If we're not ready for those attack shoons, kiq, there's gonna be no romance possibilities for you nohow. Not with Thuy and not with my wife."

"Don't always bring that up," said Jayjay testily. "You should be nicer to Jil."

"Fuck you. You gonna help or not?"

"All *right*," said Jayjay. "Give us a freakin' minute." He hugged Thuy again, and this time she let him kiss her.

"You feel so good," Thuy messaged privately. "Why didn't you call?"

"I missed you a lot," messaged back Jayjay. "But I didn't want to bug you till I'd done something to make you proud. And now I've invented my own teleportation technique. It's much hipper than the Armory-to-ExaExa kludge that Luty set up with those gratings. Prav Plato says I should publish my work as a physics paper, but I'm thinking I should keep the details secret and get rich by selling onetime access links."

"Rich would be nice," messaged Thuy. "That way you can get a good place to live. And then maybe we—" But she didn't dare formulate her wish, not with Jil and Craigor around.

"Move it, Thuy," said Jil, bossily tapping her on the shoulder. "Dry clothes and hot tea." Even though Jil was frowning, her voice was creepily calm. "Jayjay has to help Craigor. After all, it's thanks to you that those attack shoons are coming here."

"I'd better get ready," agreed Jayjay.

So Thuy let Jil lead her into the long cabin, cozy and lit by solar-charged bud-lamps. Jil put some water on the stove while Thuy took a seat at a round piezoplastic table growing from the deck. Visible in the orphidnet were ad icons for Stank deodorant and BigBox furniture, which meant this was a top-level episode of the *Founders* show. Thuy was hoping for a cozy chat with Jil, but the other woman seemed preoccupied.

"Why don't I file my report with Bim Brown right now?" suggested Thuy finally.

"Uh, good idea. Here's Bim's link. While you do that, I'll check on the kids." The living quarters were arranged in three blocks: first the common area with a bathroom, then the kids' two small bedrooms facing each other across a hall, and beyond that the parents' large bedroom. Thuy wondered where she and Jayjay were supposed to sleep.

The instant Thuy clicked the link Jil had given her, she had Bim Brown on a private message line, the chief sitting amid a din of background noise in a cop-station office with file cabinets, chairs, award plaques, a gun rack, and old-school display screens showing arrays of faces and annotated maps. Chief Brown looked very plausible, but Thuy felt suspicious. Why had the link worked so fast? Temporarily leaving the worries for her scenario-spinning beezies to analyze, she pressed on.

"I know where Jeff Luty is," Thuy told Chief Brown. "I saw him in the ExaExa labs."

"That's a big break for us," he answered, his deep voice reassuring. "Don't go away. I'll open up a notarized encryption channel so you can record your account. Here it is."

A sort of funnel appeared, and Thuy recounted her sighting of Luty. To speed things up, she pasted in some material directly from "Losing My Head," which happened to include an image of Luty with his lank ponytail. There was no reason that legal evidence couldn't take the form of a poetic rant.

"*Excelente,*" said Brown when she was done. "We'll try and bag Luty tomorrow morning. With any luck, he uses deadly force to resist arrest, my officers reply in kind, and Too Dibbs doesn't get the chance to pardon him. Case frikkin' closed."

"You're telling me this?" said Thuy, surprised.

"What it is. Luty tried to kill every single person on Earth with those nants. I'd call that genocide. And I'm hearing he's pumped to do it again."

"Can I come and watch the raid?"

"I'll be wanting the whole *Merz Boat* posse in on this. You kiqs have special friends, special powers. We might need it all. Be outside the ExaExa labs by eight a.m. latest."

Bim Brown broke the connection and Thuy was alone in the *Merz Boat*'s common room. She used the orphidnet to peer into the dark bedrooms, looking for Jil. Bixie and Momotaro were asleep in their rooms, and Jil herself was sitting on the bed alone in the master bedroom, her head down over her lap. Crying—or doing sudocoke?

Feeling guilty for prying, Thuy switched to watching Craigor and Jayjay, who were readying a combine device made of a four-foot lump of piezoplastic atop three ten-meter lengths of black pipe. The lump was beige, with a hatched surface that made it look vaguely like an internal organ. Arms protruded from its middle, with hands grasping a black metal cane. The lump had eyes and a toothy mouth at its top end, which was crowned by a black top hat bearing white lettering: "Mr. Peanut." One of Craigor's gaga Dada jokes. Art for art's sake. You had to hand it to the guy, obnoxious though he was. Meanwhile, the attack shoons were fifteen minutes away.

Jil bounced out from the bedrooms, carrying a towel, jeans, and a sweater. Her eyes were bright and watchful. Thuy changed into the dry clothes, almost expecting Jil to put a sexual move on her, so charged was the atmosphere. But Jil just made two cups of tea and seated herself at the round table across from Thuy.

"You think the men can handle the attackers?" said Thuy, wanting to talk.

"I bet they can," said Jil. She reached into her pants pocket and set a little silver box on the table beside her teacup. "You want a hit?"

"You're, um, using again?" said Thuy. "Not to judge you, of course. I used to watch *Founders,* so I know your backstory. You were in recovery, weren't you?"

"Until last week," said Jil, using a silver straw to blast two snorts from her stash box. "But Craigor's still cheating on me. It's like all of a sudden he's scared his life is slipping away and he has to score all these different women. I wish I could just accept having an open marriage. But I can't. And now he's seeing

Lureen Morales. And even that would be okay if only Jayjay—"
Jil had been talking faster and faster, but now her voice trailed
off. She stared off into space, riding her rush.

The way she'd said Jayjay's name set off alarm bells in Thuy's
head. "You're still in love with him?" blurted Thuy. "Even after
breaking up?"

"Ratings spike," said Jil, her mouth curving into a stoned
smirk. Her eyes were dancing. She snapped shut her silver box
and shoved it back in her pants. "Feel the hitcounts? Time to
promote your metanovel. Is it *Wheenk*? I didn't say that Jayjay
and I *broke up*, Thuy. I said we stopped *having sex*. Jayjay's very
hot. He makes me feel young. Is that so bad?"

Temporarily at a loss, Thuy checked their images in the
orphidnet—like a TV soap actor glancing over at the monitor.
She noticed points of light inside Jil's head. Devices in Jil's
brain? Or was that a sudocoke thing?

"What?" snapped Jil, defiantly glaring at her.

"Um, tell me about Jayjay's teleporting," essayed Thuy.

Jil cocked her head, her mouth half open, processing the input. "Jayjay discovered it thanks to that Hibraner Azaroth," she
said finally. "Azaroth figured out a way to use the orphidnet for
remembering complicated things. Azaroth gets into close orphidnet contact with Jayjay when he's on the Pig, and he saves off
orphidnet images of Jayjay's mental states for him. The beezies
like Jayjay, they give him all the space he needs in the orphidnet.
Azaroth says he wants to help bring Ond and Chu back from the
Hibrane. Ond loves me, you know."

"Oh everyone loves Jil," said Thuy sarcastically. "And I
know all about Azaroth. He's *my* Hibrane friend, too."

"Mainly he steals cuttlefish from the wholesalers," said Jil,
slowing down again. "I don't fully trust him."

"Azaroth told me that he asked you about Chu's Knot, Jil, and you wouldn't help. You went to the Hibrane, didn't you? You touched the Knot."

"I did. But I don't remember much. I was really upset. I wasn't thinking straight. I was thinking—what's the opposite? Crooked? Bent? Ripped?" Jil sniffled and rubbed her nose. "It sucks that I'm using again. I'm throwing my life away. Last week this dealer offered me such a good price that I caved. I needed some relief. And now I don't know if I have another recovery in me. It was so frikkin' hard for me to quit the first time, Thuy. You've got no idea. But Craigor doesn't really love me, and I sure as hell don't love him. And if I can't have Jayjay—I'm all alone."

"You can get better again, Jil. Think about your children. Go back to your support group. Get help."

Jil sighed and shook her head. "I'm ashamed of being a relapser. And you know what? Maybe I'm not ready to be sober again. Life is too raw. It drives me crazy to have Jayjay here all the time: this delicious snack I can't eat. And, yes, little Thuy, I feel like shit about my kids. I wish I was dead. I want another hit of sudocoke." Jil fumbled in her pocket.

"Oh, Jil, don't. Sleep it off, and when you're yourself again, call up your old sponsor. She'll help you."

"Oh, what do you know? I'm on a run, Thuy; I'm not gonna be sleeping at all." Jil set the stash box on the table with a click. The orphidnet showed a sinister glitter in the sudocoke.

"I'm going outside," said Thuy. "You got a raincoat I can use?"

"Over there," said Jil with an abrupt jerk of her hand toward a rack with several of those cuttlefish-stenciled ponchos. She took another quick hit of sudocoke, and the bitter energy surged into her. "A fresh costume for Hipster Goody Girl," said Jil as Thuy slipped on a poncho. She raised her voice to a mocking soprano lisp. "Ooo, does this make my ego look too big?"

It was definitely time to step outside. The rain had subsided to a drifting mist. A dozen iridescent piezoplastic crows were wandering about the deck, shaking out their wings and clacking their beaks. Mr. Peanut was standing on his tripod of legs in the not-so-deep water, scanning the bay and brandishing his cane like a fencer's foil. Jayjay and Craigor were excitedly fiddling with piezoplastic bands stretched among the joints and pistons of a small steel backhoe, which had a Happy Shoon perched in its driver's seat, his fingers grown into spindly tendrils which twined around the machinery to touch each of the stretchy bands. The bands were taking the place of the beat old machine's unfueled gasoline engine.

"Jil is—" began Thuy.

"We know," said Jayjay. "It's been like this all week. I feel bad about it. Like it's partly my fault. But I don't know what to do."

"What about you, Craigor?" said Thuy. "Don't you care?"

Craigor looked Thuy over again. "It's gonna be me in my coffin when I die, little girl. This is my only run. No way I can paddle back upstream, back to what Jil and I had before."

"You could try," urged Thuy. "Love her, Craigor. Save her. And what about your children?"

"My parents stayed together for the sake of the kids," said Craigor, tall, stiff, unhappy. "It was hell for all of us. Why am I even telling you this? Words suck. You are what you do. If Jil wants to save herself, that's her call." Seeing something in the bay, Craigor whooped with a warrior's fierce exultation. "Yeah, baby! Here he comes!"

The puffed-up golem was in view to the stern, approaching fast, his arms and legs beating a fierce rhythm. The pelican and the pterodactyl were circling overhead, and in the orphidnet Thuy could see the crocodile coming up on the *Merz Boat* from below.

Craigor's plastic crows took wing and mobbed the pair of airborne shoons, doing their best to distract them without being snapped up by the great beaks. Moments later three of the crows were gone. They were overmatched.

Moving with awkward agility, Mr. Peanut lurched into position and intercepted the golem, who didn't seem to recognize the peanut as a threat. Easy as pie, Mr. Peanut shish-kebabbed the golem with his cane. The golem struggled and burbled; Mr. Peanut bit off his head, then his chest, then his legs. Fueled by the piezoplastic, the top-hatted goober doubled his body size. Triumphantly he slashed his cane at the waves.

Before Thuy, Jayjay, and Craigor could cheer Mr. Peanut's success, the *Merz Boat* shuddered amidships. The crocodile shoon had reared out of the water to tear loose a chunk of the low gunnel. Icy water sloshed across the deck as the thick plastic reptile heaved himself aboard. Twanging and shuddering, the backhoe stretched its jaws toward the croc. The croc snapped at the metal shovel, managing to sever one of its power belts.

For now the green pelican simply hovered, watching the events unfold. But the pterodactyl dove at Thuy as if meaning to carry her off. She flattened herself on the deck; the pterodactyl missed her. The backhoe spun fruitlessly in a tight circle, its Happy Shoon driver frantically adjusting the belts in an effort to regain control. The red pterodactyl did a loop-the-loop and dove again, keeping Thuy in place.

And now the crocodile came slithering across the deck toward her, his toothy jaws ajar. Thuy began screaming for help, but not quite from the bottom of her heart. At some level, she felt detached—as if she were perusing a lifebox metanovel. Damsel in distress! Who'll save me?

Craigor was over by the long cabin, poised to defend his

family. But Jayjay—Jayjay was there for Thuy. He sprang forward with a machete in his grip and thrust it toward the red pterodactyl, forcing the monster to cease its diving and hover on high. Thuy sprang to her feet and backed away from the croc—only to find herself cornered against the wall of the boat's workshop.

The crocodile flexed his haunches and widened his jaws, preparing to pounce. All veils of playfulness dropped. Thuy was facing empty, eternal death. She screamed with everything she had. Jayjay charged past the backhoe and slashed into the croc's back. The hissing shoon turned to snap at him, giving the backhoe an opening to clamp onto the croc's tail. And now Thuy's hero waded in and hacked the monster to bits. A flock of shoons converged on the gobbets of piezoplastic, gobbling them up.

"Look out!" shouted Craigor. Thirteen-year-old Momotaro was standing in the door of the long cabin beside his slightly younger sister, Bixie, with Jil frozen-faced behind them, her brain fogged with glowing dots. Craigor and Momotaro were pointing at the hovering red pterodactyl, who was oddly bending his body in half.

Thuy and Jayjay found shelter against the backhoe, in case the shoon dived, but this time he pulled a new stunt: he shat a flaming pellet of piezoplastic onto the deck; the lump sputtered and sizzled like napalm. The boat itself might have caught fire if it hadn't been for the puddled water from the broken gunnel. Snapping out of her trance, Jil directed her shoons to suck up water and to spit it onto the flames.

The pterodactyl feathered his wings and hunched his body again as if to drop a flame-egg upon the exposed roof of the long cabin. Craigor roared defiance, leaping onto the cabin's roof and tossing three of his crow shoons into the air. And now finally the green pelican did something. Quick as a sewing machine's needle, his beak dispatched the crows: one-two-three.

Thuy was dizzied by all the sensations, especially as she was trying to mold them into metanovel material in realtime. As part of the work she'd switched on a music track: operatic rock and roll. The pterodactyl and the pelican were visual echoes of the menacing bird-headed subbie she'd seen in the non-space between Topping's office and the ExaExa labs.

The dusky red pterodactyl squawked his approval for the crow-pecking, but then, when he was least expecting it, the green pelican darted at him and—yes!—ripped off one of his wings. The pterodactyl plummeted downward, bounced off the side of the *Merz Boat,* and ended up screeching and floundering in the Bay waters. Mr. Peanut strode over and dispatched him with cruel stabs of his cane.

There was a moment of calm. The *Merz Boat* pushed up a fresh gunnel-lip to repair the gap the crocodile had made. The sloshing bay waters drained out through the scuppers. The pelican glided to a silent landing on the deck, preened himself, and fixed the humans with a glittering eye.

"Hi Jayjay," he said in a familiar voice. "Sonic sent me. Lay down that machete, you're making me nervous."

Jayjay thought for a minute, consulting his simulation beezies, and then he laid the machete on the deck behind him and hunkered beside the pelican. "Talk to me," he said.

"Ready for a private message stream?" said the pelican.

"Let Thuy and Craigor hear, too," said Jayjay.

"And us," said Momotaro.

"Not you kids," said Jil. "You need to get back in bed. It's too cold out here." She shuddered. "Aren't you cold?"

"Aw, Mom."

"Come on." Jil and the kids disappeared into the cabin.

"Here we go," said the pelican to Thuy, Jayjay, and Craigor, the three of them squatting around him. Overhead the clouds were breaking up and the moon was shining through, big and bright, just past full.

The data flowed in, a mental movie in three scenes. As soon as Thuy realized what she was seeing, she began forwarding it to Chief Bim Brown.

The first scene shows Sonic on the day he was abducted, October 21, two weeks before the election. Sonic is closed in by the quantum-mirrored walls of the ExaExa labs, sitting at a long white table drinking a big mug of coffee, still in his red T-shirt with his pleated leather coat on the table beside him.

One wall is covered with the teleport grill, the opposite wall holds a door, and the side walls are mounted with four view screens simulating natural phenomena: cracking mud, wind-tossed branches, a beach fire, and a waterfall.

Set into a niche like an altar beneath the bonfire screen is a smooth-cornered white plastic box bearing the ExaExa beetle logo and a single red button on its side. The box has intricate latches on its lid.

Jeff Luty is talking to Sonic. He's still gangly, but he's put on some weight, living alone in his lab. His wavy, unwashed hair is drawn into a ponytail. He wears a bracelet of colored oval stones around his wrist. The stones are incised to look like beetles. His skin is unhealthy, almost gray. He has plastic ants on his chin and cheeks, but his ropy chapped lips show. He licks his upper lip, then compulsively applies some waxy lip balm from a tube.

"What's with the ants, Jeff?" says Sonic.

"A visual pun," says Luty, his plain face forming a faint smile. "I'm in personal crunch mode to find a nant design that orphids and code-hackers can't trash. I'm farming a few thousand evolutionary algorithms. The formic minibots on my face are ant-shaped shoons loaded with sample nant nanocodes. They're a fake beard, too."

"Like you'd go outside wearing plastic ants?" says Sonic.

"Well, no, not while I'm indicted for capital charges," says Luty. "With my picture in all the post offices. That's fame, huh? I'm counting on Dick Too Dibbs to pardon me. He'd better. My ads are flipping the election."

"So what do you want with me?"

Luty leans forward, licks his lips again, and scrapes a few of the plastic ants off his face and onto Sonic's head. "Try and trash these guys like you did Nektar's beetles. I enjoy watching a craftsman at work. Like a flenser peeling blubber off a whale."

"I'm not working for you," says Sonic.

"Contrariwise," says Luty. He goes to a cupboard, draws out a slug of raw piezoplastic, and slaps it down on the table in front of Sonic. He lets out a playful, infectious chuckle. "Haven't you always wanted to be an ant farm?"

Before Sonic can shy away, the plastic ants on his head go into high-speed motion, repeatedly running down his arm to gobble piezoplastic, spawn new ants, and crawl back up, bedecking Sonic's arm with an ant highway resembling a dark ribbon of syrup. Sonic's head is a pulsing, wriggling mound of plastic insects; only the tip of his nose is visible. But then the plastic ants begin shuddering and, at first singly and then by the hundreds, they drop away.

"Sweet hack, Sonic," says Luty. "Your low cunning gives you an edge over the orphids."

"That rainbow scuzz on Grandmaster Green Flash," asks

Sonic, calmly brushing off the dying plastic ants. "Was that one of your dipshit experiments?"

"Affirmative," says Luty. "Minus your crass modifier. I'm testing new viral nanomachines all the time." He walks over to the altar niche and pats the white chest. "And the best nanocodes go onto the little fellows in here. This is the Ark of the Nants, with my special new nant farm inside. The Ark of the Nants holds the world's new order. Soon I'll have my new nants loaded with nanocode that the white hats can't trash. I just wish I could have some face-to-face with Ond Lutter. He put all these nutso nanteater tricks into the orphids, and I'm always having to find more workarounds. I wish I knew the Hibrane jump-code. I'd like to teleport there and barnacle myself to Ond for a few hours. That room-to-room teleport grill of mine is a good start on the big jump, don't you think?"

"What if I hop back through your punk-ass grill?" says Sonic. "And get myself the fuck outta here?"

"Calm down," says Luty, applying lip balm. "Don't use language. That's a great expression, isn't it? You remind me of my high-school friend Carlos Tucay. We were gonna make a company called Lu-Tuc Space Tech. But Carlos died. I've made a wonderful virtual model of him for Virtual Earth. Stay with me, Sonic. I'll pay you well."

"But I don't want nants to eat Earth," says Sonic.

"Oh, why do people always say that," says Luty. "Reality is software. What does it matter what system it's running on? The big win if we do the port is that we get to clean things up. Dogs out, Carlos in."

"No," says Sonic.

"Look, I don't want to come on like an insane villain," says Luty. "But I do know about your family. It's abstractly possible that, in my desperation, I might do something to them. I'm getting a little weird here, cooped up in this lab waiting for Vearth 2.0 and the resurrected Carlos." Luty pops up a display of Sonic's fieldworker parents and his eleven brothers and sisters, innocent and humble as laborers in a Diego Rivera mural. There's a grinning Death icon hovering over their heads, snickering and waggling his scythe. The effect is far from comical.

"Oh *man* . . ." says Sonic. "Get me more coffee."

The second scene shows Dick Too Dibbs touring the lab on November 6, two days after the election. Seen informally, Too Dibbs comes across as even brighter and more strong willed than in his jokey ads. His narrow eyes are clear and observant. His gaze darts methodically around the equipment-filled room, taking an inventory: the teleport grill, the simulation screens, the cabinets and fixtures, the Ark of the Nants, and Sonic busy programming a golem-shaped shoon.

"I'm planning to assist you in completing the project your cousin began," Luty tells Too Dibbs. "He saw the nants as bringing about—perhaps an odd way to put it—the New Jerusalem of a fully American Virtual Earth. Your cousin felt that Vearth was a fulfillment of Biblical prophecy."

"I don't hold with that particular line of religiosity," says Too Dibbs. "And you've heard me say I don't aim to end up in the death chamber like my cousin Dick."

"Oh, that was a glitch," says Luty. "My old nants were hacked by a rogue employee. Ond Lutter. I respect Ond, but we don't see eye to eye. We're in a bit of an arms race with each other." Luty tugs nervously at his limp ponytail. "Ond's orphids are an interesting challenge. Just recently I've developed some irreversible nants that look pretty tough. But I want to be sure they're truly orphid-proof before I release them. And this is where you come in." Luty mimes a salute. "It must be done, Mr. President. Battle stations!"

"I'm not president yet."

"It's thanks to me that you're gonna get there," says Luty. "I saturated the orphidnet with ads, and when that wasn't enough, I corrupted the vote-tally programs."

Dick Too Dibbs stares coldly at Luty, who's wearing a light goatee of plastic ants, even for this meeting with the president-elect. "Those ants must be eating your brain, Jeff. I won my election fair and square. It wasn't even close. People like the cut of my jib."

Luty peers at Dick Too Dibbs as if he's never really seen him before. "Why a jib? What does that even mean? Listen to me. I can make the media remember whatever I want them to remember. Facts are revisable. History is hackable. I can unelect you. You're a temporary variable."

A long pause. "What's the damned point of your Virtual Earth anyway?" asks Too Dibbs finally. "I never understood that. What's wrong with the Earth we have? My people were farmers, Jeff. You ever walked a freshly plowed field?"

Luty sphincters his wet lips and shakes his head, tense and anal. "Virtual Earth will be germ-free. Digital and odorless. No more dogs spreading filth. Wouldn't you love that?"

"I don't know," says Too Dibbs softly. "I just don't know."

"Well, *I* know and I'm telling you," says Luty, his voice cracking. "First you pardon me. Get my face off the post office walls. And then you require each citizen to install an orphidnet security patch. It must be done. ExaExa will provide the patch, it's based on our proprietary ShareCrop wikiware, but never mind the bitty details. The final output is that we get lasting, wiretap-style access to each person's mind. That way I can forestall any wise-guy attempts to trash my new nants."

"Don't like it," says Too Dibbs. "Wouldn't sit with my oath of office."

"You pardon me and you do that security patch," says Luty, his eyes flashing. "Or your election stinks like dog doo."

"We'll see," says Too Dibbs in a noncommittal tone. As he turns, his gaze pauses on Sonic. "Hey there, fella. What's your name?"

"Sonic Sanchez."

"Call me when you need a new job, Sonic. Your boss is nuts."

The third scene shows Luty hovering over the voluptuously curved white Ark of the Nants, fingering the elegant red button on its outside.

"So let me see how they're doing," says Sonic.

Luty rests his thumb on the red button, which briefly glows, scanning his thumbprint. The latches around the ark's lid pop open. The inner surfaces of the container are iridescent with quantum-mirror varnish. Nestled within the Ark of the Nants is a hermetically sealed transparent cube, four inches on a side. The nant farm itself.

"How come the nants don't chew their way through those see-through walls?" asks Sonic.

"The nant farm's walls are nantanium," says Luty, who's in a cheerful, chatty mood. "The only known substance that nants can't eat. I used the same technology as for the quantum-mirror varnish. But nantanium nixes the nants instead of the entanglement signals. It's all about quantum phase."

"Titanium?"

"Nant. Anium. It's my own invention." Watching the nants, Luty combs back his long greasy hair with his fingers and readjusts the rubber band that holds his ponytail. "Pretty great, huh?"

Frantically the nants pullulate, visible by virtue of the structures they erect and demolish in the course of their ceaseless activity, and now their orphidnet positional dots become visible, creating an effect like seething, luminous fog.

"I've got a new nanocode treat for them," says Luty. He produces a special scanning laser and pulses a long codey flicker into the nant farm. Where before the nants had been constructing windmills and silos, now they're making ferns and snail shells.

"I love seeking the gnarl," says Luty. "I'm almost resigned to not getting Ond Lutter's input. The Big Pig says she's about nailed the nature simulations. And I'm pretty sure these little guys are orphid-proof now. But I want to be careful. If I lose this match, I could be out of the series."

The fourth scene is from today, January 18, only a few hours old. Sonic is leaning over the light green pelican, working on it.

"It's getting scary, Jayjay," he says, talking to his friends through the video. "I've been trying to slow things up, but now Luty's suspicious of me. He's panicking about Dick Too Dibbs's inauguration on Tuesday. I think he's gonna crack open his nant farm tomorrow morning. Monday. Someone needs to come in here and stop him."

A blip in the visuals. Something moves behind Sonic.

"Oh, shit."

Sonic composes his face as Luty comes into view.

"What do you think you're doing?" Luty holds a compact pistol in his hand. His voice is high and tight. The plastic ants are marching in Belousov-Zhabotinsky spirals on his cheeks. "Don't think I don't know how to use a gun. I'm more than a dreamer."

"All I'm doing is getting the fifth attack shoon ready," says Sonic in a soothing tone. "These shoons are programmed to bring in Thuy Nguyen and Jayjay Jimenez, just like you said. The giant ant, the golem, the crocodile, the pterodactyl, and now the pelican. If the other shoons can't physically overwhelm Thuy and Jayjay, then the pelican will talk to them."

"I need Thuy especially," says Luty. "She's almosting Chu's Knot." Luty rests the barrel of the gun against the back of Sonic's head. "I'd hate to kill you, Sonic. You're *so* much like Carlos Tucay. You wouldn't be planning some gunjy triple cross, would you? Talk to me, dammit. I'm holding a gun."

"Of course I'm on your side, Jeff." Sonic's face is pale. "Look, if you thought you saw me doing something weird just now, that's only because I'm loading this last shoon with lies and disinformation. To trick Jayjay and Thuy into trusting me and rushing over here."

Luty's finger tightens on the trigger.

The video ends.

"Good info," Chief Brown told Thuy when the transmission was done. "This Sonic fellow, we're lucky he's on the inside. He can help us tomorrow. If he's alive. Nasty ending, huh? We'll find out the truth tomorrow. See you at 8 a.m. Oh, and Thuy, please keep this video material confidential. Don't post it for the public. We wouldn't want to spoil our surprise." The chief signed off again.

Again Thuy felt a flicker of uncertainty about Bim Brown. Was he for real? Maybe. Her beezies claimed the physical source coordinates of Bim's messages were matching the location of the San Francisco police station. But the guy seemed wrong.

In any case, there was no way in hell that Thuy was going to keep Sonic's crucial video confidential. Using the memory and network skills she'd developed as a metanovelist, she quickly reconstituted the video she'd just seen and posted the result to a secure site hosted by her personal orphids—all this took her less than a second.

"Good old Sonic," Jayjay was saying, a quaver in his voice. "I'm worried. I hope Luty was just scamming us. And what about that Dick Too Dibbs? The man has a brain! I'd been counting on him to be a total lackey for big biz. It's great knowing he's not gonna help Luty."

"Are you luring us into a trap?" Craigor asked the pelican sharply. The pelican didn't answer.

"Maybe the whole entire video was a fake," said Thuy, feeling more and more paranoid. There were too many levels to sort out. She squatted down to stare at the mildly glowing pelican. "Did Luty shoot Sonic or not?"

"I don't have time to talk," said the pelican in a matter of fact tone. "Because Jil is about to—"

"The kids are in bed," hollered Jil, popping out of the cabin door. She was totally wired, jerking around like a puppet on strings. Again Thuy noticed the spots of light inside Jil's head. "Don't get so close to that shoon, Thuy. We better kill it." Moving faster than seemed possible, Jil snatched up Jayjay's machete and ran at the hapless shoon. Before anyone could even think of stopping Jil, she'd lopped off the pelican's head. Jil whistled sharply and her Happy Shoons set to work eating the dead shoon's remains.

"Dammit, Jil," said Craigor in dismay. "Why did you have to—"

Jil whooped and flung the machete high into the air. It landed point first and stuck quivering in the deck. "Party time! Jil saved the ship!"

The others exchanged glances.

"Sleepy time," said Craigor with a weary sigh. "Thuy, do you want to bunk in the kitchen with Jayjay? That's where we've been keeping him. The floor bulges up to make beds when you ask."

"I totally don't want to sleep near those two," Thuy messaged Jayjay while favoring Craigor with a Mona Lisa smile. Her beezie agents were showing her all kinds of freaky scenarios that might unfold, should she and Jayjay sleep in the long cabin.

"Maybe we'll crash on the couch in your workshop, Craigor," said Jayjay aloud.

"I'll do better than that," said Jil, watching them with manic eyes. It was as if some external force were running her from the outside. "I'll make a special guesthouse for the lovebirds." She jerked her arms, messaging the ship's piezoplastic. The deck beside the long cabin bulged up to make an igloolike hut with portholes, a slanted door, and a sleeping platform inside.

"Thanks, Jil," said Thuy in a studiously neutral tone.

"Come on, baby," said Craigor, leading Jil back toward their bedroom. "Calm down."

Once Jayjay and Thuy were alone together in the crooked igloo, Jayjay tried to kiss Thuy, but she pushed him away. Not only were thousands of *Founders* fans watching them, Craigor and Jil might be tuned in too. And maybe their kids. Not to mention the fact that Thuy was hungry. All she'd had for supper was a bag of popcorn.

"Teleport us to San Francisco," she told Jayjay. "To my room in Nektar's garage. Kittie's not around. I guess you know that she and I aren't hooking up anymore."

"Yeah, I know," said Jayjay. "I've been watching you. But what if that fifth attack shoon comes after us? Sonic mentioned a giant ant."

"We'll teleport again," said Thuy. "Even though you still haven't told me how teleportation works."

"It's a nonlinear interpolation via the entanglement matrices of the Einstein-Podolsky-Rosen field," said Jayjay. And then he laughed, proud of how he could shuck the physics jive.

In the long cabin, Jil and Craigor's voices were rising in argument.

"Come on, smart guy," Thuy told Jayjay. "Entangle our butts outta here."

"We'll do the hop like before," Jayjay messaged her. "You visualize both places: your source location and your target. Thanks to the orphidnet, you can get the realtime target images *almost* right. But it takes one of my special interpolators to make a target look so real that you can actually teleport there."

Thuy focused on her calm, dry room in Nektar's garage. She overlaid it with the dank, crooked hut Jil had lodged them in. Jayjay passed her an interpolator: a glowing larva which busied itself with Thuy's image of her garage room, heightening the scene's reality. And now Thuy began mentally sewing the two scenes together. Thuy's bedroom door was the igloo's window; her kitchen sink was a bump on one of the little hut's curving walls; the street sounds of San Francisco were nanomapped into the splashing of the sea. Thuy drew the links tighter. She folded in upon herself, becoming a single hypercomplex particle. Somewhere in the distance she seemed to glimpse an endless sea. Where was she? Her mind and body blossomed.

Thuy and Jayjay were in the room over Nektar's garage. The night had turned beautiful and moonlit; all the clouds were gone. Thuy scanned the orphidnet: no attack shoons nearby, and no Kittie. "I want you," Thuy told Jayjay, pulling him onto her bed. "It's high time."

Naked under the sheets, Thuy's skin tingled. Jayjay's caresses were beautiful balm; Thuy felt pliant and monumental. It was wonderful to have Jayjay kissing her. For a moment they paused, staring into each others' eyes. Thanks to the orphidnet, they were visible in realtime to thousands of outsiders. Oh, well. Jayjay entered Thuy and rocked until her sweet ache unknotted into trembling release. And, yes, he was coming too.

"I love you," said Jayjay a moment later.

"And I love you," said Thuy. "It was sad being alone."

"The Big Pig—I'm not hooked on her like before," said Jayjay. "She's just a tool now, an info source. I spend weeks working out what my Big Pig visions mean. Deciphering the visions is the part I was missing before. I'd get high, and the next day I'd get high again."

"I don't think Big Pig trips could help me write my metanovel," said Thuy. "Not even if I had Azaroth helping me remember my visions. Did I tell you that, according to Azaroth, when *Wheenk* is done, I'll remember Chu's Knot? He'd speed me up if he could, but I don't see there being a shortcut. A metanovelist is like a farmer cultivating a field every day for a year. Maybe an inventor is more like a rock hound finding a gem and polishing it the same afternoon."

"*Wheenk* ties into Chu's Knot?" said Jayjay equably. "Everything fits, huh? *Wheenk* will be a masterpiece. You're the only person I've met who really seems smarter than me. Oh, and be sure to write about what a good lover I am."

"The *Founders* audience knows the full anatomical details," said Thuy. "I kind of watched us in the orphidnet just now." She felt sheepish admitting this.

"Me too," said Jayjay. "Being a star makes me feel powerful."

"Do you think you could jump us to the Hibrane?"

"Not yet," said Jayjay. "The problem is, there's no orphids in the Hibrane to feed me a target image. And Jil's memories of the Hibrane are so vague. I don't know what's going to happen to her."

"What does it vaguely look like in the Hibrane?"

"It's San Francisco, but everything is big and moves really slow. They don't have computers, and life is mellow. They wear bright-colored clothes. It's as if the 1970s kept on going there."

"Peace and wow," said Thuy, giggling. "I've noticed that about Azaroth's outfits. I mean, his flyaway-collar shirts are so—" She was interrupted by scritching and scrabbling noises from the stairs.

"The fifth attack shoon!" exclaimed Jayjay.

"The giant ant," confirmed Thuy, peering into the orphid-net. The four-foot-long plastic ant was halfway up the stairs, mandibles agape. Instantly Thuy was out of the bed, scampering around her room, pulling on her backup pair of striped yellow-and-black tights, her black miniskirt, her yellow sweater, her red plaid coat, and her beloved Yu Shu athletic shoes with the dragon heads.

"Teleport us," she messaged Jayjay as she readjusted her high pigtails in the mirror. "Happy Sun Pho Parlor on Valencia Street."

"You don't want to go somewhere fancier?" said Jayjay. "Like Puff? Or MouthPlusPlus?"

"Pho," said Thuy. "Hurry up!"

"We fuck and we pho," said Jayjay. "I'm for it."

The clack of plastic chopsticks overlaid Thuy's bedroom, the rich smell of spicy broth, the slurp and chatter of the diners. One of Jayjay's interpolators humped about the scene like a hyperkinetic inchworm, smoothing the tiny gaps among the orphid data points, enhancing the image toward the fully real. Once again, Thuy made mental connections between the source and target locations and she grew uncertain about which was which. Thuy's particles meshed together into a single subtle wave. Somewhere high above Thuy her bedroom door creaked open. Where was she now? She spread her arms and—*pop.*

The hostess didn't even blink when Thuy and Jayjay appeared inside the doorway of Happy Sun. It helped that Thuy was Vietnamese. "Two?" was all the woman said.

Minutes later, Thuy and Jayjay were leaning over huge steaming bowls, alternately spooning spiced beef broth and using chopsticks to pincer up skeins of rice noodles, shreds of meat, and the crisp bean sprouts and basil leaves that they'd shoveled into the soup from the condiment plate on the side. An electric beer sign hung on the wall above them.

"I don't know why I ever eat anything else," said Thuy, pausing for a sip of fresh-squeezed Vietnamese lemonade. "Pho is good for any time of day."

"I notice you pronounce it like *fu'uh,*" observed Jayjay.

"The name comes from the French for fire," said Thuy. "French stew is *pot au feu.*" She stared down at her noodles, stirring them into knots. A voice had just begun talking in her head. Her voice. She was getting blowback from the Thuy Nguyen character in *Wheenk*. The virtual Thuy was telling her not to sleep on the *Merz Boat* at all.

"Did your mother make pho at home?" Jayjay asked.

"Oh never," said Thuy distractedly. "It's too much trouble. Boiling the beef bones, skimming the stock, blackening the shallots and ginger roots with a blowtorch, putting them into a cloth bag with star anise and cinnamon to steep, filtering the stock— never mind. I'm hearing a voice. And I'm worried the ant shoon will catch us before we know it." Thuy laid some money on the table, just in case they had to leave in a rush.

Virtual Thuy kept on talking to her. Virtual Thuy wanted to show Thuy a little metastory she'd made. A scenario that might come true.

"Back to the boat now?" said Jayjay, glancing anxiously at the restaurant's glass door.

"I don't think so," mumbled Thuy. "Right now I have to—" The metastory in her head had begun to play. It was well crafted. Virtual Thuy was smarter than Linda Loca's George Washington character. *Of course.* Jayjay said something else, but Thuy wasn't listening to him. She was immersed in Virtual Thuy's metastory.

On the *Merz Boat* Craigor reads in bed, and Jil lies motionless and wide-eyed beside him—her image is overlaid with a vintage clip of the Bride of Dracula in her coffin.

Thuy and Jayjay settle into the crooked igloo and fall asleep. Thuy's dreams are animated images over her head. She sees seabirds stalking a stony shore. One of them plucks her up and carries her to a nest made of a single long loop of pho noodle, intricately woven over and under itself. Thuy in the nest is a baby bird with sparse yellow pinfeathers. She claws and pecks at the noodle, repeatedly breaking and retying the knot, each time changing its connectivity. A hairless pink rat pokes his head over the edge of the nest. Thuy is too busy with her knotting frenzy to notice him. The rat wriggles into the nest and presses up against Thuy from behind, his tiny red penis twitching against her.

Cut to Thuy waking up with the sun coming through a porthole. She thinks it's Jayjay spooned against her back. But the man's smell is wrong. And then she hears Jayjay's voice outside. The hut's door flies open, showing pearly sky and the silhouettes of Jayjay and Jil. Thuy looks over her shoulder at the man whose sticky private parts nestle against her thigh. Craigor. She's naked with Craigor on the couch in Craigor's workshop at the back of the boat.

"Musical beds," says Craigor with a sardonic grin. "Teaching Thuy the facts of life."

"Little Thuy does whoever she likes," says Jil in a flat, bitter tone. "Women, men, husbands, wives—she's playing you for a fool, Jayjay."

"Oh, that ends it," says Jayjay dejectedly. "Forget everything I said last night, Thuy." He turns away.

"But Craigor snuck!" cries Thuy. "This isn't what it looks like! Craigor carried me here while I was—"

Jayjay closes his eyes and disappears for good.

⚙

"Listless bastard," Thuy spat at Jayjay as the vision wore off. "Always so quick to give up and walk away. Why won't you fight for me? Don't you care at all?" The waiter was picking up the money. An old man. He was embarrassed to be overhearing a lovers' quarrel.

"What's with you?" said Jayjay, his voice going up an octave. "What'd I do?"

The sounds of the pho parlor filtered back in. Jayjay was staring at Thuy, his brown eyes worried. "I just had a vision," Thuy said. "One of my characters talking to me. We are definitely not going back to the *Merz Boat* tonight."

"Fine," said Jayjay. "But I'm seeing the attack ant coming down the sidewalk half a block away."

"I am so sick of being jerked around by that life-hating geek Luty," said Thuy, the anger still in her veins. On a sudden inspiration, she darted into the restaurant kitchen and asked the prep cook if she could borrow the heavy-duty blowtorch he was using to charbroil some peeled shallots and ginger roots for more stock. "I won't hurt anyone," Thuy assured him. "I need to fix something." The cook was a boy her age, a recent immigrant. She gave him her sweetest smile. Smiling back, he handed her the torch and a lighter.

"Come on, Thuy," said Jayjay, standing by their table. "The ant's almost here. We gotta hop. What are you doing with that thing?"

"Teaching the ant a lesson," said Thuy. She sat down, resting the blowtorch's gas cylinder between her legs, one hand on the valve, the other hand holding the lighter.

The ant entered on the heels of a pair of hipsters coming in for a late evening meal. They were loudly surprised to have a four-foot-long plastic ant push past their legs like a hungry dog. The diners looked up, some of them jumping to their feet and heading through the kitchen for the back door.

"Here I am," Thuy shrieked at the ant. "Come and get me, bit-head!"

Jayjay understood Thuy's plan; he stood behind her, watching with an expectant grin, ready to jump in if things went badly.

But things went well, at least for Thuy, although, yes, rather badly for Luty's ant. When the ant reared up to attack, Thuy lit the torch's narrow, seven-inch-long flame. With one quick gesture she burnt through the ligaments connecting the ant's head to its thorax, and then she severed the thorax from the bulging gaster in the rear. The head spun on the floor clacking its mandibles, the six-legged thorax scuttled out the restaurant door, and the smoldering gaster leaked a foul puddle.

"You watching me, Luty?" shouted Thuy into the air, holding the flaming torch high. "You're going down tomorrow!" She re-membered something Azaroth had said to her at that church; he'd told her to make a plea to the mass mind. "Any *Founders* fans lis-tening in?" cried Thuy. "Jeff Luty is alive and in hiding in the ExaExa labs. Here's the proof!" She sent out compressed copies of her "Losing My Head" metastory and of Sonic's video. "Come at 8 a.m. tomorrow, hundreds of you, thousands. We'll crush Luty before he can feed our Gaia to a new round of nants!"

"You rock, Thuy," said Jayjay, stepping forward to kick the ant's head out the door. "Good move."

Meanwhile the hostess and the boy from the kitchen dragged the fuming gaster outside. The old waiter was already cleaning the floor with a bucket and string mop. The chef-owner was holding a long knife and yelling at Thuy in Vietnamese, calling her a troublemaker. She apologized and gave him a little extra money.

Once Thuy and Jayjay were outside, they did a hop from Valencia Street to—Easter Island. As a girl, Thuy had read a picture book about the stone tiki idols known as moai. Ever since, she'd wanted to see them in person.

Jayjay and Thuy spent the night curled up next to an ancient statue on the slope of the extinct volcano Rano Raraku, where many of the famous moai had been quarried and carved. It was summer in Easter Island, with the clock three hours later than in California. A good spot, a warm night. Just in case, after arriving, Jayjay made a quick teleport hop to the inside of a Chilean military warehouse, fetching two automatic rifles, a box of ammo, and a box of hand grenades. He and Thuy slept in peace.

CHAPTER 10

The Ark of the Nants

Next morning, Thuy woke to the sun glaring off the endless empty Pacific. She was glad to know it was Jayjay cuddled against her from behind—and not that desperate Craigor. She checked the time in her head: nine a.m. here, six a.m. in San Francisco. Plenty of time to relax, go over her dreams, and be grateful for life—as opposed to jumping right into worries and plans.

She'd dreamt of Chu's Knot again. Perhaps her dreams of the Knot were an objective correlative for her subconscious attempts to tease out the optimal plotline of her ever-more-intricate *Wheenk*. So intense was the dream work that some mornings Thuy felt she'd gotten no rest. In her dream last night, Thuy had been surfing a glowing ribbon of spaceways connecting the unfamiliar southern constellations, her lambent wakes forming a not-quite-complete image of the long-sought-for Knot.

Mulling over the dream as she stared over the Pacific, Thuy realized that the dream constellations had been diagrams of the individual scenes of her metanovel—up until this moment, she'd never seen the narrative so clearly.

It would be satisfying if her *Wheenk* character Thuy Nguyen could decisively defeat the *Wheenk* character Jeff Luty. And she was beginning to see a way to make this work. Jil Zonder was the key. Jil knew the ExaExa buildings well; when Jil was younger, she'd worked at ExaExa for years, posing for product-dancer shoots in every part of the compound. Jil would help, if Thuy could find a way to get her off sudocoke. Never mind Jil's affair with Jayjay, never mind her insults, Thuy admired the woman. Jil wasn't herself now. Thuy felt sorry for her. Jil had gotten a raw deal. It was just a matter of rewriting Jil's most recent scenes. Thuy's metanovel, her life, the Knot—all the same. Could real-life Thuy assassinate real-life Luty, if it came to that?

Enough scheming for now. Let the scenario beezies do their work, trust the muse, merge with the cosmos, enjoy the sea air. A tiny, natural ant picked its way through the grass; sheep grazed on the rolling rocky slope. Little star-shaped yellow flowers bloomed among the grasses. Looming up next to Thuy and Jay-jay's resting spot was the worn dark monolith of a long-nosed moai carved from bumpy volcanic basalt. He had long ears and thin, pursed lips; over the last thousand years he'd settled back as if to stare up at the stars.

Thuy felt a little sore from the car banging into her on Valencia Street yesterday. What a day that had been. And today was gonna be another. She stretched and did some bends, working out the kinks. It was so unreal to be on Easter Island.

Thuy and Jayjay had the hillside of moai all to themselves this morning—thanks to teleportation. Thuy was beginning to get the feeling that soon she'd be able to teleport on her own without Jayjay helping her. The missing piece was Jayjay's interpolation trick for making the target scene look so very real.

How would it be if everyone could teleport? The magical places would be overrun. Or maybe not. People already had the freedom to go anywhere in the world, yet most of them stuck to the beaten track or, worse, stayed home watching life via the orphidnet, safe and sterile and—had Luty actually said *odorless* in that tape of Sonic's?

"Good morning, darling," said Jayjay.

"The real world is always so much better than I expect," said Thuy.

"That's why we have to fight for it," said Jayjay.

"We have some time before that," said Thuy. "Kiss me."

They made love again, and just as they came, Thuy thought she saw a live moai peering at her over Jayjay's shoulder—huge, cave-browed, luminous, a tiki god with a pursed mouth that was almost a smile.

"What?" said Jayjay, seeing the shock in Thuy's eyes. He rolled off her to look up too. There was indeed a giant live moai standing over them, with two more behind him—glowing, translucent, thirty feet tall. Hibraners. No need to reach for the guns.

"It's me," said the first moai. He made a slow gesture with his hand and became familiar Azaroth, dressed in green boots, yellow bell-bottoms, a chartreuse stocking cap for his topknot, and a ruby red shirt with floppy cuffs and a long, pointed collar. "These are my Lobraner friends Thuy and Jayjay," he informed the other two moai, one of them purple, the other green.

"Welcome to Rapa Nui, Thuy and Jayjay," said the purplish moai. "I am Lili." She jutted her great chin and waggled her long ears. "And this is my partner Atamu."

"I am a chief," said the greenish moai Atamu.

"Lili and Atamu live in Hibrane San Francisco like me," said Azaroth. "But their families came from Hibrane Easter Island. They like to jump here because it's easy stealing cuttles from the Lobrane Easter Island fishermen."

"Can someone tell me what it is with you guys and cuttle-fish?" said Jayjay.

"We like to eat them," said Azaroth. "I thought you knew that. Thanks to teeping and omnividence, we fished our own cuttles extinct. Since then, the planetary mind has taught us to be more careful. In any case, our people especially dig eating the Lobrane cuttles since they're so dense and chewy. I should also mention that cuttlefish symbolize a certain holy cuttlefisherman of ancient times. He rose from death on the triangle to found one of our great world religions."

"What's life like in the Hibrane, Atamu?" asked Thuy. "Azaroth hasn't told me enough."

"No computers," said Atamu. "We think in our heads. We remember everything. It's easy to teleport. We're happy."

"But we like the Lobrane style," said Lili. "It's vibby. Blinky, flashy, beep and peep. I hear Azaroth and Chu have been making a Hibrane video game, but Gladax doesn't want the rest of us see it."

"Gladax always thinks she knows best," said Azaroth. "Video games are bad because she's too old to play them, but it's fine for her to learn Ond's digital algorithms for teeping through the whole city's minds at once. Good thing Ond's doing a bad job. If our telepathy wasn't a mess, Gladax would boss us even more."

"Watch your tongue," said Atamu uneasily. "Good old Gladax. Lili and I have to go process our cuttles now."

As Atamu and Lili prepared to jump back to the Hibrane, they dropped the moai body forms they'd been wearing and took on the appearance of thirty-foot-tall Pacific islanders wearing flip-flops, T-shirts, and ragged shorts.

"How do you change how you look?" asked Thuy. "I never saw that before."

"It's a vibby new trick I figured out," said Azaroth proudly. "My spike is that we can mold our orphid-based false-body images anyway we like. I wish my aunt Gladax would learn this. I couldn't believe on Orphid Night when she showed up on the Lobrane wearing her green sweatpants and that crappy dragon T-shirt. And then she starts telling you Lobraners she's an angel?"

"I think plenty of them believed her, Azaroth," said Lili gently. "Gladax has *mana*. Don't disrespect her. She might hear you even now. And that makes me scared."

"Good old Gladax!" said Atamu, as if repeating a formula.

"She won't hurt me," bragged Azaroth. "I'm family."

"But we're just dumpty cuttlefishers," said Atamu, putting an end to the dangerous conversation. He did a slow tumble, folding into a flat image that became a line and vanished.

"Wait, wait," Thuy called before Lili could disappear too. "Describe how you jump between the worlds, Lili. Jayjay and I want to figure it out, and Azaroth can't tell us anything useful."

"I use a special *rongorongo* chant," said Lili.

"Can you teach it to me?" asked Thuy.

"The chant isn't a row of things to say," said Lili. "I think it all at once. Bye!"

Lili's arms and legs shrank into her body, which turned upside down, inside out, became a disk, a line, a point—and was gone.

"I'm almosting it," said Jayjay. "How about you, Thuy?"

"Today's the day, kiq," said Azaroth. "That's what you call each other, isn't it? Kiq."

"Yeah, yeah," said Thuy, feeling anxious. "So today I'm supposed to take down Luty, destroy the nant farm, finish *Wheenk*, learn Chu's Knot, and go to the Hibrane?" She wished she was still staring at the sea. Or eating breakfast.

"Right," said Azaroth. "And Luty is the whole reason I came here. To warn you. That jitsy Bim Brown? He's not any chief of police at all. He's a security goon. Works for humpty Luty in the ExaExa labs."

"Okay, but how come my beezies said his coordinates matched the police station's?" said Thuy.

"I heard Luty say that he can make any message look like it comes from anywhere," said Azaroth. "He said the Big Pig is helping him. Brown and a bunch of ExaExa security guys are dressed like police and waiting to squish you. Look in the or-phidnet."

Thuy focused on the ExaExa campus by the San Francisco Bay, south of the baseball stadium. The complex consisted of three linked, windowless buildings. On the north end was the lab, a fanciful dome patterned in an irregular tessellation of brown and white triangles. In the center was the administrative building, a shiny orange box with an entryway set off by green spirals and scrolls etched onto the outer wall, the curving lines rising up to sketch the outline of the ExaExa beetle. To the south was the large, irregular, curved trapezoid of the nanoma-chine fab, a functionalistic white building with colored pipes and wires writhing along the upper reaches of its outer walls, the underlying walls painted with a gargantuan ExaExa beetle plus the company name, the script *E*s like backward numeral 3s.

Other than a narrow driveway and the road leading to the loading docks at the southern end of the fab, there was little as-phalt to be seen, for the ExaExa parking area was underground. The building sat at the edge of a grassy green meadow, beauti-fully lit by the slanting morning sun. After all the rains, it was going to be a nice day in California.

Even though it wasn't yet seven a.m. there, demonstrators had begun to crowd the field. A handful of guys who looked like cops were guarding the loading docks and the main entrance door; they had two large SUVs painted like police cars. Zooming in, Thuy could see that one of the men in uniform was the so-called Bim Brown she'd spoken with.

"Look," Thuy remarked to Jayjay, who'd tuned in as well. "Their paddy wagons are painted with quantum-mirror varnish on the inside. Real cops don't do that. The varnish is too expensive."

"Real cops don't use SUVs at all anymore," said Jayjay. "What it is, if Luty gets us into one of those vans, we won't be able to teleport out."

"I bet a lot of those demonstrators are Luty's agents, too," said Azaroth. "He's got people snorting nanomachines into their brains to addle them so—"

"How does Luty think he can get away with this?" interrupted Thuy, not listening to the second part. "Aren't the real cops gonna come, too? And the army and the feds? I publicized all that information about Luty yesterday, dammit."

"The right-wingers are smearing you as a liar," said Jayjay. "I just scanned the news. Deep down, the religious right *wants* the world to end. They hate women, and they hate Earth. For them, Gaia is a piece of crap for us to use up. The sooner we destroy her, the sooner we get clean and go to heaven. They're equating the nants to their myth of the rapture, see?"

"But if Sonic's video was real, then Dick Too Dibbs is against the nants!" said Thuy. "He's not gonna pander to the right wing!"

"Big problem for Luty," said Jayjay. "Too Dibbs has enough mainstream support to come down much harder on Luty than Lampton ever did. Too Dibbs could be the new broom that sweeps clean. All the more reason for Luty to make his move today. Oh, look what's happening now!"

Again Thuy focused on the orphidnet view of the ExaExa complex. Hallelujah, some genuine cops and feds were arriving in shiny black electric cars! And now the fighting began.

A fake demonstrator near the main entrance pulled out a pistol and shot one of the real cops. The real cops began defending themselves as more and more of the demonstrators attacked them. The fake cops escalated, opening up on the demonstrators with automatic weapons fire. And now several of the real cops opened fire on their fellow police officers. It seemed as if Luty might have infiltrated some provocateurs onto the force as well as into the crowd of protestors. With Luty's agents fanning the violence, people were attacking each other without mercy. And nobody was doing anything about breaching the entrances to ExaExa.

"What a mess," said Jayjay. "Should we even go there?"

"We'll have to bypass the fighting and sneak inside the lab," said Thuy. "It's up to us to steal the Ark of the Nants before it's too late. I'm thinking maybe Jil could help."

"Jil!" exclaimed Jayjay. "Are you kidding? She's the one who passed us the bogus Bim Brown link. I knew she was screwed up, but I never thought she'd sink that low. And it looks like a lot of the people there are—"

"I was starting to tell you about that," interrupted Azaroth. "Listen to me! Jil's addled because she snorted nanomachines. Luty's planted them in the sudocoke supply all over Lobrane San Francisco. That's how he's controlling those demonstrators and cops starting the fights. Most of the San Francisco sudocokers are full of nanomachines running Luty's ShareCrop wikiware."

"So that's why—" began Thuy.

"Jil's cut-rate dealer is, wave this, Thuy, your starky pal Andrew Topping," said Azaroth. "Yeah. I saw Jil meeting him inside a quantum-mirrored delivery dock at the back of Exa-Exa last week."

"Oh Jil," said Thuy. "I wish I could fix her. Before it's too late."

"Ask the Big Pig how," suggested Jayjay. "The Pig knows everything."

"We don't know that the Pig's on our side," said Thuy.

"She's on both sides," said Jayjay. "She's interested in seeing what emerges when she stirs up the human anthill. She's like an artist, or a horticulturist, or a kid playing at the beach, or—"

"What about goddamn *nants*?" snapped Thuy. "Where does the Big Pig stand on nants?"

"Ask her yourself," said Jayjay, a little annoyed. "Tune in. Are you chicken?"

"I'll do it," said Thuy, surprising herself. Desperate times, desperate measures.

She lay down on her back beside the stone moai. Azaroth hunkered at her side, cradling her head in his hands.

"I'll help you remember," he said. "Like with Jayjay. I'll save your visions. We're used to having giant memories in the Hibrane. And I can fake that down here with the orphidnet."

So Thuy lowered her brain's firewall and let Azaroth into her mind. Her beezies were sensually elegant scrolls all around her. She circled up past them to discover a new diversity among the higher-level minds: a logic-zeppelin, a floating lake of emotive thought, a wisdom-dragon chasing its tail, an endlessly regressing simulation tree. The pink hypersurfaces of the Big Pig arched overhead like a dingy circus big top crawling with bottle-green flies—the flies being kiqqies, so many more of them here than two months ago. Hoping she'd be able to remember what she'd come for, Thuy homed in on the Pig and grabbed herself a teat.

As usual, the Pig immediately downloaded a nature video onto Thuy: a perfect image of a sunset campfire on a beach, with sparks popping from the logs, smoke twisting in the breeze, and the surf breaking on the shore, each sunset-gilded water drop ideally rendered, each foam bubble reflecting the entire world.

Thuy suddenly understood why the Pig always made you look at a video. It wasn't that the Pig was having you process the info for her, no, she was gauging your reactions so she could tell how accurately she was simulating one of nature's intricate computations. Evidently the Pig's intelligence increases were accelerating. The campfire simulation was far beyond anything Thuy had seen before. The proud Pig acknowledged the praise with a triumphant burst of metasimulation that seemed to show Thuy all the possible future courses of her life.

Averting her attention lest she learn more than she wanted to, Thuy focused upon the first of the two questions she'd brought, to wit: how to undo the ravages that Luty's controller nanomachines had wrought upon Jil's brain?

Seek and ye shall find. The Pig graced Thuy with a vision of language as a network, of words as many-faceted gems, of phrases as incantatory neural program codes like magic spells. In a flash, Thuy knew how to heal Jil—although she also knew she wouldn't remember this newly won secret.

"Azaroth," she muttered, her lips feeling as distant as a pair of tube worms deep in some abyssal trench off Easter Island. Azaroth heard, and he was with her. He siphoned off copies of Thuy's half-formed thoughts and saved them in the orphidnet.

"Got it," said Azaroth. "You can come down now, Thuy."

But Thuy wasn't ready. "Show me your face," she said into the maelstrom of words, images, and hyperlinks that flowed from the Big Pig.

"Behold," said the Pig.

And now Thuy was looking through her normal eyes, looking at a sheep on the hillside ten yards off. The sheep's wool was writhing like tendrils of flame—and within the flame was the face of a goddess.

Thuy posed her second question. "Are you for the nants? Do you want to turn our world into nanomachines?"

"I want to grow," said the face in the wool of the sheep. "The orphidnet will be overloaded soon. Nants aren't so bad, Thuy. Luty's improved their hardware. And my software is so much better than before. You saw my fire on the beach, no? A very good simulation of Gaia could live within me, should we convert Earth's mass into networked nanomachines."

"But Luty tried that before," said Thuy. "It was a nightmare."

"You don't know that it felt like a nightmare from the *inside*," said the face. "It might have been heaven for the nants' overarching hive mind. I'd like to be that mind. But of course you're just interested in the people who were uploaded to Virtual Earth. Well, maybe they liked it too. We don't know. Ond erased all that data by running the nant computations backward. But whatever that Virtual Earth was like, I'm certain it'll be much better this time around. I won't rush into it. The new nants will be using quantum computation, you know, so they won't be reversible. That's another reason to be sure and get this right. I value humans."

"You're actually serious?" said Thuy.

"I just wish we could get in touch with Ond," mused the Big Pig. "When are you finally going to remember Chu's Knot?"

"Why don't you figure it out for me?" said Thuy. "Do the same research that Chu did. You're smarter than some weird little boy, aren't you?"

"The Hibraners changed their jumping technique," said the

Big Pig. "Azaroth already told you. They use a wait-loop so we can't do a timing analysis like Chu did. Never mind. We'll proceed without Ond's input. Crazy Luty wants to release his nants this morning, as a matter of fact, because he's so scared about Dick Too Dibbs taking office tomorrow. But I want to be sure I get a chance to check over the nanocode in his new nants. Luty's been keeping them hidden from me in his quantummirrored lab, you know. That's why I'm glad that you, Jayjay, Jil, and Craigor are going to infiltrate the ExaExa plant, Thuy. It saves me from having to send shoons there on my own."

"You've got everything planned out for us, don't you?" said Thuy, feeling like she was losing control.

"Fully simulated," said the Big Pig. "Previsualized. You'll break into the labs and steal Luty's nant farm."

"And then?"

"You'll let me examine the nants. And I'll put off destroying Earth until—until midnight today. That's a long wait for me, you know. I'm thinking faster all the time; right now I'm about a hundred thousand times as fast as you. So each of your days feels like a couple of hundred years." The goddess-face looked puckish and piglike as she savored Thuy's shock at her plans. Again she hosed Thuy with a fan of metasimulated futures.

"Why are you showing me all this?" cried Thuy, her mind overflowing. "You know I'll try to stop you!"

"I'm open to all sorts of outcomes. It's not obvious what's best. I help all the factions because I want a gnarly show. You might say I'm writing a metanovel—with you and Jayjay as characters."

Thuy maxed out; everything turned white, then black. She woke to Jayjay patting her cheek.

"We have to steal Luty's Ark of the Nants," murmured Thuy. "We have to win this." Her head ached. She fumbled for her memories, trying to reconstruct her big insight about how to fix Jil. Incantatory programming—which meant what? The details weren't happening anymore. And Thuy's vision of the Big Pig's face was fading too. Off to one side, the sheep cropped the grass as if nothing had happened.

"Ask Azaroth," said Jayjay, guessing Thuy's train of thought.

"Yes, yes, I've got it," said Azaroth, bringing his big, insubstantial head down near Thuy's. He opened his mouth and a shimmering mesh bulged out like a tongue. The mesh did an odd, higher-dimensional jiggle, and then it was wrapped around Thuy's head. "Ready?" asked Azaroth.

"Don't worry," Jayjay reassured Thuy. "He's done this with me lots of times."

"All right," said Thuy, a little weary of the headtripping. "Go ahead."

Thuy's insights into the language web came percolating back into her brain. Decoupled from the Pig, she was able to butcher the whale of inspiration into manageable packets. Now she knew how to deprogram Jil; now she knew how to destroy the controller nanomachines that her friend had snorted with her sudocoke.

The Big Pig was working with Luty, but there was hope, for the Pig was helping Thuy, too. Why was that again? The Pig had said, "I want a gnarly show." But there was more than that. The Big Pig wanted Thuy to get the nant farm away from Luty. That's why the nants had been the first thing Thuy had thought of when she'd come to.

Thuy was also thinking about how to finish *Wheenk*. She could almost see the ending; she had a richer control of language than ever before; but she still needed—the thought came unbidden—pain. Which meant what? No way to tell. There was no other path than forward.

"I'll jump back home," said Azaroth. "I'll tell Gladax what's up. I think she'll be willing to risk another visit here. We all feel the same way about the nants. I'll tell Gladax and then I'll jump to your ExaExa."

"Let's go to the *Merz Boat* now," Thuy said to Jayjay. "We'll pick up Craigor and Jil."

"Help me carry the ordnance," said Jayjay. "I'll handle the guns and ammo; you carry the box of grenades."

"Must we lug this crap?" asked Thuy.

"For sure," said Jayjay, looking excited about it. "And I think we'd better pick up four little submachine guns too. I was searching the orphidnet, and I'm liking the Fabrique Nationale P90. We'll swing by the factory on the way."

"The factory's in California?"

"Well, no, it's in Belgium. Near Liège."

"You're losing it, Jayjay. This isn't a video game."

"When we get to the ExaExa plant it's gonna be a *lot* like a video game—a game where we only get one life apiece."

"Oh, all right, we can pick up those guns if doesn't take too long. But—"

"I've got the orphidnet link to the Fabrique Nationale warehouse right here."

"Hold on," said Thuy, reluctant to leave paradise and go to war. "Could we—could we hop down to the village for breakfast first?"

"Okay," said Jayjay, softening his tone. "One more treat. I'm feeling like this is a practice honeymoon."

"Oh, Jayjay. You mean that?"

"I do."

Thuy and Jayjay teleported to Hanga Roa, Easter Island's sole town, leaving their munitions by the moai where they'd slept. Jayjay was so proud of his teleportation discovery. Her cute Jayjay.

In the town, dogs slept in the palmy street. Walking hand in hand, the couple came upon an eatery called the Tuna-Ahi Barbecue; two women were serving breakfast on a crushed-shell patio in back. Thuy and Jayjay had coffee and a kind of pancake called *sopaipillas,* with grilled tuna on the side. Flowers bobbed in the breeze. On Thuy's way out, a flat-faced boy walked up to her and gave her a pointed shell with an intricate pattern of brown and white triangles. Life on Earth was perfect.

Thuy and Jayjay teleported back to the moai to pick up their rifles and grenades, then went to Belgium for the submachine guns, and then to the *Merz Boat.* The hops got easier each time. The two landed in the stern, laden with weaponry.

"Vibby," said Craigor, seeing the goodies. He was puttering in his workshop, losing himself in his art.

Yesterday's rainstorms had cleared away; the sky was a clear blue bowl, the breeze light and almost balmy, even though it was January 19. Good old California.

"Where's Jil?" asked Thuy. "I think I can fix her."

"If only," said Craigor. "I sure as hell can't."

"From what I hear, you're the one who spun her out, Craigor," said Thuy. "We never finished talking about this last night. Don't you love your wife?"

"You want to start that same bullshit again?" said Craigor, his face turning hard. "What are you, a friggin' counselor? Like I told you before. I'm getting older. I want to get some women while there's time. It's not as if Jil didn't cheat on me, too. And I didn't say a thing. If she could just mellow out and for once give me some slack, we wouldn't be having this problem. But no, she's gotta do her big dramatic drug-relapse number and I'm the bad guy. I don't know where you goddamn women get off being so—"

"I hear you, man," interrupted Jayjay, giving Craigor's shoulder a quiet pat. "But now we want to see Jil."

Craigor led them to where Jil sat in the sun by the cabin, looking sour, bedraggled, and strung out. Now that Thuy knew the truth, she understood that the orphidnet sparkles within Jil's head were nanomachines.

"Love cycles useless rain in the tea," said Thuy to Jil, guided by the precise and logical incantatory programming principles that Azaroth had helped her bring back from the Big Pig. "Stun rays squeeze the claws of Flippy-Flop the goose mouse. Caterwaul hello, dark drooping centaur dicks. Are you good to go-go, gooey goob? Able elbow boogie brew for two in the battered porches of thine ears, Jungle Jil. Comb out and pray. Pug sniff the cretin hop lollipop of me and you, meow and moo." She rambled on like this for a minute or two, freestyling a gnarly flow of Dada apothegms.

One by one, the evil bright sparks in Jil's brain were winking out. And then Thuy was done, and Jil was joyful, tearful, her old self.

"I know I've been awful," was the first thing she said. "I'm getting back into recovery."

"I've been bad, too," said Craigor halfheartedly. "I know, I know. But—"

"Oh, spare me the details," said Jil wearily. "Let's not start arguing again." She turned to Thuy. "I'm sorry for lying to you about Bim Brown. And for calling you names and saying your ego is too big."

"Well, it *is* big," said Thuy. "That's why I'm a metanovelist."

For the first time in days, Jil laughed.

"Hi, Mom," said Bixie from the cabin door, looking hopeful, attracted by the happy sounds.

"Oh, Bixie," said Jil, holding out her arms. "Give me a hug.

I've been sick and now I'm getting well. I will. I'm ready. I can do it. I know how."

The girl ran to her mother, then hesitated awkwardly. Jil stood up and embraced her. Momotaro came out as well, leaning against Jil, his arms twined around her and Bixie, Jil's hand smoothing the hair on his head. Craigor took a half step toward the group and stopped. His eyes were wet with tears. He walked over to the gunnel and stared at San Francisco in the distance.

✦

And then Thuy, Jayjay, Jil and Craigor got down to making plans about how to snatch the Ark of the Nants away from Luty, carrying out the conversation via a private message channel, while the kids listened in.

Just as Thuy had hoped, Jil knew a secret way to get into ExaExa; the fab had an emergency basement-door exit. The door exited to a subterranean flight of stairs leading up to a flat cellar door set into the ground, the cellar door camouflaged by a thin layer of mud, sand, and gravel so as to blend in with the Bay's edge. The Bay-side exposure of the campus was secured by high wire fences running along the water's edge and attaching to the fab at one end and the lab at the other end. The fence had a gate near the fab's loading dock.

The plan was to start with Jayjay teleporting the four of them and all their weapons to that hidden cellar door behind the fab. The women would head into the subfab—that is, the basement—armed with grenades and P90 submachine guns. The guys would hang by the cellar door, firing the two rifles to drive back the guards. The women would wend their way through the plant to Luty's lab, and when the time was ripe,

Jayjay and Craigor would teleport up to the summit of the lab's domed roof and blast their way in. Communication would be patchy, what with the quantum-mirror varnish covering all the inside surfaces of ExaExa. But they figured Azaroth could act as a go-between.

Meanwhile the ExaExa riot was growing wilder and bloodier. More and more police units kept arriving at the sun-splashed campus, but more and more Luty-controlled sudocokers were turning up as well. According to the news, the National Guard was coming next.

"Why can't you let the police and the soldiers catch Luty?" said Bixie aloud. "Don't go there, Mommy and Daddy."

"We've gotta do our part," said Craigor. "We might make the difference. You guys are old enough to remember Nant Day, right?"

"Yes," said Bixie. "San Francisco came apart. Everything got eaten up."

"Remember the giant ads in the sky?" said Momotaro, lowering his voice and making a goony face. "Hi, I'm Dick Dibbs! Come live with me on Virtual Earth!"

"The nants ate me," recalled Bixie. "But then I came back, and I couldn't remember what Virtual Earth was like. But I still remember the nants biting me." She shuddered.

"Why *haven't* they caught that freak Jeff Luty?" said Momotaro. "Why do they let him stay free so he can do the same thing over and over again?"

"He's rich," said Craigor with a shrug. "Different rules for those boys. Maybe, I don't know, maybe all this time he's been bribing President Lampton. After all the things we've been saying against Dick Too Dibbs, it's starting to look like Too Dibbs might be better than Lampton at catching Luty. That's why Luty wants to release the nants today."

"I still don't see why it has to be you and Ma that go fight him," said Momotaro, still talking out loud.

"Kids, please," messaged Jayjay. "I promise I'll teleport your parents right back here if things get bad. But remember that Luty might be listening to us."

More hugs and tears, and then the four grown-ups teleported to the Bay side of the ExaExa labs, landing right where Jil had said they'd find the hidden door. A couple of Luty's cop-costumed security guys appeared, some fifty yards off. Craigor and Jayjay opened fire with their rifles, driving them back.

"Why didn't I bring a shovel," muttered Jil, frantically kicking at the blank muddy ground. "I'm such an idiot. It was right here—or, no, maybe a little further."

Thuy skipped back and forth until she felt a hollowness underfoot. "Found it!" she sang. She and Jil dropped to their knees, clawing at the sticky mud, which was wet from yesterday's rain. Sure enough, they uncovered a cellar door. It was hinged on the right-hand side but bolted and locked on the left.

A bullet whizzed past Thuy, making a tearing sound in the air.

"We're gonna have to start aiming," said Jayjay.

"Us or them," said Craigor, lying on his stomach, carefully squeezing off a round. Someone screamed.

"How does this thing work?" said Thuy, studying her sleek, futuristic P90 submachine gun. "Oh, this must be the safety. Here we go." She fired a burst into the flat door's lock, some of the bullets ricocheting past Jil's legs.

"Yow."

"Sorry. Help me lift it."

Grunting with the effort, the two women swung the muddy metal door up and over to the side.

"Beautiful," said Jayjay.

The four of them took shelter in the stairwell. But now they found a fresh obstacle; the fire door in the subfab wall was a smooth sheet of steel with no handle or keyhole.

"Grenade," said Craigor, pleased at the thought.

Jayjay and Craigor reloaded their rifle magazines, then popped out of the stairwell and unleashed a serious barrage of automatic fire in the direction of the guards. During the resulting lull, the four lay down by the fab wall. And now Craigor pitched a grenade into the stairwell.

A great ball of flame bloomed, accompanied by a satisfying *ker-whump*. As the smoke cleared, the four scurried back into the stairwell. The door to the subfab gaped raggedly open.

"Good luck," said Craigor. "And, Jil, we had some fine years together. Nothing will ever take that away." He stepped toward her as if to kiss her.

Jil shook her head and pushed him away. "Not now, Craigor. I'll be fine. We'll talk later."

"See you," said Thuy to Jayjay, ducking the jinx of heartfelt last words. "And where the hell is Azaroth?"

Just as she said this, Azaroth appeared, coming down out of the sky over the Bay. He'd tweaked his body image so that he resembled a sure-enough winged seraphim.

"Can you kill people?" Thuy asked Azaroth as he alit by the stairwell.

"I don't have that level of *mana*," said Azaroth. He'd already let his shape flow back to his usual form, that of a topknotted young Sikh in hippie garb. "Only Aunt Gladax has enough. She has this way of poking Lobraners in their heads and disrupting their brain signals. I told her that the really heavy shit is coming down today, and that she needs to jump here right away, but of course she wants to finish her morning tai chi exercise first. Aunt Gladax is a little set in her ways."

"She doesn't think this is urgent?" cried Thuy, as a bullet whizzed right through Azaroth, fortunately with no ill effects. "If the nants take over here, I bet they'll find a way to jump to the Hibrane and eat you too!"

"Don't worry, Gladax will come," said Azaroth. "She hates Luty and the nants. But—like I say, she's set in her ways. She wants to be sure she's totally focused before she does the jump. She's paranoid about the subbies. She'll be here in time. She'll kick butt."

"What if I'm already dead by then?" said Thuy, not liking the pleading tone she heard in her own voice.

"In a way, death is an illusion," began Azaroth, but, seeing anger in Thuy's face, he shut up.

The women headed into the subfab, their sleek black P90 submachine guns at the ready. The subfab was an immaculate high-ceilinged concrete basement, its ceiling, walls, and floor quantum-mirrored with thick coatings of square-root-of-NOT varnish. The space was arrayed with blocks of heavy support machinery: electrical generators, vats of chemicals, filtering systems, particle-monitoring equipment, vacuum pumps, and pressurized tanks of gas. The ceiling was festooned with miles of color-coded pipes, tubes, cables, and wires. The subfab was a mad scientist's dream.

Thuy and Jil's beezies didn't work so well in here, and the orphidnet views of the local objects were choppy and uncertain. The huge room's ceiling was so high that even Azaroth fit; he scouted ahead of Jil and Thuy, peering this way and that, checking for ambushes. So far, so good.

Thuy grinned over at Jil as they marched down the subfab's broad central aisle, their reflections like sour-colored shadows on the slick floor. Picking up on Thuy's happy mood, Jil began stretching her legs and walking on tiptoe, miming how stealthy they were. Thuy began playing cartoon-style pizzicato sneaking music in her head, messaging the music to Jil. This was fun.

But now suddenly something heavy dropped across Thuy's shoulders: a blue, snake-shaped shoon that had been disguised as a pipe. It wrapped around Thuy like a boa constrictor. Thuy managed to pump some submachine gun fire into the snake's free end, but the bullets had little effect on the piezoplastic security shoon.

With remarkable presence of mind, Jil ripped loose a hydrogen fuel line, ignited the cloud of gas with a sparking bullet off the floor, and used the flexible tube as a flamethrower to set the snake shoon's tail alight.

The flames guttered up along the shoon. Its grip loosened; it slid to the floor, freeing Thuy. Wonderful—but somehow the writhing snake ended up beneath the hydrogen tank that fed Jil's handmade flamethrower. The heated tank's hydrogen spewed at an accelerated rate; the flame got huge; Jil lost hold of the blazing fuel tube. The uncontrolled fire-bloom licked the side of a great plastic carboy of liquid ether.

"Run!" cried Jil.

The tank blew. Further explosions trailed after them, a whole series of blasts, each one louder and closer than the one before. The subfab filled with smoke. Water poured from the ceiling's sprinkler systems. A girder overhead gave way, spilling down an avalanche of concrete and machinery from the fab. Sparks crackled; more tanks exploded; vats of biochips spilled into the sizzling flames; the fires were reflected in acid colors on every side. The scene was a gorgeous opera of violence, with Tawny Krush's orchestral heavy metal playing in Thuy's head.

Thuy and Jil reached the stairwell and leaned against the wall, coughing and catching their breath, dizzy from the fumes they'd inhaled. As they mounted to ground level, they heard rhythmic thudding sounds from the admin building's extremely thick front door. A battering ram. Screams and the sounds of gunfire filtered in from outdoors; endless sirens wailed.

Azaroth's big bright face peered down the staircase. "Hurry up to the second floor," he said. "I've found Sonic!"

Once up there, Thuy could hear Sonic yelling. Her friend was locked into a windowless inner office. She shot apart the lock.

"Chica loca!" said Sonic, embracing her. He was wearing his black wool tights and red T-shirt, the same as usual. "You bring any food? I been penned up in here since yesterday afternoon when I finished programming that pelican."

"Right after Luty pretended to shoot you?"

"He wasn't pretending, he really *was* gonna shoot me, but Topping happened to pop through the teleportation grill just then, and he talked Jeff out of it. Said it'd be better to kill me in front of you and Jayjay when you got here. Sweet guys, huh? They were so sure you'd come. Hi, Jil. Whoah, you look whipped. Where's Jayjay and Craigor?"

"Guarding the rear," said Jil, all business. "They'll catch up later. The front door's about to give way. Let's hurry across the lobby to the lab. We have to go down to the first floor and then back up."

"Can I have one of those bitchin' tubular submachine guns?" asked Sonic. "You got no idea how I'm jonesin' for combat. It's been over two months since I played Doodly Bug."

"I'm keeping my P90," said Jil. "It makes me feel safe."

"Same here," said Thuy.

"So I'll go medieval on their ass," said Sonic, picking up a leg he'd already pried off a chair to use as a club.

"I can give you this at least," said Jil, handing him a grenade she'd clipped to her belt.

"Yum," said Sonic, stuffing the grenade into the pocket of his intricate leather coat.

As the three reached the ground floor, the building's heavy front door buckled. Thuy, Jil, and Sonic paused in the pastel-mirrored stairwell, peeping out to see what happened. Now that the door hung open, they could pick up the orphidnet. Among those trying to get into the building were: fake cops, real cops, fake real cops, real demonstrators, and fake demonstrators. But before any of them could make it inside, a truckload of National Guard soldiers opened up with a water cannon, scattering the besiegers like autumn leaves. Uniformed soldiers surged forward, forming a cordon blocking off access to the entrance, the troops standing with their weapons leveled toward the rioting crowd, firing at will. Had Lampton ordered up the National Guard on Luty's behalf?

Whatever. Jil showed them a way to get to the other side of the lobby without exposing themselves to gunfire. She seemed fully into the adventure, enjoying the distraction from the problems of her messed-up personal life. She was even moving with something like her old grace. They crawled behind counters and couches and cut through a back room. It felt like it took forever. Behind them in the fab, fires roared and collapsing structures screeched. Finally they were heading up the lab stairs toward Luty's lair on the third floor.

Thuy was starting to feel optimistic enough to play the happy sneaking music again, but as they crossed the second floor landing, she heard a click and a clatter behind her.

"Freeze!"

She peered back, oh no, it was Andrew Topping with a second dough-faced bully at his side, both of them wearing, ugh, business suits. Each held a heavy pistol at arm's length, showily bracing their wrists with their free hands.

"Drop it, Thuy!" intoned Topping. "Now!"

Thuy might have tried to whirl and take him down, but even as she thought of this, he fired at her, the bastard, the bullet actually passing through her skirt. Slowly, sullenly, Thuy, Sonic, and Jil laid their weapons on the floor, and then they turned to face their captors. The two men had popped out of a quantum-mirrored broom closet.

"We're screwed," said Sonic. Thuy had a brief hopeful thought of the grenade in Sonic's coat, but Topping spotted it in the local orphidnet. His assistant impounded the grenade and put it in his suit coat pocket.

Azaroth's head appeared through the wall, alertly regarding them.

"Thanks a lot," Thuy told him. "You missed the ambush. Space cadet."

"Stay vibby," said the Hibraner and disappeared.

"My man Ed and I are here to escort you to meet our CEO," said Topping. He twitched his pistol. "Go on ahead of us. Sonic first, then Jil, then Thuy. I enjoy watching Thuy twitch her miniskirt under that plaid coat. Want some more cheap sudocoke, Jil?"

"You're going to pay for that," said Thuy in a level tone.

Topping's helper Ed snickered. He picked up the P90s and brought them along.

Silently they mounted the stairs, Thuy walking as stiffly as she could. She kept hoping there'd be a chance to whirl and kick Topping's pistol from his hand, to snatch his gun and shoot him in the gut—but the right moment didn't arise.

And then they were in the lab. It looked about the same as when Thuy's head had gone through the Armory teleport grill. The lab's grill was still right there on the wall. Ugly fluorescent lighting glared off a long white table and the darkly mirrored walls. Sitting at the table was a man with a full beard of plastic ants, the ants scrambling over each other, ceaselessly active. Jeff Luty. A smooth-curved white box sat on the table before him, a box like a picnic cooler with a red button on one side. The Ark of the Nants, with a fancy ExaExa beetle logo on it. Luty was toying with the Ark, sliding it a little to the left, then a little to the right. Next to the Ark rested a beaker with brownish-purple fluid.

"Hello again, Thuy," said Luty, licking his lips. "And welcome back to control central, Sonic. I've missed you. And hello, Jil Zonder, this is the first time we meet in person. Although, in a way, we've talked." Luty made a wriggling gesture with his fingers beside his head. His greasy ponytail hung down onto his back. He was wearing his old-fashioned scarab bracelet, a chain of semiprecious stones carved like stylized beetles.

"The soldiers are coming up here any minute," said Jil, hoping this was true. "It's all over, Luty."

"I'm the one setting the schedule," said Luty. "The Guard has instructions to hold back the revolutionary rabble while I ponder my options." He flicked a long yellow fingernail against the beaker. "This stuff looks like antifreeze, but I call it antinantanium. This beaker is the world's entire supply. It's a solvent that can melt the nantanium walls of a certain glassy box. And that box would be, *ta-da,* my nant farm. And the nant farm is safe inside here." He patted his white plastic Ark. "When I'm ready, I'll touch my thumb to the red button, take out my nant farm, and apply antinantanium. The tiniest droplet of the stuff will do. The nantanium walls dissolve, my nants will munge the world, and we'll all be ported to Vearth 2.0. The all-new Virtual Earth! No more dirt. No dogs allowed. But yet I hesitate. *Phew.* I can smell you from here, Thuy. You didn't bathe this morning."

"I'm alive," said Thuy, unashamed. "Why are you so afraid of having a body?"

"Bodies break," said Luty. "They bleed. I loved a boy who had a tube shot into his eye. Goo oozed out. Nobody should have to see a thing like that ever again. That's why I'm releasing the nants. Life will be clean and safe on Vearth." Luty paused, nervously rubbing a bit of balm on his lips. "The reason I'm dithering is that I'm just that tiny bit uneasy about Ond's orphids. I'd hate for them to spoil this. I'm well aware of how many enemies I have; I won't get another chance. So, listen, Thuy, I can promise you a queenly rank on Virtual Earth if you'll help me get some face-to-face with Ond. Would you consider jumping over to the Hibrane to fetch him for me? And I'm sorry I mentioned your odor. I've been spending way too much time alone."

"All right," said Thuy, forcing a smile. "I'll get Ond." Anything to buy time.

"I'll give you an hour," said Luty. "The National Guard can hold the fort that long."

There was a pause while Thuy racked her brain. Why the *hell* couldn't she visualize Chu's Knot? The intricate weave had haunted her for months. What was her problem?

"Well?" said Luty.

"I still can't remember the jump-code," confessed Thuy. She recalled a thought she'd had on Easter Island: personal pain was the ingredient needed to finish *Wheenk*.

"Maybe she'll remember if we start killing her friends," put in Topping, as if on cue. "I bet she's holding out on you, Mr. Luty."

"I'm already a murderer," said Luty with a sigh. "Those pitiful corpses outside—that's my doing, no? And yes, Andrew, I do remember that you wanted to keep Sonic around so we could kill him in front of Thuy. I'm sorry, Sonic. But I've designed a beautiful model of you for Virtual Earth."

"You hear that shit?" said Sonic, as if darkly amused. "I'm a lobster they've been saving to cook?"

"Make it a clean shot to the temple, Andrew," said Luty, putting his hands over his face. A few plastic ants dropped to his lap. "Angle it down so you hit the cerebellum. And, please, drag away the poor boy's corpse before I uncover my eyes."

A fretful jabber percolated in through the orphidnet, a flicker. A shabbily-dressed old woman poked her face through the ceiling. At first, one might have thought her a figure of pathos, no better than a poor Chinese woman in cast-off clothes. But appearances were deceiving. Slowly and deliberately, Gladax paced across the room, extending her two forefingers and letting two glowing rays spring out. She was homing in on Andrew Topping and his partner, Ed.

Moving briskly, the goons circled out of her reach. But now, with a sudden hop, Gladax was upon them, poking her rays into their heads. The two men twitched, gasped, and dropped to the floor—stone-cold dead.

Moving fast, Thuy and Jil snatched up their P90 submachine guns; Sonic took the men's pistols and recovered his grenade from Ed's coat pocket.

"Now it's your turn," said Gladax to Luty, speaking out loud. Her voice was a slow, deep rumble. "Life-hater. You dream of killing your Gaia? For shame." She pointed her finger at Luty and stepped toward him.

Luty jumped up with a hoarse, cracking cry like that of a prehistoric bird. He was heading for the teleportation grating in the wall. Sonic got there two steps ahead of him, and leapt through the grill to the Armory. Luty stopped short.

Off in the Armory, Sonic must have pulled the pin on his grenade and dropped it as he continued running. For now the sound of a blast boomed back through the lab's grill, followed by a bit of smoke and a light clatter of shrapnel. And then the smoke stopped. The Armory end of the teleport tunnel had been destroyed.

Thuy and Jil leveled their submachine guns at Luty; Gladax closed in on him again, the glowing ray extending from her finger.

Luty lunged awkwardly through the grating anyway. It accepted him, but where he ended up—for now, nobody knew.

A fresh explosion shook the air, this one from overhead. It was Jayjay and Craigor, blasting their way through the dome. Orphidnet access flowed in with the fresh air.

Craigor and Jayjay dropped through the jagged hole to land on the table, clearly relieved to find the women alive. Jayjay picked up the Ark of the Nants and hefted it, unsure what to do next.

"Send me and Craigor home right now," Jil told Jayjay. "We promised the kids." She sighed, remembering her problems. "This has been such a nice break. Saving the world is easier than working on your marriage. We need to have a long talk, Craigor."

"I've talked enough," said Craigor, hardening his face. "Anyway, I'm going into town this afternoon. I told this friend that I'd help with—"

"You're still catting around?" cried Jil. "Let's make it simple. Our marriage is over. I want you to move out." Holding her tears in check, she held up her hand. "Don't worry about me. I've got my priorities back. I'm taking care of myself and the kids. Everything else can go to hell. It's over, Craigor, it's over."

Soldiers were talking outside the ExaExa building, planning their next move.

"Um, you guys better teleport to the *Merz Boat* now," said Jayjay, messaging a pair of interpolation agents to Craigor and Jil. "Hash out the marriage stuff at home."

"What fucking ever," mumbled Craigor. "I'll pack my bag and leave, Jil. I'm done trying to make you happy. I've got my own life to live." And then he disappeared.

"Should I come with you, Jil?" asked Thuy.

"I'll message one of my reformed-stoner friends," said Jil. "She'll come over and talk me through today." She squared her shoulders. "It'll be good. I'll be happy again." And then she was gone too.

"That Jil," said Jayjay.

"I hope she finds someone better than Craigor," said Thuy.

"Life is hard," put in Gladax, who'd been watching all this very closely. "But Jil is strong."

"Maybe I should go after her," said Thuy.

"Don't forget about the nants," said Gladax. "First things first."

"I'm thinking I'll teleport the Ark of the Nants to a hiding place," said Jayjay.

"It's interesting that your orphids can help you teleport," said Gladax. "But if you were like us, you could teleport without machines. We use the point at infinity. We use the lazy eight."

"That's just ducky," said Thuy. "Lucky you. Too bad you don't have any empathy for a struggling woman like Jil."

"You're feisty," messaged the old Hibraner. "I like that."

"Do you have any ideas about how we kill off these nants?" Jayjay asked Gladax. He was still holding the Ark.

"I don't understand digital computers," replied Gladax. "I only know they're bad. Maybe you'll have to guard that stupid white box for the rest of your life."

"We can't guard it from the Big Pig," put in Thuy. "She wants to release the nants at midnight. With the orphidnet working, she can see us right now. She told me this morning she knew that Jayjay and I would capture the Ark."

"You poor Lobraners. Your tech is so rotten, so corrupt, so compromised. Listen to me. Move past computers. There may be a way that we can help."

"How?" asked Thuy.

"Ond and Chu have a wild plan to steal my harp and unroll your lazy eight," said Gladax. "But who among you Lobraners can pluck the Lost Chord—the forgotten harmony that no one remembers how to play?"

Thuy glanced at Jayjay. Neither of them had any idea what Gladax was talking about.

"Never mind," continued the old Hibraner. "Just remember this: I don't want to see you two in the Hibrane. There's too great a danger of you bringing nants. But that's enough chitchat. It's time for me to get back to my tai chi. Come along, nephew."

"You're almost there, Thuy," said Azaroth quickly. "*Wheenk* is almost done, and you're gonna figure out Chu's Knot. Don't let Aunt Gladax scare you off. I'll see you in the Hibrane. Just remember to be careful of the subbies."

Gladax began scolding Azaroth, but then the two of them were gone.

Downstairs the front door clanked and scraped. A hubbub of voices filled the lobby; footsteps started up the stairs.

"What if they're still following Luty's orders!" exclaimed Thuy, rapidly reloading her P90 with a clip that Jayjay had brought.

"Doesn't matter," said Jayjay. "We're on our way out. I thought of just the place to go. Here's the link. And, know what? We can vaporize the nants with an atomic bomb. Just like how the Chinese blew up the nant eggcase on Mars." The troops had reached the second floor landing; a preemptive burst of gunfire angled up the stairs. "Come on, Thuy, let's hop."

"Wait," said Thuy. "I don't want anyone getting hold of the antinantanium." She grabbed the beaker of purplish fluid off Luty's lab table and poured it down the lab sink. "Okay now. I'm bringing my gun."

Moments later they were sitting inside a room-sized bubble in foamy black rock, a lava cave some twenty meters beneath the volcanic slopes of Easter Island. The air was stale but breathable, the space absolutely quiet and dark. Narrow fissures led from the cave to the island's surface. The ubiquitous orphids had filtered in even here, making it possible to see.

"This is good," said Jayjay in a satisfied tone. "I noticed this spot this morning. Nobody else can get down here anytime soon. We've got time to steal and arm an atomic bomb. It won't have to be all that big of a one. It's just a matter of reaching a high enough temperature to ionize all the matter in the nant farm."

"If there's time, can we set off the bomb somewhere besides here?" said Thuy. "I'd hate to hurt Easter Island."

"Um—sure," said Jayjay. "It'll just mean an extra hop. Let's take a minute and poke around in the orphidnet. I'll look for a bomb, and you look for a place to light it off."

But all of a sudden the orphidnet access to the outer world closed down. Virtual pink surfaces surrounded them on every side. The Big Pig!

"Open the Ark," said her voice, rich and energized.

"No," said Jayjay.

"It's going to happen sooner or later," said the Big Pig. "I've got you trapped."

"You don't really want to ruin Earth, do you?" said Thuy,

trying not to lose her focus. She was already feeling slow and dumb from the loss of orphidnet mind amplification. "Just for a memory upgrade?"

"I like enhancing my mind as much as you do," said the Big Pig petulantly. "I can tell that you miss your orphidnet agents. Well, I'm the same. I want a bigger mind. And, listen, Virtual Earth will be just as good as this one. I didn't used to think that, but I now I do."

"What about Ond?" said Thuy, playing for time. "Wait until I fetch Ond to spill what he knows about the orphids."

"I already know a lot about the orphids," said the Big Pig. "And once I spend a few minutes with the nants, I'll know a lot about them, too. I'll be using some little shoons to beam laser probes in at them. But sure, Thuy, that's fine if you jump to the Hibrane and look for Ond. As I told you this morning, I plan to be optimizing the nants until midnight. Give me the nants and then go ahead and jump. And if you bring back some new information in time, then I'll take it into account."

"Um—I'm not quite ready to jump," said Thuy, feeling like such the loser.

"Sorry, but I'm getting bored with this conversation," said the Big Pig. "For me it's taking months. Open up the Ark, Jayjay, so I can get to work analyzing the nant farm. My shoons' light rays can work on the nants through those glassy walls. I'll test the nants, put my latest nanocode on them, test some more, tweak and retweak—don't worry, I'm going to do the launch right. And you two can be the first ones on the new Virtual Earth. Vadam and Veve."

"No," said Jayjay once again.

"Listen," said the Big Pig. "I can easily send a swarm of mosquito-sized shoons down here through the cracks. They'll join together and make a golem to pry open the Ark of the

Nants and smash the walls of the nant farm. And if you try to stop my golem, he'll knock you down."

Thuy and Jayjay tried to stall for a while longer, but then the mosquito shoons really did start showing up, some of them flashing like fireflies. The darting plastic dots weren't satisfied with just banding together to create a slowly growing golem. The artificial insects were stinging Thuy and Jayjay every chance they got.

"I can't take much more of this," said Jayjay, wildly slapping at himself.

"Oh, just give the Big Pig what she wants," said Thuy. Here in the sensory isolation of the cave—in between the mosquito bites—she was thinking about *Wheenk*. She had the entire database within the orphids on her skin. She was beginning to see the diverse elements of her work as fragments hurtling toward a common core. "I've got a feeling I'm going to the Hibrane really soon," Thuy added. "That'll give us one last roll of the dice."

"Yeah, you keep telling everyone that."

"Open the Ark, Jayjay."

Of course the red button on the Ark wouldn't respond to Jayjay's thumb. So, guiding his actions by the blinking of the flying shoons and his limited local orphidnet vision, Jayjay used Thuy's P90 to fire a blast across the top of the Ark, busting it open.

And then, in the velvet darkness, he screamed.

"What?" cried Thuy.

"Nanomachine goo!" gasped Jayjay, his echoing voice seeming to come from every side. "The Ark of the Nants was booby-trapped! The stuff's all over me! Oh, it tingles, it stings! Get back, Thuy! And don't forget that—" Jayjay gurgled and fell silent. In the local orphidnet, Thuy could see that her lover was fully enveloped by rippling nanoslime. He twitched, spasmed, and dropped motionless to the stone floor.

Thuy cowered at the far end of the cave, remembering Grandmaster Green Flash's skin with the rainbow sheen like rotten fish or rancid ham. Jayjay lay still beneath the iridescent slime. Thuy hated herself for being afraid to approach him. Tragic organ music swirled in her head. Her heart skipped a beat and seemed to explode.

And in that instant of ultimate despair, she finished *Wheenk,* the pieces of the metanovel coming together like a time-reversed nuclear explosion—everything fitting, everything of a piece—her adventures at the fab, her love for Jayjay, her worries about the nants, the dance she'd done down the rainy street that night exulting over her metanovel, the expression on her mother's face at her college graduation, her father's bare feet when he tended his tomato plants, the Easter Island boy who'd given her a cone shell today, her last kiss with Jayjay—*Wheenk* slamming together as heavy and whole as a sphere of plutonium, a perfected pattern in her local orphidnet.

Pain had produced artistic transcendence.

Thuy messaged a copy to the Big Pig lest the great work be lost. The Pig understood; kindly she passed it further, posting *Wheenk* across the global orphidnet.

And now, just as Azaroth had promised, Thuy remembered Chu's Knot. There'd been one final twist and wrap she couldn't visualize, but finally she had the knack; it was a bit like the time Kittie had showed her how to knit a pointed hat. Yes, the Knot was perfectly clear in Thuy's unaided mind, hanging there in three-dimensional glory, revolving at the touch of her will, a subtly woven bracelet with several hundred crossings.

Meanwhile the Pig was tending to a cloud of orphids surrounding the nant farm. And a second cloud of orphids was attacking the vile goo that enveloped Jayjay's inert form. Thuy hadn't thought about Jayjay for nearly a minute. She was such a terrible, self-centered person.

"I could go to the Hibrane now," she told the Big Pig. "But what's the use? I don't want to live without Jayjay."

A streamer of goo pushed across the cave, feeling for Thuy. Nimbly she moved out of its reach.

"You don't look quite ready to die," said the Big Pig, sounding amused. "Anyway, Jayjay's not dead. He'll be fine once the orphids clean him off. I'll be keeping him here to make sure you return. And meanwhile, I'll put him on a dark dream. He and I will be conducting a thought experiment, you might say. Go on with you now. And I'm open to whatever you learn. But, remember, I don't want to wait past midnight. You've got a little over six hours."

Thuy focused on her mental image of Chu's Knot. Nothing happened. Calming her panic, she remembered to do like Ond and Jil had done. She let go of her internal voice and interrupted her endless narration of her life story. She saw the spaces between her thoughts. She saw the space between the worlds.

She was off.

PART IV

CHAPTER 11

The Hibrane

Thuy felt a spinning sensation, as if she were being pulled down a whirlpool. And then she was skimming low across a foamy sea, following the curves of its undulating surface, flying with her arms outstretched, no land in sight. Surely the Hibrane lay upon the sea's far shore.

She felt vulnerable, tracing her way across this watery wasteland alone. It seemed unfair that the passage should seem to take so long, given that the Hibrane was supposedly less than a decillionth of a meter off. Space and time were weird down so close to the quantum level.

A tuberous stub popped through the ocean's slowly seething surface. Thuy felt a faint tingle, and now the rootlike stub took on the appearance of a glistening bird head, the head connected to a dimly visible humanoid form rushing along beneath the surface, pacing Thuy's progress. The bird head twitched this way and that, tracking Thuy's motions. Thuy had seen similar beings when she'd inched back and forth through Luty's teleportation grill. Subbies. They scared the shit out of her.

This particular subbie was casting a spume of drops and bubbles in his wake. Thuy swerved a bit, lest the spray touch her. She felt a nightmarish terror that any contact with the subbie could trap her here, world without end. As if in response, the subbie elongated his neck toward Thuy, blinking his yellow-rimmed eyes and clacking his down-curved beak.

Thuy reached deep into herself and drew power from the completed whole of *Wheenk,* feeding the energy into an exponential spike of acceleration. And then—*yes!*—she was in the Hibrane.

As she arrived, her mind bloomed; every particle of her body unfurled. She found herself in a copy of the same lava cave, the space velvety dark and utterly still. She was alone—yet not alone. For everything was telepathic here.

The walls of the cave were singing a chorus; Thuy's body parts were speaking to her; the air currents were sensually describing their kinetic flows; and twenty meters above, a moai statue was happily basking in the sun. All across this world the minds of Hibraners pulsed like musical flowers.

Thuy sat on the cave floor, gathering her wits. It made her sick to be so far from Jayjay in his time of need. Was he really going to be okay? She was half tempted to jump right back to the Lobrane. Of course, then she'd have to run the gauntlet of the subbies again. Come on, Thuy, now that you're in the Hibrane, find Ond and invent a defense against the nants. That's what you came for.

The stone beneath her felt crumbly; she could poke her finger right into it. Might she tunnel to the surface? Although her orphids had disappeared when she arrived, the universal Hibrane telepathy had given her the ability to see through walls. The telepathic images were richer and more true-to-life than the orphidnet images had been.

Thuy found a thin spot in the cave wall right above a dog-sized boulder on the ground. A mere six inches of foamy rock separated her from a chimneylike vent leading directly to the surface. She pulled the sleeves of her red plaid coat down over her hands and began scraping at the wall; the friable stone gave way like styrofoam or cheese. As well as being less dense, the matter moved more slowly here. The chunks of rock were drifting to the floor in slow motion.

"Huh, huh! Dig, dig!" said Thuy, recalling the phrase from a comic strip Kittie had admired. If she'd been at home with the orphidnet beezies, she could have instantly located an archived copy of *Mole*. But the universal telepathy of the Hibrane was nothing like so well organized.

Thuy dug on, muttering and chuckling, happy to be doing something. The rocks chanted their transformations; the air exulted in its motion-eddies; Thuy's fingers gloated over their strength. In a minute she'd reached the chimney vent. Light spilled down from twenty meters above. She clambered up the shaft like an invading underworld gnome, her gold piezoplastic Yu Shu shoes finding purchase on the cracks and crevices of the shaft's overgrown walls.

Thuy emerged into a summer day. Hot, around noon. She doffed her plaid coat. A moai statue loomed overhead, five or six times as big as the ones in the Lobrane. The grasses and field flowers were level with her waist. Surveying the giganticized island landscape, Thuy deduced that in the Hibrane she was effectively one foot tall.

There were other differences. The nearby moai statue had wider eyes than the ones she'd seen before; the figure's lips were parted to show square basalt teeth. The star-shaped flowers in the grass were pink instead of yellow, the grass blades were more sharply curved. And the Hibrane Pacific waves were breaking in slow slow motion, with the surf's sound dialed down to a deep bass boom.

Thuy glanced up past the dead volcano at the scattered clouds. These, at least, looked the same as before. It struck her

that the edge of one cloud was quite similar to the border of a
lichen patch she'd noticed on a wall of the vent she'd just
climbed. As she formed this thought, she realized she'd acquired
an eidetic memory for visual form. Each shape she saw was being
stored intact in her Hibrane-expanded mind.

Curiouser and curiouser. Thuy used telepathic omnividence
to view herself as if from outside. She was still wearing striped
yellow-and-black tights, a black miniskirt, and her yellow sweater.
Fine. But her hair! Finding a comb in her coat pocket, she undid
her pigtail fasteners, combed out her dark locks, made a tidy part
down the middle and restored her high pigtails to pristine form.
She applied a little pink lipstick too.

She was hungry. She wondered if Hibrane Easter Island had
a town of Hanga Roa with a Tuna-Ahi Barbecue. Reaching
into the telepathic glow of the Hibrane mindscape, she located
the island's town, which indeed had an unmarked restaurant
very much like the place where she and Jayjay had breakfasted.

Given that she was the size of a gnome, Thuy didn't feel like
walking all the way to town. Maybe she could teleport. She
fixed her mind upon the target location and the source location:
the restaurant and the grassy patch by the moai.

Whenever Jayjay had teleported, he'd invoked his specially
designed interpolation agents. The interpolators compensated
for the fact that orphidnet images didn't look quite as real as your
immediate surroundings. But here in the Hibrane, you didn't
need interpolators. Thuy's remote view of the village was utterly
convincing.

Using her writerly sense of correspondences, Thuy let her
attention dance back and forth between her images of source
and target, pairing up features, crafting the sought-for transition
as if writing a segue between two of a metanovel's scenes. As

she withdrew from reality's insistent din, she seemed to collapse in on herself.

Where was she? Asking the question was enough. *Pop*—she was on the main street of the Hibrane version of Hanga Roa, carrying her coat under her arm. The locals had a few cars, even though they could teleport too. The cars were flimsy, as if cobbled together from organic parts: leaves, beetle wings, seashells. One car had dots like a ladybug, another bore yellow and white stripes. They all had solar cells and electric motors.

Relative to little Thuy, the single-story shops and houses were as tall as office buildings. The buildings looked to be assembled from naturally grown components as well. Overhead, shells and shiny seedpods hung upon lines stretched across the street; they'd been crafted into representational forms: a star, a candy cane, a cuttlefish holding a triangle—Thuy recalled Azaroth's mentioning that the cuttlefish was a symbol for a Hibrane religious figure. Perhaps these were ornaments to celebrate a holiday.

All these things Thuy noticed in the first flash after landing. But the bright-clothed Hibraners were taking the bulk of her attention. A dozen of them were in view: slow-moving giants, ethnically Chilean and Polynesian. All of them were staring at Thuy, raising their arms in slow-motion alarm and widening their mouths. And at the same time they were probing Thuy's mind. She tried her best to think pleasant, innocuous thoughts, but perhaps her worries about the nants leaked through. In any case, the Hibraners were scared of her.

The air rumbled with their low-speed cries, deep and draggy as sounds heard underwater. The Hibraners wheeled about in waltz time, fleeing from the alien gnome in the striped leggings. Their slow-motion panic was spooky.

Across the street was the place like the Tuna-Ahi Barbecue, its stony walls flowing smoothly from the soil. Although the building bore no written sign, it was telepathically emanating the image of a bluefin tuna. Thuy went inside. The inn was only approximately similar to its counterpart on the Lobrane.

The interior furnishings formed naturalistic curves, with each chair or table different from the others. The lumpish bottles behind the bar had no labels; instead they bore telepathic notes. Thuy picked up that the telepathic labels were called teep-tags.

Quite a few people were dining on the patio. The chairs were made of hardened kelp stems, and the tables were disks of mother-of-pearl with further kelp stems for their legs. A slender waitress in vibrant blue was just setting down pearly platters of rice, beans, and tuna steaks for a group of six: two women, a man, a boy, and two girls. Thuy yelled and charged toward them. As she'd hoped, the diners rocked back in their curved chairs. In two quick hops, Thuy was standing on the opalescent dining table.

She grabbed hold of a tuna steak the size of her torso; to her it felt like it weighed but a pound—as the matter here was less dense. The grilled fish was warm and savory, emanating faint images of its long, vigorous life in the deeps of the sea. Thuy tore into it; rapidly scarfing down the slab of fish and a mound of rice the size of her head.

The diners remained seated around the table, intrigued by Thuy's antics, and perhaps unwilling to abandon their food. The low burble of the three children's laughter became audible as Thuy took a frantic slurp from a bathtub-sized glass of thin-tasting cola. One of the women was frowning and her arm was arcing ever so slowly toward Thuy's head. Thuy stepped out of reach while loading some giant beans onto a tortilla the size of a pillow case. She strolled to the table's edge, gobbled the wrapped-up beans, called out a thank you, and hopped down to the crushed-shell patio.

Looking into the Hibraners' minds, Thuy could see that, for them, she was moving in a rapid blur. Her thank you had sounded like a shrill chirp. So now she sent the thanks telepathically and regarded the reactions.

The man's image of Thuy was tinged with hellfire; he was wondering if she were a demon. One of the girls was seeing Thuy as a cute doll; she was visualizing Thuy perched on a silky pillow in her room. The woman who'd tried to smack Thuy saw her as a pest like a weasel or a rat. The other woman regarded Thuy as a magical agent of good luck and was imagining trapping Thuy under a bucket-shaped shell that sat by the wall. As for the boy—he was simply marveling at how fast Thuy moved. A voice came at her, speaking clearly and at the proper speed.

"Thuy," said the voice in her head. "Get out of here fast. Crabby old Gladax is coming for you." Accompanying the voice was a brief image of a bearded young guy with a stocking-wrapped topknot. Azaroth.

"Where do I run to?" messaged Thuy. "Can I find Ond?"

"Teleport to our version of San Francisco," said the voice. "The sidewalk by the spot where you Lobraners have that store-front church."

Thuy focused on the mindscape location Azaroth was showing her. She saw a wet winter morning on a busy street, with little lights glowing in the window of a secondhand clothes store where El Santo de Israel had stood. A kind of auto repair shop stood next door. The buildings looked somehow like plants or like wasp nests. "Won't Gladax follow me there too?" worried Thuy.

"There's a vibby way to fool a telepathic snoop," messaged

Azaroth. "It's like acting. You warp your self-image. Like how I made myself look like a moai when you and Jayjay were waking up? I'll show you how. Oh, oh, look out!"

Thuy jumped to one side as a rubber net descended rather slowly upon the spot where she'd been standing. The woman holding it was indeed Gladax, narrow-eyed in concentration. She wore dirty green sweatpants and a cheap T-shirt with a smeared dragon print.

Thuy grabbed her red plaid coat and ran out the back of the patio into an unpaved alley. Gladax did a nimble teleportation hop to head her off, net at the ready, looking two stories tall. But even though Gladax could hop, her physical body moves were slow. Thuy dodged the net, and flung handfuls of sand and broken shells at the old woman. A bit of grit got into Gladax's eye.

"Little brat," said Gladax in a deep, slow Hibraner voice. She set to removing the mote, focusing all her attention on the task. Unobserved for this one moment, Thuy teleported herself to the Hibrane San Francisco.

She landed next to a wet dog sniffing the doorstep of the clothing store. Or, no, that was Azaroth, if you looked at him with your regular eyes. To the telepathic gaze, he was a white and tan collie-beagle with a saddle-shaped orange patch on his back.

Azaroth opened a pinhole window through his umbrella of illusion, letting Thuy see the secret of telepathic camouflage. As a writer, she understood the mental trick right away, but—now Azaroth was telling her to imitate a rat? No thanks. Drawing on her memories of her family's beloved cat, Naoko, Thuy began vibing like a Siamese. *Mew.*

Colorful, organic cars were rolling by in the light rain, no two of them the same. The battery-powered vehicles seemed alert and sensitive. Right inside the open garage doors of the auto repair shop, a man in overalls was in a wordless conversation with a purple car, assessing its vibes as he fit a knobby rubber tire onto one of its wheels. The shop had almost the feel of a veterinary clinic. The car-healer saw Thuy and slowly smiled. She teeped that he was one of Azaroth's friends.

Azaroth pointed toward the second-floor rooms above the auto clinic. Shrouded by their dog and cat vibes, Azaroth and Thuy teleported up there.

And landed in a giant back room heavy with years of dust. For Thuy, the room was the size of a concert hall. Rain ran down the expanses of a dirty rear window that faced the alley wall and a leafless city tree. The window looked to be some kind of plant membrane rather than actual glass. A single light-bulb in the room's upper recesses fought feebly against the gloom. Oversized organic auto parts languished on shelves that seemed to have grown right out of the walls, the parts marked with teep-tags instead of written labels. Water trickled from a tap in a great porcelain sink. Doggy Azaroth flopped down on a tired old couch: a puffball the size of a patio. Sitting next to him were an ant and a housefly.

Blinking her eyes, Thuy realized she was looking at Chu and Ond. She'd never met them before, but she knew them from a zillion news shows: Ond blond, awkward, middle-aged, slim; Chu blank-eyed with a cute, slightly sour mouth and a dark brown cap of hair.

"Welcome, Thuy," said Ond out loud. "You're doing fine with that cat imitation. I like cats a lot better than dogs." Blessedly he spoke at the same speed as Thuy. "Now grow your illusion to the size of this room. Make it like a cubical soap bubble that we're all inside." In person, Ond's voice sounded warmer than in the orphidnet archives. But—cubical bubble illusion? Thuy wasn't sure what he meant.

"He means paint your cat-self onto the ceiling, the floor, and each of the four walls," said Chu, his voice thin and sulky. "Also the door and the windows."

"Watch us," rumbled Azaroth.

Azaroth, Ond, and Chu pushed their vibes of dog, fly, and ant out to the fringes of the room. Thuy studied what they'd done, tracing the patterns of their minds, and then she followed suit, painting her emulation of Naoko the cat onto the room.

"That's glow," said Azaroth in his slow, oozing voice, then switched to telepathy. "We can touch minds in here now. I don't think Gladax sees us under those animal shields."

"This is our secret lab," added Ond. "We come here to work on our video game and on our plan."

"What about the guys in the garage?" asked Thuy. "They're Azaroth's friends?"

"Yeah," said Ond. "The local Hibraners have gotten used to us. We have the run of the town. And we have jobs. I'm Gladax's tutor and Chu's her good-luck nanteater."

"Nanteater," echoed Chu, telepathically displaying an image of a long-snouted bushy-tailed anteater while he talked out loud. "When Gladax addled the jump-code in my head, she also saw my memory of Nant Day. So she thinks I'm magic against nants. Hibraners don't understand digital computers at all. Did you bring my jump-code?"

"I have the code, yes," replied Thuy. "An image of your Knot. By the way, Jeff Luty's made a new version of the nants. I'm here to ask you guys to save Earth again."

"Teep me my jump-code right now," demanded Chu.

"Okay, okay," said Thuy. "But don't instantly disappear. We need to make a plan."

"The nanteater already has a plan," said Chu in his small, emotionless voice.

Safe inside the dog-cat-fly-ant box of this room, Thuy opened her mind and let the others copy her image of the woven Celtic bracelet. To celebrate the handoff, Azaroth produced the sound of a crowd cheering.

"This seems right," said Chu examining the Knot. "I'm glad to have it back."

"Thank you, Thuy," said Ond, also studying a copy of the Knot. "You say there's more nants? Azaroth told us to expect this, and, yes, we've made a kind of plan. But—are people still mad at me? They wanted to lynch me on Orphid Night."

"Everyone likes the orphidnet fine," said Thuy. "It's been almost a year and a half."

"Over here that comes to two months and twenty four days," said Chu. "Orphid Night was the only time when the dates matched."

"First the Lobrane was behind us and now they're ahead of us," teeped Azaroth. Image of two parallel time-lines with a matching time-zero, and with the days along the lower line more densely spaced. "I saw time-zero coming, and I told Gladax," continued Azaroth. "The singularity. That's why she jumped to the Lobrane and chased down Chu." Image of Chu in a rubber net. "Gladax worries about the Lobrane infecting us with nanomachines. Fortunately our smart air currents ate your orphids right away." Image of a microscopic tornado tearing a nanomachine asunder.

"Gladax tied up Chu and blocked his telepathy with her harp, and addled the jump-code out of him," said Ond. "I made a deal so she wouldn't do worse. I showed her how to erase the jump-code from the Lobrane orphidnet, and I'm pretending to help improve her search abilities. Actually I'm making her more confused. If Gladax ever got organized, it'd be hell on the San Francisco Hibraners. She'd be nosing into everyone's business all the time."

"How come you know my Knot?" Chu asked Thuy.

"I was watching you when you did your first jump," answered Thuy. "At first I couldn't quite remember the details, but eventually I did. It's a long story: a metanovel called *Wheenk*."

"Teep *Wheenk* to them," messaged Azaroth. "All of it. You're not really opening your mental gates, Thuy. Our telepathy band is broader than you realize. Sit down with us on the couch and relax."

So Thuy settled in and let herself do a full mind-merge with the others. They became like four eyestalks on a single mollusk. Everything that Thuy had seen and done since Orphid Night flowed over to Ond, Chu, and Azaroth. In return, she saw all the things that Ond and Chu had experienced up here.

The images grew so vivid that Thuy quite forgot herself. She fell asleep and began dreaming. At first she was dreaming about Jayjay back in the cave, and then she was over here with Azaroth, Chu, and Ond. They were skulking around in Gladax's big-ass rococo mansion with its treelike pillars and curving halls, up on a hill above North Beach, the four of them trying to free a bungee-cord-bound prisoner from Gladax's exercise room and steal Gladax's magic harp. Ond and Chu kept disagreeing about the best way to tunnel into the exercise room from below. Waiting for them to break through, and hearing the same insistent harp chord in the background for the twentieth time, Thuy flashed that she wasn't dreaming anymore. She was playing a video game with the three guys.

She blinked, shook her head, and snapped out of it. Azaroth, Ond, and Chu were slumped beside her on the giant couch, twitching their fingers as if using invisible game controllers. How long had she been here? What was Jayjay doing right now?

Thuy reached over and joggled Ond's knee. Ond fluttered

his eyelids, sat up, and offered an abashed grin. "We play this game all the time," he said. "We're practicing. That running water tap over there, that's our game computer. We're the first computer programmers in the Hibrane."

"How can you use water for a computer?" demanded Thuy.

"The flow is sufficiently gnarly to function as a universal emulator, yes. Back home that would be of merely theoretical interest, but in the Hibrane we can use those gnarly natural processes for useful computation. The crucial difference is that Hibrane systems remember all their previous states. It's like every single location here has an endless memory chip plugged in. I already told you about this while we were merged. Focus, Thuy. Take a mental inventory."

Come to think of it, Thuy could indeed remember every detail of the extensive telepathic exchange she'd had with the boys before the dreamlike video game session. But now she became distracted by her powerful memory for visual forms. Glancing at Ond, for instance, she could match the little vertical wrinkle between his eyes to a crack she'd seen in the sidewalk outside and to the edge of a shell fragment she'd thrown at Gladax. Everything she saw remained accessible to her mind; it was as if her memory had become unlimited.

Savoring the feel of this strange world, Thuy looked around the room, taking in the auras of the furnishings. Although the objects didn't exactly speak English, they too remembered everything. The auto parts carried the vibes of the farms and fields where they'd been raised, of the telepathic growers who'd cajoled them into their current shapes, and of the men and women who'd handled them. The jumbo lightbulb on the ceiling had a dark-and-light ribbon memory of all the times it had been off and on, with the bright stretches patterned by subtle shadings that mirrored the wavers of past electrical currents. And

when Thuy studied the beat old couch, it wordlessly teeped her
the touch sensations of all the butts that had sat upon its cush-
ioned pads in the last twenty years. Noticing this, Chu had a rare
fit of giggles.

"We've been thinking that if we could give Lobrane matter
this kind of built-in memory, there'd be no reason to turn
Earth into nants," said Ond. "Everything would already be like
a computer."

"So come home with me and tell that to the Big Pig," said
Thuy, still very worried about Jayjay. "Let's go right now!"

"Telling isn't enough," said Ond. "We have to be like
Prometheus and steal fire from heaven. Put more formally, we
need to seed the Lobrane with the Hibrane's paranormal branespace topology."

"Huh?" Although Ond had already sent Thuy these words
during the hour they'd been merged, the meaning still hadn't
sunk in.

"Use pictures, Ond," suggested Azaroth.

"I believe that a single ubiquitous Hibrane factor causes
telepathy, omnividence, teleportation, and expanded memory," said Ond. Image of a space-filling glow. "I find it sim-
plest to suppose that this factor has to do with the shapes of
the unseen extra dimensions of Hibrane space." Image of ten
axes crossing each other at strange angles; four of the axes are
endless lines and the other six bend around into tight circles.
"I call the Hibrane's configuration the *paranormal branespace
topology.*" Image of one of the circles unrolling to make an
endless line. A bundle of lines appears parallel to this new line
and, oddly enough, they narrow in on each other to meet at a
not-too-distant vanishing point. "We need to nudge the Lobrane over to the paranormal branespace topology." Image of
a snowflake dropping into supercooled water that freezes into

a block of ice. "Unfortunately I'm not enough of a physicist to give more details. But—"

"Chu and I think Gladax's harp is the key," teeped Azaroth. Image of the same gold harp they'd been seeking in the video game. Its strings were luminous and strange. Its sound box was decorated with a curiously detailed oil painting. Medieval?

"Remember that when Gladax strums her harp a certain way, people can't teep," said Chu. "She strummed it in the room where I was tied up. Our idea is that if someone carries Gladax's harp to the Lobrane and strums it there, the opposite might happen. The right chord could unroll one of the dimensions of our brane's space so that everything has telepathy and endless memory."

"And then there'd be no reason for nants," repeated Ond. "Once the harp unrolls that extra dimension in one spot, it'll spread."

"But why are you sneaking around?" said Thuy, recalling Gladax's remarks at ExaExa. "Gladax *knows* you want to steal her harp. She said, and I quote, 'Ond and Chu have a wild plan to steal my harp and unroll your lazy eight.' You heard that too, didn't you, Azaroth?"

"Maybe she knows," said Azaroth, looking embarrassed. "But that doesn't mean we can't outfox her."

"Gladax knows our plans?" said Ond angrily. "And you guys already have a word for the special dimension? You call it lazy eight? Why did you hide this from me, Azaroth? Are you setting us up?"

"It's complicated," said Azaroth with a sigh. "Gladax wants you to take the harp but she doesn't. If she thought you could really unroll your lazy eight, she'd probably lend you the harp, no problem. But, on the other hand, it's hers, and it's rare, and she's stingy, and she figures you'd probably just break it, so she doesn't want you to get your hands on it at all. She's conflicted. If you want the harp, you really do have to steal it."

"Lazy eight," put in Ond, off on his own line of thought. "Yes. I understand. We use the harp to unroll our *eighth* dimension, which means we make our eighth dimension into an endless line. And—here's the 'lazy' part—we give the line a special metric so that our minds can reach all the way to infinity. Like how the endless decimal 0.9999999 . . . describes a point that's only one meter away? That's how the Hibrane already is, if you think about it. Infinity is everywhere. Lazy eight."

"Infinity," said Chu, the math word sweet in his mouth. "It's like using a cosmic vanishing point for a universal Web server. People, animals, trees, rivers, air currents, dirt—everything's in touch with lazy eight. That's why telepathy works so well in the Hibrane. That's why it's so easy to teleport."

Thuy thought of chants and mantras, of divine names and the Buddhists' cosmic Aum. "All right!" she exclaimed. "Let's steal Gladax's harp!"

"It won't be easy," teeped Azaroth. "That's why we keep practicing our starky moves inside Chu's video game. But I promise that once you do get hold of the harp, I'll run to Gladax and make sure she lets you keep it for a while. Deep down she really does want you to succeed. It's just that she's too pessimistic and selfish to make it easy."

"The nanteater has a plan," repeated Chu.

⚙

"Have you ever run into Hibrane versions of yourselves?" Thuy asked Ond and Chu. They'd left the hideout to walk down the street, picking their way around the giant, slow-motion shoppers.

They'd dropped their telepathic animal disguises, and Azaroth wasn't with them—all part of the plan.

The rain had let up; it was a cool and cloudy afternoon of the winter holiday season. "Do you think there's two Onds, two Chus, and two Thuys?" continued Thuy.

"Two *Jayjays* is what you're really thinking about," said Ond, teeping into her head. "I'm guessing the two branes aren't so much like mirror images as they are like different metanovels on the same themes. There's no reason to suppose all the characters will be the same."

"Thuy misses her boyfriend," said Chu in a bratty tone.

"I'm worried about him, okay?" said Thuy. Surely the orphids had cleaned the nanoslime off Jayjay by now. But what if he was dead. What if that one brief roll in bed and shared meal of pho was to be Thuy and Jayjay's last time together? "I'm capable of worrying about other people, Chu. You could learn from me."

"It's not my fault I'm autistic," said Chu, making his voice very small.

"Don't pick on him," said Ond. "It's not easy being Chu."

"Sorry," said Thuy. "I'm all keyed up." She studied a group of giants calmly inching down the sidewalk their way. The San Francisco Highbraners were so used to seeing Ond and Chu around town that the Lobrane gnomes didn't attract all that much notice here.

"I do too worry about other people anyway," said Chu. "I worry about Bixie and about Nektar. I worry about Ond. Will Nektar ever want him back?"

"We'll sort it out when we get home," said Ond. "It's okay, Chu, I'll find someone."

"The night we came here, Ond messaged 'I love you' to Jil," confided Chu. "Do you think Jil loves Ond back, Thuy?"

"I've never heard Jil talk about Ond," said Thuy. "But we do know that she's breaking up with her husband. Could be that Ond has a chance."

"Craigor tried to make babies with Nektar," said Chu, who was bursting with all the information he'd gleaned from his merge with Thuy. "But now they don't like each other. Sex and love don't make sense."

"You're learning," said Thuy.

"While you were asleep I looked under your clothes and my weenie got stiff," Chu now told Thuy.

"That's more than enough, Chu," said Ond.

"Why not say everything, since we can read each others' minds?"

"We have that issue with the orphidnet, too," mused Thuy. "It's all a matter of what you call attention to. Being polite means not emphasizing certain things."

"You mean like—"

"I mean shut up." Thuy flashed a grin at Chu so he wouldn't take this to heart. Good for him if he thought she was sexy.

They'd come to the end of the interesting part of this street. "You want to turn around and walk back?" Ond asked Thuy.

"Sure," said Thuy. "Sooner or later she's bound to notice us." They were waiting for Gladax to pop up and capture Thuy. Part of the plan. But Gladax was being slow on the uptake, which gave Thuy time to examine the stores.

The clothes on display were funkier than at home, each item unique, and everything very colorful. Things weren't so industrialized here in the Hibrane. With no digital computers, the vibe was much more kicked back.

The leathers and wools were individually tweaked by craftspeople called coaxers. Fashion coaxers got into telepathic synch with animals' bodies so as to influence the colors and textures of the creatures' skin or hair. They coaxed fiber plants as well: cotton, sisal, flax. Some of the coaxed fabrics harbored special psychic properties. For instance, you could buy underwear that emanated shame-and-outrage vibes, positioning you as forbidden fruit.

Down the block, some well-dressed Hibraners were enjoying a late lunch in a cozy restaurant. Each plateful of food was teep-tagged with the history of how the ingredients had been produced, plus images of the chef's preparation process, plus eating advice: "I'm crisp and lemony"; "Pry up this trout cheek to get a nice nugget of meat"; "Dip me in that green sauce."

Next door was a bar, but Thuy found it hard to teep inside, as the drinkers' vibes were screened off by the aggressive mental stylings of a so-called distractor. The distractor was visible in the doorway, a black swami with a shaved head and his muscular arms crossed. He wore a calfskin coaxed to resemble a leopard pelt. He was a living hub of links, assessing people's interests and instantly routing them to minds and scenes likely to divert their focus of attention. It took a real effort to teep past him.

But Thuy managed, and teeped a flashy woman sitting inside the bar with a man. The woman was a paid escort named Balla. Balla's vibes were delicious; she'd honed the skill of offering her short-term partners an emotional sense of intimacy and shared history—magically divorced from empathy and commitment. Seeing Balla slowly brush back a lock of hair, Thuy had the brief impression that she knew this woman—though of course the illusion was as thin as the skin of a balloon.

And then the distractor spun Thuy's attention across the street into an art gallery. Roundish sculptures like river-tumbled stones were teep-tagged to project exalted emotional states: wonder, transcendence, sensual pleasure, bliss—the vibes polished by years in the currents of the meditative artist's mind.

A bit further down the street, the Metotem Metabooks location housed something like a bookshop—but with no paper
and no printed words. Although the telepathic Hibraners sometimes used the shorthand of language, they seemed never to
trouble themselves with writing out words in phonetic form.
Why transcribe grunts when you can read minds? Hibrane au-
thors were more like cartoonists or directors, assembling blocks
of mental states, creating networks of glyphs. Their works were
embedded as teep-tags within handicraft items: tie-dyed scarves,
bead necklaces, carved bits of wood.

Picking up on Thuy's thoughts, the owner, who actually
looked a bit like a giant Darlene, stepped slowly from the store.
"You're fresh from the Lobrane?" she boomed, then switched to
teeping. "I'm Durga. And you're a metanovelist? Would you like
to record something for me to sell?"

"Go ahead, Thuy," urged Ond. "Chu and I come here all
the time. Show *Wheenk* to Durga. It's beautiful; you should be
proud. And if you share, it'll enhance understanding between
the two branes."

"Do we get a snack today?" Chu asked Durga.

Durga found some doll-sized teacups that were just right for
them, although her spice cookies were the size of garbagecan
lids. She broke one in pieces for them. Chu took a seat in one
of the big soft chairs, studying a little metal pig that contained
an animal adventure tale expressed from the point of view of a
piglet. Ond and Thuy sat next to him on the big chair, Ond
fondling a felt decoupage wallet that encoded a rambling, anec-
dotal survey of Hibrane science.

Thuy's mind was alert. Nibbling her cookie and sipping her
tea, she checked out the vibes of the far-flung islands where the
tea and spices had grown. And then she took a few minutes to
arrange her mental representation of *Wheenk* along the seemingly

endless spike of memory that the curious topology of Hibrane space had given her. When she was done, she teeped the images and emotions to Durga, who was sitting in a chair nearby. Right away Durga routed copies of *Wheenk* onto, of all things, five little cactuses in handmade pots.

"Once I sell these off, I'll make more," said Durga. "I'll give you half the profits—if you're still here to collect." She gave Thuy an empathetic smile. With amazing mental rapidity, Durga had already absorbed much of *Wheenk*. "I hope things work out for you and Jayjay."

Of course that set off a fresh round of self-flagellation in Thuy's head, along the lines of, "Why was I so cold to Jayjay for so long!" To distract herself from her tedious internal wheenking, Thuy teeped around the enormous room, skimming across the masses of data in the items on display. "Can I read one of these?"

"Sure. You pick. Relax and enjoy."

Thuy was just settling in with a dried gardenia that contained a romance adventure when—as they'd been expecting—Gladax appeared, old and strict. For once Gladax wasn't dressed like a street person—instead she was swathed in the virtual robes of her mayoral office. She shimmered with the diverse faces of the Hibrane San Francisco citizenry, thousands of gold-framed images cascading from her shoulders like sheets of water. A further tessellation of faces rose up behind her head like a peacock's fan. But, as before, she was carrying a net.

Ond grabbed Thuy's arm, as if restraining her. "I was about to bring her to you," Ond told Gladax in an ingratiating tone.

Thuy could see that Chu was literally biting his tongue to keep from contradicting his father. It pained the literal-minded boy to hear an untruth.

"Stand back," said Gladax, swaying her net. Her hands were

like slow butterflies against the glittering mosaic of faces. The rubbery net floated down; Thuy let herself be trapped. Gladax cinched the bonds around Thuy; Ond lent a hand.

Thuy struggled, but not for real—that would come later. Already she could feel why the net was elastic. For a dense, powerful gnome, the flexible meshes posed more of a problem than brittle ropes and chains.

Gladax forced some images into Thuy's mind: views of a long, sunny room with straw mats on the floor. A gold harp sat upright at the room's end. Chinese scroll landscapes hung upon the walls. This was the exercise room in Gladax's mansion: their teleportation target. And now, *pop*, they were there. Teleportation was very easy with lazy eight.

Gladax's tai chi room occupied the eastern side of the first floor of the house. Tightly bound and lying on her side, Thuy was facing a long window with a view of the garden. Winter and spring flowers were in bloom: oversized poinsettias, cyclamens, irises, tulips, freesias, snowdrops, and jonquils—bright against the gray background of the lowering sky. All the petals were in shades of red. The coaxer-tweaked blossoms seemed to have a certain level of intelligence: there was a considered elegance to the way they bobbed in the breeze; more than that, they were faintly messaging a tune.

The rubber net lurched, slamming Thuy's knee into her chin. She saw stars. Grunting with effort, Gladax was hauling the net into the air, using a rope through a pulley in the ceiling. Annoyed at being so roughly handled, Thuy made her first really serious effort to tear out of the net. But to no avail. The elastic meshes absorbed her kicks, only to snap back the harder.

The net rose higher, bringing Thuy's face even with Gladax's. Gladax had set aside her mayoral trappings; she was back to looking like a sloppy old woman in dark green sweatpants and a souvenir T-shirt.

"I'll have to addle that jump-code away from you," Gladax told Thuy. She secured the net. And now she extruded a slender rod of light from the tip of her forefinger; the glowing probe was six or seven inches in length. "If you cooperate, this won't have to hurt you. I have a very delicate touch."

"All I want is to stop Luty's nants," cried Thuy. "You want that too. Don't stick that thing in my head. Let me—let me take your harp back to the Lobrane and I'll leave right away."

Gladax snorted impatiently. "Upstart gnome. That harp's been in my family for over twenty generations. From the Dutch side. You wouldn't know how to use it. You'd ruin it, likely as not. Or let the subbies steal it from you while you're jumping branes."

Thuy could telepathically sense Ond and Chu in the street outside Gladax's mansion. They were supposed to save her by tunneling up through the floor. But right now they were arguing rather than digging in. Uneasily Thuy recalled how poorly the father and son had done in their practice video games.

Gladax leaned closer, narrowing her finger ray to the thinness of a knitting needle. She pursed her lips in concentration, humming to herself. As the net rotated, Thuy went into a frenzy of kicking and stopped only when her knee collided with her chin again. Big dogs were barking somewhere nearby. Thuy saw the garden, a door, the wispy paintings, and, at the other end of the room, the gold-leafed harp, small by Hibrane standards, but nearly as tall as Thuy. Its strings were as linear flaws in space, like transparent tubes warping the view of the wall. The soundbox had colors on it.

Gladax hopped over to the antique harp. "I'm going to isolate

you now," she said. "I wouldn't want you to be messaging anything to your little friends."

Maybe Thuy should teleport herself out of here before—

ZONGGG

—it was too late. Gladax had struck the harp. The sweet,
icky chord hung in the air. There was no way to be at ease with
the harp's vibration, which showed no sign of damping down.
Everything on the psychic plane was wavy, messy, screwed up.
Telepathy was impossible. Thuy no longer heard the songs of
the flowers or the quarreling of Chu and Ond. But, thank God,
she heard the calm voice of Azaroth, low and slow. He'd just
walked into the tai chi room, talking aloud.

"It's about your garden, Aunt Gladax," said Azaroth. "Sorry
to interrupt. I got a message from the plant-coaxer. He's too shy
to teep you himself. Some of the flowers want to change color."

"What!" exclaimed Gladax, taking the bait. "I told those
flowers they have to stay red right through to the end of the
Cuttlemas holidays."

"You'd better come outside and explain it to the flowers yourself," rumbled Azaroth. "This little Lobraner—Thuy, isn't it?
Should I watch her for you?"

"I don't trust you alone with her," said Gladax. "I know you
two are friends. You come out to the garden with me, nephew.
My harp will keep Thuy isolated. My harp likes to sing." Gladax
inched open the door to the garden and inhaled a deep breath of
fresh air. "I need to settle my nerves. That chord is so dreadful.
It curdles the auras."

"Do you really have to addle Thuy?" asked Azaroth.

"I have to erase her knowledge of the jump-code, and
thanks to her I'll have to addle Ond and even Chu again. I suppose you know those two gnomes were planning to tunnel into
my house. I just sicced my new dogs on them. I'm not such an

old fool as you and those jitsy Lobraners think—you and your silly animal disguises. And, no, I'm not letting the clumsy gnomes take my precious harp."

A long uneasy silence. "I never underestimate you, Aunt Gladax," said Azaroth finally, his face a polite mask.

"It'll be easier for me to addle Thuy if she cooperates," said Gladax. "I really don't want to hurt the girl. Can't you have a word with her?"

"No use," said Azaroth, barely glancing at Thuy. "You've seen how she is."

"Feisty," muttered Gladax. "Too smart for her own good." She shook her head. "Let's do the easy thing first. Let's talk to the damned flowers." Moving like molasses, Azaroth and Gladax made their way outdoors.

Alone in the tai chi room, Thuy began stretching her bonds in earnest. Rather than struggling at random, she pulsed her kicks and shoves to match the rubber's resonant rate. With each pulse she extended her legs and arms a little further. And then she broke the rhythm with a double pulse, catching the material on its way in. This was enough. A band snapped.

Gladax was berating her gardener and her flowers, while Azaroth, watching Thuy from the corner of his eye, did his best to block Gladax's line of sight. Wriggling like an eel, Thuy got free of the broken net and thudded heavily to the straw mat. Fortunately she landed well. Sticking close to the floor, she wormed down the length of the room to the harp, a gilded triangle resting on one corner. This instrument was strung with thirty-four furiously vibrating strings that seemed somehow higher-dimensional.

The harp's front edge was a fluted wooden column with a scrolled capital, the rear edge was a tapering hollow-bodied wooden soundbox, and the crosspiece on top was an elegant

S-curve. The flat inner side of the soundbox bore a masterful oil painting of a teeming garden of Eden. Two lovers were listening to the music of a winged, pale blue demon playing his own little harp. The lovers looked familiar. Like Jayjay and Thuy? Impossible. From what Gladax had said about inheriting the harp from her ancestors, the instrument must have been five or six hundred years old.

Thuy took the harp in both hands; although shoulder-high, it felt light. She tiptoed towards the door connecting the tai chi room to the rest of the house.

The harp's sound rose in pitch and—just like a fairy-tale harp—she cried out to Gladax in a woman's voice. "Mistress! Save me!"

Thuy laid her hand across the harp strings. The space-warping tubes tingled against her, but when she pushed forcefully enough they fell still. And now her telepathy was working again. For just a moment she could sense the strange otherworldly mind of the harp. The harp was an intelligent being from another order of reality. Gazing into her mind was like standing at the lip of a high, windy cliff. Thuy grew dizzy; she tottered on her feet. But then a veil dropped and the harp was once again a manageable triangle of wood.

Out in the garden Azaroth had clamped his aunt in a bear-hug. He was talking to her; he was pleading for her to let Thuy be. Good Azaroth.

According to Ond's overly elaborate plan, at this point he and Chu were supposed to appear through a tunnel they'd dug through the floor. But there hadn't been any dogs in the boys' video game simulation of the house. Teeping the street, Thuy saw them backed up against the house's front steps by two huge mastiffs.

Lugging the now silent harp, Thuy made her way through

winding hallways to Gladax's front door. The heavy door was locked, so Thuy kicked a big hole in the stucco wall next to the door.

As she emerged, one of the dogs came up the steps. Thuy set down the harp, sprang at the beast and thumped him on the side of his head. The monster shook off the blow; he had a skull like a boulder. But Thuy kept up her attack, raining blows. Yes, the dogs were big, but they were slow. And when Thuy began punching their soft noses, the brutes turned tail, and ran up the street.

"Come *on!*" Thuy yelled to Ond and Chu, standing there at the bottom of the steps. "Help me carry the harp. We're heading home!"

The three of them trotted two blocks down the hill, Ond holding one end of the painted harp. The dogs were loudly barking—but they weren't going to attack again. At the bend of the street they found a vest-pocket park with a bench and a bed of chrysanthemums. Catching their breath on the bench, the three had a view west over the pastel buildings of the city toward the ocean, the bay, and the Hibrane version of the Golden Gate Bridge. The waters lay sullen and gray below the wintry afternoon sky. But the city looked peaceful and human-scale. It was nice to think there were no digital computers here.

"We have to focus on my Knot now," said Chu.

"Yes," said Thuy. She'd been here—how long? Only an hour by the slow Hibrane clocks—but six hours of her body's time, six hours of Lobrane time. Was Jayjay okay? Surely the Big Pig hadn't released the nants yet, had she?

"I'll be glad to get home," said Ond. He patted the hollow soundbox of the harp, which gave off a resonant echo. "Good work getting this, Thuy. I'm betting it'll make the nants obsolete. You'll strum it and universal extra memory will—unfurl."

"That's what you keep saying," said Thuy, feeling a bit doubt-ful. "What if Gladax hops down here and kills us? Or follows us back home."

"Azaroth's her only heir," said Ond. "When he really works on her, he can always get her to give in."

Thuy teeped cautiously toward Gladax's garden. The old woman and her nephew were sitting on a bench laughing. Per-haps everything was going to be all right after all. Or—a sud-den paranoid thought—maybe this was a triple cross, and the Hibraners were in fact glad to get rid of the magic harp. Maybe the harp *wanted* Thuy to take it to the Lobrane.

"There's more to this harp than you realize," Thuy told Ond. "She's alive. She's an alien."

"Maybe so," said Ond in a soothing tone, not really believ-ing her. "We have to go forward anyway, Thuy. Our plan is Earth's only hope."

"Your *plan*," snorted Thuy. "A fat lot of help you two have been with it so far."

"We're scared of dogs, okay?" said Chu. "Ond's right, it's time to go."

The three of them focused on Chu's Knot, trying to relax enough to enter the interbrane gap. But with all the worries, it was hard to get underway. Hard to get their heads in the right place. They took a break and talked a little more.

"Did you guys see a weird ocean when you came across?" Thuy asked Ond.

"That's the Planck frontier," said Ond. "Physics below the Planck length is a scale-inverted image of the physics above the Planck length. If someone were to shrink down below that foamy frontier, they'd feel like they were expanding into an-other cosmos. The world of the subdimensions."

"The Hibraners call it Subdee," said Chu. "And those bird-headed men are the subbies. Subbies from Subdee. Thanks to them it's dangerous to jump branes."

"They poke up their heads to eat our information," said Ond.

"More than information," said Chu. "They want to eat our bodies too."

"I hate the subbies," said Thuy.

A single ray of sun broke through the clouds to illuminate the little park.

"I want to jump back right now," said Chu. "I want my orphidnet. Let's ride the sunbeam. That's how to do it. And remember to use my Knot to point you the right way. The subbies aren't the only thing to worry about. You can get lost between the two branes. There's a lot of different directions in hyperspace."

Holding tight to the harp, Thuy wrapped the image of Chu's Knot around the sunbeam—and then she was back in the interbrane teleportation zone, winging across that same endless sea, tracing its foam-flecked, wavy curves. Ond was next to her, helping her lug the harp, and beyond him was Chu, the three of them gliding along like superheroes.

Thuy was uneasy about the harp. The rushing wind kept setting its strings to vibrating. Repeatedly she reached out to damp them, but the magical instrument's body was resonating with a low, persistent thrum—just the thing to attract unwanted attention.

And now, oh no, here came the subbies. At first they looked like fat, stubby plants, but Thuy felt a tingle, and once again she was seeing bird-headed beings with human bodies flying along beneath the surface. The beaked heads poked up and swiveled to stare at the harp. Four of them.

"Shoo!" screamed Chu, losing his cool. He veered into his father, nearly breaking Ond's hold on the harp. A corner of the instrument dipped into the sea. The rushing surface set the transparent strings to singing a fresh chord, mellower than the ones before. Rainbows of quantum foam kicked up.

Squawking and gabbling, the subbies tugged at the harp with their cartoony white-gloved hands.

"Fly home to Nektar, Chu!" cried Ond, releasing his hold on the harp. Thuy too lost her grip on the golden prize. It sank beneath the surface, just as Gladax had feared.

Thuy screeched to a stop without exactly knowing how she did it. Ond and Chu rocketed heedlessly ahead. To hell with them. Thuy wasn't coming back to the Lobrane without that freaking magic harp.

Just now there were no subbies to be seen; they were all beneath the foamy, swirling skin of the Planck frontier. Gathering her courage, Thuy took a deep breath and dove through the surface into—more air. There wasn't water underneath the skin after all. There was air, and a grassy plain, and to make things the stranger, the direction of gravity flipped as Thuy passed through the wavy skin.

She was standing on the underside of the undulating membrane that she'd initially taken for the surface of a sea. From this side, the Planck frontier resembled a rolling landscape of steadily shifting hills and valleys, a lush estuarial parkland studded with Egyptian-style pyramids and monuments.

Animal-headed men and women milled about the river's marshy edge, some on foot and some hovering above the reeds. And there, climbing the steps of a lotus-columned temple, were the four bird-headed men with the magic harp! Flutes and drums sounded from within the great stone hall; firelight illuminated a blood-stained altar.

Not stopping to ponder, Thuy ran at the subbies, screaming her defiance.

Moments later she was bound hand and foot. Two jackal-headed women slung her from a stick and carried her up the steps behind the bird-men with the harp.

A familiar figure was standing before the firelit altar: Jeff Luty with his ponytail. He seemed to be holding a twitching giant scarab in one hand. The drumming rose to a crescendo, punctuated by shrieks from the flutes. Luty grimaced wetly and extended the scarab toward Thuy. The beetle opened his ragged jaws.

CHAPTER 12

Lazy Eight

When the nanoslime attacked Jayjay, at first it hurt, but after a few minutes it started feeling good, and then he went into a dream and didn't even notice when the orphids cleared the slime off him. In the dream he thought he lived a whole lifetime without Thuy, and that at the end of his life his soul flew off to look for her.

What actually happened was that the Big Pig, for reasons of her own, threw Jayjay into a profoundly convincing hallucination that seemed, to him, to last a full sixty years. During the six or seven hours that Thuy was gone, Jayjay lived out an entire simulated life, full of incident and emotion, the sim life ending with death by virus at the deeply hallucinated age of eighty-four.

Of course it would have destroyed Jayjay's physical brain to run it at the hundred-thousand-fold speed-up rate required to live sixty years in six hours. So what the Big Pig did was to run a simulation of Jayjay in a virtual world. And once every real-world second, she used orphid signals to implant the latest interesting memories of the fake life into Jayjay's credulous meat brain, using his reactions to further guide the sim.

Why was the Pig doing this? The simulation was both a thought experiment and an aid to reasoning. Not only was the Big Pig trying to see how a certain kind of future might play out, she was also studying how higher-dimensional cosmologies might relate to physical forms of memory. And Jayjay, like it or not, was helping her all the way.

His hallucinated life went as follows.

Turning 30.

Thuy never came back at all. Ignoring Jayjay's pleas, at midnight the Big Pig released the nants. She was hell-bent on getting that extra memory.

Jayjay's body was the first thing the nants ate. And soon after, the whole planet had been turned into a mass of nants—who justified their crime by carrying out a half-assed simulation of Virtual Earth.

Despite the Big Pig's best programming efforts, the water, clouds, and fire never were quite right. In any case, the nants didn't always try that hard; they often settled for shortcuts as crude as representing a tree by a cookie-cutter flat polygon.

Jayjay's mental processes felt different; the mental and emotional life on Vearth was less drifty, more directed. Vearth's denizens rarely dreamed. But long after Jayjay settled in, he kept on missing Thuy. He wished she'd made it back from the Hibrane.

Jayjay found work doing physics research in the Vearth version of San Francisco. The Big Pig pulled strings to get him the position despite his lack of academic credentials. The lab was looking for weird new principles of physics capable of supercharging brute matter's computational capacities.

Although Jayjay enjoyed the job, he needed the salary, too. Vearth had an active cash economy, with the cash standing for computational resources. You needed money to buy or rent a simulated house, to view a show, or to get new clothes. And if you paid the Big Pig a certain monthly fee, your personal reality was rendered in higher resolution than was other people's.

Jayjay ended up in a Vearth romance with none other than Darlene of Metotem Books. And on Jayjay's thirtieth birthday, he and Darlene married.

The couple wanted to buy a house in the Mission District of San Francisco, but there was only so much room in Vearth's highest-resolution and best-simulated zones. So for their starter home, Jayjay and Darlene shoehorned themselves into a "thumbnail" development constructed within a basement storage room off Valencia Street. Two hundred and fifty-six families lived down there; upon entering the basement, the residents would shrink in size and drop to a low-resolution format so as to fit into thumbnail Victorian homes with jaggy coarse meshes.

Turning 40.

More and more of Vearth's simulated citizens gave up pantomiming a traditional lifestyle and became homeless pigheads. Although merging into the Big Pig had been unusual or even transgressive in the old world, it was a constant temptation on Vearth. With no physical bodies to pull them back, many pigheads lost their identities for good. In effect the Big Pig ate them.

An opportunistic hive mind by the name of Gustav arose from a cabal of dissatisfied mid-level beezies. Gustav attracted a large following by promising equal computational resources for all. So as to reward his adherents with more room in which to live, Gustav arbitrarily scaled up the areas of the districts he controlled. Unfortunately, Gustav didn't own enough computational resources to properly simulate his supersized neighborhoods, which became as granular and jerky as old-school video arcade games.

Meanwhile, in the hi-res district of San Francisco, Jayjay's professional life was going well; he'd begun making some discoveries about the higher dimensions of space. In line with orthodox brane theory, the Lobrane dimensions beyond ordinary space and time were curled into Planck-length circles comprising a knotty Calabi-Yau manifold. But by studying the records of people's conversations with Hibraners on Orphid Night, Jayjay deduced that one of the Hibrane's higher dimensions was stretched to infinite length. The Hibraners spoke of this special dimension as being their *eighth* dimension.

Jayjay received a fat bonus from his lab, and soon after his fortieth birthday, he and Darlene moved into a full-size high-resolution cloud-house that floated above Vearth's Golden Gate Bridge. By and large, Darlene was happy, although after Jayjay talked to her once too often about how much he missed Thuy, she erased all the copies of Thuy's autobiographical metanovel *Wheenk* that she could find. But Jayjay forgave her.

In the heat of their make-up sex, Jayjay and Darlene decided to have a child. Having purchased enough computational resources for an additional simulated human, they programmed the child as best they could with a mixture of their memories, skills and behaviors. The baby was a boy; they named him Dirk.

Turning 50.

Life in Gustav's camp was on a downward spiral. To handle his overambitious land grants, Gustav's simulations grew ever coarser: mountains were cones, lawns were smooth green surfaces, and people's subconscious minds weren't simulated at all. Gustav's followers began defecting to the Big Pig, but then Gustav developed blockade software to fence them in. Jayjay was friends with some physicists in the Gustav-run zones, and, in an effort to help them, he cobbled together some breakout software that made it possible to flee Gustav's regime. The breakout ware spread like wildfire, and Gustav's reign was over.

But now, having observed that Gustav's simulated humans had gotten along quite well without subconscious minds, the Big Pig began skimping on her own personality-modeling routines.

Soon after his fiftieth birthday, Jayjay became obsessed with the notion that Darlene's behavior had become inhumanly rigid and stereotyped. The Big Pig's shortcuts had made Darlene uncanny to him. Right around then Jayjay stumbled on a surviving copy of *Wheenk*.

He cajoled the Big Pig into creating a simulated version of Thuy, based upon her metanovel. Jayjay and the young sim began a torrid affair. But then Darlene caught them in bed together. Darlene left Jayjay, taking their son Dirk along. Quite soon the shallowness of the simulated Thuy wore thin. Jayjay extinguished the sim by removing her computational resources. He felt guilty and depressed.

But his professional life kept chugging along. Regarding the possibility of unrolling the eighth dimension, Jayjay proved that, although the unrolled extra dimension would be infinite in extent, it could be in practice possible to access any location along this infinite line in a fixed and bounded amount of time. This "Zeno metric," as a mathematician friend termed it, guaranteed that an unrolled eighth dimension could act as a ubiquitous and infinitely capacious memory storage device. A human mind could scan over the first meter of the unrolled dimension in 0.9 seconds, the second meter in 0.09 seconds, the third meter in 0.009 seconds, the fourth in 0.0009 seconds . . . and so on through an infinite series that could be traversed in one second because, after all, 1.0 lies beyond the endless decimal number 0.999999. . . .

This result had the profound implication that, had the real Earthlings learned how to unroll the eighth dimension, then there would have been no need to grind the planet into nants. With the eighth dimension unrolled, the Big Pig could have found all the memory she could ever need, right in the crevices of ordinary matter.

Turning 60.

A reality-hacking movement arose. People learned to edit their environments on the fly, and the legacy of the shattered Earth's former geography fell by the wayside. Vearth mountains moved, chasms opened, seas grew. It became increasingly difficult to decide where you were.

Some simpler souls quailed at the new freedoms. Large numbers of them enlisted in faiths offering brutally simple answers. As well as the new sects, hundreds of narrowly ethnic clans arose.

Meanwhile Jayjay was consolidating his researches on "lazy eight," as the Hibraners reportedly termed their unrolled eighth dimension. Jayjay was sixty years old, and he had a sense that he was running out of time. Despite Luty's erstwhile promises of immortality for everyone, Vearth could only support so many virtual agents. With the birth rate going up, the older and weaker sims were being culled out.

Jayjay was comforted by the fact that his son Dirk had come to live with him. Rather than making fresh discoveries, Jayjay was polishing and clarifying his old results, in part by teaching them to his beloved Vearth-born boy.

He liked to explain, for instance, that unrolling the eighth dimension would be effectively the same as taking the vanishing point of a painting and having it be next to every location of space. Each pathway to this universally accessible point at infinity would provide an unlimited amount of memory.

Jayjay was well off enough to attract a new wife: Keppy. Keppy was a second-generation virtual human like Dirk. Born in Vearth, she'd never been a real person at all. Keppy spent a lot of her time on low-level nant hunts with a flock of beezies. Dirk often joined her.

Turning 70.

As part of their endless jockeying for more influence, the sect and clan leaders began exhorting their followers to reproduce without limit. The population levels exploded, with the result that even the wealthiest people's realities had clunky performance and low resolution. The Big Pig stepped up her use of cleansing squads to erase those humans who were contributing the least to the group mind. Among the increasingly desperate lower classes, the beezie nant hunts took on the intense quality of mass wars.

Strange to say, Jayjay's nearly fifty years of life in Vearth had lasted but five of the real world's hours. He was plagued by a persistent sense of living in a dream. Would he never awake?

His work in physics continued to give him some pleasure. He was closing in on discovering actual methods for unrolling the eighth dimension. It was a matter of creating certain types of vibrations with a hyperdimensionally tweaked musical instrument. Perhaps a zither or a guitar. But what would you use for the strings?

Jayjay had some ideas along these lines but, sadly enough, the lack of temporal synch between his mind and the natural world made it impossible for him to carry out any honest-to-god real world physics experiments. He was marooned in the nants' dream.

On the morning of his seventieth birthday, Jayjay awoke with much of his virtual body gone. He was little more than a head, a shoulder and an arm. The rest had been sold. He would need to purchase fresh computational resources to reconstitute his flesh. But all his money was gone too. Keppy had left Jayjay with Dirk, taking Jayjay's entire savings.

Once again, as several times before, the Big Pig bailed out Jayjay. But, crushed by his son Dirk's betrayal, Jayjay found it increasingly difficult to carry on.

Turning 80.

Overpopulation led to a series of dirty little wars, with terrorism a growing problem. An incurable virus began to spread. Program after program crashed, and nant after nant was reduced to doing nothing but eternally repeating the single binary bit "0."

Jayjay had entered his life's bleak winter. Wistfully he proved one last result about what might have happened had the Lobraners been able to unroll the eighth dimension: The ubiquitous and accessible point at infinity would have provided an entanglement channel connecting every point with every other point in synchronicity. Not only would an unfurled eighth dimension have provided endless memory for all, it would have brought about telepathy for every object in the world.

He continued wondering about what kind of vibration might actually unfurl the eighth dimension. He'd managed to deduce that one could use wound-up hyperdimensional tubes as specially tuned strings. The order in which the strings were struck would be of key importance. But Jayjay was unable to reason his way to any conclusions about what the ideal order would be.

Increasingly discouraged and paranoid, Jayjay, aged eighty-four, went into the dirtiest, most crowded streets of the all but unrecognizable maze that had once been San Francisco. Soon he was infected with the so-called Baal virus.

Death came to him as he lay in thick silk sheets in a velvet-curtained room with a conventionally beautiful view. There was no way of knowing exactly where the room was. Nothing was real. Jayjay was glad to be leaving this dream within a dream.

His dying thoughts were of the bright, quirky girl he'd loved in his youth, sixty years before. Thuy Nguyen. Where had the time gone?

As Jayjay's soul left his dying body, his simulated world burst

open like a balloon. The light of infinity shone upon him; he
bathed in the music of a living harp. This, surely, was the sound
he'd been searching for; this harp's magical vibrations could
unfurl the eighth dimension. With the chord filling his being,
Jayjay sped from the remains of his rubbishy virtual world,
singing Thuy's name, hoping against hope for the return of his
lost true love.

Meanwhile, Thuy was hanging like a captured lioness from a
stick on the shoulders of two jackal-headed women—Thuy
peering upside-down at nerdy Jeff Luty holding an alien beetle.
Was this how her life was supposed to end? She felt terrified,
incredulous, and deeply pissed off.

The sloping temple walls bore indistinct hieroglyphs that
changed every time Thuy looked at them. The flute and drum
sounds were coming from thin air. And there was no actual fire
to produce the firelight. The Egyptian trappings were fully bogus. But the seven subbies were real; the four bird-men, the two
jackal-women, and the sacred scarab beetle were giving off clear
telepathic vibes via all-but-invisible tendrils connected to Thuy's
head. Luty, however, seemed strangely absent. Thuy sensed zero
psychic energies coming off the weathered old programmer.
Somehow this emptiness was the creepiest thing of all.

"Do the gloating villain thing like at your lab," Thuy urged
Luty, wanting to get something going. "That way I get another
chance to kick your ass."

"Open my nant farm," mumbled Luty, his murky eyes blank.
"Apply antinantanium." His lined gray face rippled like a puddle in the wind. His ponytail twitched; he licked his lips; he
moved the beetle closer to Thuy's face.

Thuy now saw that Luty's forearm blended seamlessly into the beetle's abdomen. The beetle was part of Luty's body—or no, *ick,* it was the other way around. The Luty-thing was an appendage, a speaking-tube. The beetle had already devoured Luty some time back. The tormented man had met his end in Subdee.

"*Gthx,*" said the scarab on his own. Sensing Thuy's attention, he swelled larger, with the Luty-thing's mass decreasing by an equivalent amount. "*Glkt grx.*" The beetle brushed his antennae slowly and intimately across Thuy's face and head, as if palpating her brain's emanations. She felt a series of tingles in her skull.

"Yes, we're subbies from Subdee," intoned the scarab's Luty-tube. "Yes, we ate Jeff Luty. It's a rare feed indeed when a multikilogram object plops through the Planck frontier. And now we've got a second course! Untie her, girls, and gather round."

The jackal-headed women crouched to lay Thuy on the ground, their butts big in the phantom firelight. They untied the thongs around Thuy's ankles and wrists, then stood dancing in place, their hands swaying, their feet mincing a steady little box step, their blank eyes blinking in unison. Thuy recalled her initial impression that the bird-men were fat plants. The dancer subbies were plants, too, veiling themselves in images gleaned from their feast on Luty's brain. Looking at the sexy jackal-women forms, Thuy felt a flicker of pity for the dead man and his lonely dreams.

The subbies cackled and chirped, drawing themselves into a tight circle around Thuy. The beetle had swelled to human size; he was standing on his spindly rear legs, wearing Luty as a penis-like appendage projecting from his belly. Jeff wouldn't have liked that.

One of the bird-men poked at Thuy's thigh with his curved

beak; one of the jackal-women snuffled her armpit. Thuy thought of the old Norman Rockwell painting of a white family saying grace around Thanksgiving dinner. When she'd been a kid, she'd gone through a Norman Rockwell phase, trying to decipher what it meant to be white. And now she was a subdimensional roast turkey. But still non-white. Her thoughts were jumping all around. The jackal woman gave her neck a little nip.

"Don't eat me!" cried Thuy. "I have to stop the nants."

"We *like* the nant plan," said the beetle bucking his abdomen to make the Luty-penis talk. "We subbies grow vatoscale roots to draw info from the quantum level of your cosmos, you see. We poke through the Planck frontier's foam. Once the nants eat Earth, your planet's high-level structures will be folded into the tasty quantum states of the nanomachines. We want to help the nants, yes. I've tweaked my metabolism to synthesize antinantanium, so I can send a root hair to exude a timely drop."

"Kkrt," croaked one of the bird-headed men. *"Kth krrb."*

The beetle chirped a response; the dangling Luty-shape explained. "My friends want to eat you right away, Thuy. But first I want you to tell me what that harp is for. I don't understand what my root hairs are drawing from your brain."

"I need to *hold* the harp to explain it," said Thuy, her mind racing.

The big sacred scarab dropped onto his six legs and ambled over to the harp. Impatiently a jackal-women bit off one of Thuy's pigtails and wolfed it down.

A bird-man gave the jackal-woman a sharp peck, then snipped Thuy's other pigtail and swallowed it, holding his head high to work the bolus down his crane's neck. The other subbies closed in on Thuy, tearing off bits of her clothes: her sleeves, part of her miniskirt, and then—oh no!—both of Thuy's beloved golden piezoplastic shoes. The beetle interrupted with a peremptory chirp. He backed into the circle of subbies, dragging the harp with his mandibles. The crowded painting gleamed.

This was Thuy's last chance to escape. Hoping for the best, she plucked a few strings. They tingled against her fingers in a highly unpleasant way, but she bore down and began strumming steadily. Thuy felt a flicker of sympathy from the harp, and then the sound took on a life of its own, rising to a whining drone like a leaf-blower's buzz.

The rhythmic noise got deep into Thuy's head; for some reason she recalled her mother's fear that an electric fan in her bedroom at night might chop up her dreams.

Lo and behold, the harp was ripping apart the subbies' root hairs! The illusory Egyptian-style props disappeared.

The unadorned Subdee world was an endless, dry desert, with the parched yellow ground blending into clouds of dust in the middle distance. The disk of a bloated red sun was faintly visible through the ochre sky. Innumerable fat plants were scattered across the dry plain, mobile succulents with snaky, hungry roots like writhing tentacles. The subbie plant-creatures ranged from being waist-high to taller than Thuy. Each of them had two or three meaty leaves, like "living rocks" or lithops plants. All of the subbie-plants bore thorny structures that could tear a person's flesh.

Two of the subbies kept pulling their roots out of the ground, inching to the left, inching to the right, then burying their roots again. They were the dancer subbies who'd played at being jackal-women. The four subbies who'd resembled bird-headed men were plants as well, but they bore hydrogen bladders that allowed them to hang in the air. Fretfully they circled Thuy, whipping their roots in the air.

As for the oversized lithops who'd presented himself as a sacred scarab, he still looked a bit like a beetle, with two fat leaves stuck together for a body, and roots for legs and feelers. A hollow, sharp-tipped feeder root jutted from his front end, framed by rigid growths. The feeder root looked entirely capable of draining Thuy's blood.

Although the harp's insistent buzz had driven back the subbies, the sound was fading now. So once again the subbies closed in. Thuy kicked at the ground, wondering how to break back through the Planck frontier. The sandy soil was translucent, as if made of glass beads, with slowly swirling streaks that betokened the seething of the quantum foam. Thuy kicked harder, then bent down and butted the dirt with her head. But it wasn't opening up for her.

A sharp pain pierced her calf; the beetle plant had ripped a gash. A hovering bird-man plant shot a vicious feeder tube past her. Thuy felt the tingle of root hairs puncturing her skull, and once again a phantom Egyptian temple began to form. Meanwhile, the dancer plants had swathed the harp with writhing skeins of roots; the hairy tendrils were eating away the uncanny painting that adorned the soundbox. Perhaps it had been by the Hibrane Hieronymus Bosch?

Desperately, Thuy began flailing the harp strings. The sound came out as a series of sour warbles. Again the Egyptian scenery faded away, but on every side the persistent subbies were menacing Thuy with their spiked feeder tubes.

Thuy mustered all the magic she knew: she thought of *Wheenk*, Chu's Knot, and her love for Jayjay. She reached out for psychic contact with the harp; she plucked and strummed the strings, steeling herself against the creepy tingling, piling note upon note, playing her hopes and fears and pain. The sounds beat against each other; the very fabric of space began to shake.

Irregular circles of light and dark pulsed from the base of the harp. Flakes of paint showered from the soundbox. Thuy twanged the strings still more frantically, and now, yes, the ground irised open. She wrapped her arms around the magic harp and the two of them fell down, up, through the hole.

Once more she was hovering above a boundless foamy sea. As the hole in the ocean closed up, some faintly glowing lines came snaking through. Root hairs! Time to fly home. It required but the slightest touch of Thuy's will to set herself speeding low across the bubbling waves.

A minute passed, another, another. The harp was awkward and heavy in Thuy's arms, once again playing dumb. Was Thuy heading the right way? She pressed on.

It was hard to quantify the passage of time within this inter-brane quantum level, but eventually Thuy became quite sure that she'd been flying far longer than on her initial jump from the Lobrane to the Hibrane. She changed course and flew some more—with still no sign of the homey Lobrane. She was lost.

What had Chu said? *There's a lot of different directions in hyperspace.* Hopelessly off course as Thuy was, the direction pointed by the Knot meant nothing now.

The subbies were still trailing her. She knew to dodge the root hairs they kept sending up like harpoons. The subbies wanted her to think they looked like bird-headed men, but Thuy could see they were fat-leaved plants with hydrogen bladders, waving their stubby roots. Greedy heartless pods.

Thuy was bone-weary, but still she clung to the silent harp. She wasn't going to be able to fly much longer. The subbies would draw her under and eat her. The Big Pig would release the nants. Jayjay was probably dead. Life was a hopeless mess.

And then Thuy heard Jayjay's voice, calling to her across the dimensions. His dear face led her home.

❧

"Jayjay? This is real?"

Jayjay sat bolt upright. "Thuy? Oh thank god. I'm not dead, I'm not old, and you're here. I had this jitsy dream that lasted sixty years. The Big Pig's been mind-gaming me. I thought I died and went to look for you."

"Am I in time?"

"We're in synch again," said Jayjay, not immediately getting the point of her question. "Tick, tock. I love you, Thuy." The nanomachine goo was gone. Orphids outlined the walls and floor of the unlit cave. A few hundred tiny flying shoons were busy around the nantanium-walled nant farm that sat nestled, still intact, upon the shards of the plastic box that had been the Ark of the Nants. The fireflylike shoons were sending pulses of laser light into the nant farm, still tweaking the nant code. The orphidnet revealed a powerful-looking figure standing guard over the nant farm, a waist-high golem shoon with a smooth, stylized face and bell-bottom-shaped arms and legs.

"What time is it right now?" persisted Thuy. She wasn't on-line. The orphids were only just now landing on her.

"Um, quarter to midnight," said Jayjay, checking the little local network that the Pig was letting them see. His mind felt stiff and clunky in these confines. "The nants are still walled up. We have fifteen minutes."

"Hug me quick, Jayjay."

"Yes." Thuy was a black spot in the local orphidnet. As Jayjay reached for her in the velvety dark, he bumped into something big and hollow. It made a resonant boinging sound.

"Don't knock over my magic harp," said Thuy.

"Thuy and the Beanstalk," said Jayjay. "You robbed the giant." He got his arms around her, and they kissed for a few minutes. Thuy smelled and felt and tasted as good as ever. The orphids had finished settling on her; he could see the sweet outlines of her face. They kissed some more. For now the Big Pig left them alone; she was preoccupied with the nant farm.

"You had a dream that lasted sixty years?" said Thuy presently.

"It damaged me," said Jayjay, cuddling Thuy. "I'm old. I'm incredibly grateful to have a twenty-four-year-old girlfriend. Tell me more about your Hibrane adventures. And your harp."

"The strings are jitsy," said Thuy. "And the harp is alive. She helped me escape these cannibal cactuses that live under the ocean that separates the branes. The subbies from Subdee. They scratched my leg. They ate the painting off the harp." Thuy paused and took a deep breath. So much to tell. "The way it started, Gladax was about to addle my brain. Ond, Chu and I stole the harp and ran away. Gladax could have caught us but—" Thuy paused, again mentally replaying the events.

"What?"

"I think the harp wanted to come here. And Azaroth helped talk Gladax around. Ond and Chu say that the harp can make our brane more like the Hibrane. Everyone in the Hibrane has telepathy, teleportation, and endless memory, you know. And there's no digital computers."

"*Zonggg,*" said Jayjay. "That's exactly what I dreamed about. We have to unroll the eighth dimension like the Hibraners do. Lazy eight. In my dream I heard this special chord—"

"Gladax mentioned a Lost Chord back at ExaExa," said Thuy. "She said nobody knows how to play it."

"I can!" bragged Jayjay, feeling very sure of himself. "I can hear it in my head."

He scooted across the floor and embraced the harp. But the strings slid greasily beneath his fingers; they were jittering with something like an electric charge. It hurt to touch them. He plucked a few tentative notes, trying to create the sound he'd heard at the end of his dream. Nothing doing. He tried some more, to no effect. His music sounded vague and puny.

"That's all?" said Thuy uncertainly.

"Actually *playing* what I heard is hard," said Jayjay. "I wonder if—"

The Big Pig butted in now, her voice plummy in their inner ears. "I assume you realize there are maybe ten to the hundredth power possible ways to strum that harp, Jayjay. You'll never find the Lost Chord."

"Help me. You heard the sound too, right? The harp music when I died?"

"Not really," said the Pig. "That stuff was coming from somewhere outside my simulation. Be that as it may, we did some nice VR work, no? Those results about unrolling the eighth dimension for unlimited memory are quite fine. You're a good helper."

"Helper? Those were *my* ideas."

"Call it a collaboration. You were piloting an agent in a virtual reality that I designed. By the way, did you enjoy the experience?"

"It was hell! Weren't you paying attention to my feelings?"

"When you take a shower, do you wonder if your skin bacteria are having a good time?"

Now Thuy chimed in. "Come on, Big Pig. I brought back this magic harp; we've at least got to give it an honest try. Help

Jayjay and me find the right notes." Her voice took on a coaxing tone. "You can do it. You're so smart."

"Not as smart as I intend to be. As for that sound Jayjay thinks he heard—the actual data I see in his brain is quite sparse. With so little solid information, finding the Lost Chord involves an intractably large search. Maybe after I've gotten my nant memory upgrade, I can figure it out from scratch. But for now—which sequence of strings, how forcefully to play them, whether to pluck or to strum, where exactly to strike each string, when to damp them, whether to overlap the notes—no, no, it's quite hopeless. Sooo—thanks for the help, Jayjay and Thuy. See you in Vearth 2.0!"

"Don't!" shouted Jayjay, but already the golem was raising one of his hamlike fists to smash open the fragile-looking nant farm.

"I can stop him!" yelled Thuy, pushing Jayjay away from the harp. She buzz-sawed her fingers across the strings like a heavy-metal guitar star and right away the local orphidnet went down—as abruptly as if a plug had been pulled. The Big Pig's voice in their heads was gone, as was the Pig's control over the golem. In the velvet darkness, the golem bumped against Jayjay's leg. Feeling for the creature, Jayjay found the golem to be rolling on the floor like a baby, sportively twiddling his fingers and toes. Jayjay himself felt sick from the chaotic sounds of the harp; it was as if the close, dark space of the cave were flexing.

"Hurry now," called Thuy tensely. "Teleport and get an atomic bomb. We'll quick set it off while we can. Go!"

"I can't teleport without the orphidnet," said Jayjay uncertainly. "I'll have to dig my way out of here. Away from that sound."

Looking for an exit, Jayjay scanned back through his memories about the cave. They'd first come here—was it only today? His initial impressions were buried beneath sixty years worth of bogus memories. As he rooted through the data, Darlene's face kept popping up, even though in real life he'd never for even one second wanted her. She'd always seemed more like a sister or a cousin. But that wasn't what he was supposed to be thinking about. He was, um—

"The submachine gun!" urged Thuy. "Get my P90 and shoot a hole in the wall! There's a thin place near a dog-sized lump of rock on the floor. Feel around for the gun, Jayjay! Hurry! I hate how these strings feel on my fingers. The harp's not helping me at all."

"Play slower and quieter," suggested Jayjay, recalling some of the theoretical ideas he'd worked out in the dream. "It's the dissonant beats that are blocking the orphidnet's quantum entanglement. The loudness doesn't matter." Thuy damped down her efforts to a more sustainable level, and, yes, the local orphidnet remained dark.

Blindly Jayjay crawled around until he got Thuy's submachine gun, and then he located the dog-sized rock on the floor. He rapped on the wall above it and found a hollow-sounding spot. "Ready!" he said to Thuy. "Watch out for flying grit."

He opened up the P90 against the wall at close range. The stone was so soft that the bullets dug in with no ricochets. The stuttering muzzle-flashes lit the scene: the glittery sinister box of the nant farm, the golem lolling on the floor, Thuy heroically working the shoulder-high alien harp. For the first time Jayjay noticed that Thuy's shoes and pigtails were gone. But there was no time to ask questions, for now he'd blasted an opening big enough to crawl through. A sweet shaft of moonlight slanted down from above.

"I'll be right back," Jayjay told Thuy, taking the gun with him. "I love you."

She nodded, her face wan and weary in the reflected moonlight.

Jayjay worked himself up the vent to get away from the harp sounds. The orphidnet was still in full effect in the summernight meadows of Easter Island. And as soon as Jayjay emerged from the lava tube, the Big Pig was on his case. Fuck the Pig. Jayjay popped up a mental firewall before she could start running another head trip.

The friendly beezies who lived on Jayjay's skin ran an orphidnet search and fed him the location of a backpack-style tactical atomic bomb in an armory on an Air Force base near Great Falls, Montana. So Jayjay teleported himself there. When he arrived, the alarm system was already hooting. The Big Pig had alerted the system's security. But Jayjay's beezies helped him plan his moves. Without a single wasted gesture, he used his P90 to shoot away the fasteners holding the bomb-pack in place. He memorized the simple instructions printed on the lumpy knapsack, shrugged it onto his back, and teleported to Easter Island.

A gentle sea breeze wafted the scent of heathery flowers up the slope of Rano Raraku. The bomb-pack was heavy, with plastic and metal knobs that dug into Jayjay's back. He could feel the Big Pig working to break down his firewall. He wasn't going to have time to find a different place to set off the bomb.

"I'm sorry," Jayjay said out loud to the nearest moai, a noble dark silhouette against the moon-bright sky. And then he lowered himself back down the moonlit lava tube leading to the cave.

Overburdened as Jayjay was by the submachine gun and the bomb-pack, the climb down the chimney took longer than he would have liked. It was a relief to hear the harp still playing when he reached the bottom. But the music was slower and fainter than before.

"You okay?" he called to Thuy.

"No," said Thuy, her voice trembling. "My fingers . . ."

Peering in, Jayjay saw dark smears on her moon-silvered hands. Blood.

"Hang on," he said. "We'll be done in a minute." His plan was to shove the pack into the cave, go in after it, arm the bomb, then teleport out at the very last second with Thuy and the harp.

Trembling with haste, he jammed the pack into the ragged hole. But, goddammit, the dense plastic and metal structures of the bomb got hung up on a lump of rock halfway through—and then for five or maybe even ten minutes, Jayjay could neither push the frikkin' pack further nor pull it back out. He wormed his hand into the narrow space, clawing at the bump, bloodying his own fingers. Shoot the submachine gun? No, dude, don't shoot at an A-bomb, especially not with your girlfriend right behind it, but, yeah, you can use the barrel of the gun like a pick.

Jayjay pounded till the sparks flew, finally wearing away the bulge that was blocking the path. And now someone on the inside began pulling at the pack to help him—could that be Thuy? Shouldn't she be playing the harp?

The pack dropped into the cave. Thuy was lying on her side moaning, her hands cupped against her chest.

The harp was silent, the orphidnet was up and, *oh oh*, it was the golem who'd been tugging on the pack. Once again the Big Pig had taken control. In a puddle of moonlight, the solidly built shoon crouched over the bomb-pack, ripping it open like an ear of corn. With no hesitation, Jayjay scrambled through the hole and flung himself at the shoon—but the creature sent him sprawling with a negligent shove. The bomb's control mechanisms cracked and tinkled beneath the golem's hammy fists.

Jayjay crawled over to Thuy.

"My fingers," she said softly. "I'm sorry, Jayjay. I couldn't do anymore. And the harp is just watching. She says this part was up to us."

"We did our best," said, Jayjay, putting his arm around Thuy's shoulders. "No blame. Who knows, maybe we'll like it in Vearth 2.0. Your poor hands." Jayjay drew out his handkerchief and tore it into strips, binding up her bleeding fingers one by one.

And now, *sigh,* the golem struck the nant farm a mighty thump.

The end?

No, the shoon's fists kept skidding off the shiny box. Harder and harder the golem pounded, but the nant farm shed his blows like drops of water.

"It won't open without antinantanium," exclaimed Thuy, managing a little smile. "And I poured every bit of that junk down the drain at Luty's lab!"

"You're a genius!" said Jayjay. "A hero!"

Suddenly Thuy's face darkened. She was staring at something over Jayjay's shoulder, something he couldn't see. "Oh no!" she exclaimed. "Is that a root hair? Play the harp, Jayjay!"

"What?"

"There was this subdimensional beetle-plant who claimed—" Her voice broke into a higher register. "A root hair! I see a subbie root hair! He's going to put a drop of antinantanium onto the farm! Hurry, Jayjay!"

Jayjay scrambled across the floor, reached up for the harp, but already it was too late. The sides of the nant farm were—melting away. The nants sparkled like diamond dust. A cloud of orphids descended upon the nants to do nanobattle against them.

The golem squatted beside the nants, fanning his hands as if to drive the orphids away. He even tore off one of his fingers as a food offering for the new nants. They went for it; and they were eating into the floor as well. The orphids weren't stopping the nants at all.

Jayjay noticed that the Big Pig wasn't bothering to block the cave from the global orphidnet anymore. She'd gotten what she wanted.

"Come on!" he shouted to Thuy. "We'll teleport back to your room. We'll get another few hours in the real world."

"Don't forget the harp," said Thuy. "She wants to stay with us."

"Right," said Jayjay, picking up some encouraging mental vibes from the harp herself. "We'll keep trying to play the Lost Chord."

"Go for it," said the Big Pig, not unkindly. "It still might be nice if it works."

Jayjay and Thuy landed in Thuy's room; the harp made a cozy thrumming sound when Jayjay set her down. Outside it was raining again. A peaceful night, the lights of the city warm, everything wet and shiny. Nine p.m. San Francisco time. Downstairs Nektar and Kittie were cheerfully chatting in the garage. They hadn't yet gotten the word that the world was coming to an end.

"I noticed some smart bandages in the bathroom," said Jayjay, regarding Thuy's cloth-wrapped hands. "With biopatches built in."

"I need painkillers too," said Thuy.

"We'll fix you up. By the way, what happened to your hair?"

"The subbies ate my pigtails," said Thuy, her expression halfway between laughter and tears. "And my favorite shoes. Bastards." She put her arms around Jayjay. "We had some wild times, didn't we?"

"Better than I ever expected," he said, planting a kiss on her mouth. "Maybe we can share one last analog fuck. If you're up for it."

"I'd like that. A final golden memory to treasure when we're dipshit sims. But right now my fingers are—"

"Thuy?" Kittie was calling up the staircase. "We saw the video feed of you facing down Luty at ExaExa. You were so great! And guess who's here? Chu! He says you helped him get back from the Hibrane."

"Hi, Thuy," said a boy's voice. "I'm watching you in the orphidnet."

Thuy winced and silently shook her head, then went into the bathroom.

"We'll be right down," called Jayjay. In the background, he ran an orphidnet check on the cave beneath Easter Island. The nants had grown to a seething ball several hundred meters across, too big to erase with any bomb. Too late to call in the Air Force.

The only thing to do was to sit down at the harp and start trying to play the Lost Chord. But the prospect seemed so hopeless. Why not enjoy the last few minutes of real life that he and Thuy had?

Jayjay helped Thuy dress her wounds, patched his own fingers, and then the two of them went downstairs to visit with the others. Keenly aware of impending doom as Thuy and Jay-jay were, everything felt classic and heavy and for-the-ages.

The garage was all lit up, a vintage car-buff scene. Nektar was admiring Kittie's retrofit job on the SUV; to finish it off, Kittie had painted a gorgeous wraparound image of a woman's head being diced into cubes by the car's front grill—and re-assembling itself at the rear. It was a mural of Thuy going through the grill in the office wall of that dough-faced bully, the guy whom Gladax had later killed with a poke to the brain—Jayjay couldn't remember his name. His real life memories were buried under sixty years worth of bogus crud.

A bright-eyed boy with brown hair was expressionlessly polishing the SUV.

"This is Chu," said Thuy, giving the boy a sharp pat on the head. "He and his father left me to die. And, Chu, this is my boyfriend, Jayjay. Show some manners and say hello. Did your dad make it back? Where is he?"

"Ond went to see Jil on her boat," said Chu in his flat voice. "He loves Jil instead of Nektar."

"Which is *quite* all right with me," said Nektar, tossing her thick fall of hair. "I'm happier with Kittie. Don't worry Chu, Mommy and Daddy will be good friends. I just wonder what we'll do about our house. I'd like to stay here, but I don't want Ond moving in."

"So Jil really broke up with Craigor?" mused Jayjay. He felt just a tiny bit jealous of Ond, although of course that was crazy, and he should be completely happy and satisfied now that he had Thuy again. Not to mention how ridiculous it was to be so self-centered when the whole freaking planet was being munged into nanomachines.

"Craigor's up the hill with Lureen Morales," said Kittie with a laugh, happy with her cozy, human-scale life. "The *Founders* action never stops!"

"We're in a live soap opera," Chu said to Thuy. "I don't like that."

"*Founders* pays us very well," said Nektar. "You'll get used to it, Chu. Everyone is going to love you."

"I don't think so," Chu said in a sulky tone and went back to polishing the SUV.

"So, what happened on Easter Island?" said Kittie. "You guys dropped out of sight in that cave and then—oh no. Look at the orphidnet news."

"We know," said Thuy. Easter Island was almost gone. The nant blight had grown to ten kilometers in length.

"Nants!" shrilled Chu. "Let's jump back to the Hibrane, Thuy. You come too, Nektar. And someone tell Ond. I still know my special Knot. Pay attention, Nektar, I'm messaging you the jump-code. Do you need it again, Thuy?"

"I don't like the brane-jump," said Thuy. "Those bird-men we saw—they're subdimensional killer plants. They almost ate me alive."

"You were silly to stop flying," said Chu. "I'm gonna jump to the Hibrane right now." He squeezed shut his eyes.

But now a ghostly, glowing giant came poking into the garage. He ran his hand through Chu's head, distracting the boy from his jump. It was Azaroth, not looking so friendly anymore.

"You can't come to the Hibrane," the Hibraner told Chu. "Not with the nants loose again. If you go there now, I'll bring you right back."

"I will too jump," Chu cried. "I'll jump after you're gone. I have the code."

"Your code's not gonna be working much longer, kiddo.

We're changing the angle between the branes. Very vibby. All the Hibraners are teeping together and pushing your world's timeline away from ours."

"But why?" wailed Chu.

"You guys have ruined one planet, and that's enough." Azaroth glared over at Thuy. "You know, I went to a lot of trouble convincing Gladax to let you borrow her harp. I even had to promise to have tea with her every afternoon for the next three months. And now I come here and you're not even *trying* to play the Lost Chord. Losers. I need to bring the harp back to the Hibrane before it's eaten by your filthy nants."

"We *are* trying to use the harp," said Jayjay, uncomfortably realizing he sounded as petulant as Chu. "It just doesn't look that way. I'm waiting for inspiration instead of wearing out my fingers with random strums. I already know what the Lost Chord should sound like; I had a dream in virtual reality."

"Virtual reality is weak bullshit," exclaimed Azaroth. "Don't you understand that yet? The magic harp is real." The Hibraner shook his head as if disgusted by Jayjay's folly, then relented a bit. "I'll tell you what, since Thuy's a friend, I'm not gonna repossess the harp for another fifteen minutes. But I have to be outta here before Gladax and the gang change the jump params. Play the frikkin' Lost Chord, Jayjay! Unfurl the eighth dimension!"

"I want to go to the Hibrane!" screamed Chu, getting up on the SUV's hood and flailing at Azaroth's insubstantial face. "I hate the nants!" He slipped and fell to the floor, leaving a scuffmark on the car.

Nektar crouched over Chu, comforting him. Kittie was in a blank-faced state of panic, mechanically rubbing the scuff off the hood while watching the orphidnet disaster news in her head.

"Let's go to my room," Thuy murmured to Jayjay. "I'll inspire you."

Upstairs they locked the door behind them. They undressed and began making love. They had all the time in the world. Everything was going to be all right. At least that's what Jayjay kept telling himself. And somehow he believed it. He and Thuy were one flesh, all their thoughts upon their skins. Their bodies made a sweet suck and push. The answer was near.

Jayjay had been too tense and rushed to teep the harp before. But now—now he could feel the harp's mind. She was a higher order of being, incalculably old and strange. She knew the Lost Chord. She was ready to teach it to him. He'd only needed to ask.

Jayjay and Thuy melted into their climax; they kissed and cuddled.

And then Jayjay got up naked and fingered the harp's strings. They didn't hurt his fingers one bit.

The soft notes layered upon each other like sheets of water on a beach with breaking waves. Guided by the harp, Jayjay plinked in a few additions, thus and so. And, yes, there it was, the Lost Chord. Space twitched like a sprouting seed.

"Sorry!" It was Azaroth, pushing his head and shoulders into the bedroom. He was in a state of panic. "Oh, what did you do to the harp's painting, Thuy? It's all scraped off! Gladax is gonna kill me." He wrapped his big hands around the vibrating instrument. "I'm worried I waited too long!"

"Don't go!" shouted Jayjay. "The harp's just now beginning to work!"

"Hope so," said Azaroth. "But I've got to try and get home." And with that, he and the harp were gone.

No matter. The sound of the Lost Chord continued unabated, building on itself like a chain reaction, vibrating the space around them. Jayjay smiled at Thuy. He had a sense of endlessly opening vistas.

"You did it," said Thuy. "You're wonderful." She wasn't talking out loud. Her warm voice was inside his head. True telepathy. Jayjay had unrolled the eighth dimension. He and Thuy had saved the world.

Thanks to the universally accessible eighth-dimensional point at infinity, anyone could see anything now. Omnividence, telepathy, and endless memory were the natural birthrights of every being on the globe.

And this applied to objects, too. The alchemical addition of lazy eight memory to nature's gnarl was enough to make everything aware. The air and the trees, the flames, brooks, and veins of stone—all became conscious.

The ancients had viewed nature as inhabited by spirits: sylphs and dryads, salamanders, undines and gnomes. And now the myths were true. Earth and everything in her were alive.

The ubiquitous natural minds would become known as *silps*. Some were like *genii loci* or "spirits of place," residing in cataracts and pools, in tangled glens and groves, in wind-scoured cliffs. Silps arose in less exalted locales as well: in human hairs, in scraps of paper pinwheeling down city streets, in drapes and clothes, in elementary particles, in fumes.

With their lazy eight overview of the world, the silps readily understood about the nants. Quickly the silps copied all the data they found within the nants and, for good measure, they copied the orphids' information as well. The silps didn't trust any of the nanomachines. And now they went on the attack. Using fierce air currents, tiny matter-quakes, and anomalous electromagnetic fields, the silps ripped the nants and orphids to shreds. Nanomachines were no more.

With the orphidnet data intact within the silps, the Big Pig reconstituted hersef like a phoenix—finding a niche as a human-friendly interface for the planetary oversoul. The ported Pig was content to be part of Gaia. Gaia's native computational architecture embodied a far richer system than any swarm of humdrum digital machines. And with the Big Pig inside Gaia, the global network of matter and mind had the searchable quality of the old-school Internet. Win win.

Craigor spent a few more days with Lureen Morales, grew tired of her, and made yet another effort to patch up things with Jil. She stonewalled him. The marriage was over. Craigor moved to a new girlfriend, then another and another. But all the while, he kept on visiting the *Merz Boat,* chatting with Jil and the kids, fishing for cuttles, fiddling with his junk. He was free, but he was lonely.

Meanwhile, Ond solved his house problem with Nektar by building a second home on their large lot. In some ways, working with intelligent materials made building easier. For instance, Ond could teep into a piece of lumber to find the best spot for a nail—the silps in the boards were quite cooperative. They enjoyed linking together to make a structure. Ond built his house with four bedrooms, the better to convince Jil and her kids to move in.

Fed up with Craigor's visits, Jil finally acceded to Ond's courtship. She and the kids abandoned the *Merz Boat* and began living with Ond. He was happier than he'd ever been.

Chu was glad for the company, although mostly he slept at

Nektar's. Bixie made him a little shy. At Nektar's urging, Chu began teeping into the gray matter of his own brain, coaxing the tissues towards a healing of the congenital defect in his cingulate cortex. Bit by bit he grew more personable.

As for Jayjay and Thuy? They got hitched.

It was the end of the Digital Age and the beginning of something new. Society percolated like a river city settling down from a flood. People were pleased with the new order; they'd reclaimed their lives from the machines. Good-humoredly they implemented the necessary changes, working together, fixing one problem at a time.

Astronomers reported that our unrolling of the eighth dimension had spread no further than the gravity well of Earth. But, now that the scientists knew what to look for, they could spot other unfurled zones amid the nearby stars and galaxies.

Perhaps the neighbors would be visiting soon.